Tree-House Comix Proudly Presents

CAT KID COMIC CLUB
COLLABORATIONS

WORDS, ILLUSTRATIONS, AND ARTWORK BY

DAV PILKEY

WITH DIGITAL COLOR BY JOSE GARIBALDI

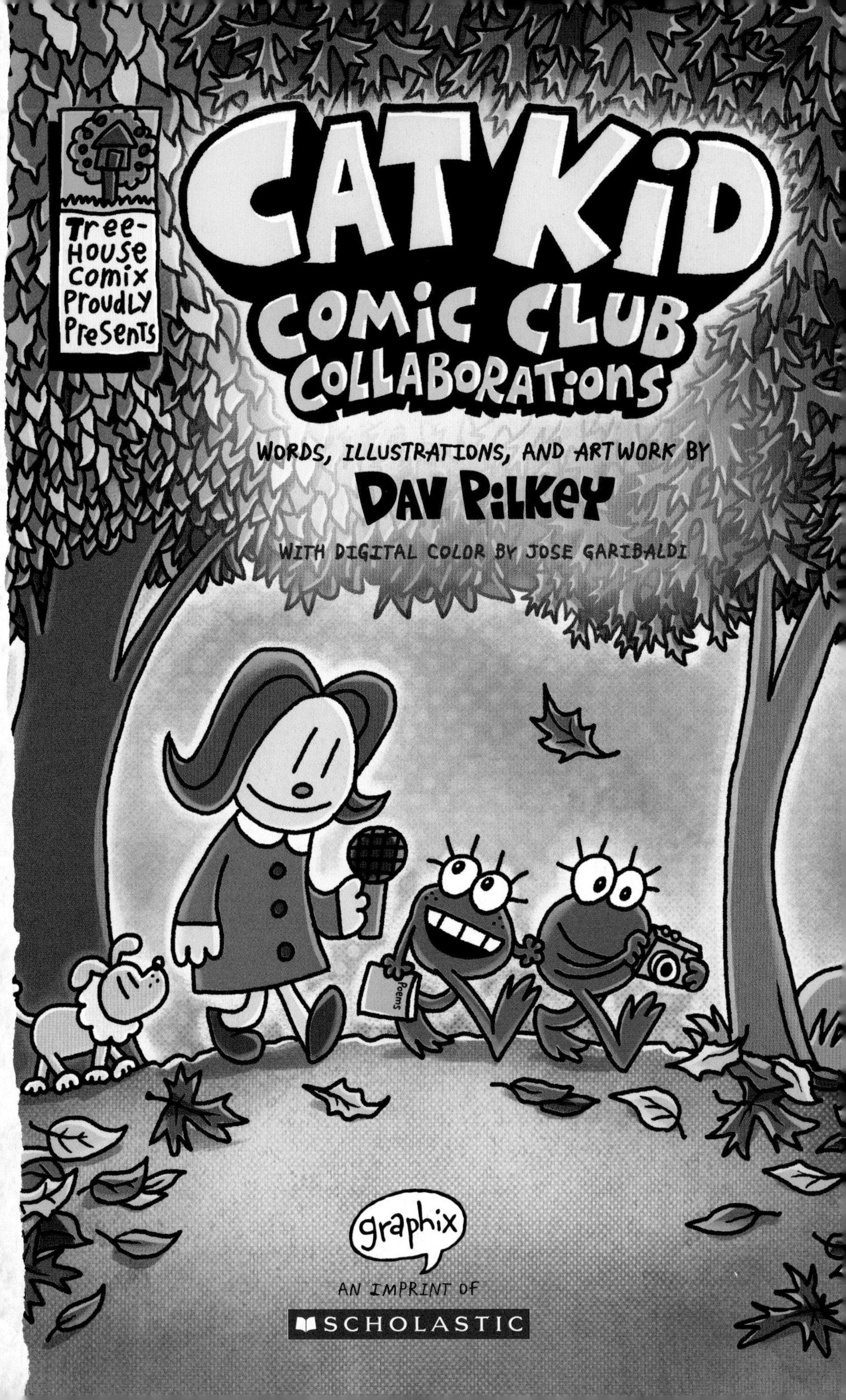
Poems

graphix

AN IMPRINT OF

SCHOLASTIC

Library of Congress Control Number 2022938034

978-1-338-84662-1 (POB)   978-1-338-84663-8 (Library)

10 9 8 7 6 5 4 3 2 1   22 23 24 25 26

Printed in Mexico   189
First edition, November 2022

Illustrations, 3-D models, photography,
and hand lettering by Dav Pilkey.

All mini comics colored by Dav Pilkey using pencils, markers,
pastels, ink, crayons, and colored pencils. 3-D models built out
of recycled cardboard, putty, wood, wire, plasticine, tape, glue,
broken toys, candy, graham crackers, frosting, gum, polyester
batting, styrofoam, and other repurposed items.

Digital Color by Jose Garibaldi | Flatting by Aaron Polk

Editor: Ken Geist | Editorial Team: Megan Peace and Jonah Newman
Book design by Dav Pilkey and Phil Falco
Creative Director: Phil Falco
Publisher: David Saylor

Chapters & Comics

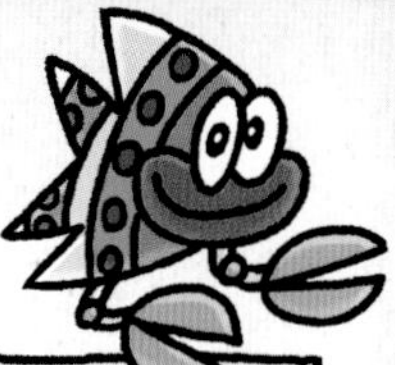

To Cece Bell, Tom Angleberger,
Oscar, and Charlie

CHAPTER 1

OFF TO A BAD START

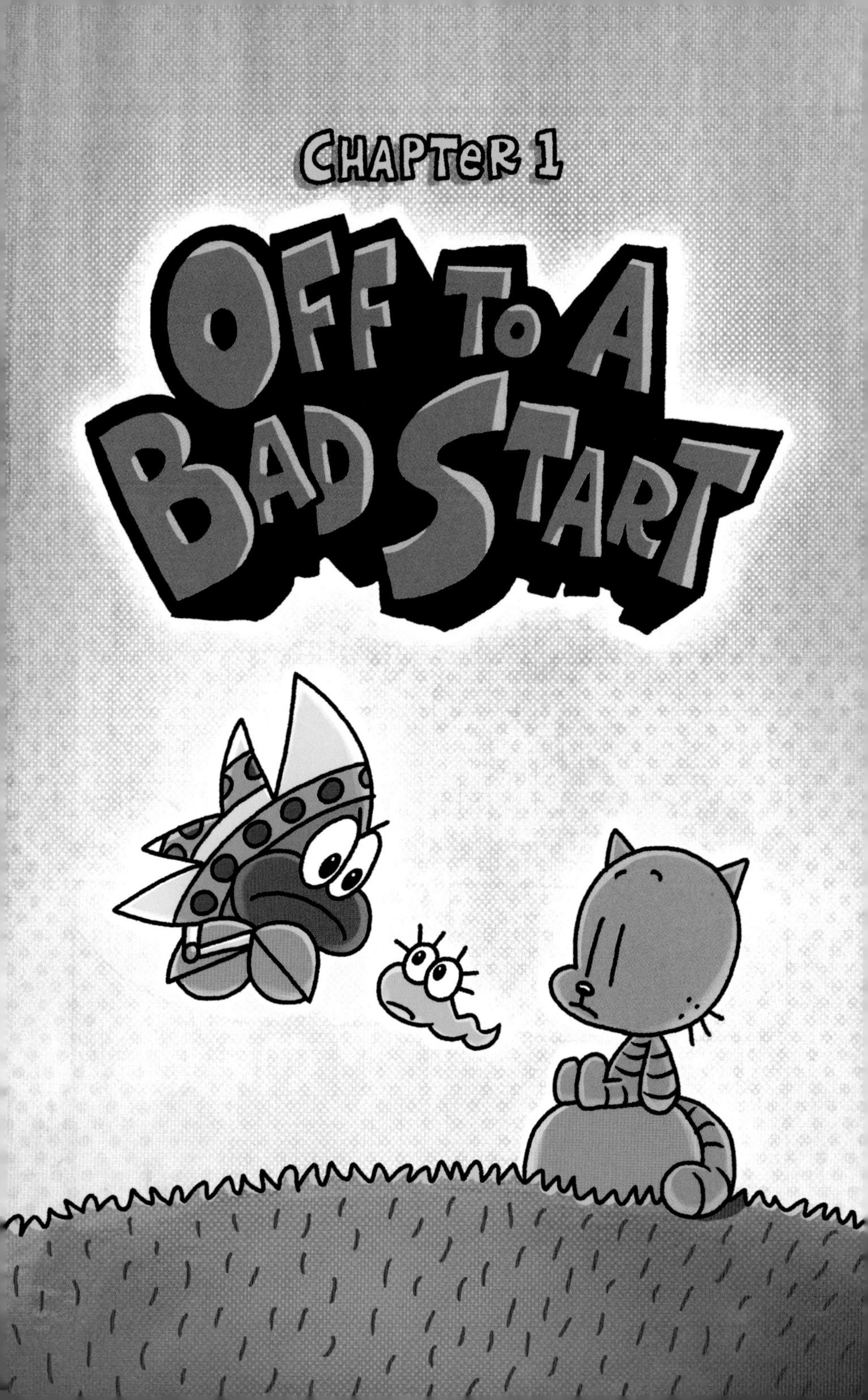

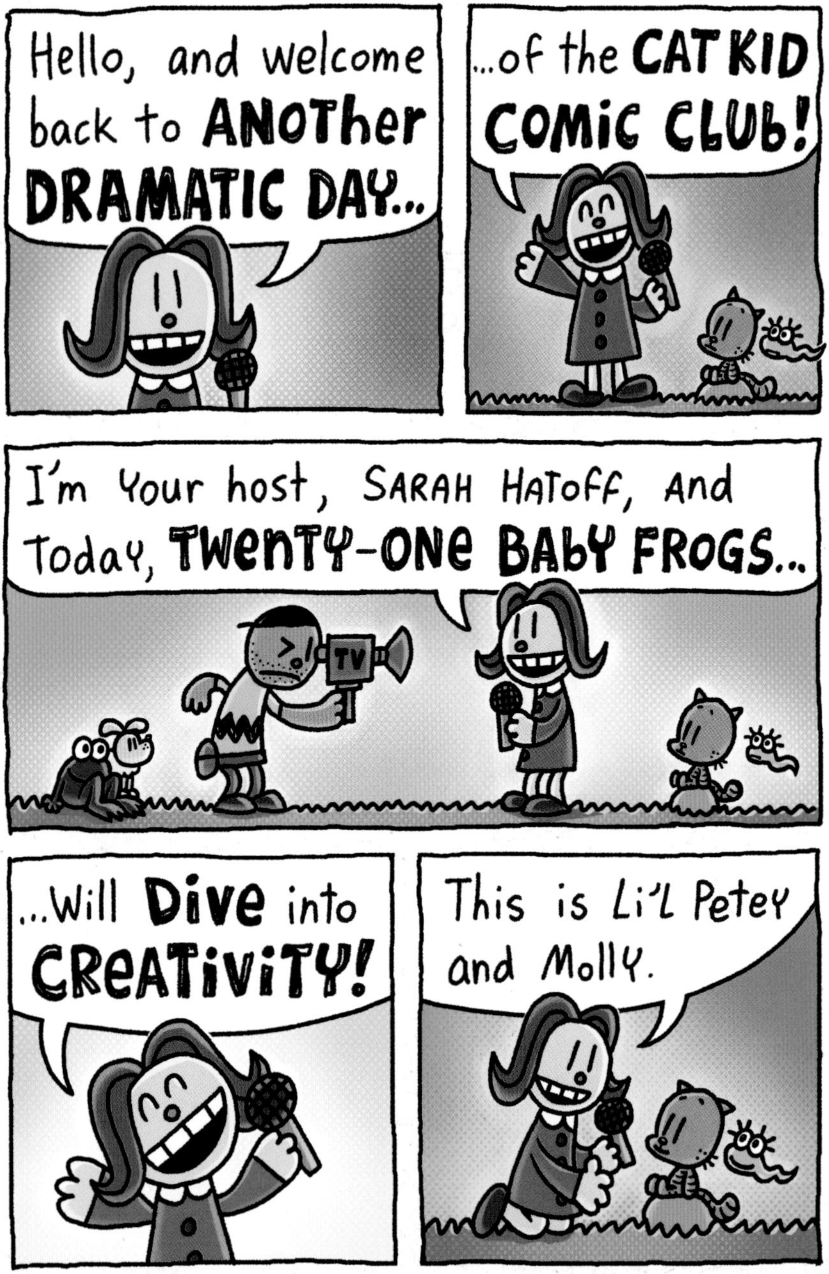
Hello, and welcome back to ANOTHER DRAMATIC DAY...
...of the CAT KID COMIC CLUB!
I'm your host, SARAH HATOFF, And Today, TWENTY-ONE BABY FROGS...
TV
...Will Dive into CREATIVITY!
This is Li'l Petey and Molly.

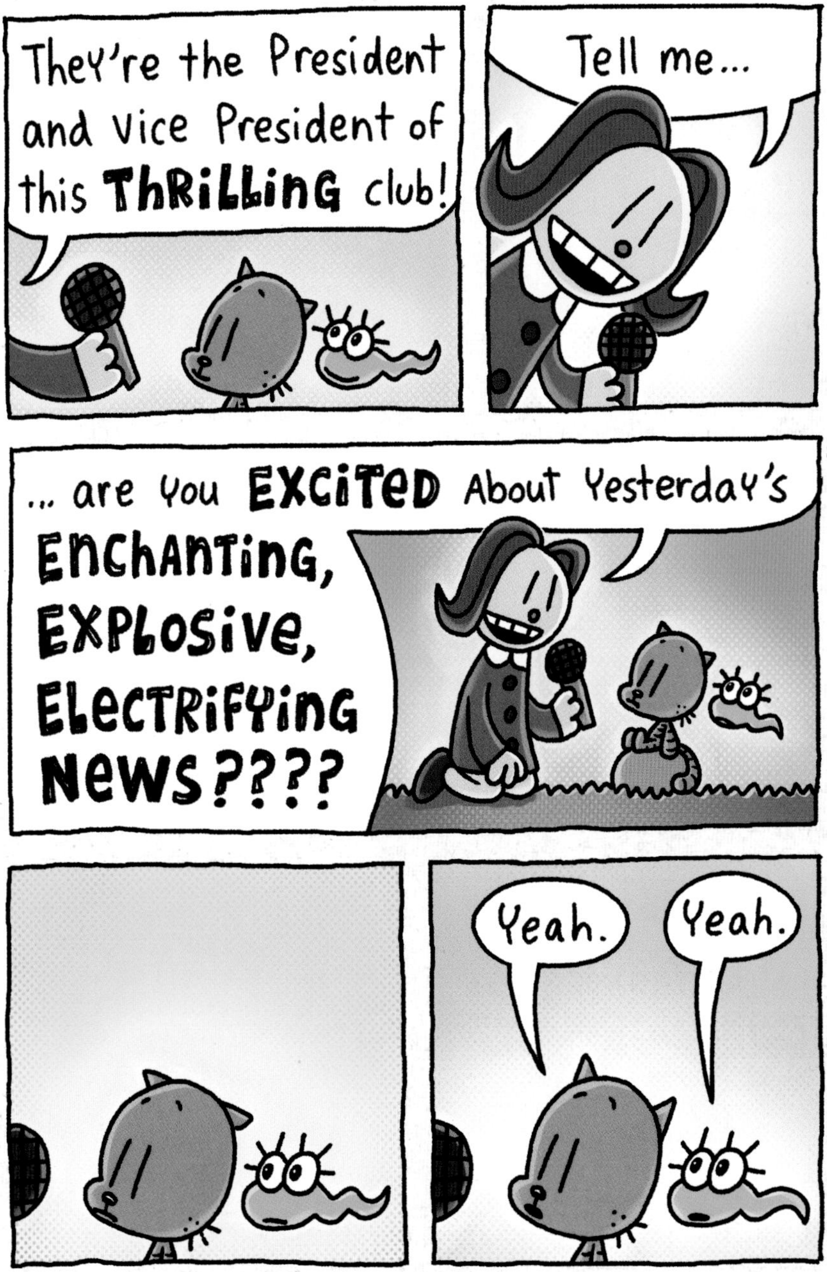
They're the President and vice President of this THRILLING club!
Tell me...
... are you EXCITED About Yesterday's ENCHANTING, EXPLOSIVE, ELECTRIFYING NEWS????
Yeah.
Yeah.

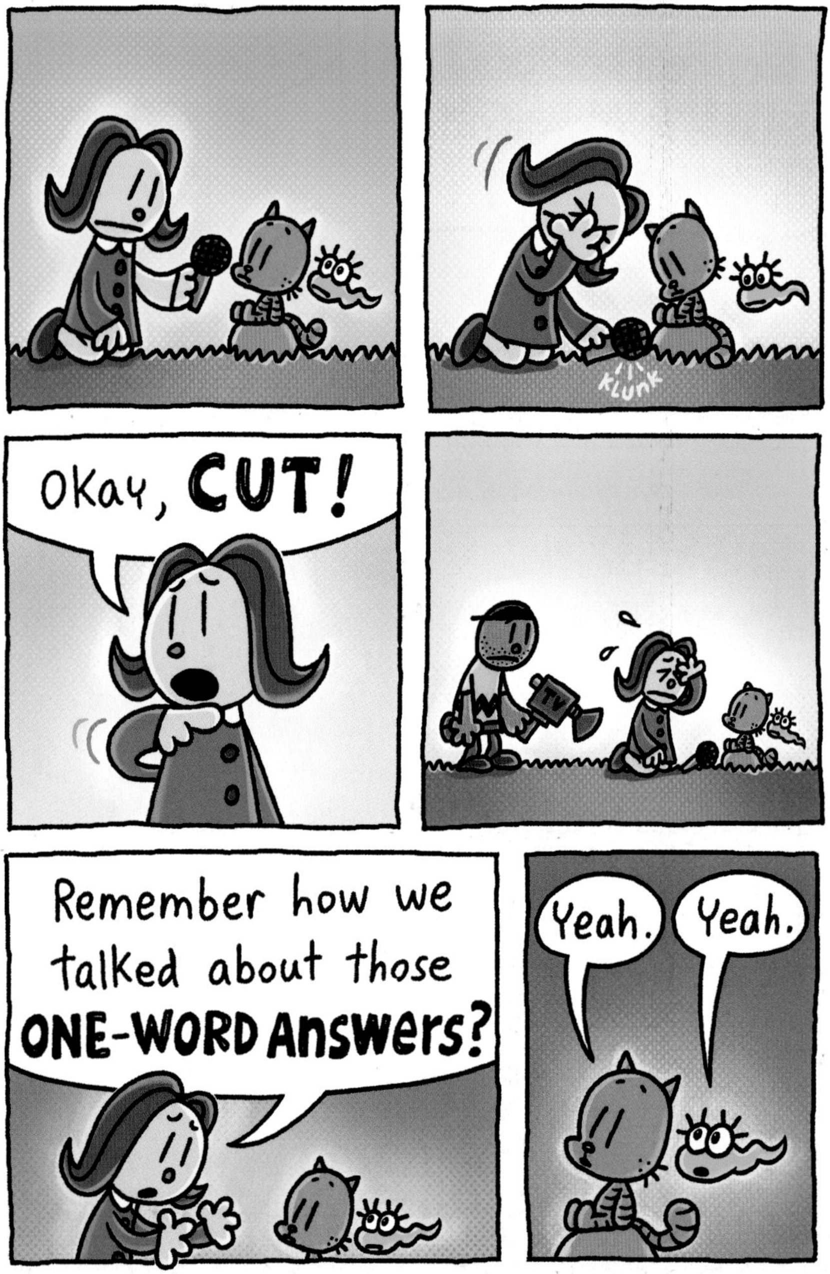
KLUNK
Okay, CUT!
TV
Remember how we talked about those ONE-WORD Answers?
Yeah.
Yeah.

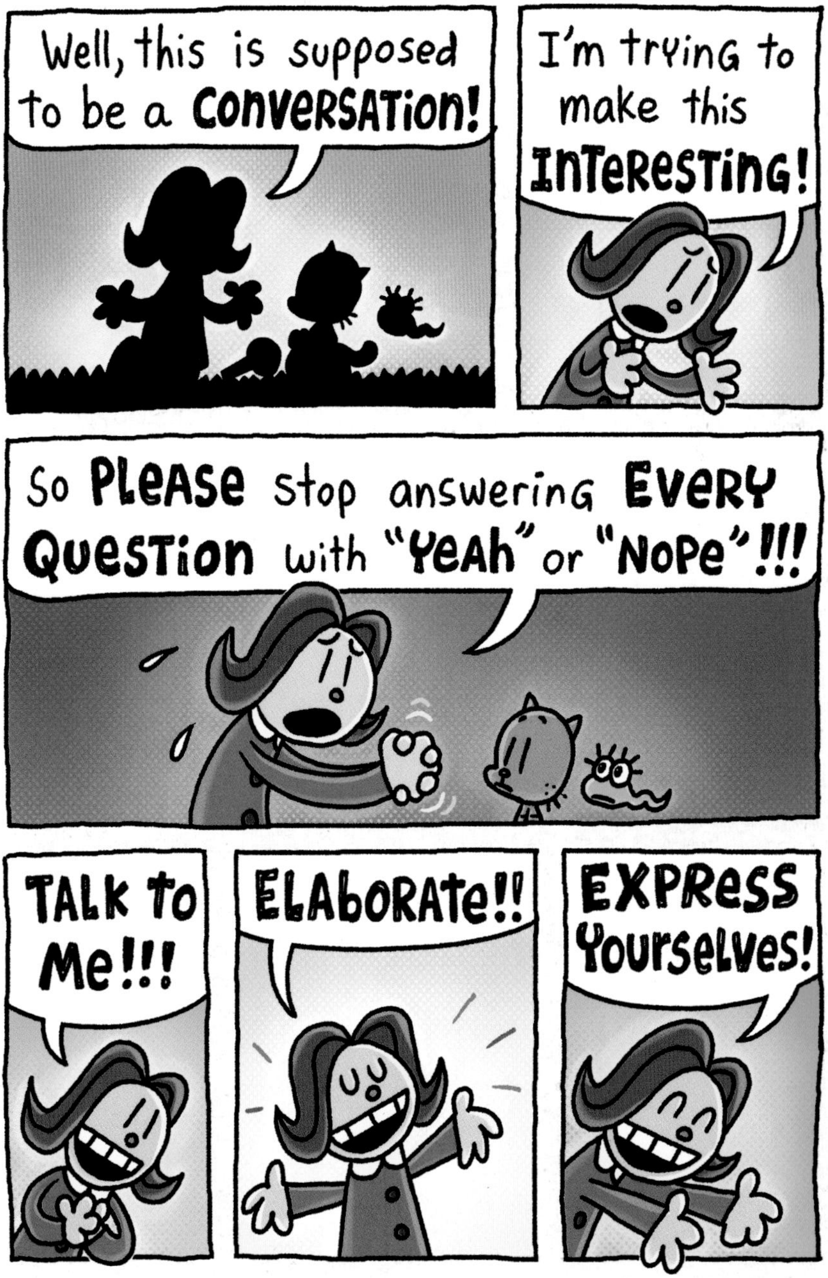
Well, this is supposed to be a CONVERSATION!
I'm trying to make this INTERESTING!
So PLEASE stop answering EVERY QUESTION with "YEAH" or "NOPE"!!!
TALK TO ME!!!
ELABORATE!!
EXPRESS YOURSELVES!

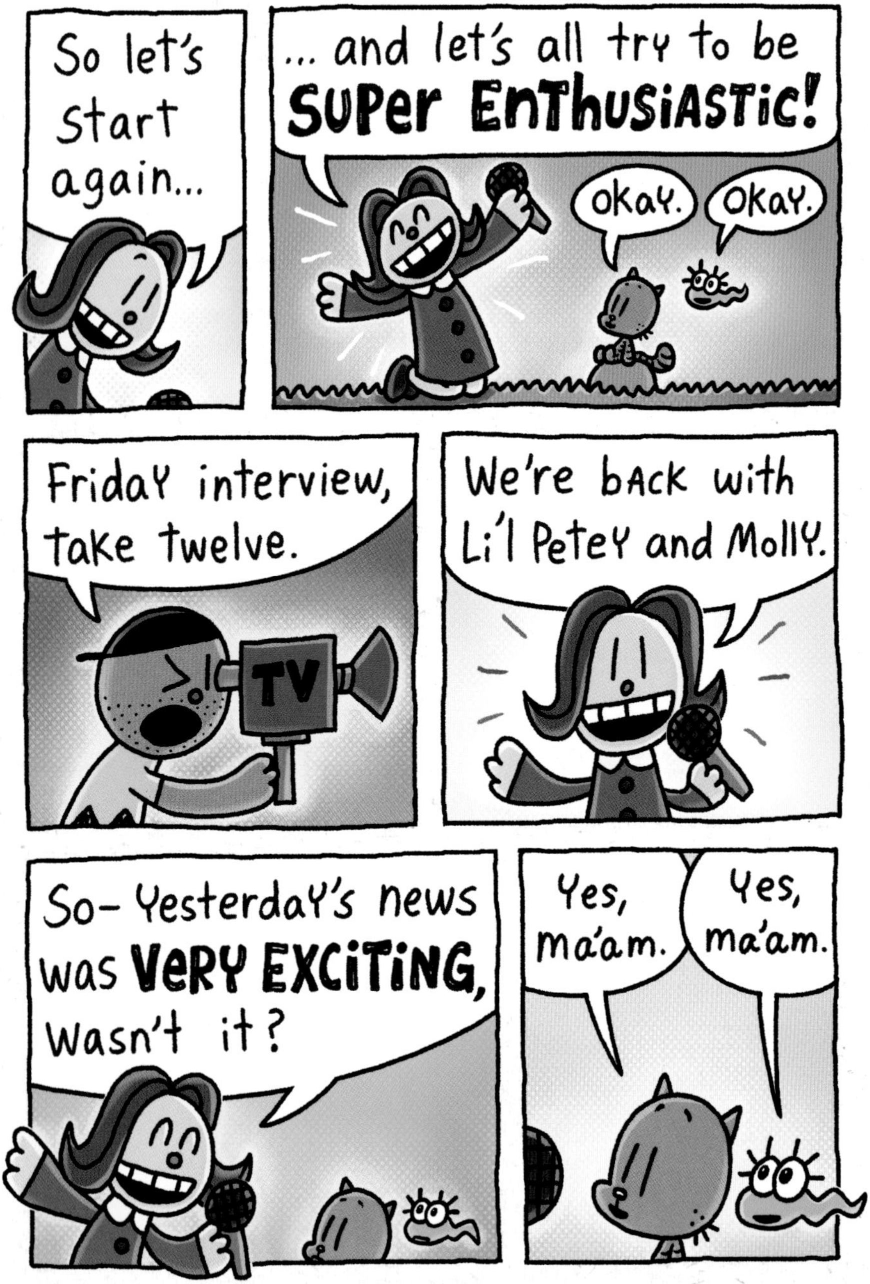
So let's start again...
... and let's all try to be SUPER ENTHUSIASTIC!
OKAY.
OKAY.
Friday interview, take twelve.
TV
We're back with Li'l Petey and Molly.
So– Yesterday's news was VERY EXCITING, wasn't it?
Yes, ma'am.
Yes, ma'am.

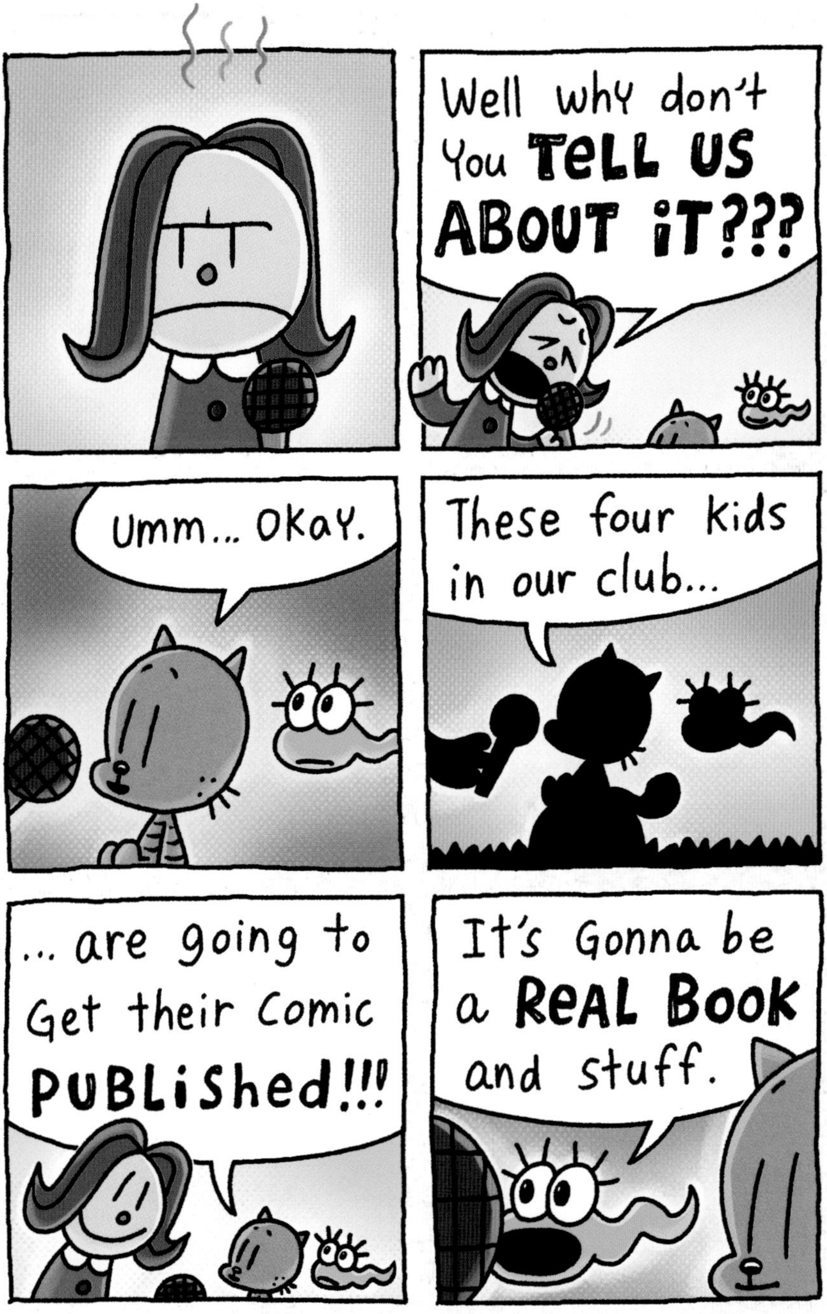

Well why don't You TELL US ABOUT iT???
Umm... OKaY.
These four kids in our club...
... are going to Get their Comic PUBLiShed!!!
It's Gonna be a ReAL BOOK and stuff.

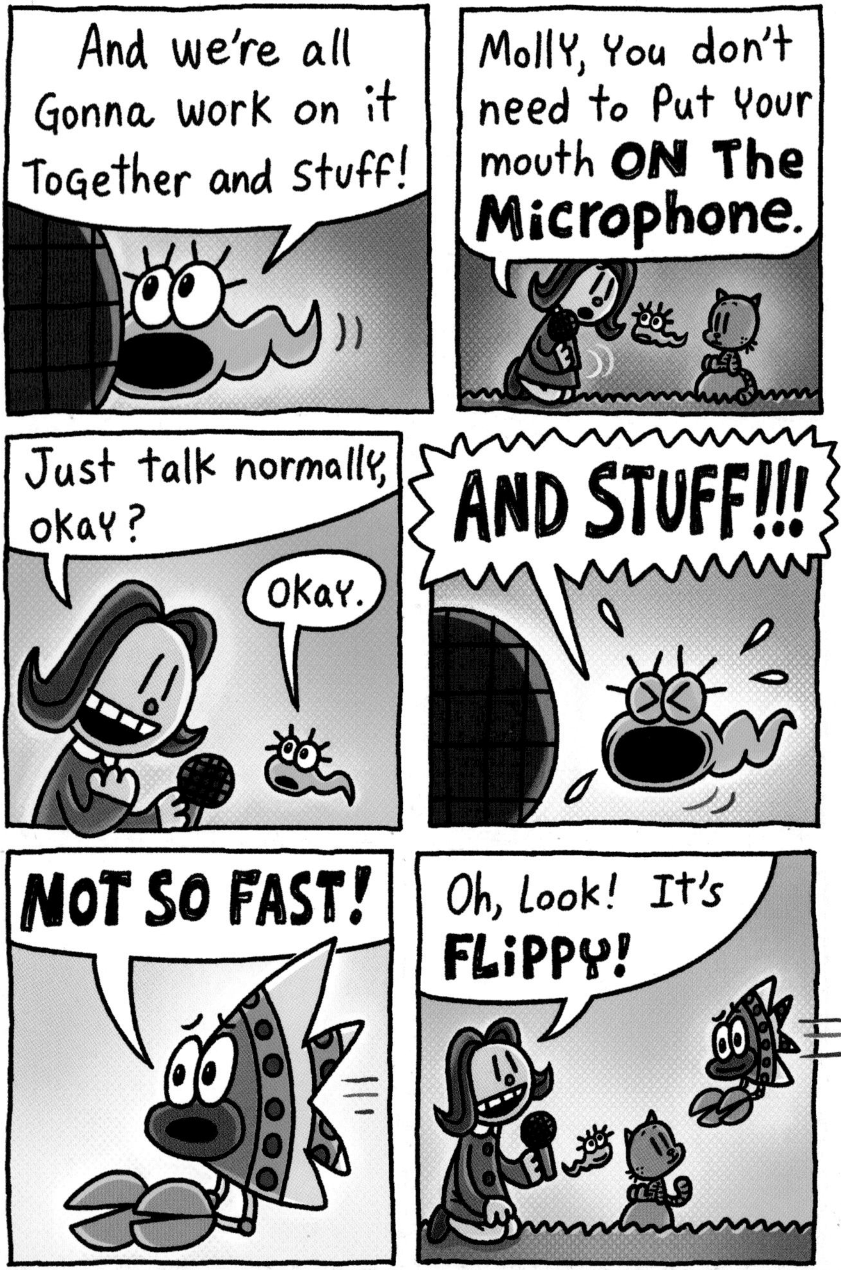
And we're all Gonna work on it Together and Stuff!
Molly, You don't need to Put Your mouth **ON The Microphone.**
Just talk normally, okay?
OKay.
AND STUFF!!!
NOT SO FAST!
Oh, Look! It's **FLIPPY!**

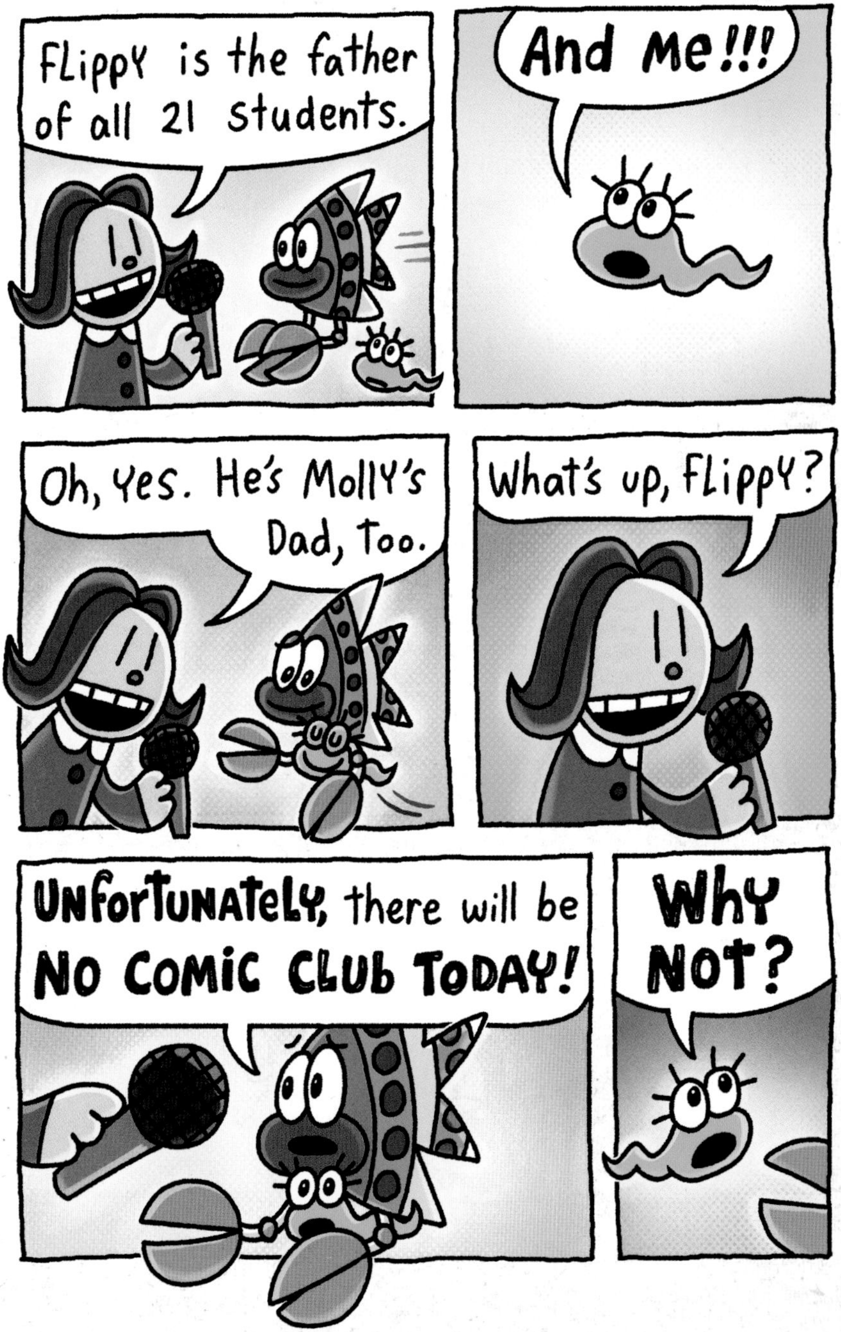
Flippy is the father of all 21 students.
And Me!!!
Oh, yes. He's Molly's Dad, Too.
What's up, Flippy?
UNFORTUNATELY, there will be NO COMIC CLUB TODAY!
Why NOT?

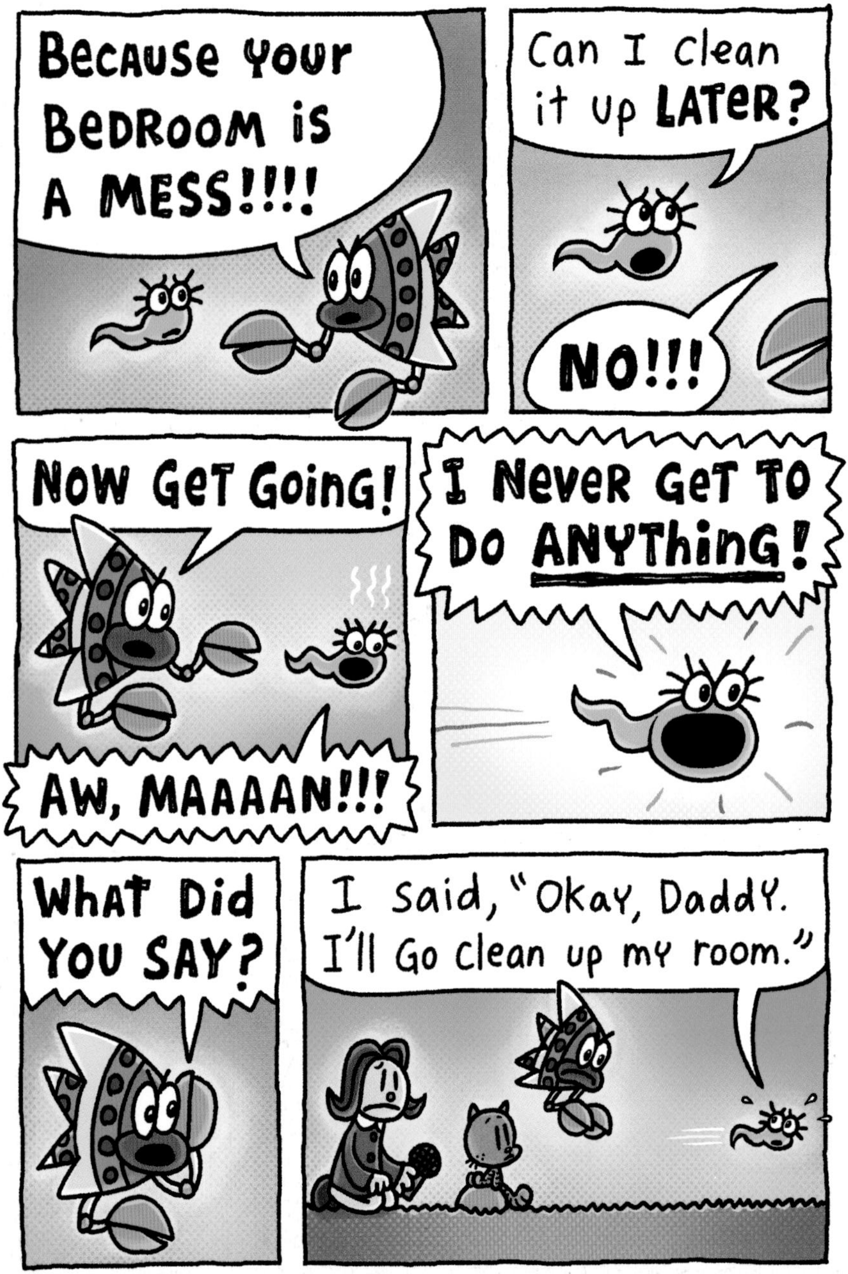
BECAUSE YOUR BEDROOM IS A MESS!!!!
Can I Clean it up LATER?
NO!!!
NOW GET GOING!
AW, MAAAAN!!!
I NEVER GET TO DO ANYTHING!
WHAT DID YOU SAY?
I said, "Okay, Daddy. I'll Go clean up my room."

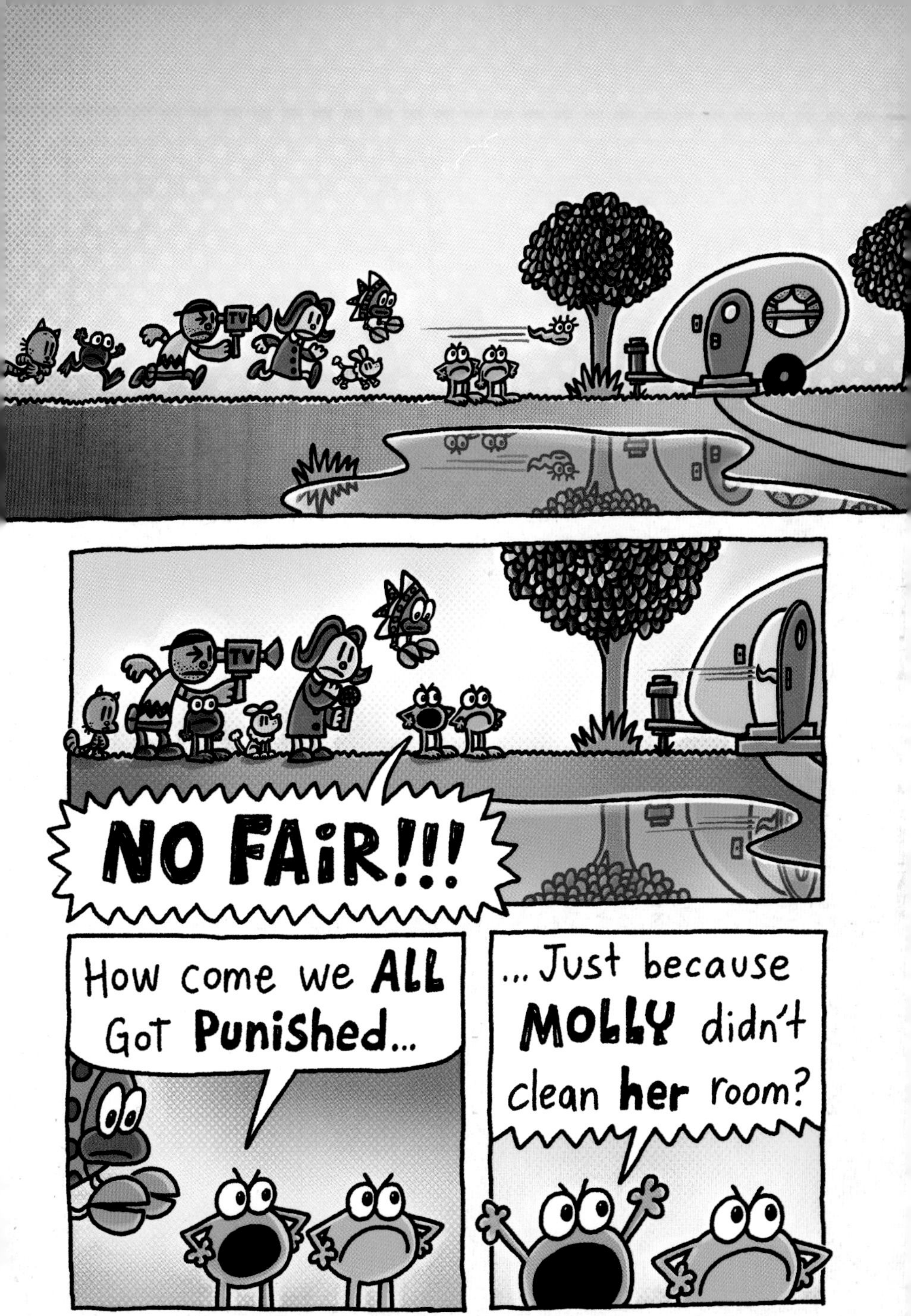
TV
TV
NO FAIR!!!
How come we ALL Got Punished...
...Just because MOLLY didn't clean her room?

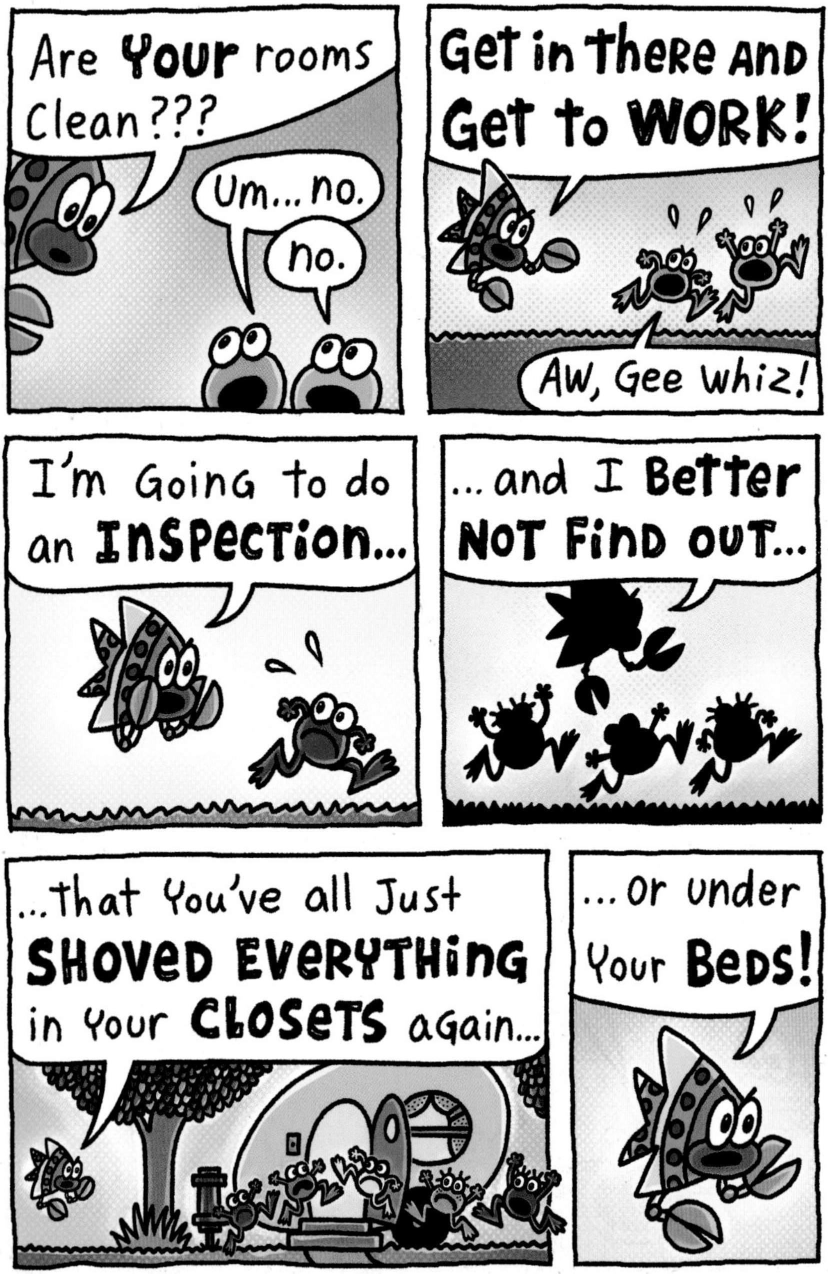
Are YOUR rooms Clean???
Um...no.
no.
Get in There AND Get to WORK!
AW, Gee whiz!
I'm Going to do an INSPECTION...
...and I Better NOT FIND OUT...
...that You've all Just SHOVED EVERYTHING in Your CLOSETS again...
...Or under Your BEDS!

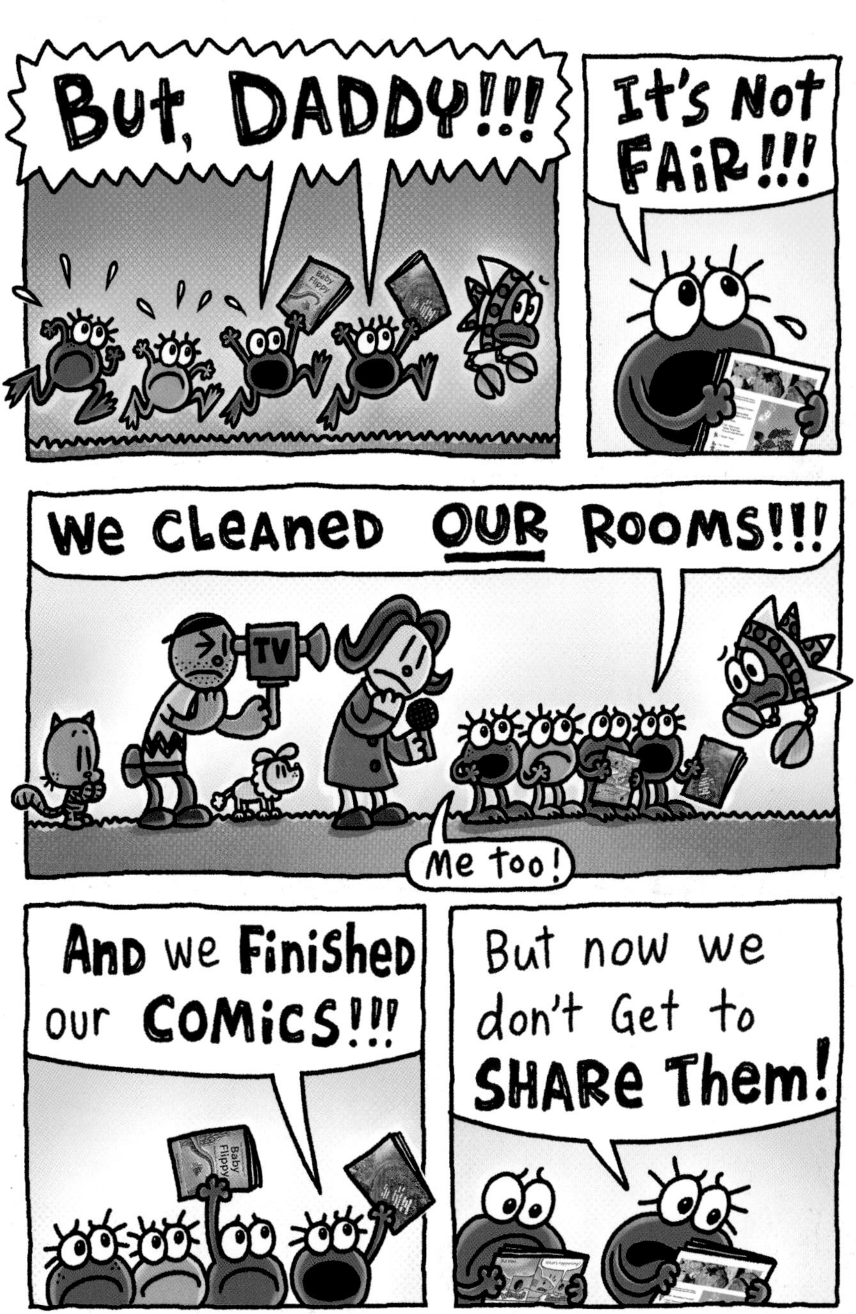
But, DADDY!!!
It's Not FAiR!!!
We CLeaned OUR Rooms!!!
TV
Me too!
And we Finished our COMiCS!!!
But now we don't Get to SHARE Them!

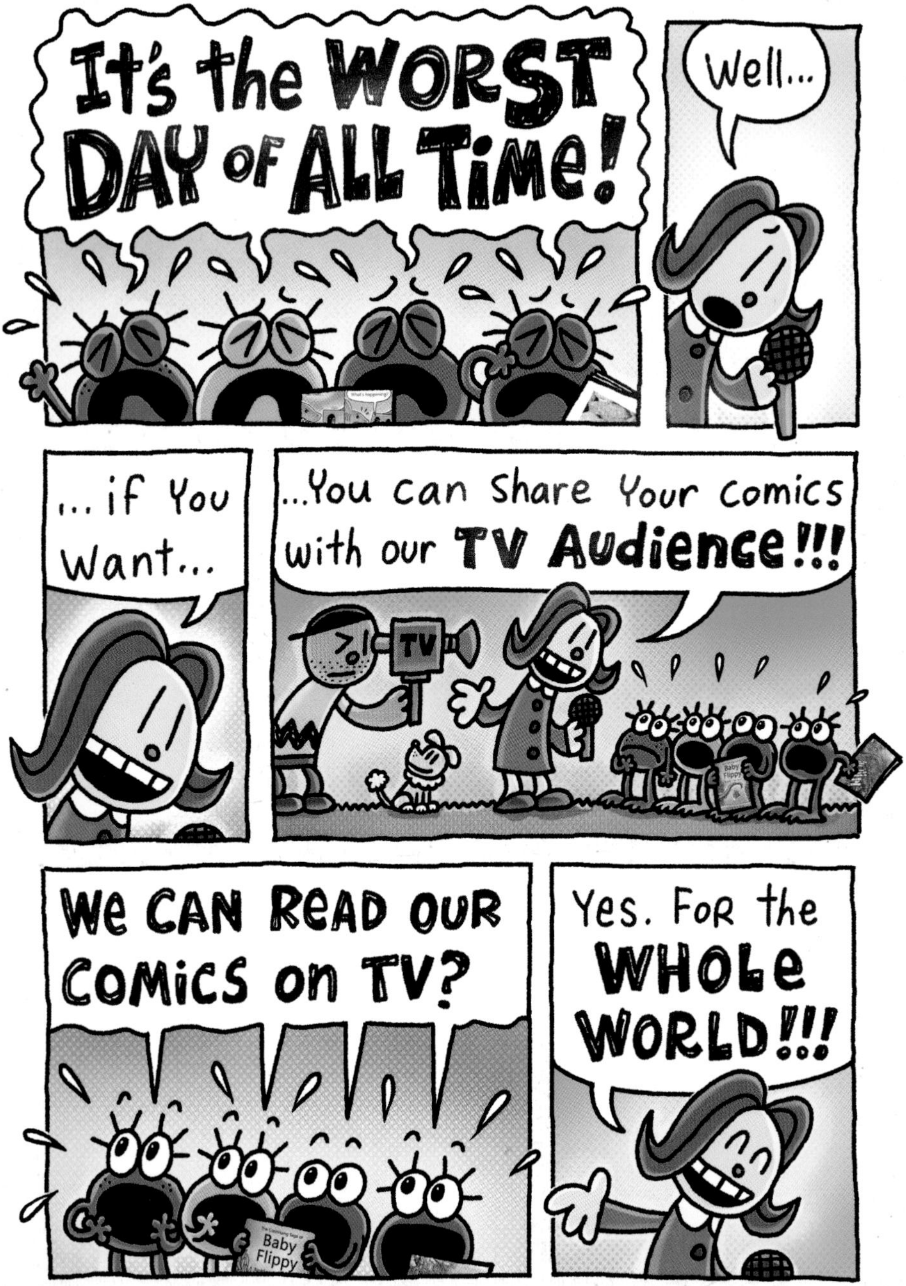
It's the WORST DAY OF ALL TIME!
Well...
...if You want...
...You can share Your comics with our TV Audience!!!
TV
Baby Flippy
We CAN READ OUR COMICS on TV?
Baby Flippy
Yes. For the WHOLE WORLD!!!

CHAPTER 2

The Best Day of All Time

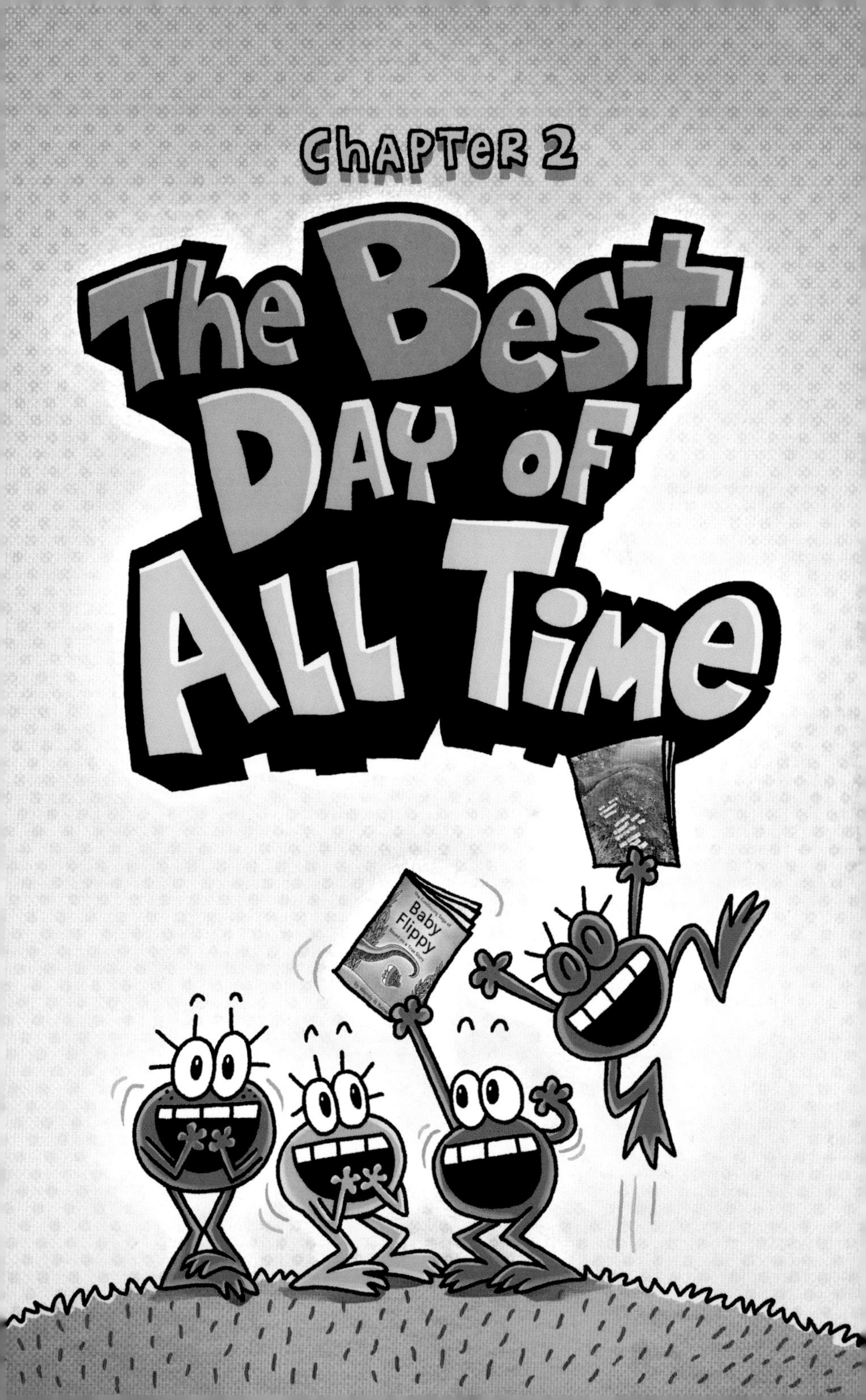
Baby
Flippy

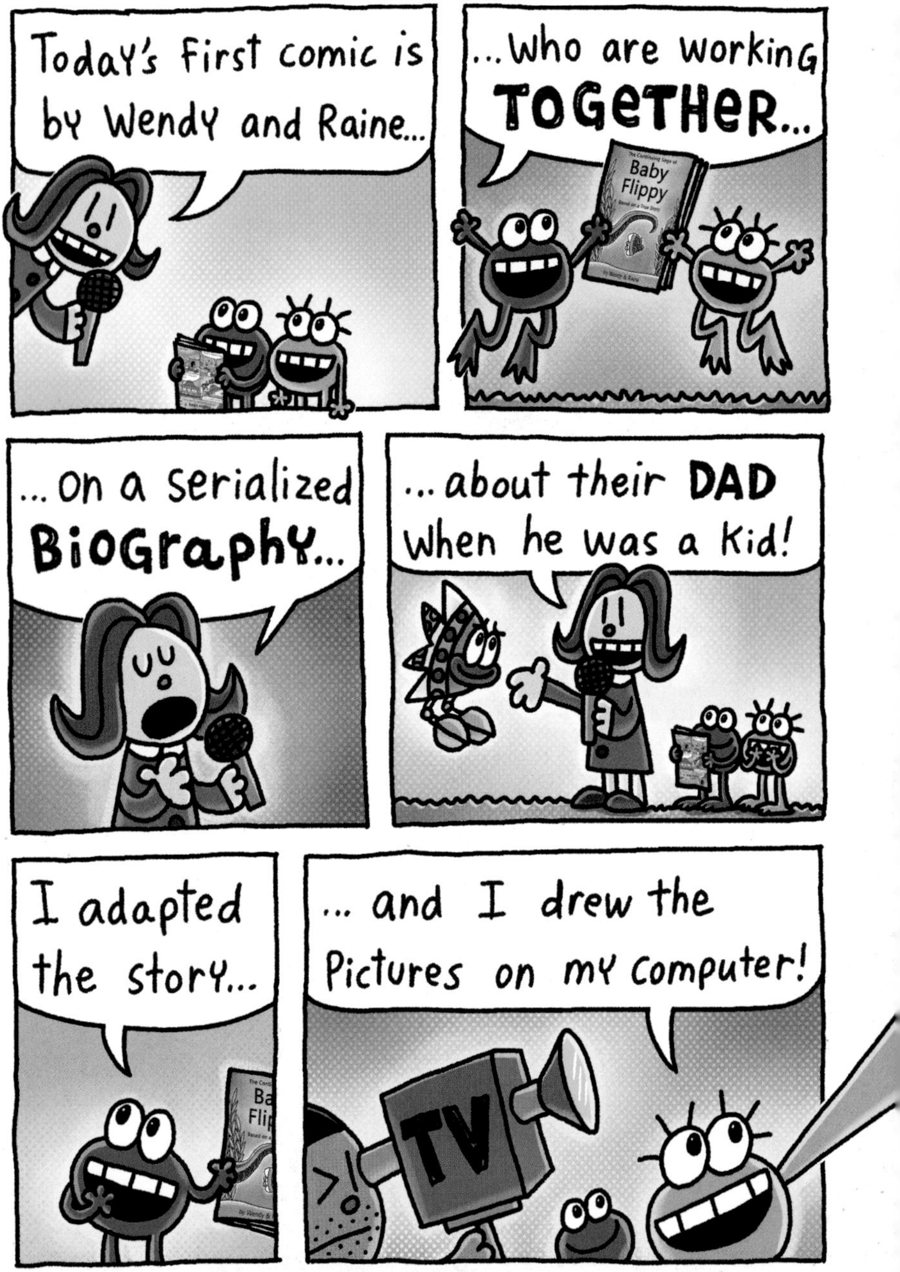
Today's first comic is by Wendy and Raine...
...Who are working TOGETHER...
The Continuing Saga of Baby Flippy Based on a True Story
...on a serialized BIOGRAPHY...
...about their DAD when he was a kid!
I adapted the story...
...and I drew the pictures on my computer!
TV

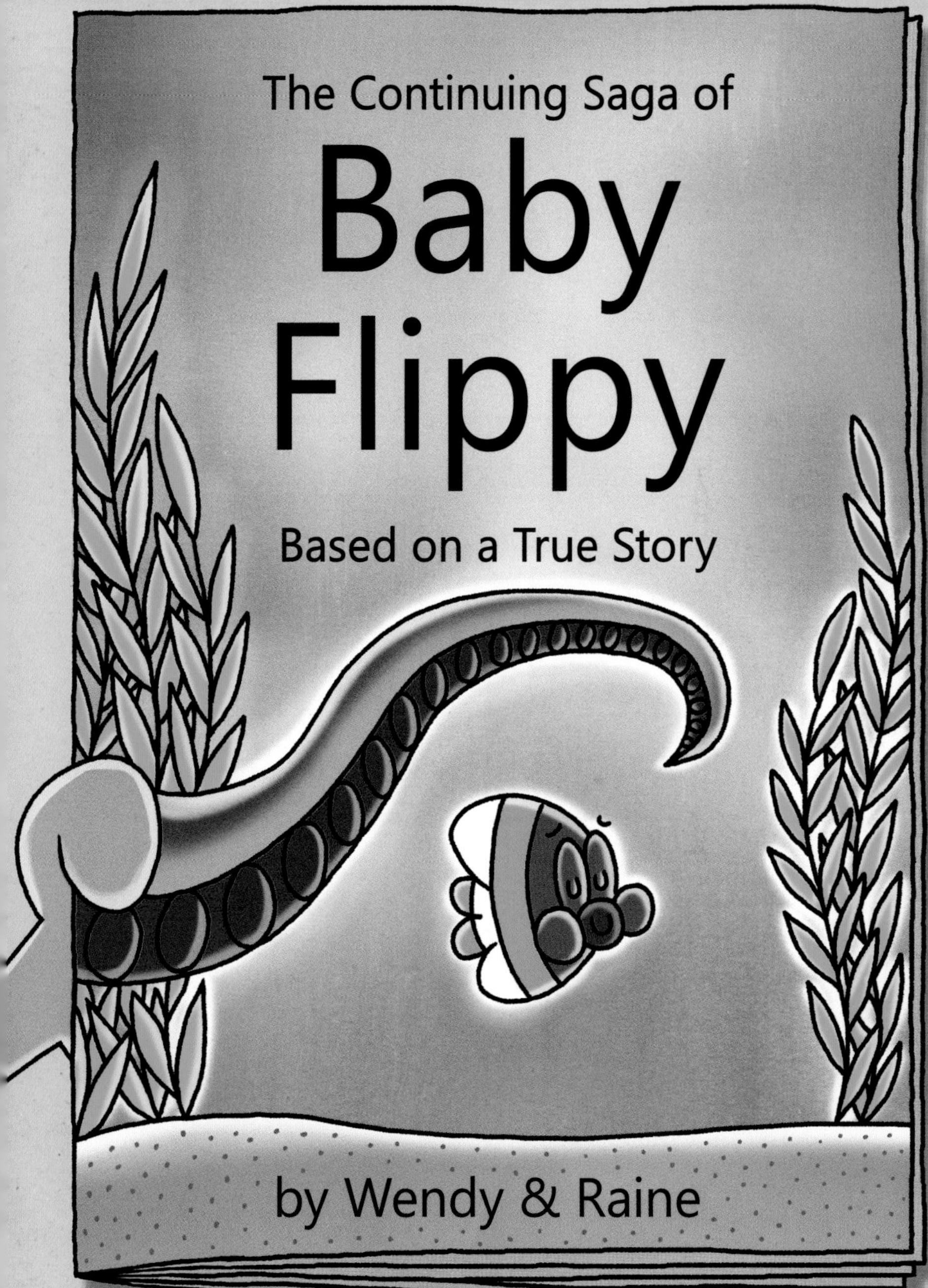
The Continuing Saga of
Baby Flippy
Based on a True Story
by Wendy & Raine

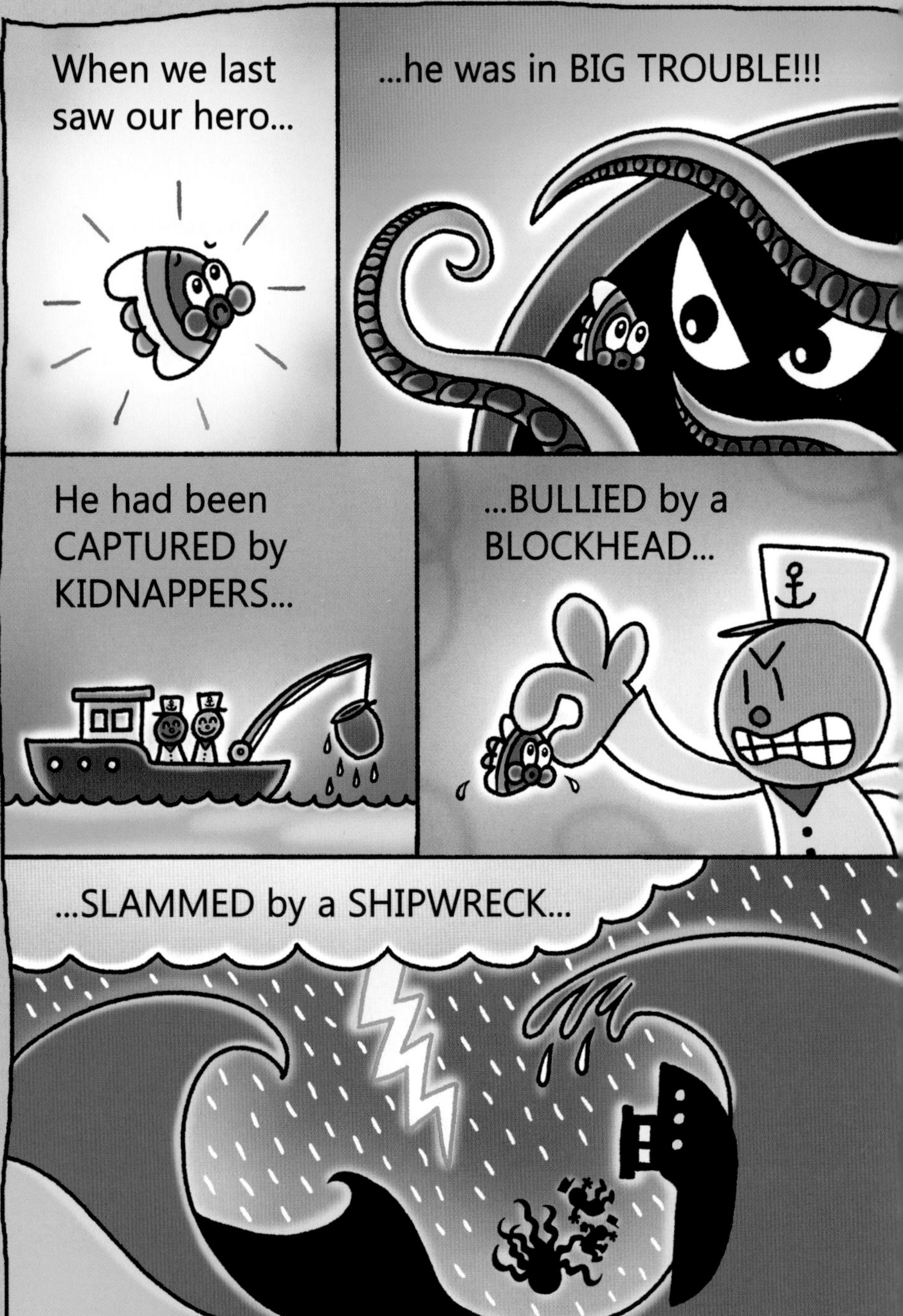
When we last saw our hero...
...he was in BIG TROUBLE!!!
He had been CAPTURED by KIDNAPPERS...
...BULLIED by a BLOCKHEAD...
...SLAMMED by a SHIPWRECK...

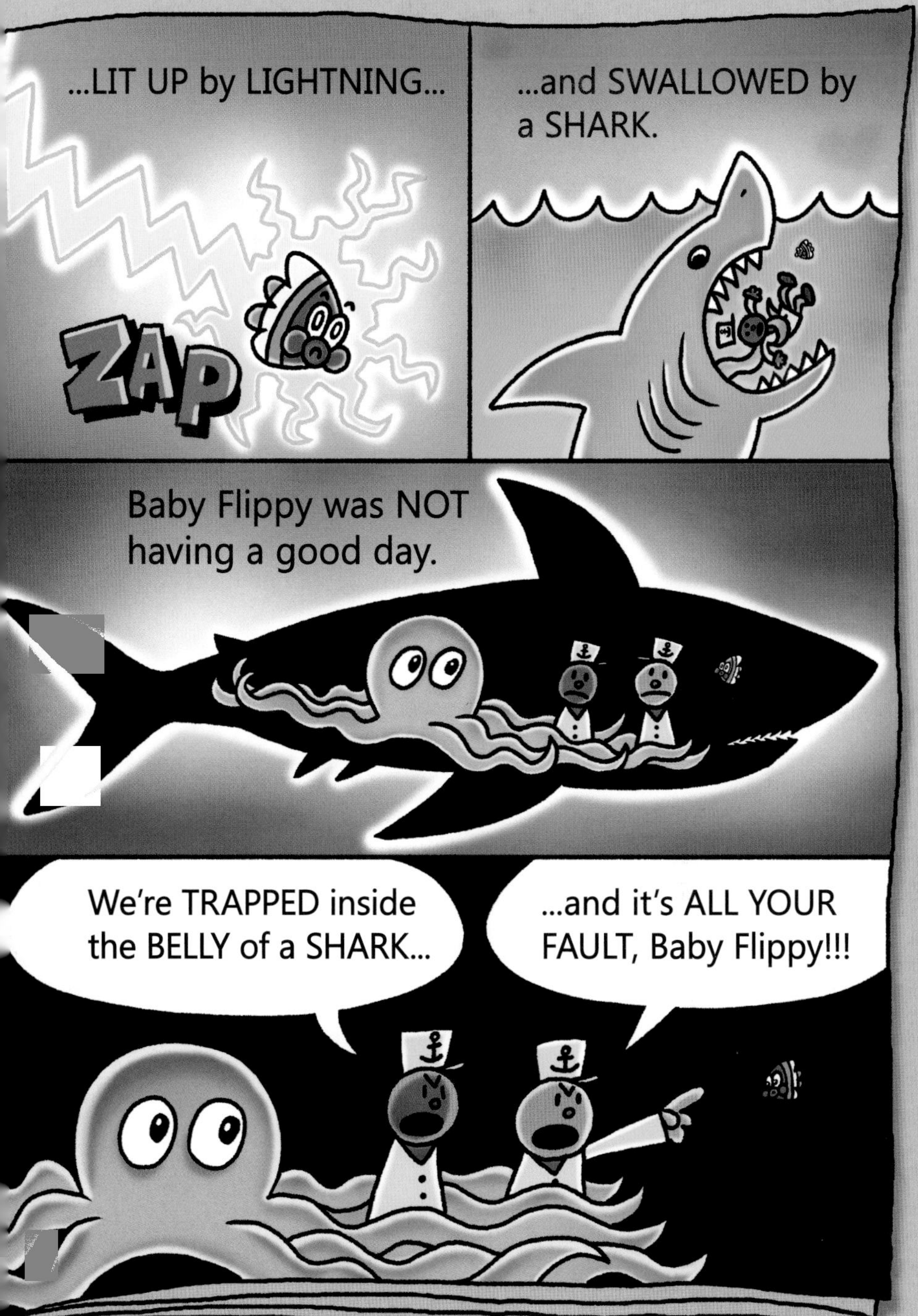
...LIT UP by LIGHTNING...
ZAP
...and SWALLOWED by a SHARK.
Baby Flippy was NOT having a good day.
We're TRAPPED inside the BELLY of a SHARK...
...and it's ALL YOUR FAULT, Baby Flippy!!!

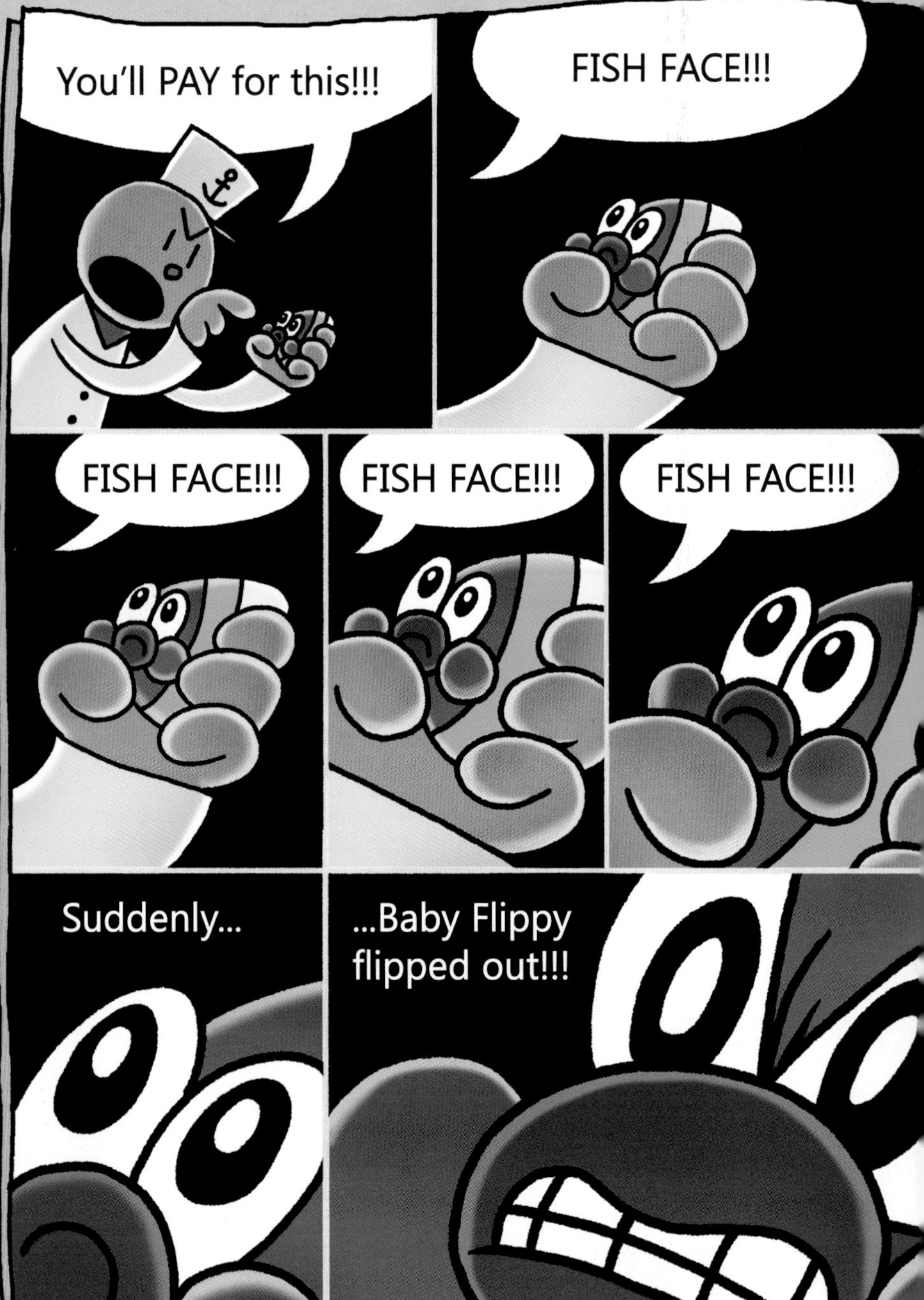
You'll PAY for this!!!
FISH FACE!!!
FISH FACE!!!
FISH FACE!!!
FISH FACE!!!
Suddenly...
...Baby Flippy flipped out!!!

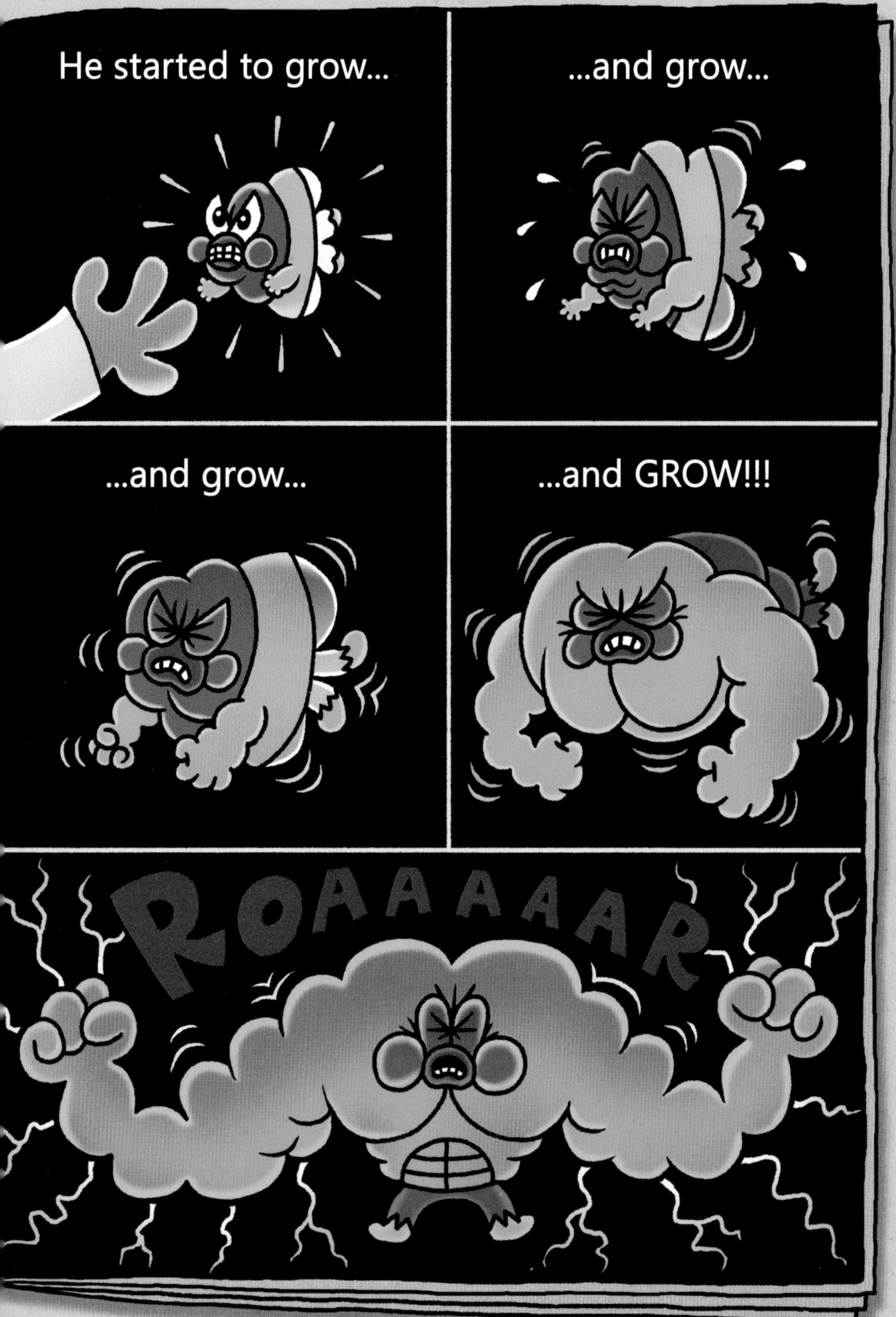
He started to grow...
...and grow...
...and grow...
...and GROW!!!
ROAAAAAR

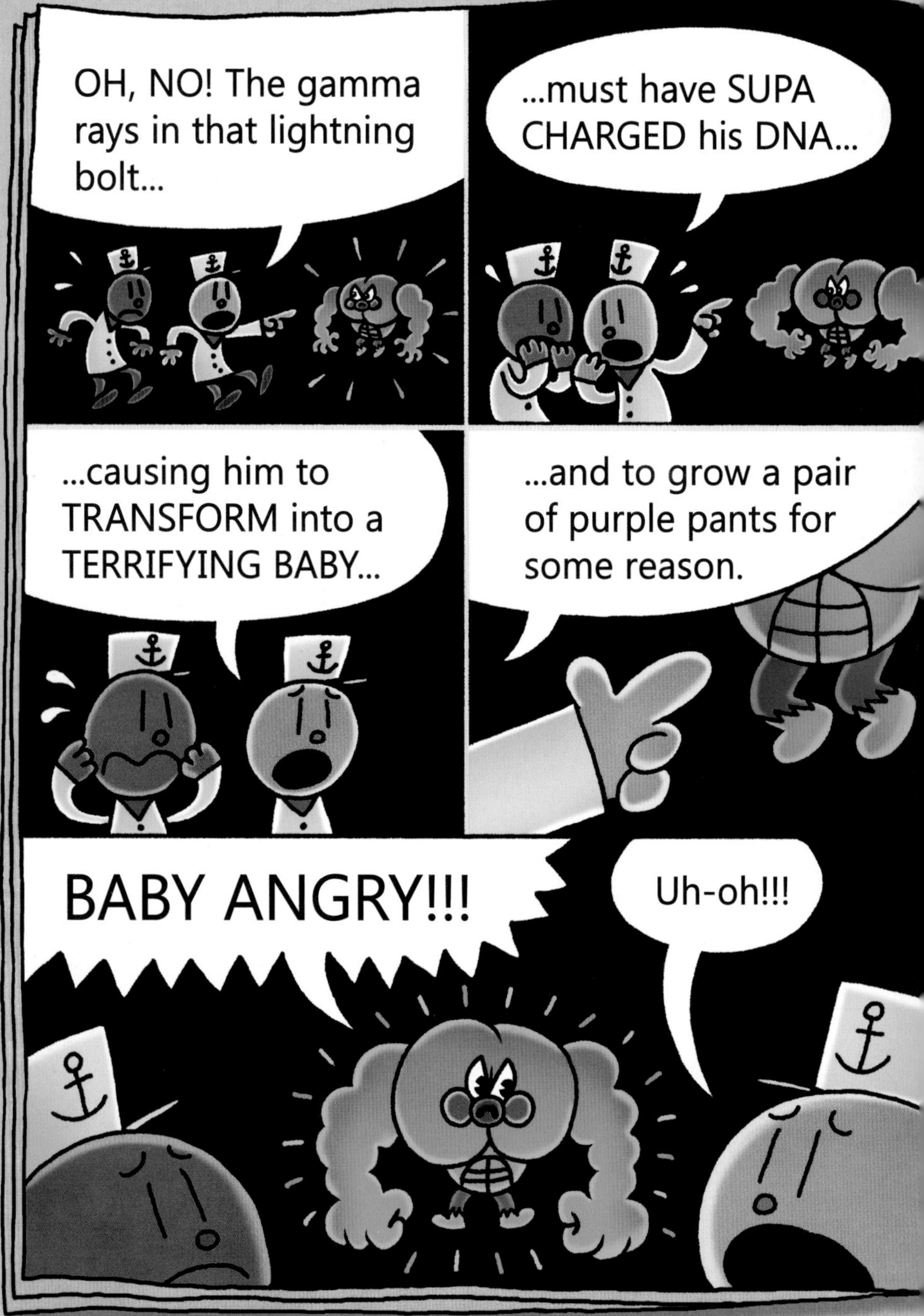
OH, NO! The gamma rays in that lightning bolt...
...must have SUPA CHARGED his DNA...
...causing him to TRANSFORM into a TERRIFYING BABY...
...and to grow a pair of purple pants for some reason.
BABY ANGRY!!!
Uh-oh!!!

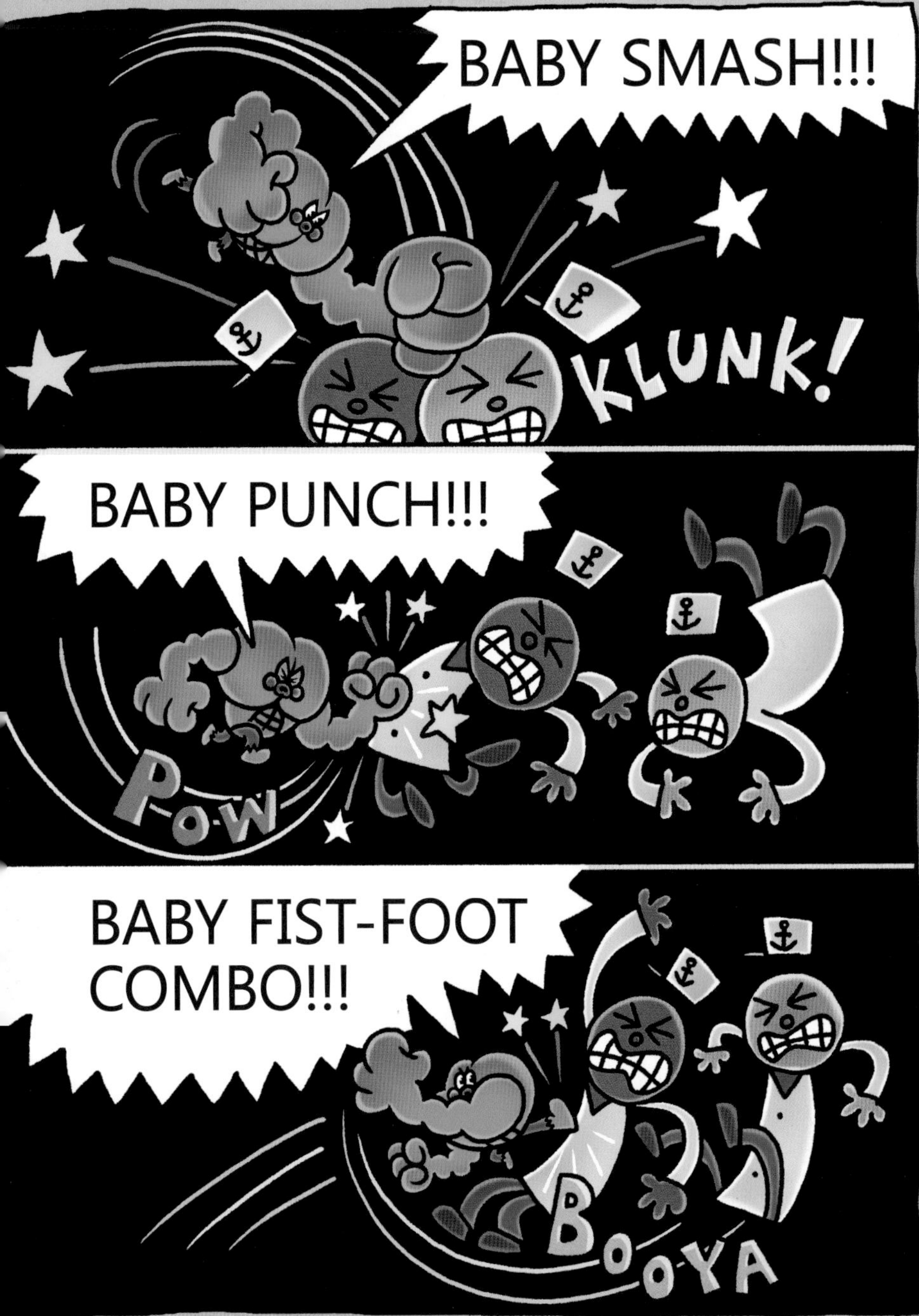
BABY SMASH!!!
KLUNK!
BABY PUNCH!!!
POW
BABY FIST-FOOT COMBO!!!
BOOYA

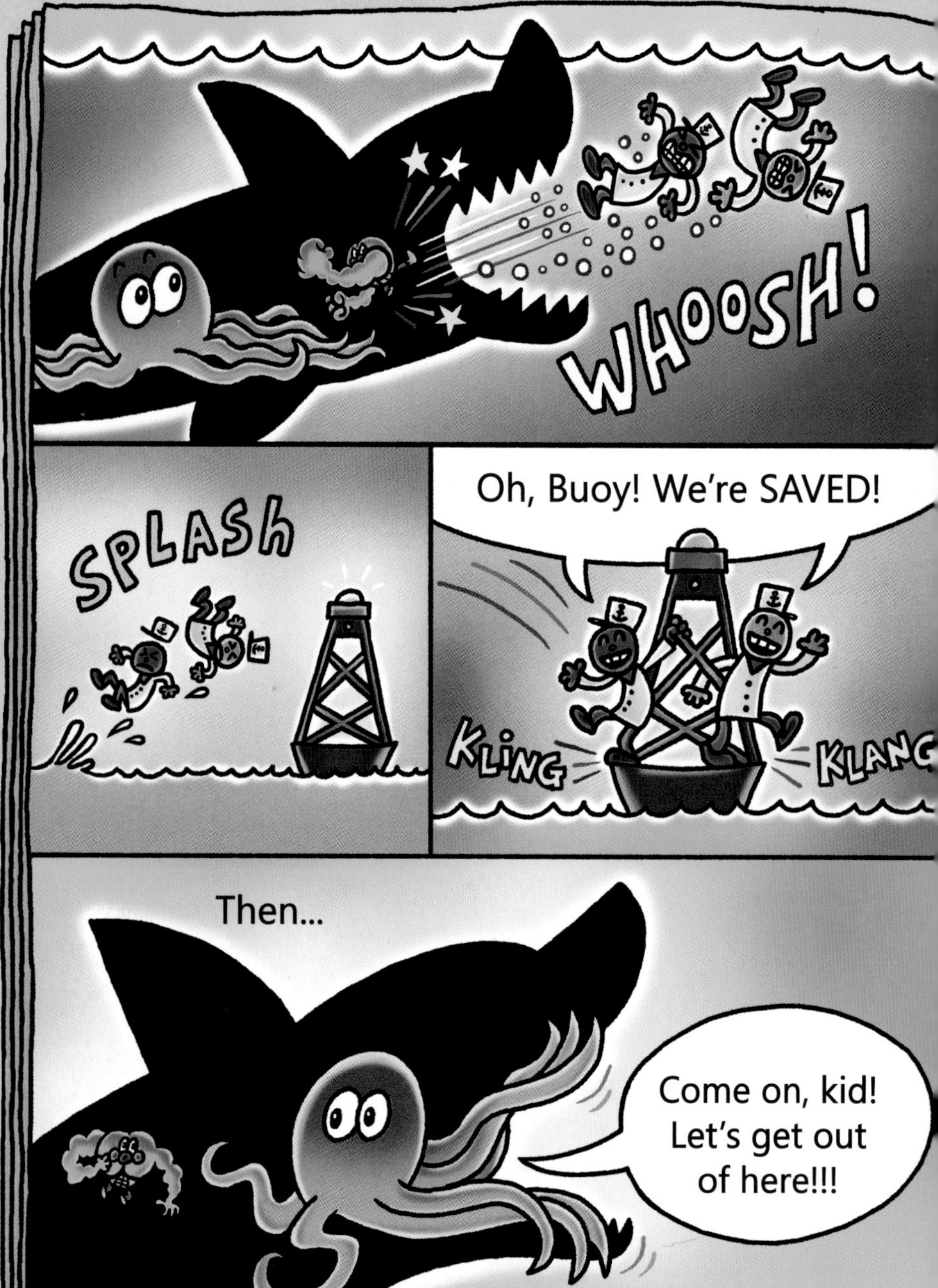
WHOOSH!
SPLASH
Oh, Buoy! We're SAVED!
KLING
KLANG
Then...
Come on, kid! Let's get out of here!!!

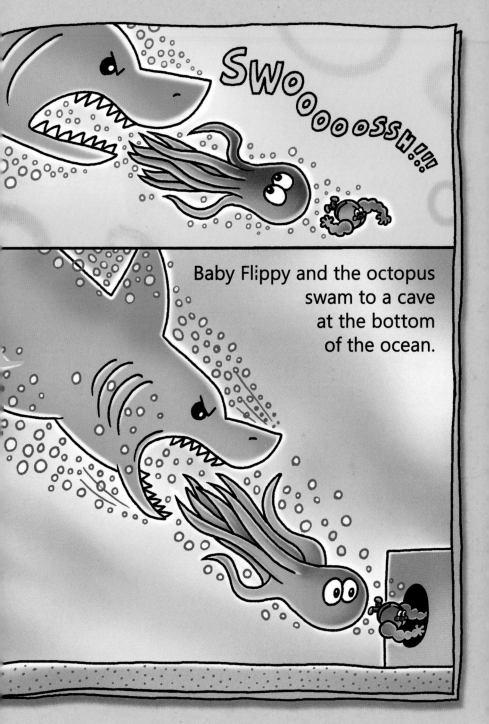

Baby Flippy and the octopus swam to a cave at the bottom of the ocean.

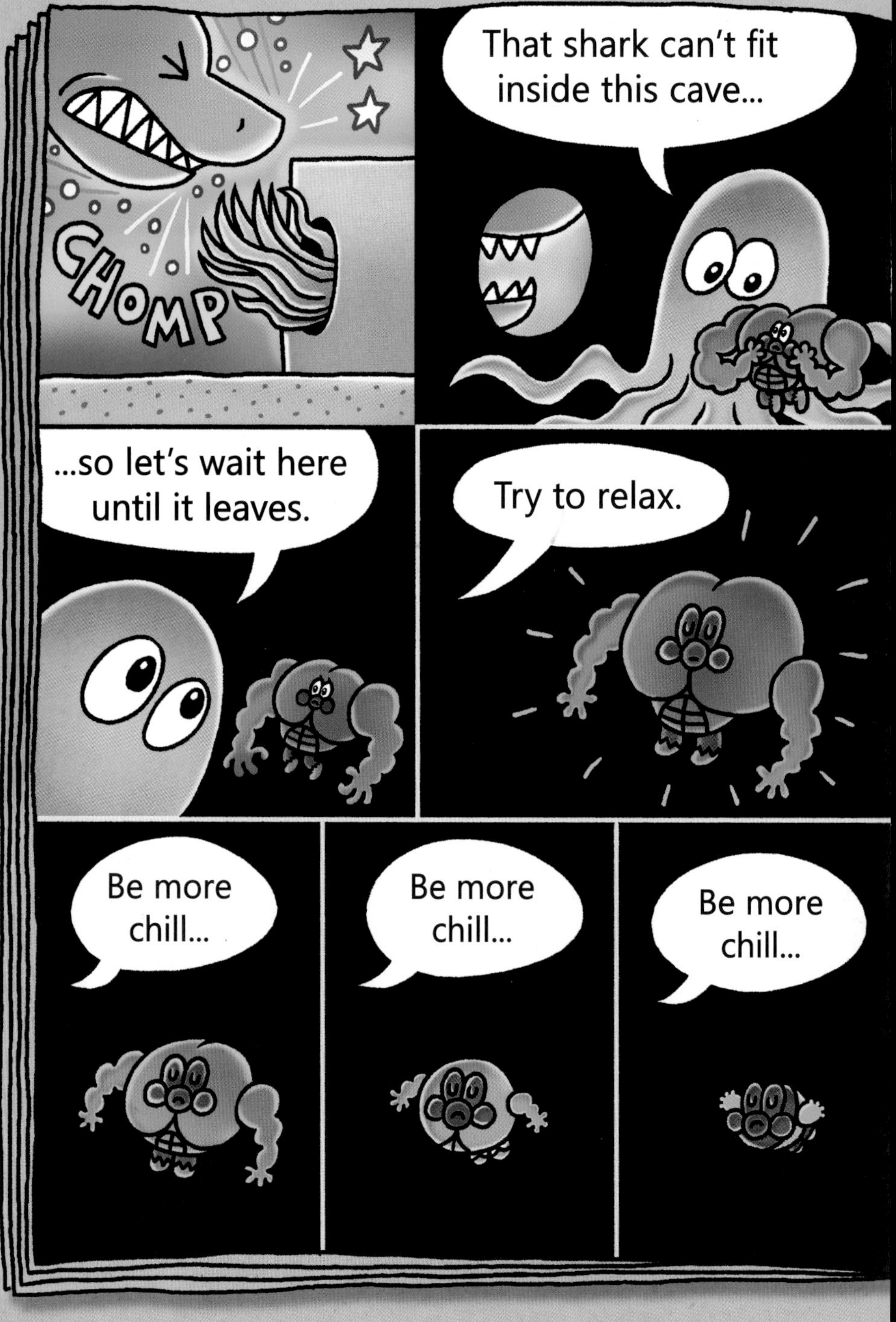
CHOMP
That shark can't fit inside this cave...
...so let's wait here until it leaves.
Try to relax.
Be more chill...
Be more chill...
Be more chill...

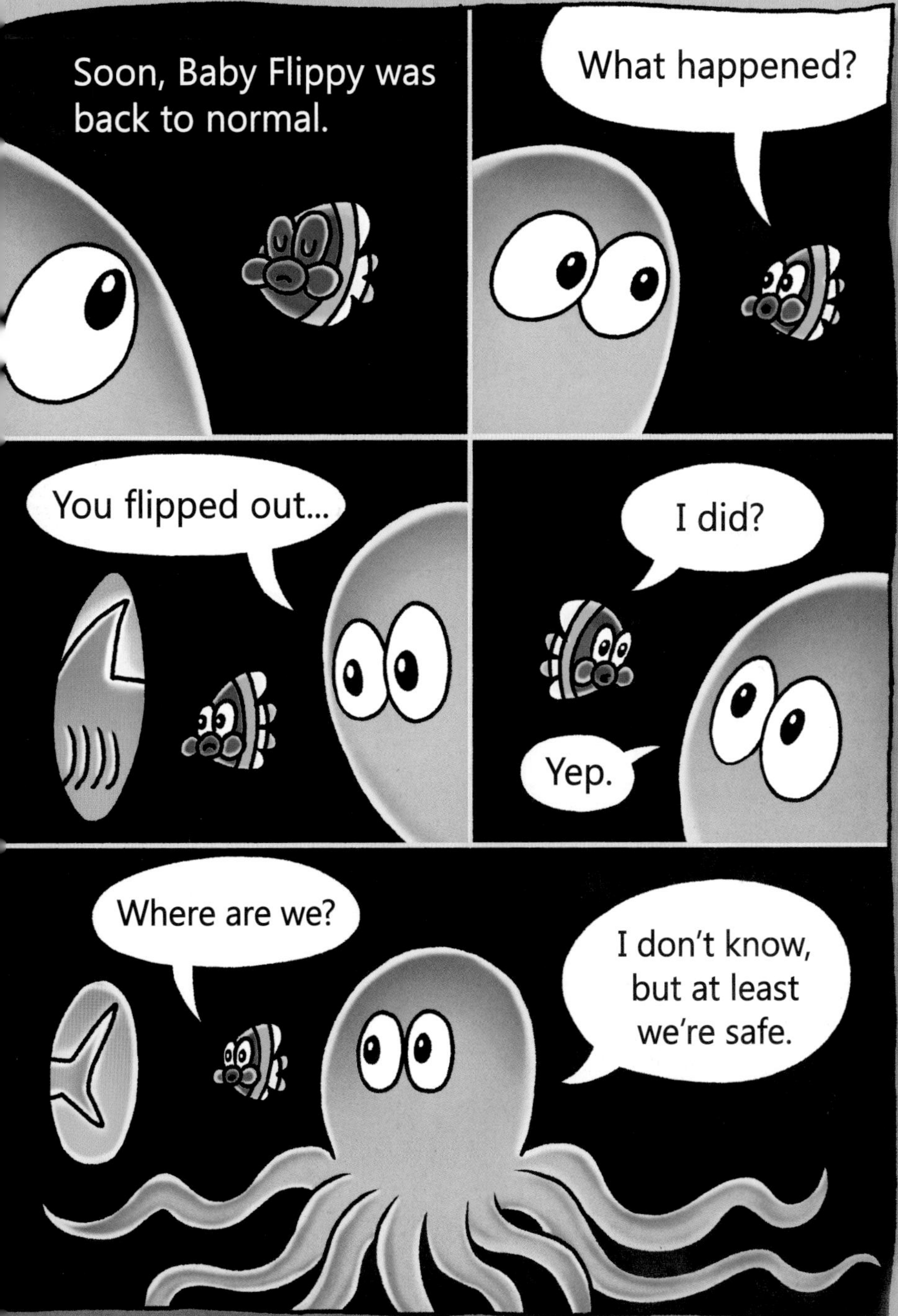
Soon, Baby Flippy was back to normal.
What happened?
You flipped out...
I did?
Yep.
Where are we?
I don't know, but at least we're safe.

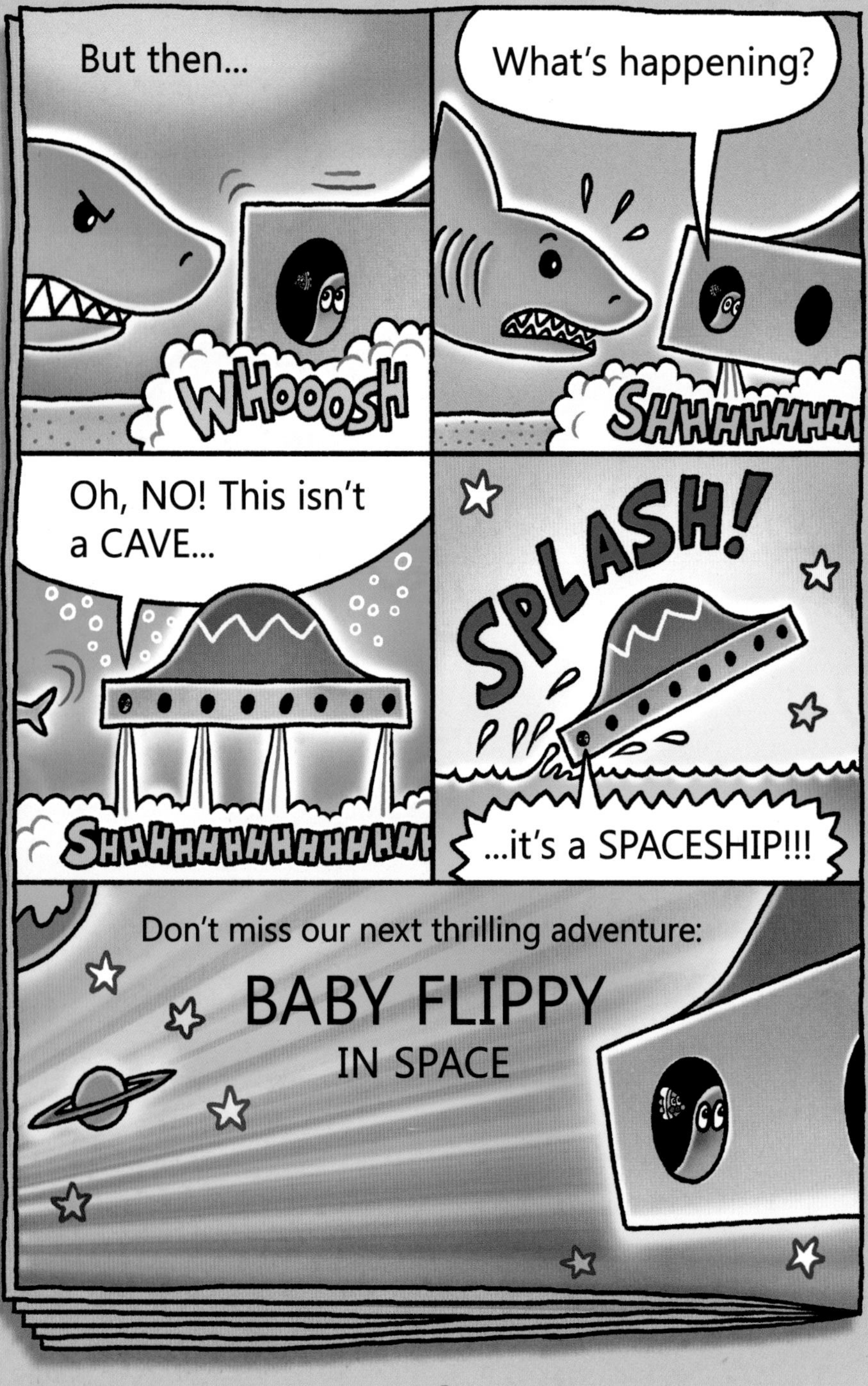
But then...
WHOOOSH
What's happening?
SHHHHHHHH
Oh, NO! This isn't a CAVE...
SHHHHHHHHHHHHHH
SPLASH!
...it's a SPACESHIP!!!
Don't miss our next thrilling adventure:
BABY FLIPPY
IN SPACE

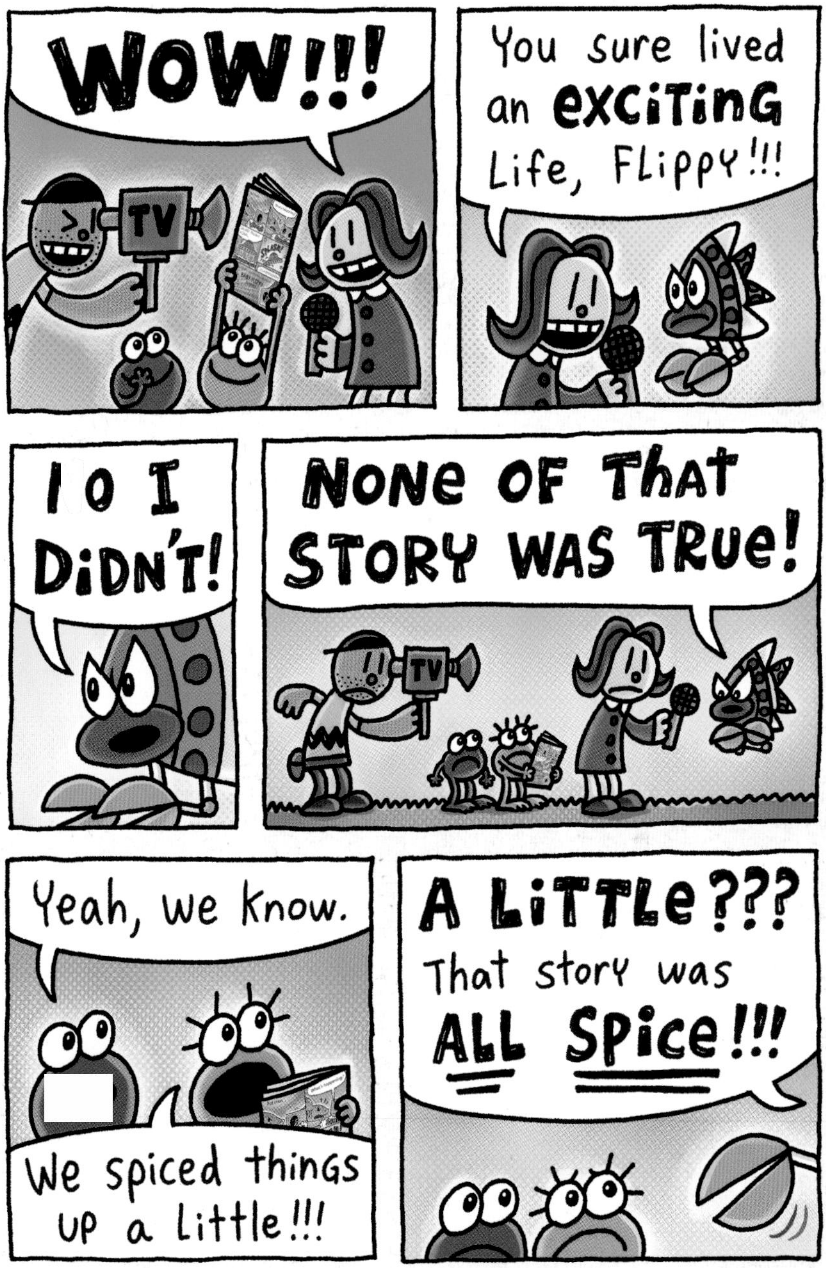
WOW!!!
You sure lived an EXCITING Life, FLIPPY!!!
NO I DIDN'T!
NONE OF THAT STORY WAS TRUE!
Yeah, we know.
We spiced things up a little!!!
A LITTLE???
That story was ALL Spice!!!

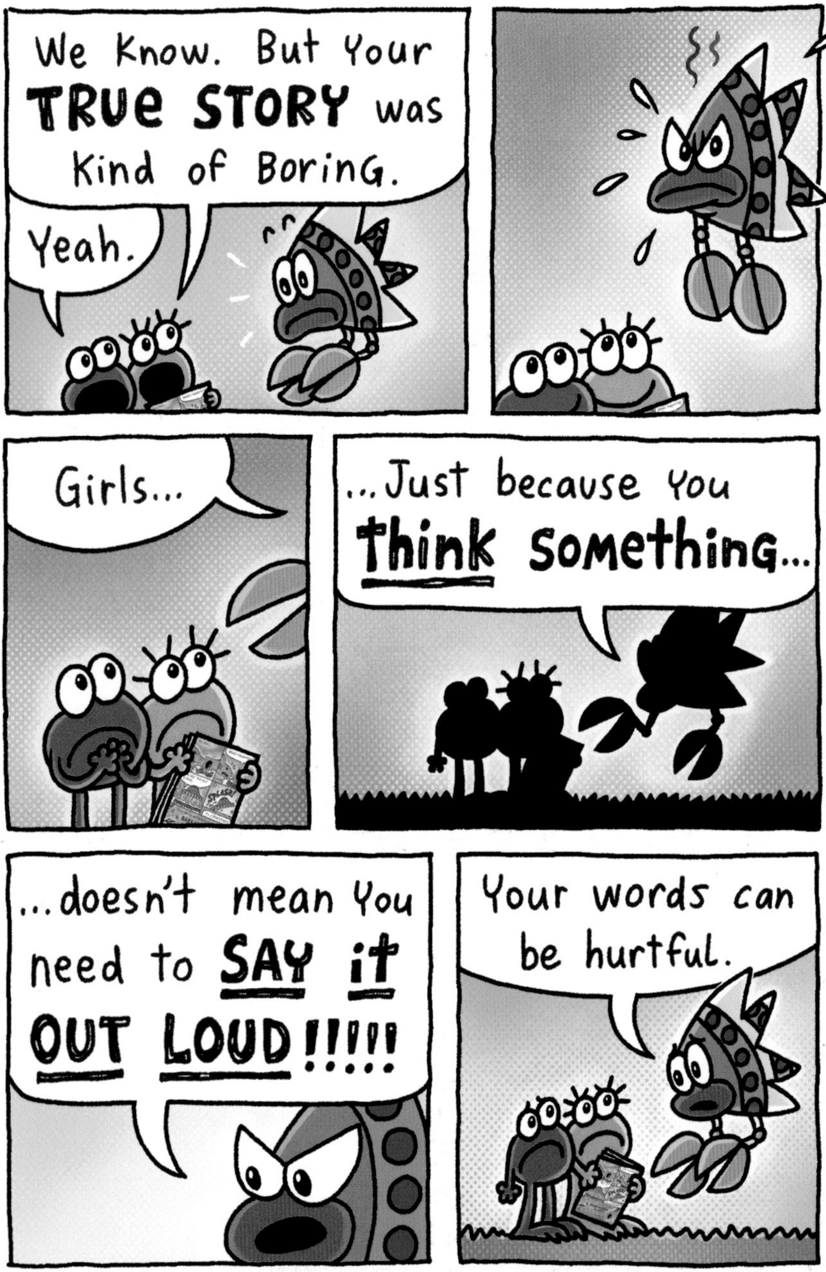
We Know. But Your TRUE STORY was Kind of BorinG.
Yeah.
Girls...
...Just because You Think Something...
...doesn't mean You need to SAY it OUT LOUD!!!!!
Your words can be hurtful.

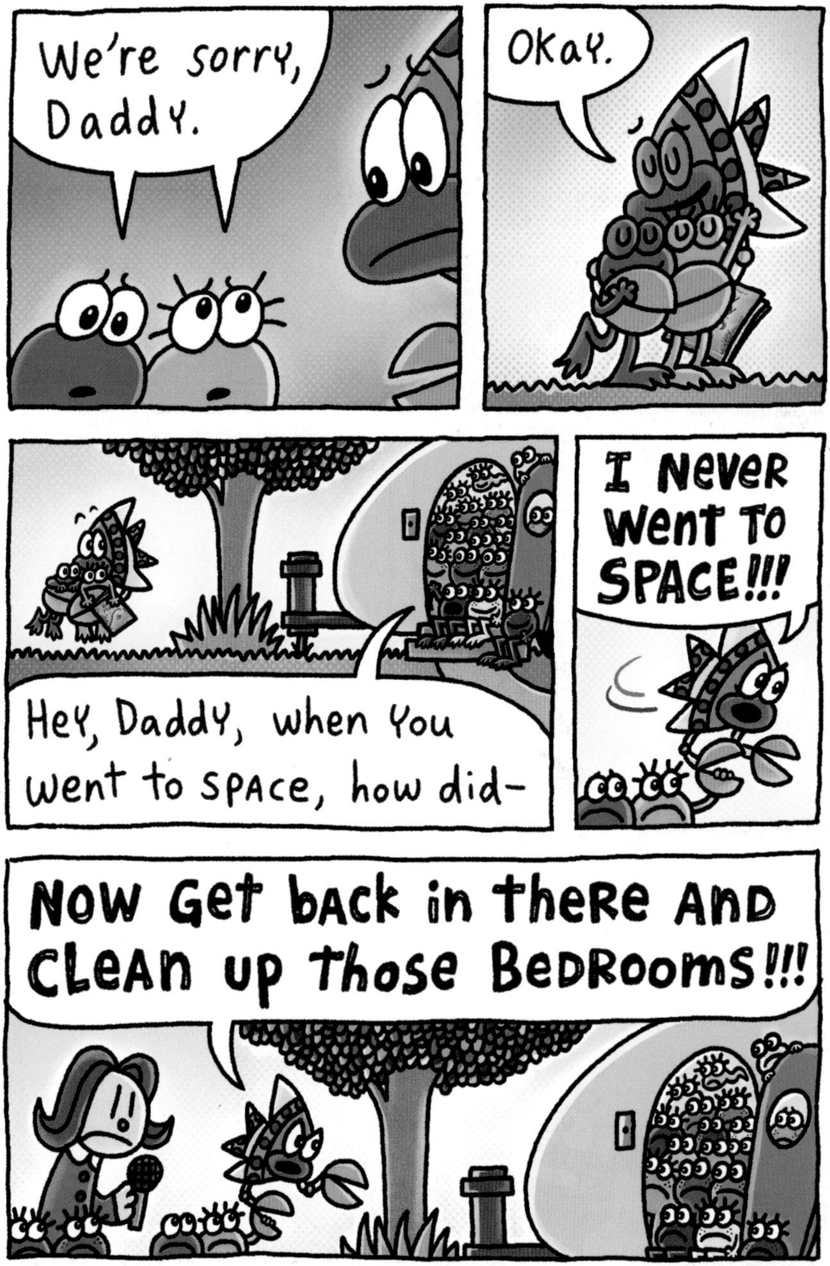
We're sorry, Daddy.
Okay.
Hey, Daddy, when you went to space, how did-
I NEVER WENT TO SPACE!!!
NOW GET BACK IN THERE AND CLEAN UP THOSE BEDROOMS!!!

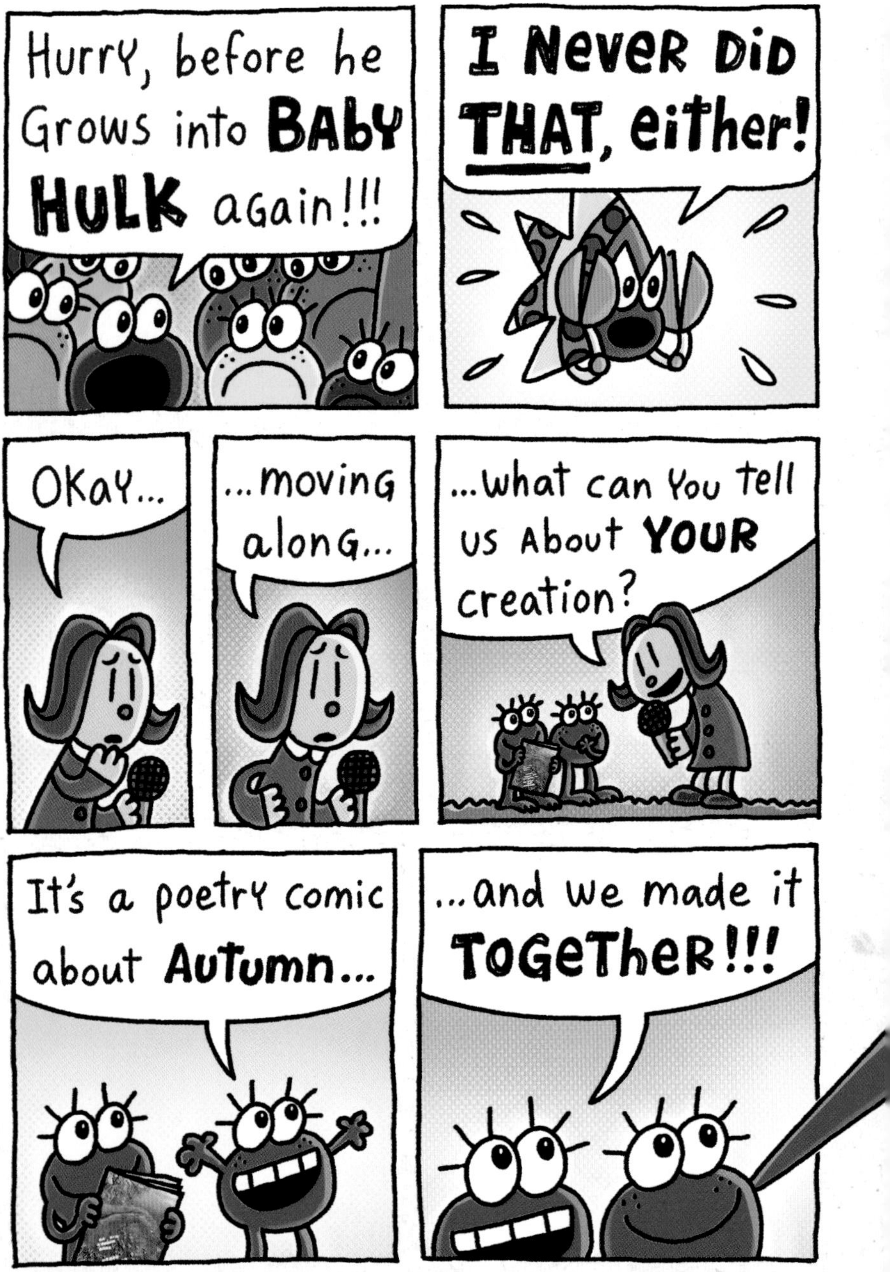
Hurry, before he Grows into BABY HULK again!!!
I NEVER DID THAT, either!
OKay...
...moving along...
...what can you tell us About YOUR creation?
It's a poetry comic about AUTUMN...
...and we made it TOGETHER!!!

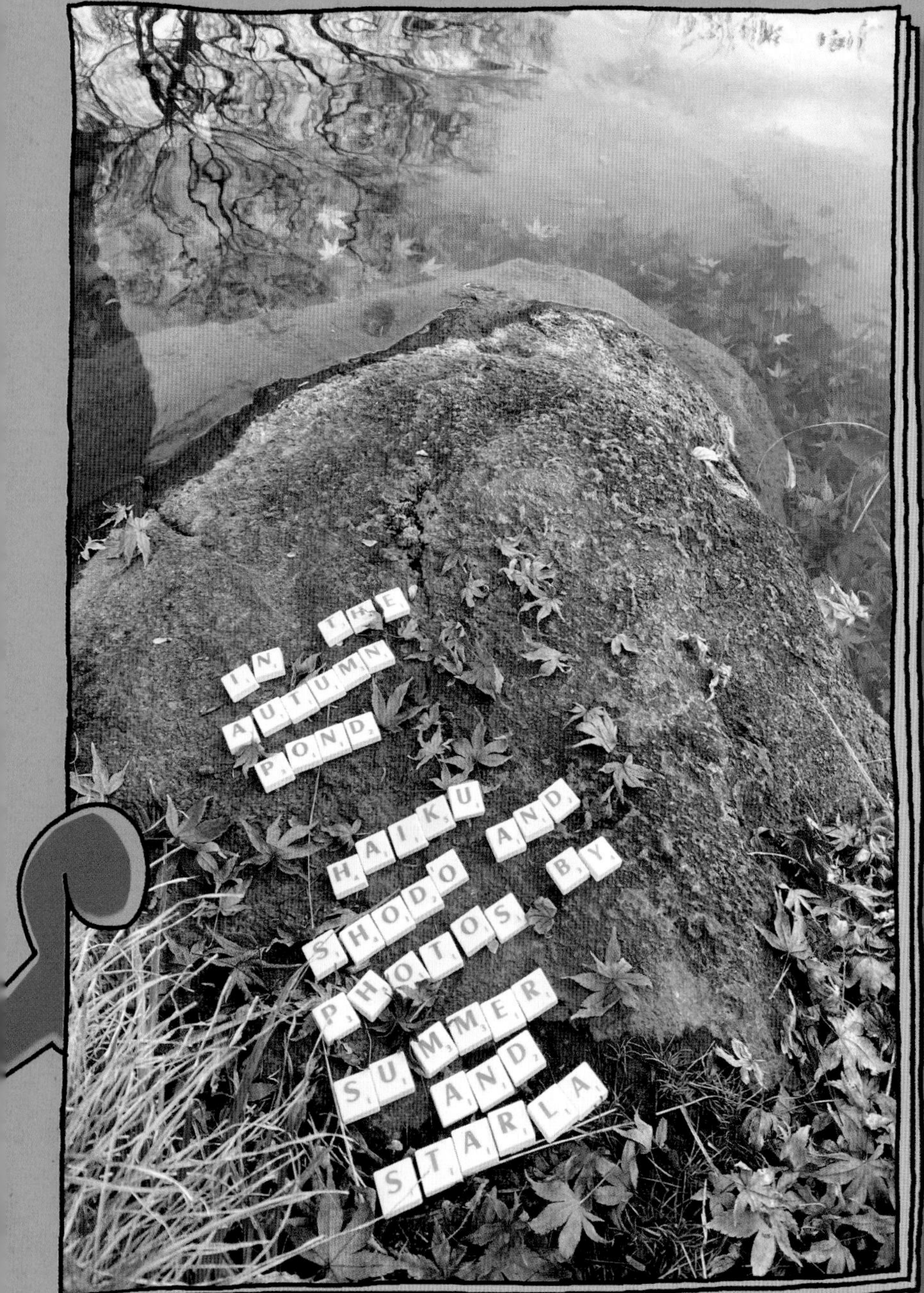
IN THE
AUTUMN
POND
HAIKU AND
SHODO BY
PHOTOS
SUMMER
AND
STARLA

反
響
音

in the autumn pond
every leaf casts a shadow
each sound, an echo

見性

the sun shows the way
but the sun is not the way
there's a difference

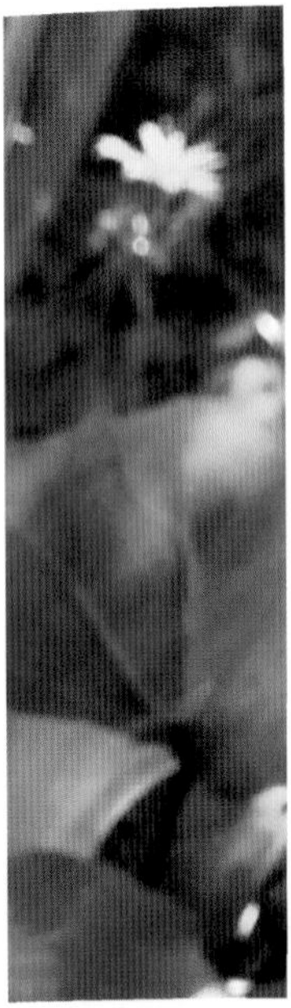

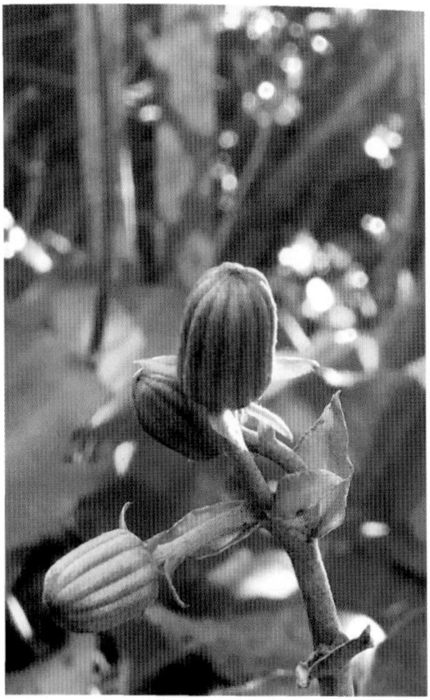

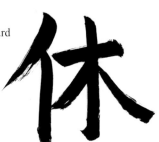

autumn days grow cold
yet in that winding downward
promises appear

休

乱舞

each star shines brightly
sparkling crisp on frigid twigs

dancing in breezes

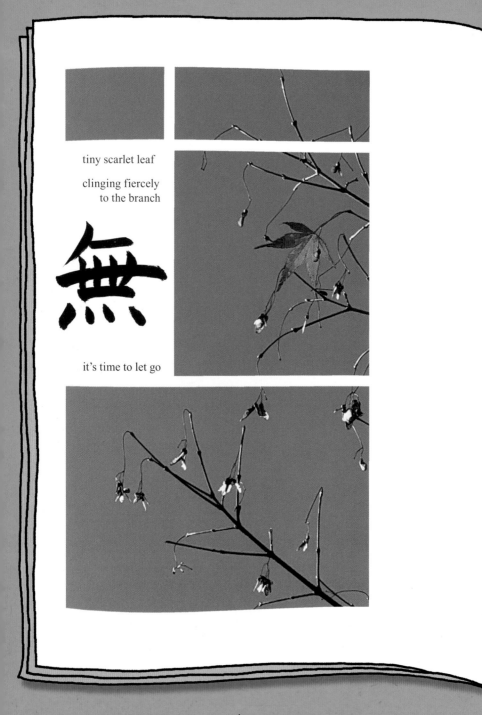

tiny scarlet leaf

clinging fiercely
to the branch

無

it's time to let go

little fallen leaves
your journey is not over

旅

now you are a path

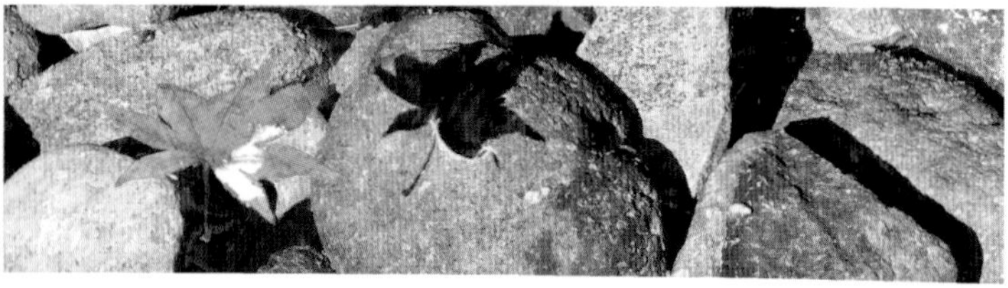

Each Shodo character can have many meanings.
These are some of the meanings for the ones we painted.

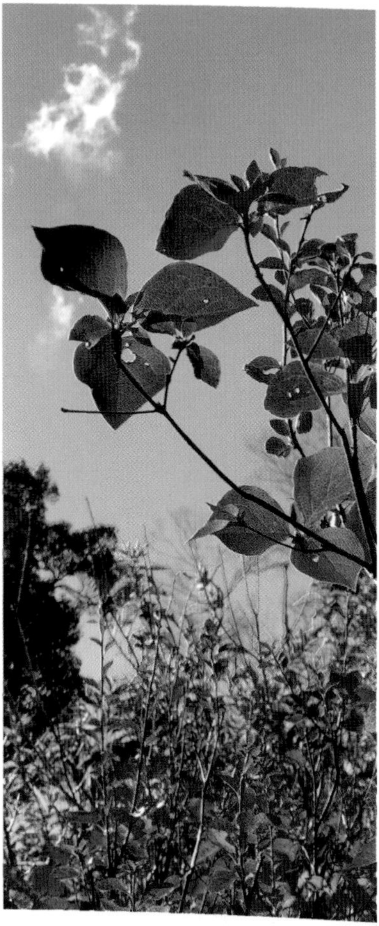

反 = "han" – One meaning is "to return."

響 = "kyou" – Sound or reverberate.
Together, "hankyou" means "echo."

見 = "ken" – Seeing.

性 = "sho" – Nature, essense.
Together, "kensho" means
"to see one's nature from within."

休 = "yasumu" – To rest.

乱 = "ran" – Disorder.

舞 = "bu" – Dance.
Together, "ranbu" means
"boisterous dance."

無 = "mu" – Nothing. In this case,
it means "although we may lose
everything, new opportunities arise."

旅 = "tabi" – Journey.

Nao'omi Kuratani, Akemi Kobayashi, Shunsuke Okunishi,
A New Dictionary of Kanji Usage (Tokyo; Gakken Co., LTD., 1982).

Summer and Starla would like to
acknowledge and thank the artists who
continue to inspire them, including:

Shoko Kanazawa, who is one of Japan's
most highly respected Shodo artists. She
paints from her heart with giant brushes.
She also has Down's Syndrome.

And

Shozo Sato, author of *Shodo: The Quiet Art of Japanese Zen Calligraphy* (Rutland:
Tuttle Publishing, 2014).

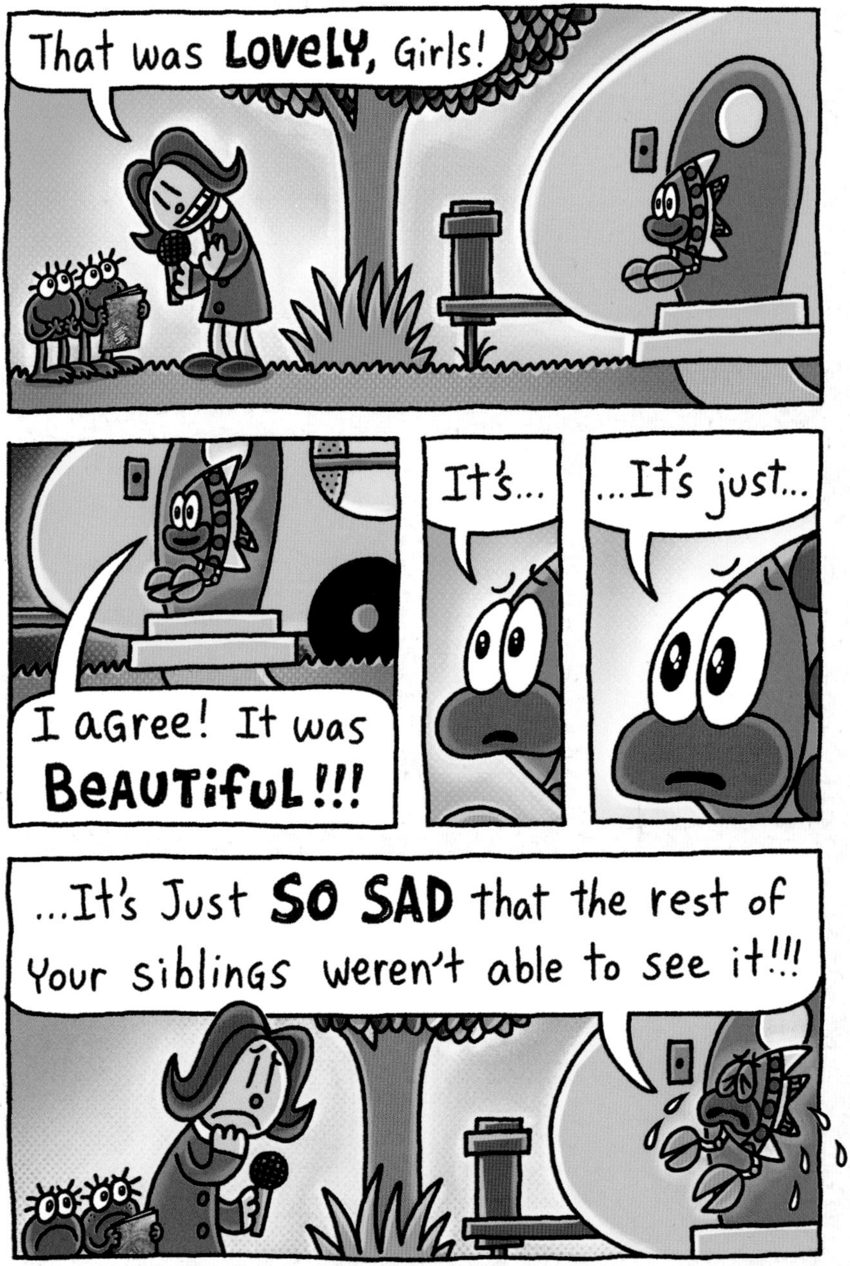
That was LOVELY, Girls!
I aGree! It was BeAUTiful!!!
It's...
...It's just...
...It's Just SO SAD that the rest of Your siblinGs weren't able to see it!!!

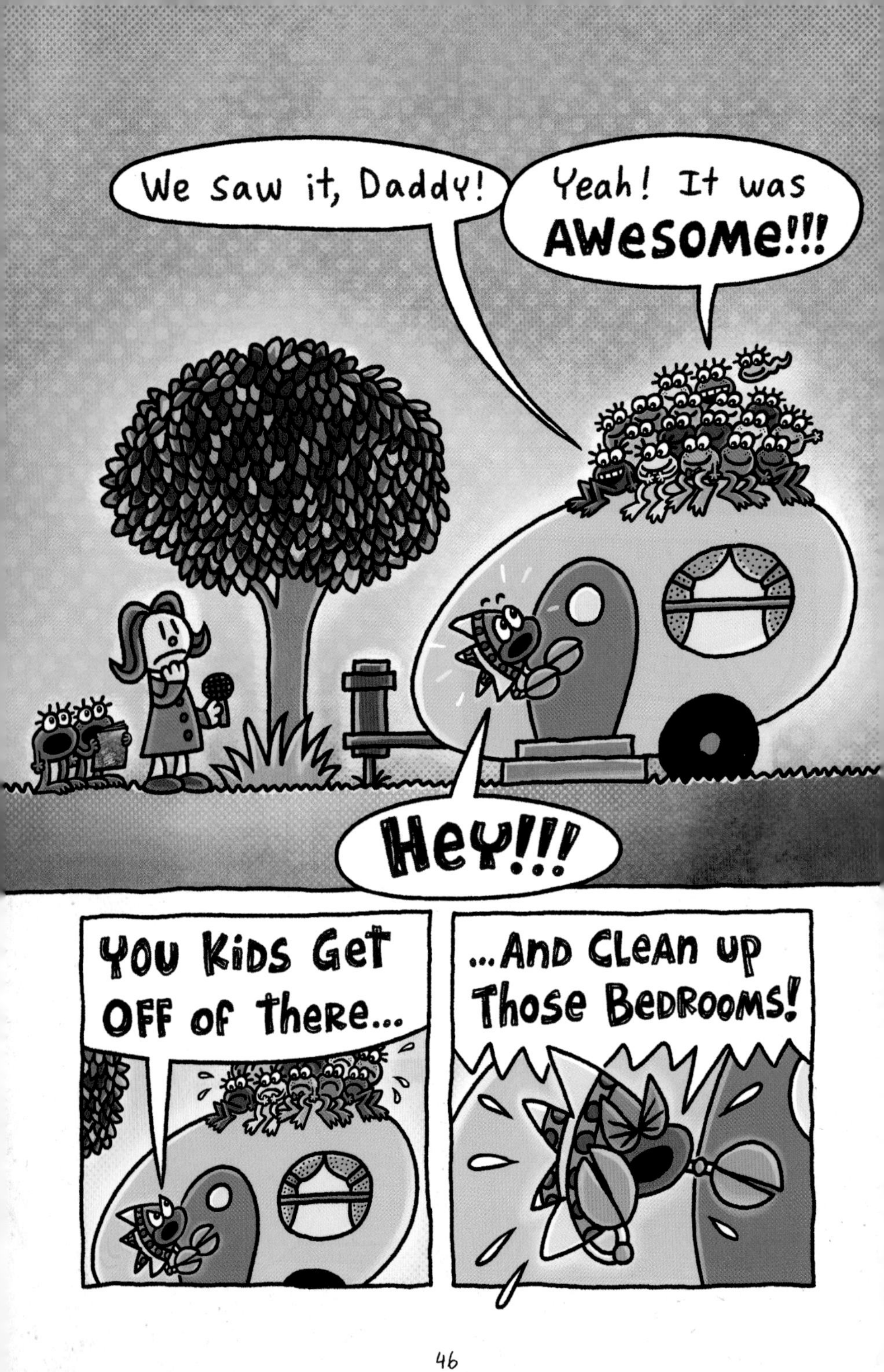
We saw it, Daddy!
Yeah! It was AWESOME!!!
HEY!!!
YOU KIDS GET OFF OF THERE...
...AND CLEAN UP THOSE BEDROOMS!

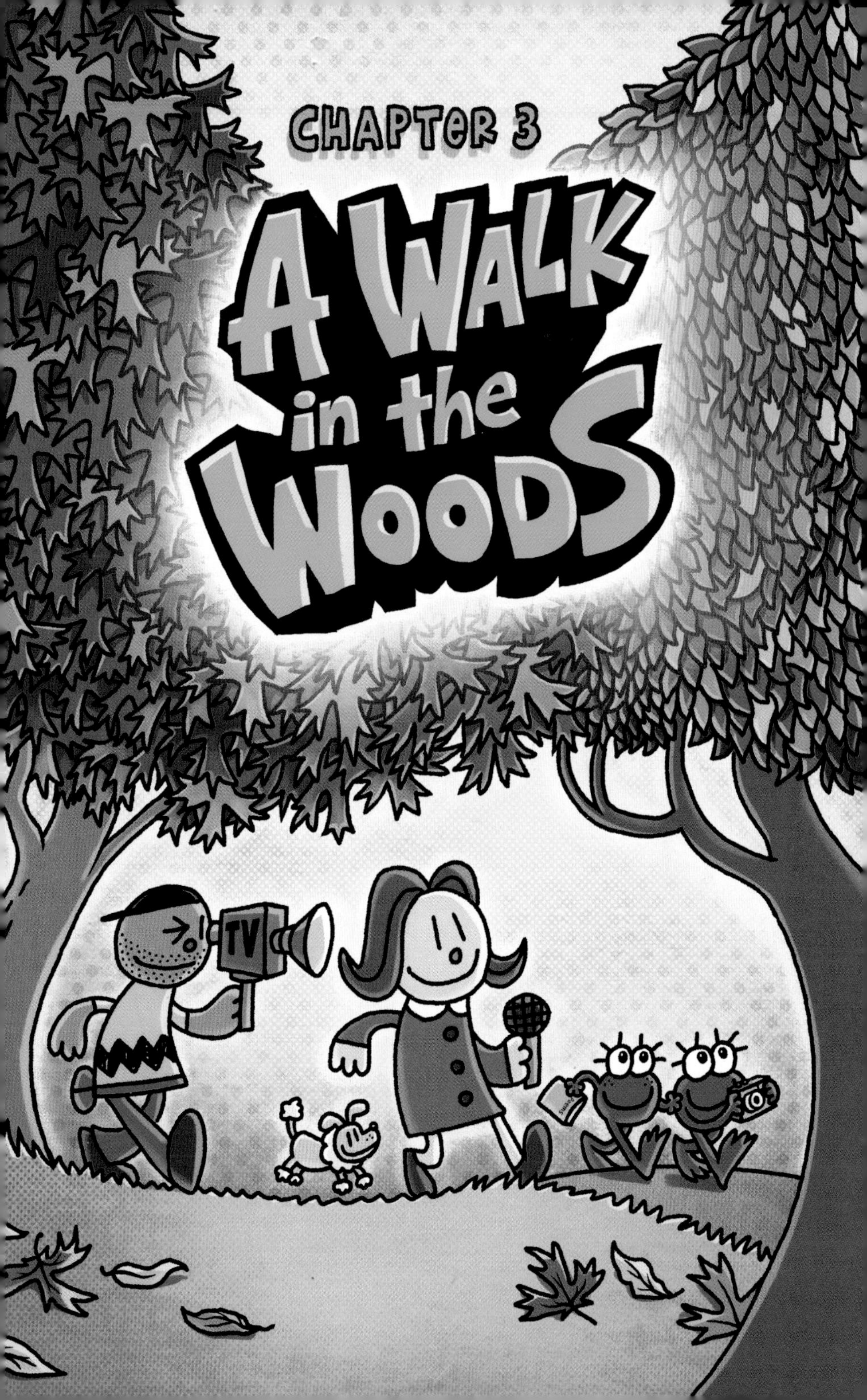
CHAPTER 3
A WALK
in the
WOODS
TV

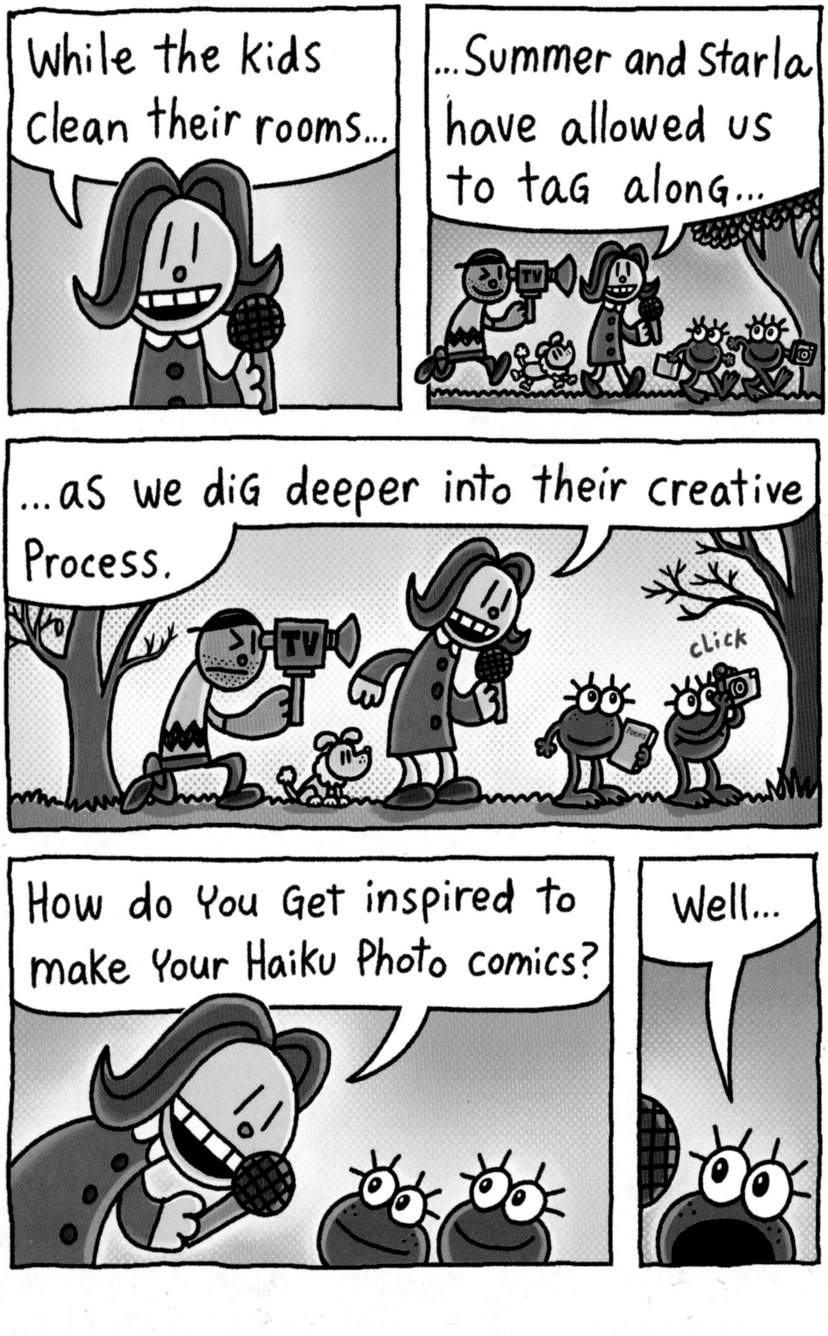
While the kids clean their rooms...
...Summer and Starla have allowed us to tag along...
TV
...as we dig deeper into their creative Process.
TV
CLICK
Poems
How do You Get inspired to make Your Haiku Photo comics?
Well...

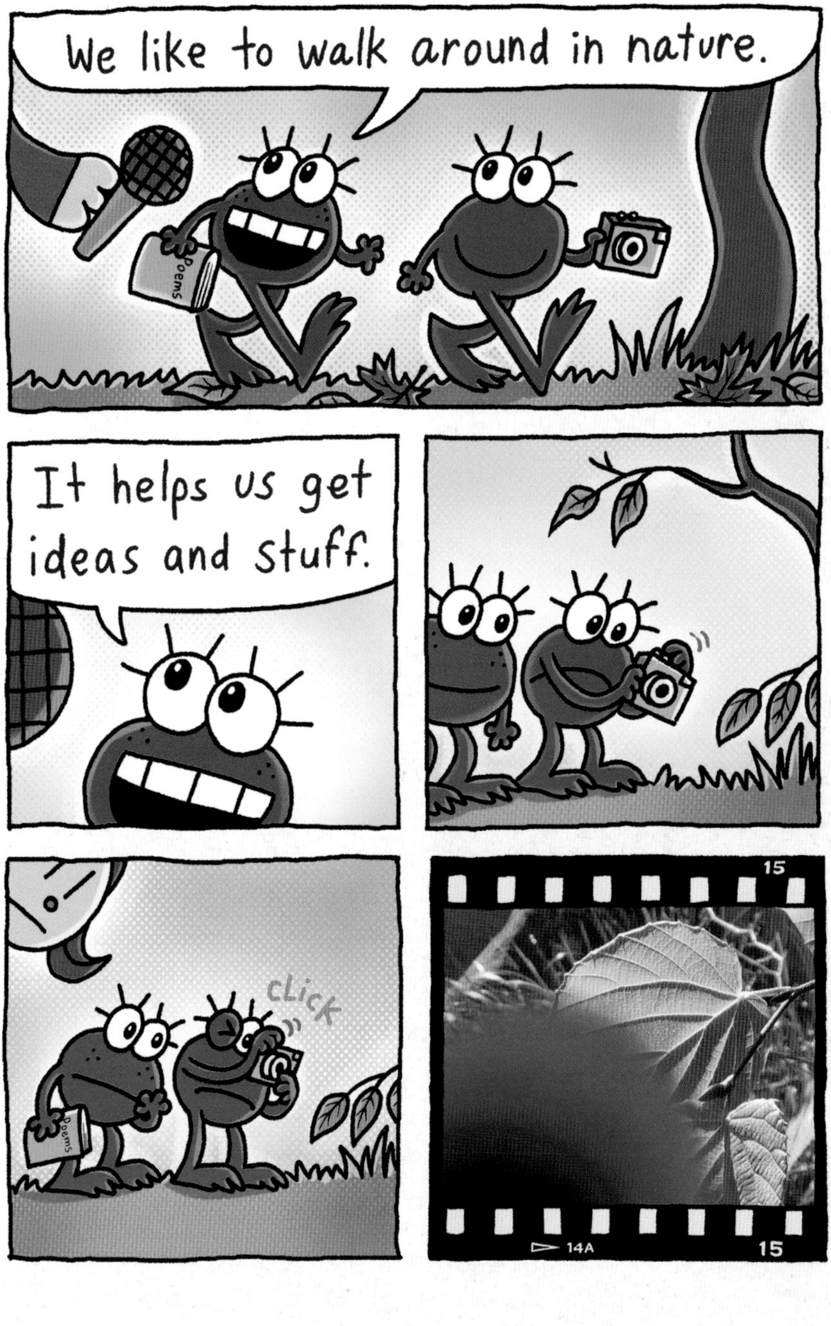
We like to walk around in nature.
Poems
It helps us get ideas and stuff.
Poems
CLick
15
14A
15

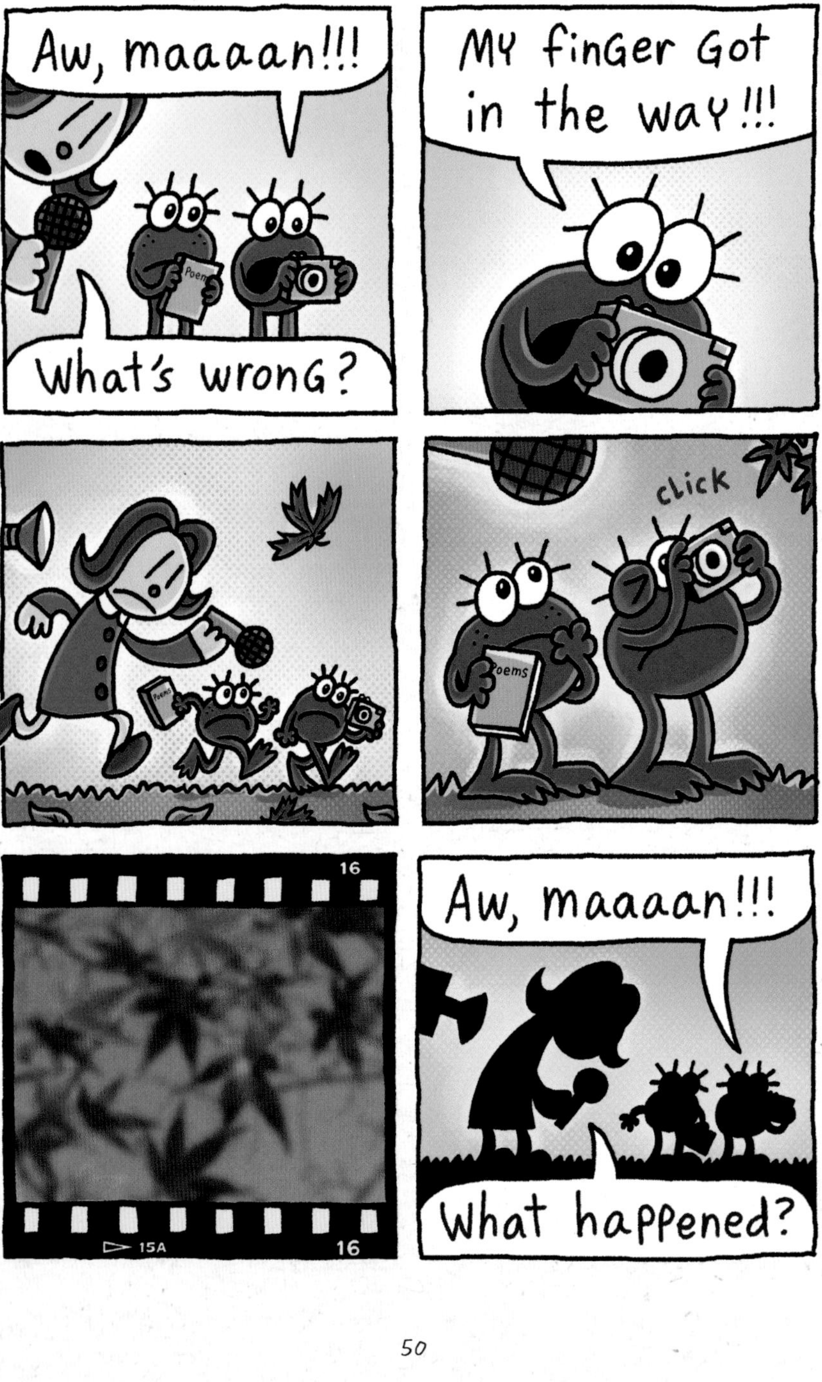
Aw, maaaaan!!!
What's wronG?
MY finGer Got in the way!!!
Poems
click
Poems
16
16
15A
16
Aw, maaaan!!!
What happened?

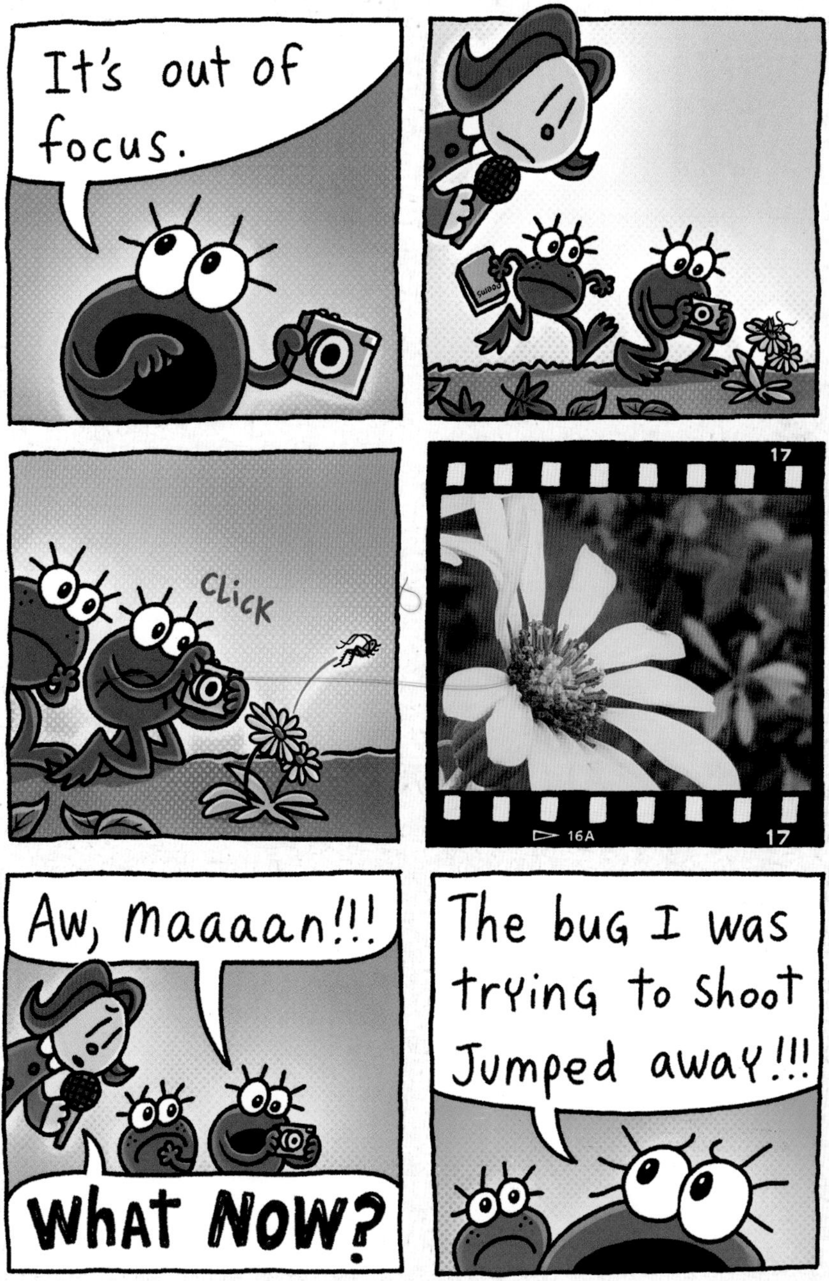
It's out of focus.
CLICK
17
16A
17
Aw, maaaan!!!
WHAT NOW?
The bug I was trying to shoot Jumped away!!!

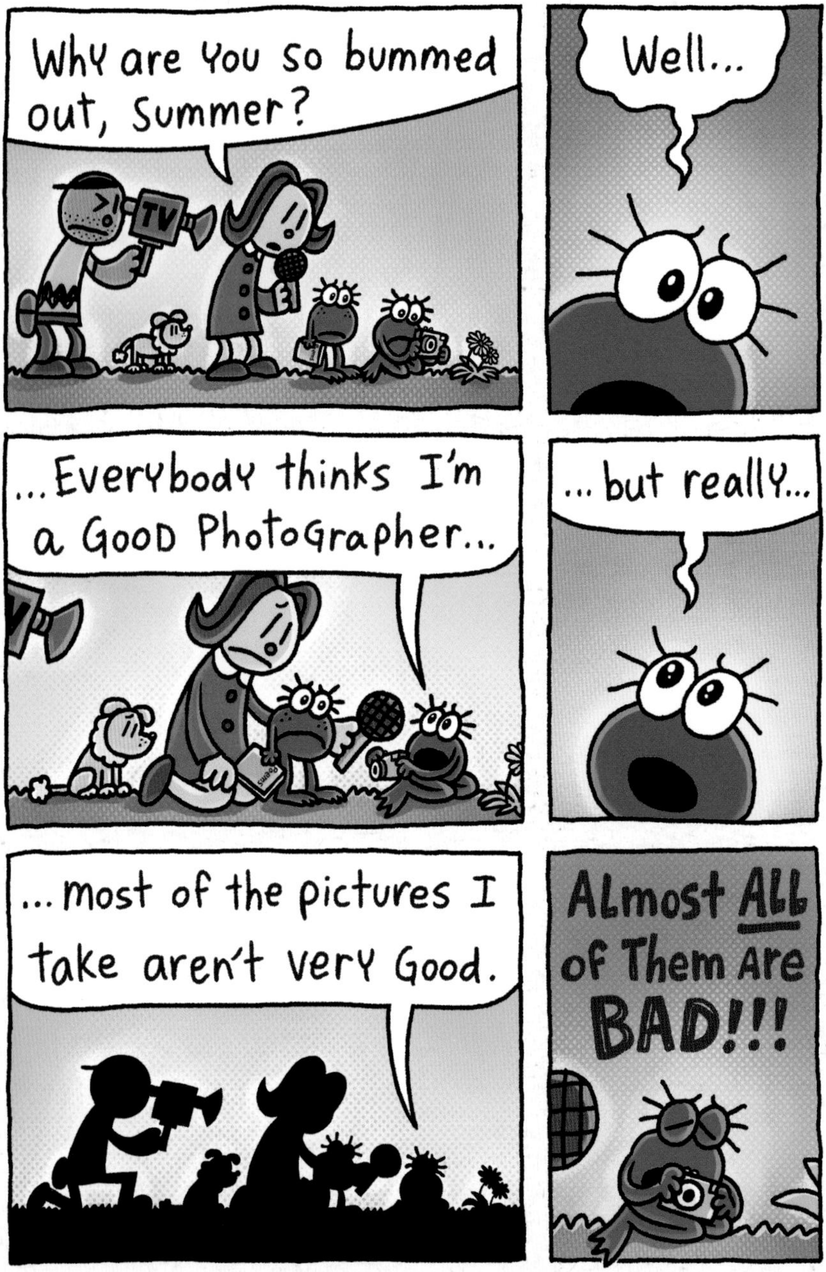
Why are you so bummed out, Summer?
Well...
TV
...Everybody thinks I'm a good photographer...
...but really...
...most of the pictures I take aren't very good.
Almost ALL of them are BAD!!!

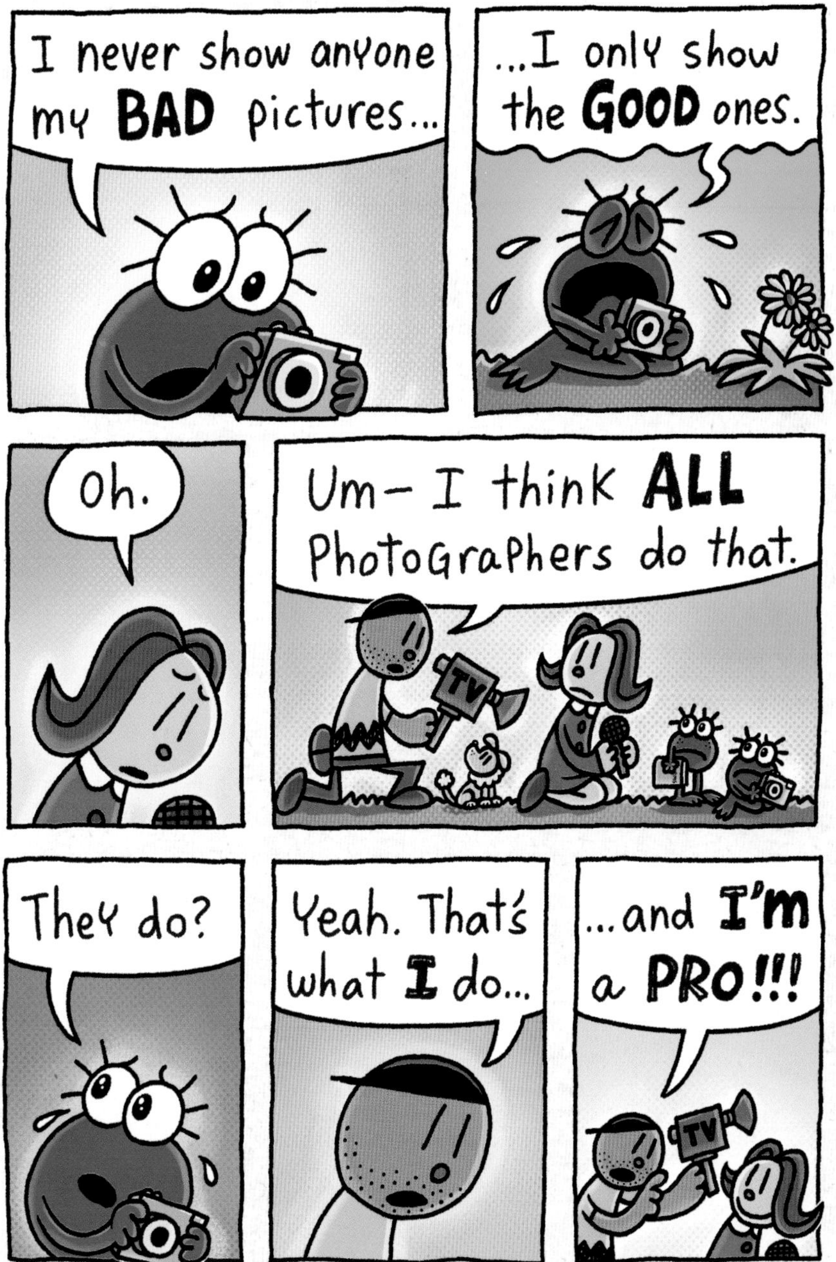
I never show anyone my BAD pictures...
...I only show the GOOD ones.
Oh.
Um- I think ALL Photographers do that.
TV
They do?
Yeah. That's what I do...
...and I'm a PRO!!!
TV

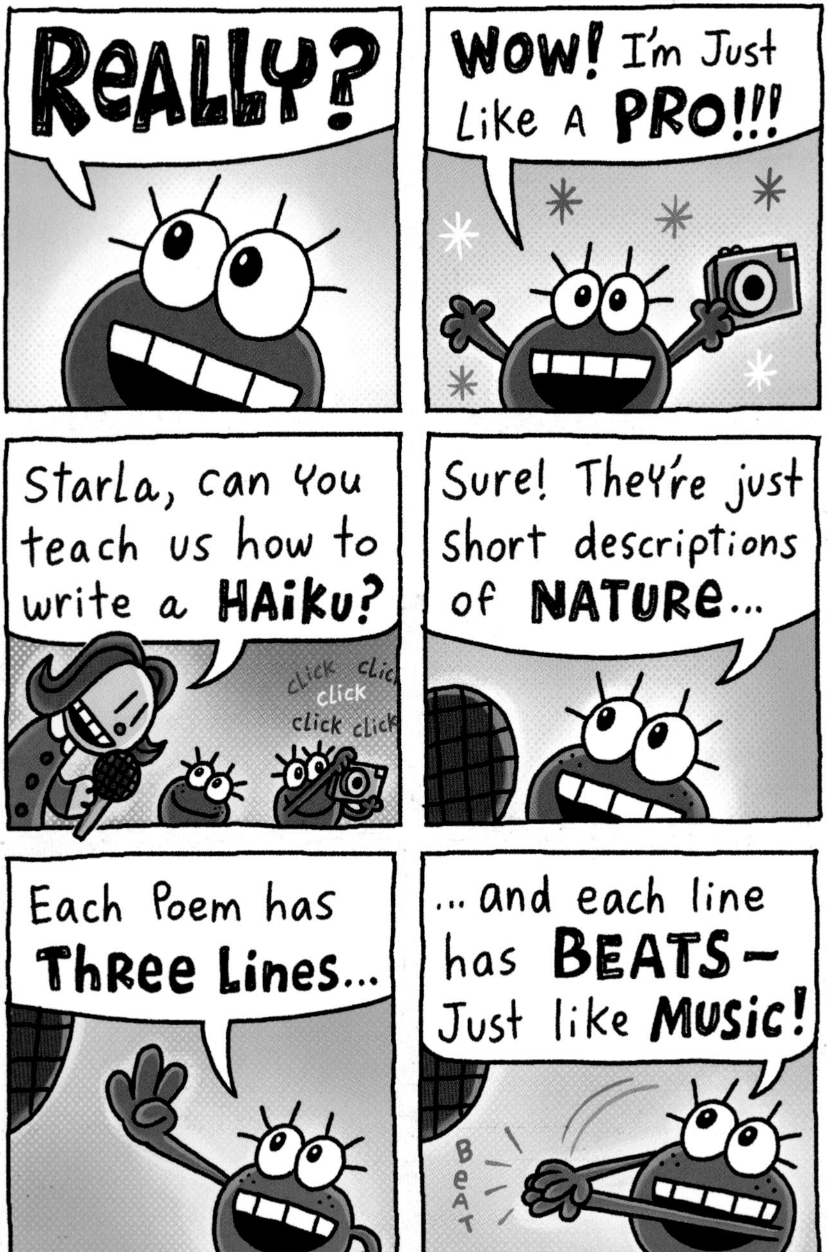
REALLY?
WOW! I'm Just Like A PRO!!!
Starla, can you teach us how to write a HAIKU?
click click click click click
Sure! They're just short descriptions of NATURE...
Each Poem has Three Lines...
... and each line has BEATS— Just like MUSIC!
BEAT

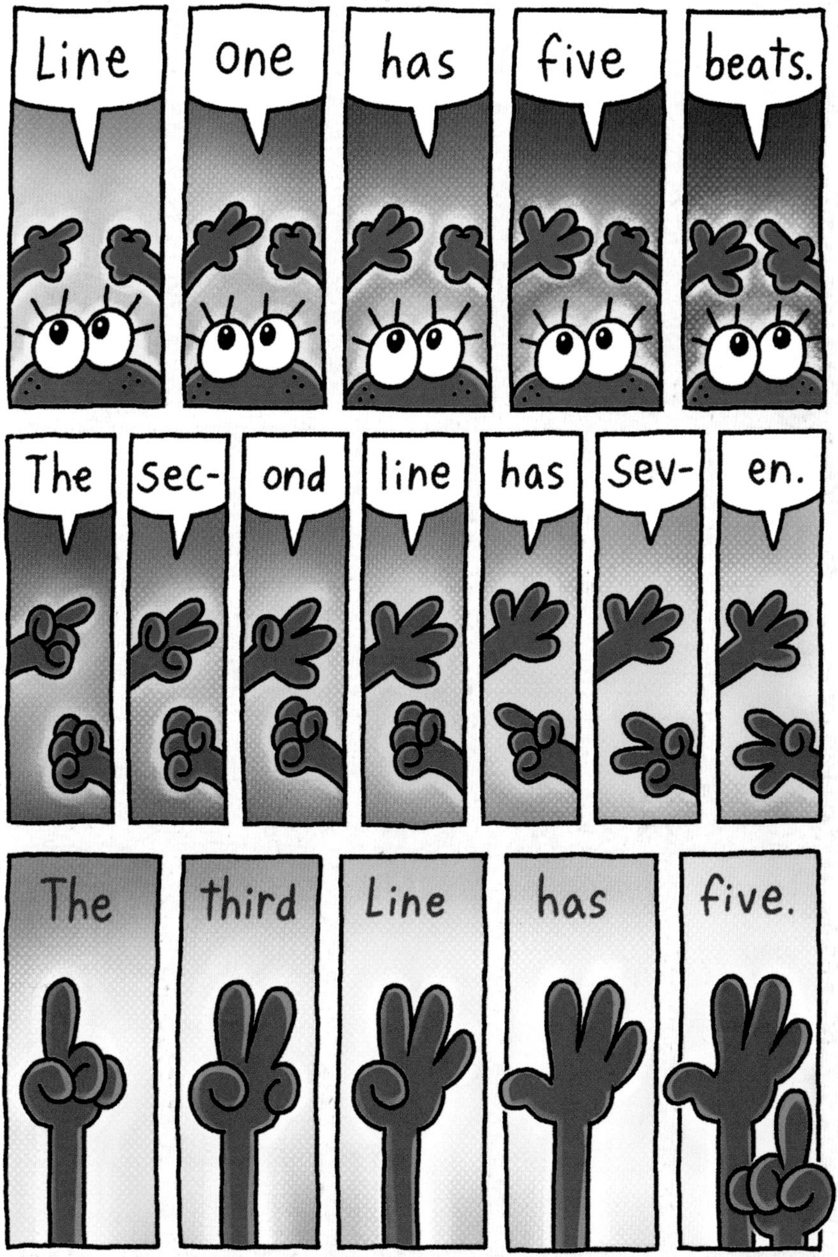
Line
one
has
five
beats.
The
sec-
ond
line
has
sev-
en.
The
third
Line
has
five.

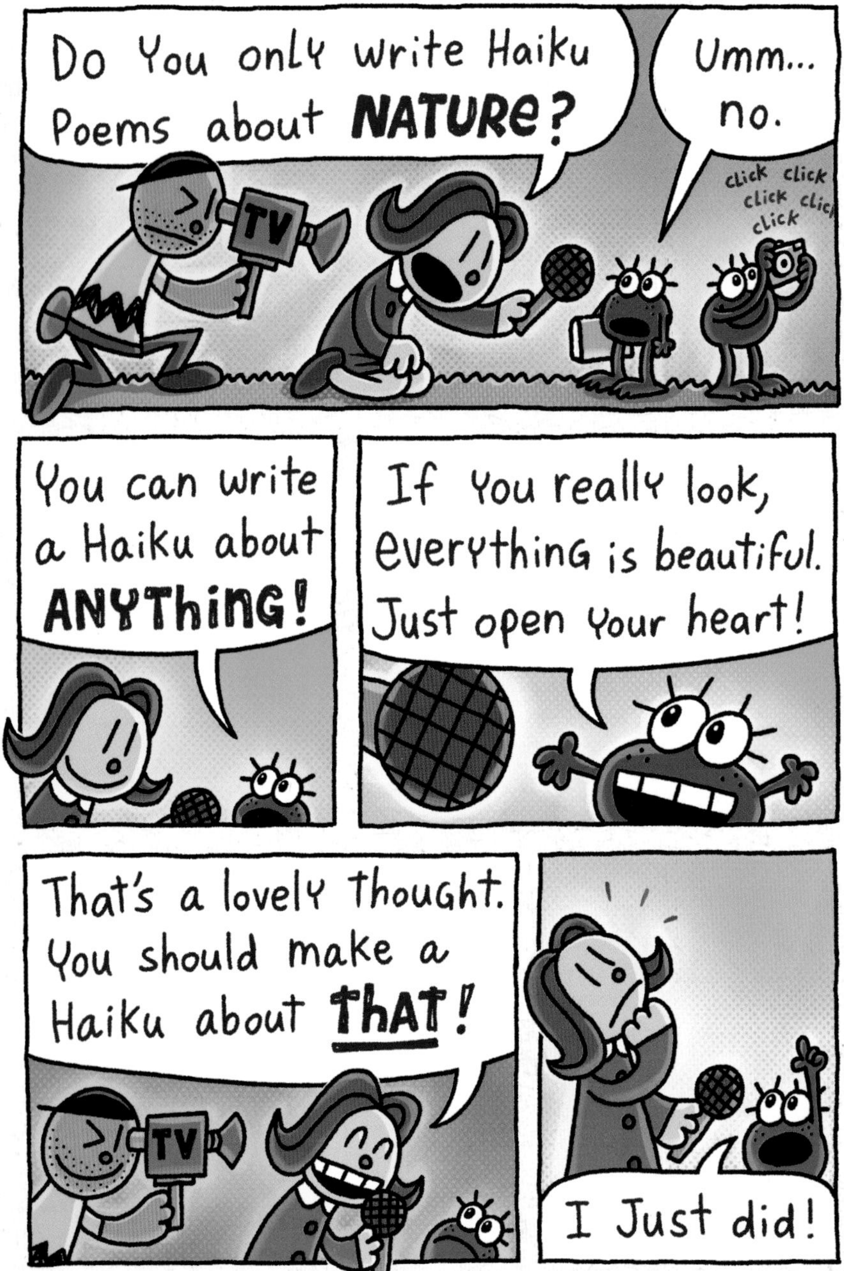
Do You only write Haiku Poems about NATURE?
Umm... no.
click click click click click
You can write a Haiku about ANYThinG!
If You really look, everything is beautiful. Just open Your heart!
That's a lovely thought. You should make a Haiku about THAT!
I Just did!

CHAPTER 4

Gilbert and Curly Heed the Call

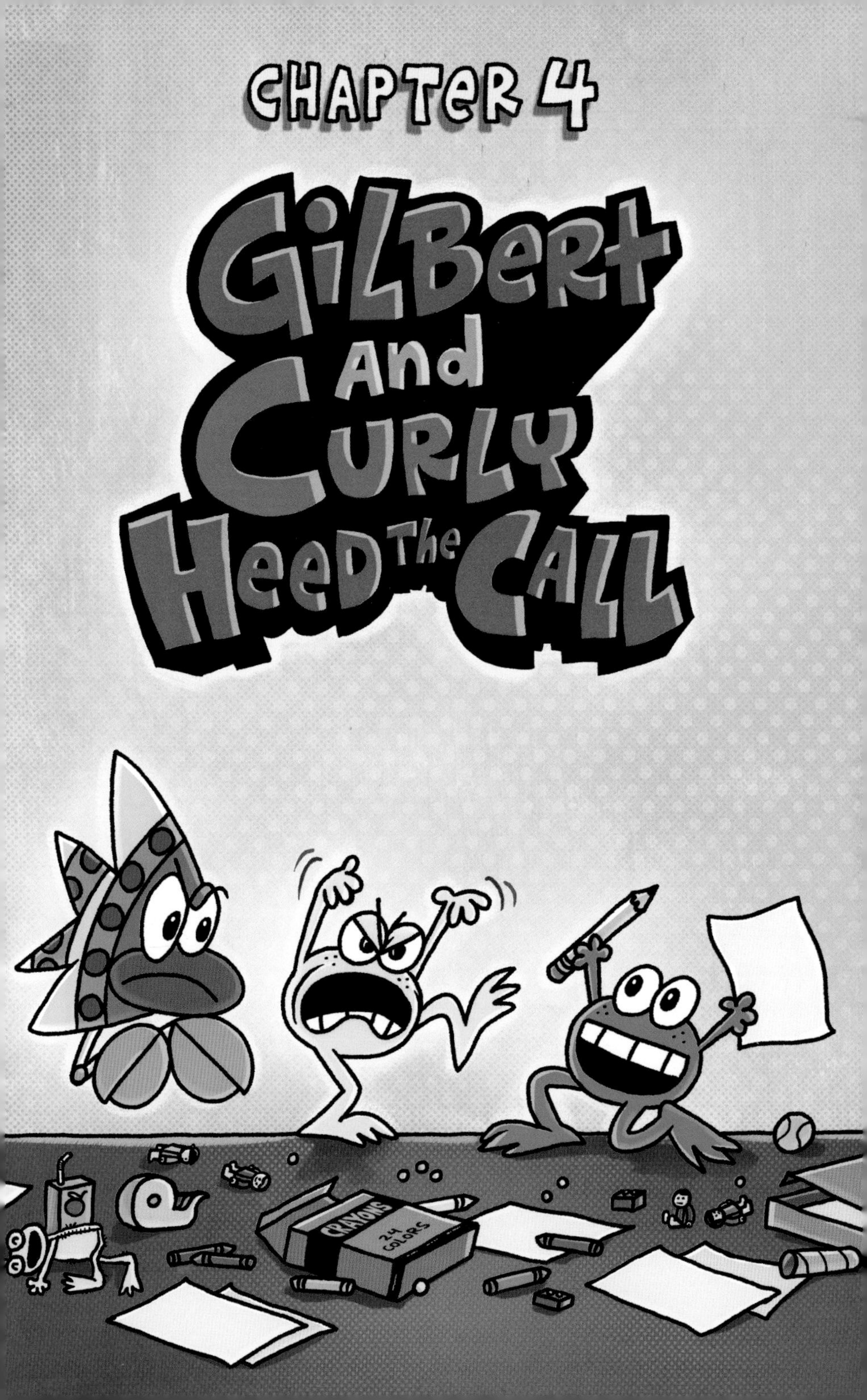
CRAYONS
24 COLORS

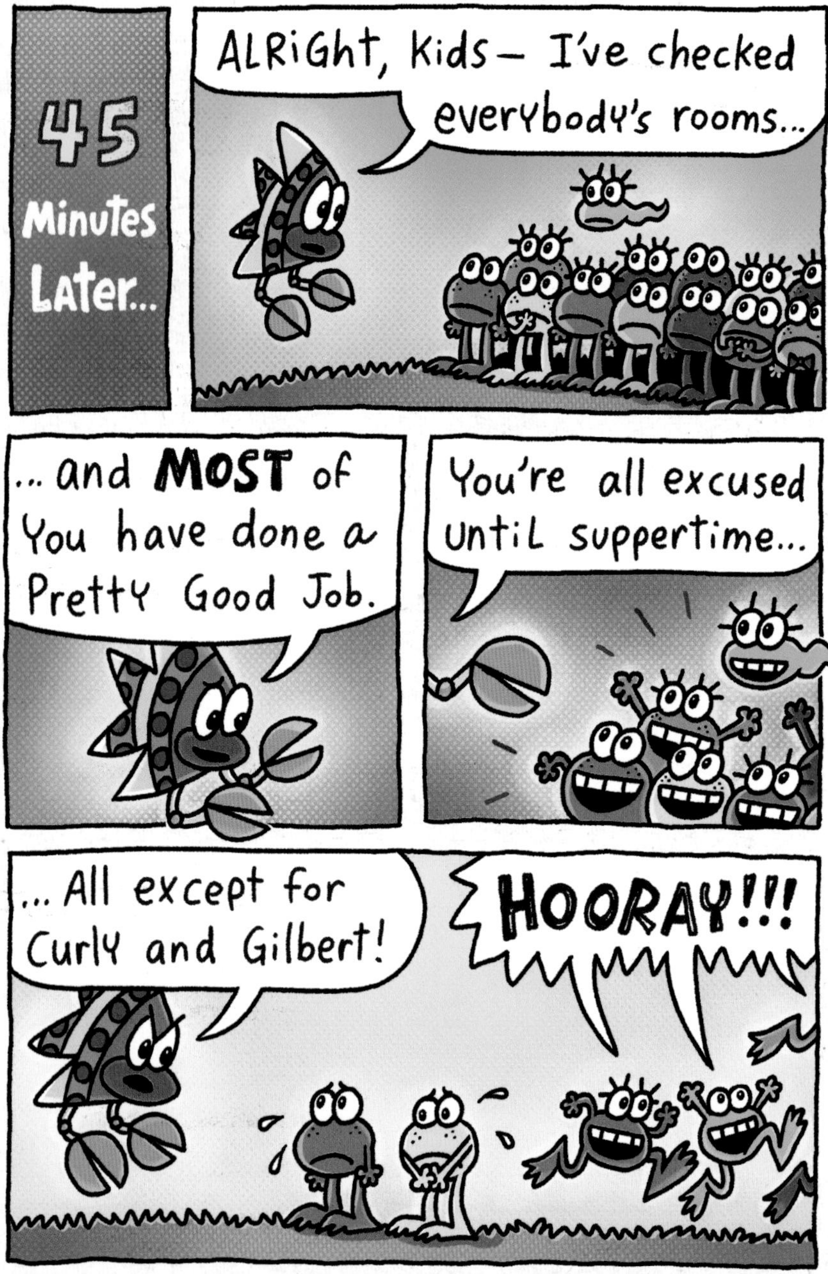
45 Minutes Later...
ALRiGht, Kids— I've checked everybody's rooms...
...and MOST of You have done a Pretty Good Job.
You're all excused until suppertime...
...All except for Curly and Gilbert!
HOORAY!!!

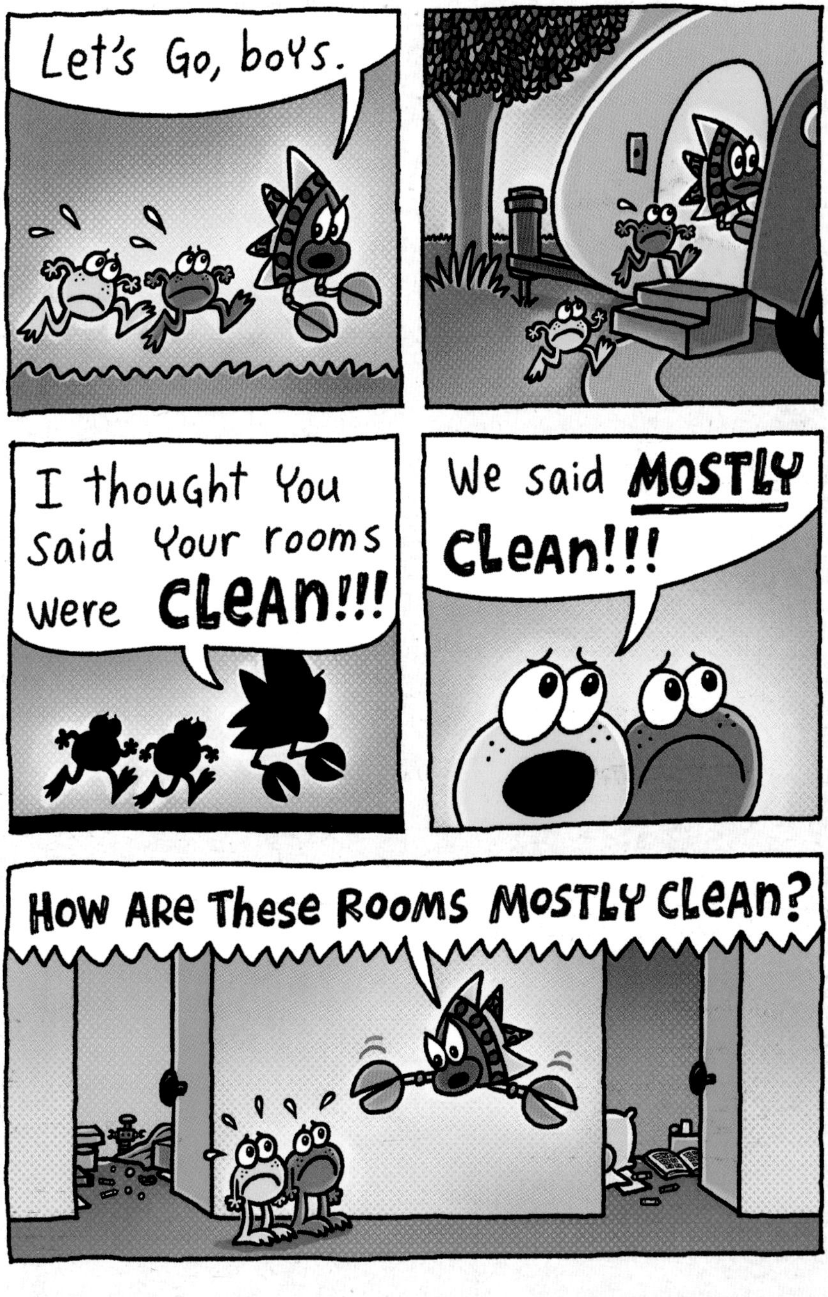
Let's Go, boys.
I thought You said Your rooms were CLEAN!!!
We said MOSTLY CLean!!!
How Are These Rooms MOSTLY CLean?

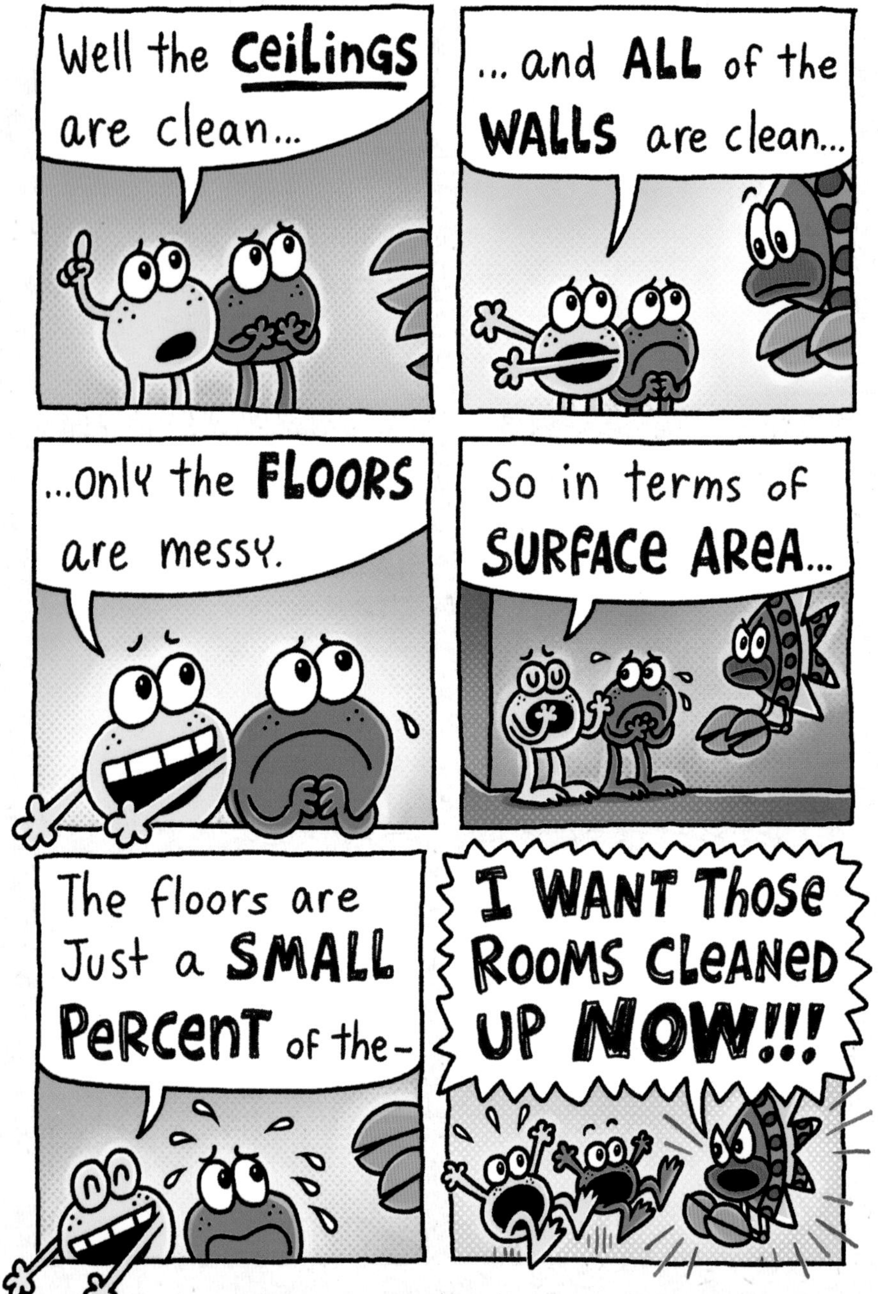
Well the CEILINGS are clean...
... and ALL of the WALLS are clean...
...only the FLOORS are messy.
So in terms of SURFACE AREA...
The floors are just a SMALL PERCENT of the-
I WANT Those ROOMS CLEANED UP NOW!!!

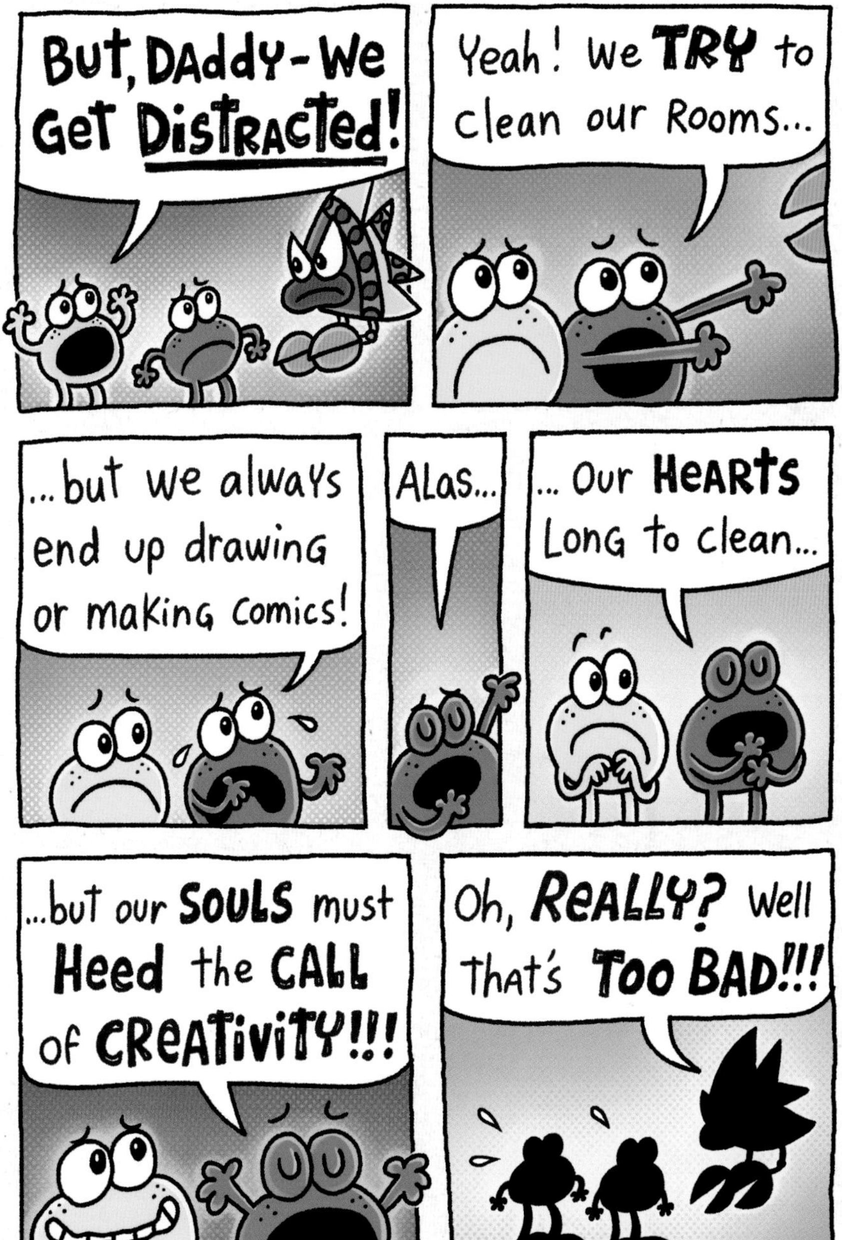
BUT, DADDY- WE GET DISTRACTED!
Yeah! We TRY to clean our Rooms...
...but we always end up drawing or making comics!
ALas...
...Our HEARTS Long to clean...
...but our SOULS must Heed the CALL of CREATIVITY!!!
Oh, REALLY? Well That's TOO BAD!!!

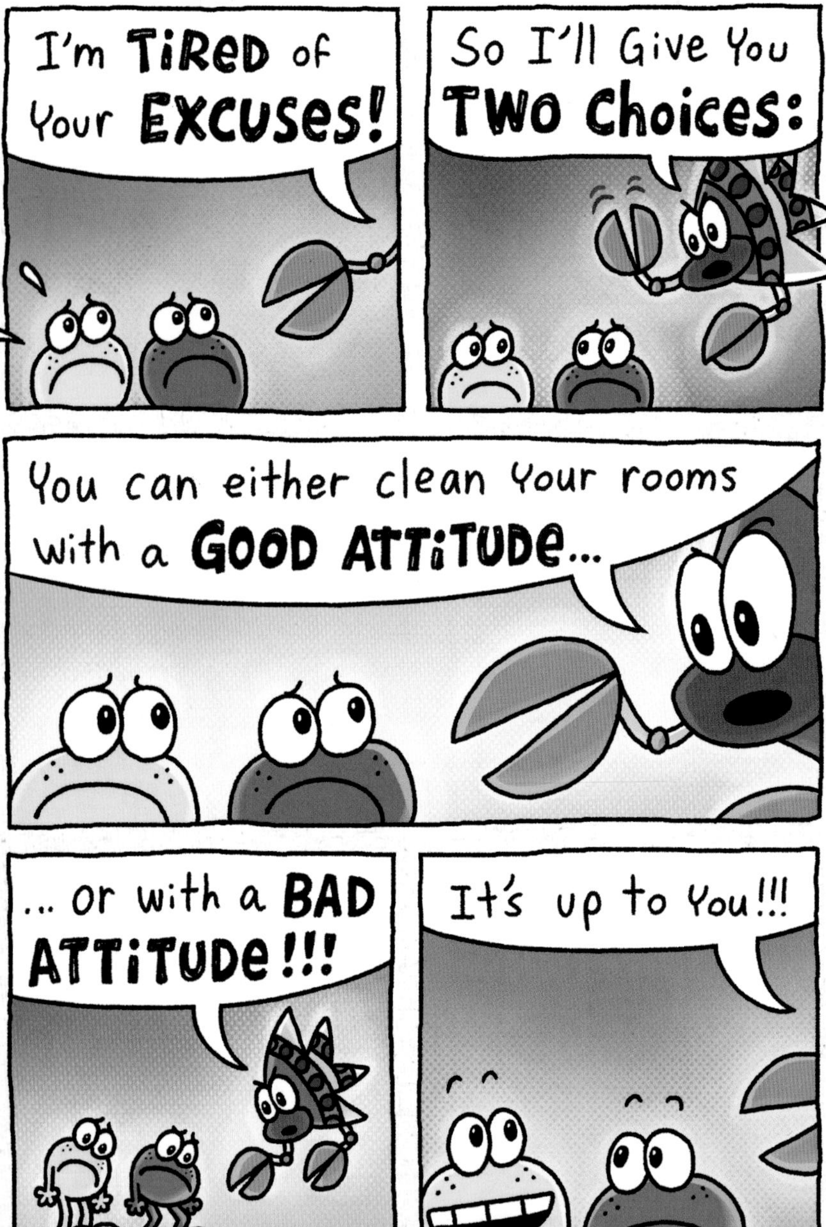
I'm TIRED of Your EXCUSES!
So I'll Give You TWO Choices:
You can either clean Your rooms with a GOOD ATTITUDE...
... or with a BAD ATTITUDE!!!
It's up to You!!!

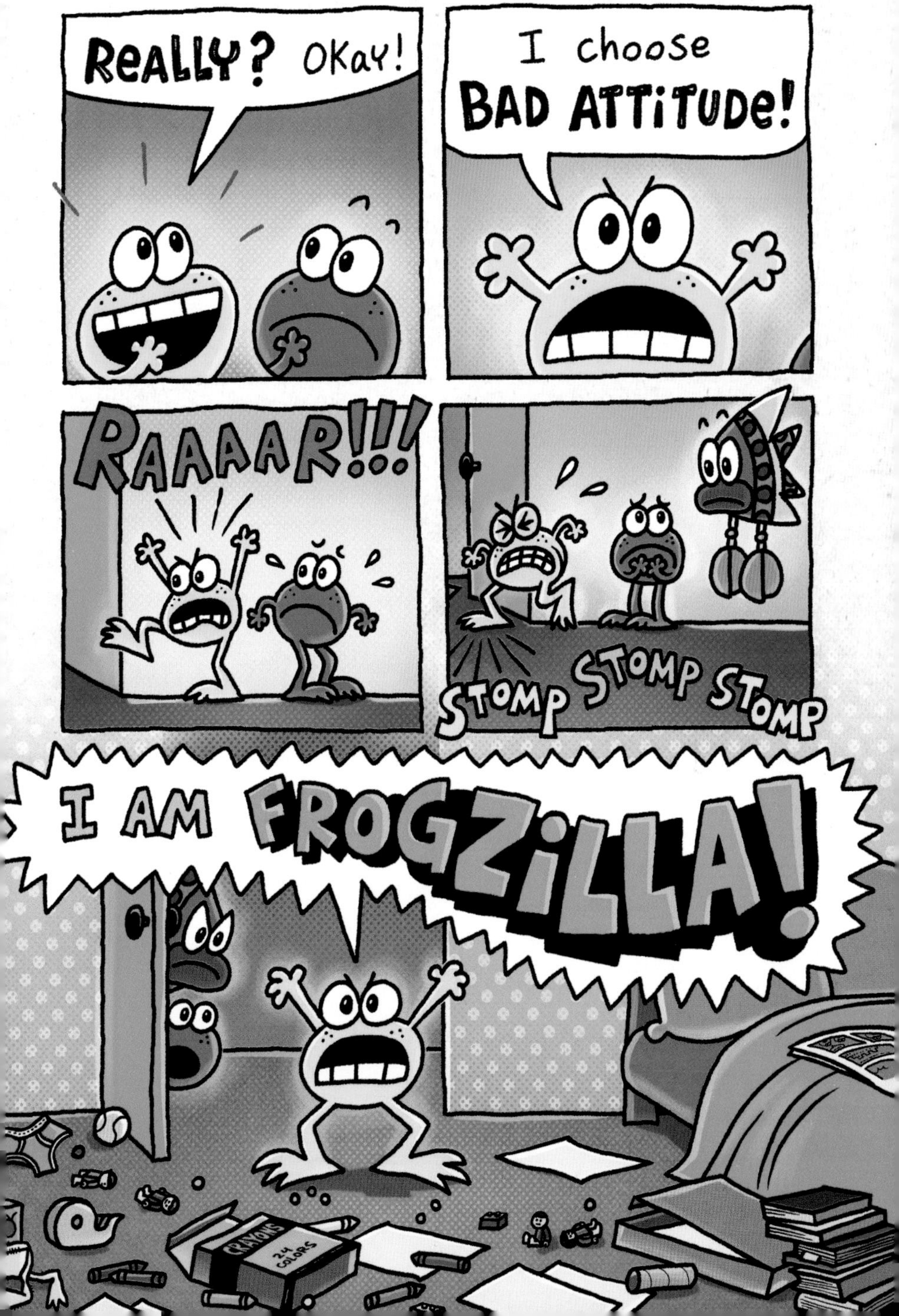
REALLY? OKay!
I choose BAD ATTITUDE!
RAAAAR!!!
STOMP STOMP STOMP
I AM FROGZILLA!
CRAYONS
24 COLORS

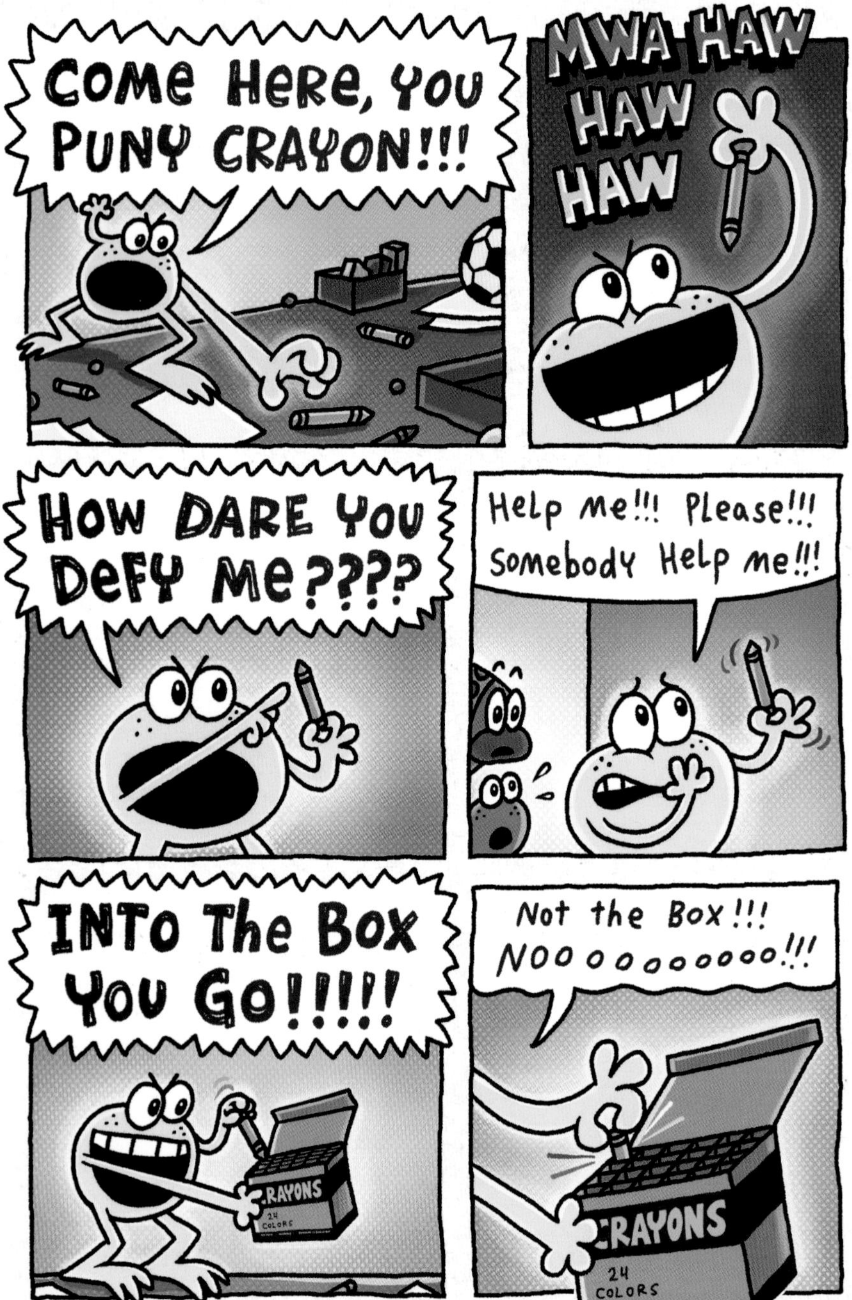
COME HERE, YOU PUNY CRAYON!!!
MWA HAW HAW HAW
HOW DARE YOU DEFY ME????
Help me!!! Please!!! Somebody Help me!!!
INTO The Box You GO!!!!!
CRAYONS
24 COLORS
Not the Box!!! NOOOOOOOOOO!!!
CRAYONS
24 COLORS

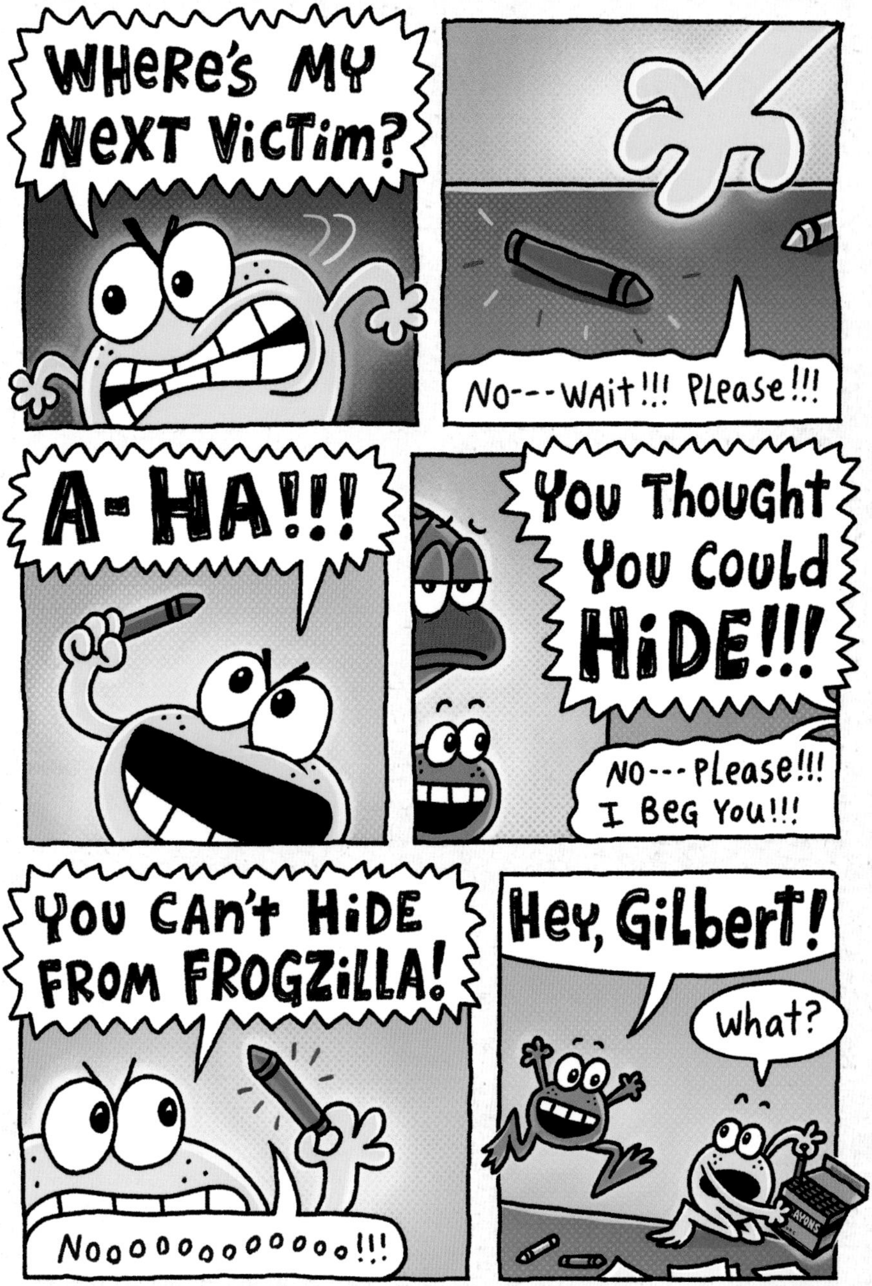
WHERE'S MY NEXT VICTIM?
NO---WAIT!!! PLEASE!!!
A-HA!!!
YOU THOUGHT YOU COULD HIDE!!!
NO---PLEASE!!! I BEG YOU!!!
YOU CAN'T HIDE FROM FROGZILLA!
NOOOOOOOOOOOOO!!!
HEY, GILBERT!
WHAT?

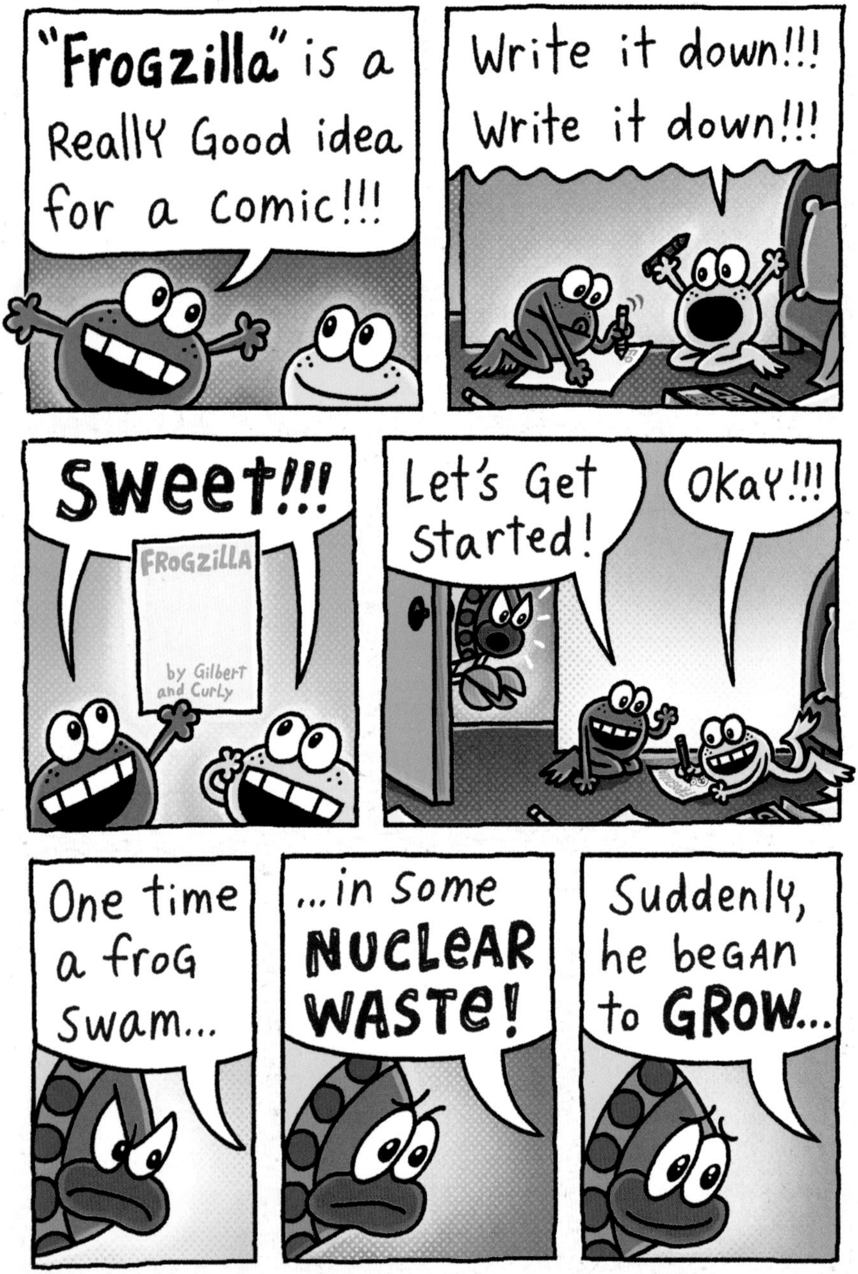
"Frogzilla" is a Really Good idea for a Comic!!!
Write it down!!! Write it down!!!
SWEET!!!
FROGZILLA
by Gilbert and Curly
Let's Get Started!
OKAY!!!
One time a frog swam...
...in some NUCLEAR WASTE!
Suddenly, he began to GROW...

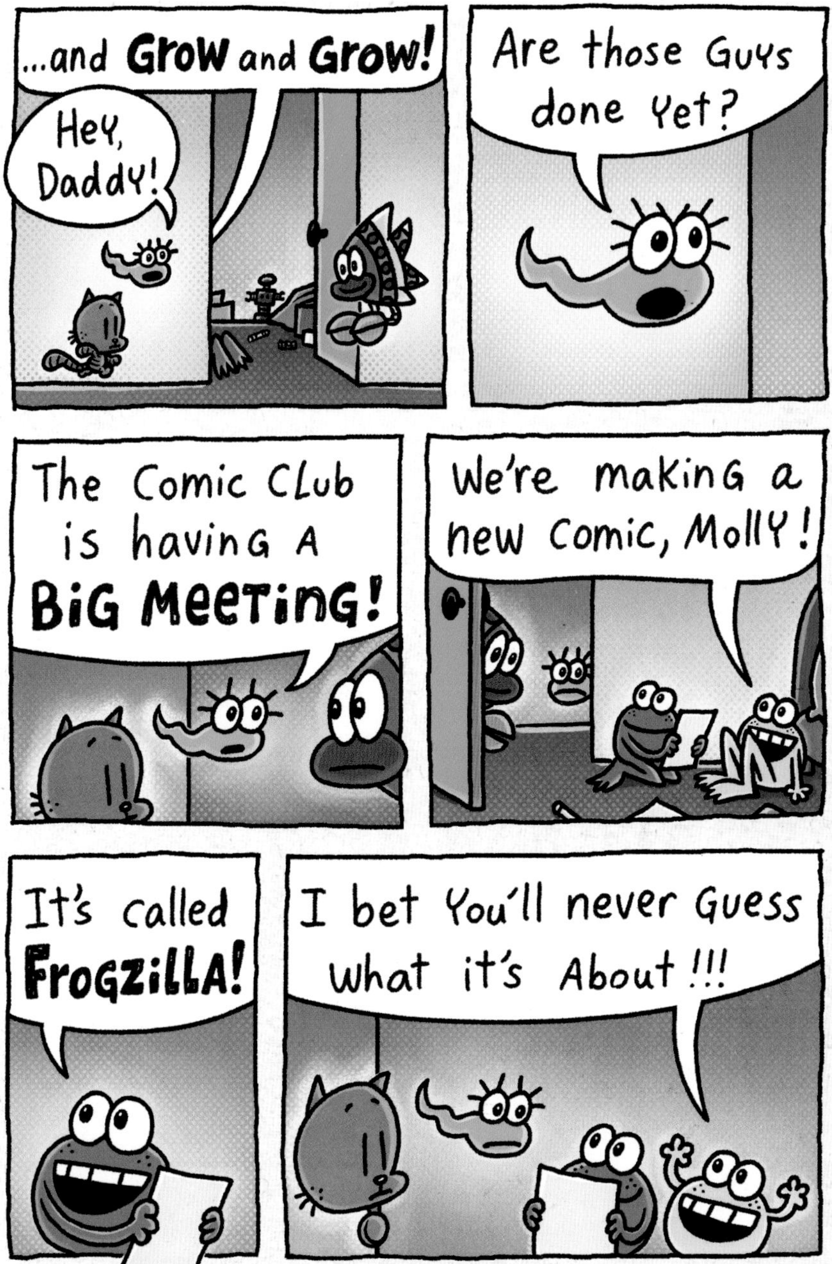
...and GROW and GROW!
Hey, Daddy!
Are those Guys done yet?
The Comic Club is having a BIG MEETING!
We're making a new comic, Molly!
It's called FROGZILLA!
I bet you'll never guess what it's about!!!

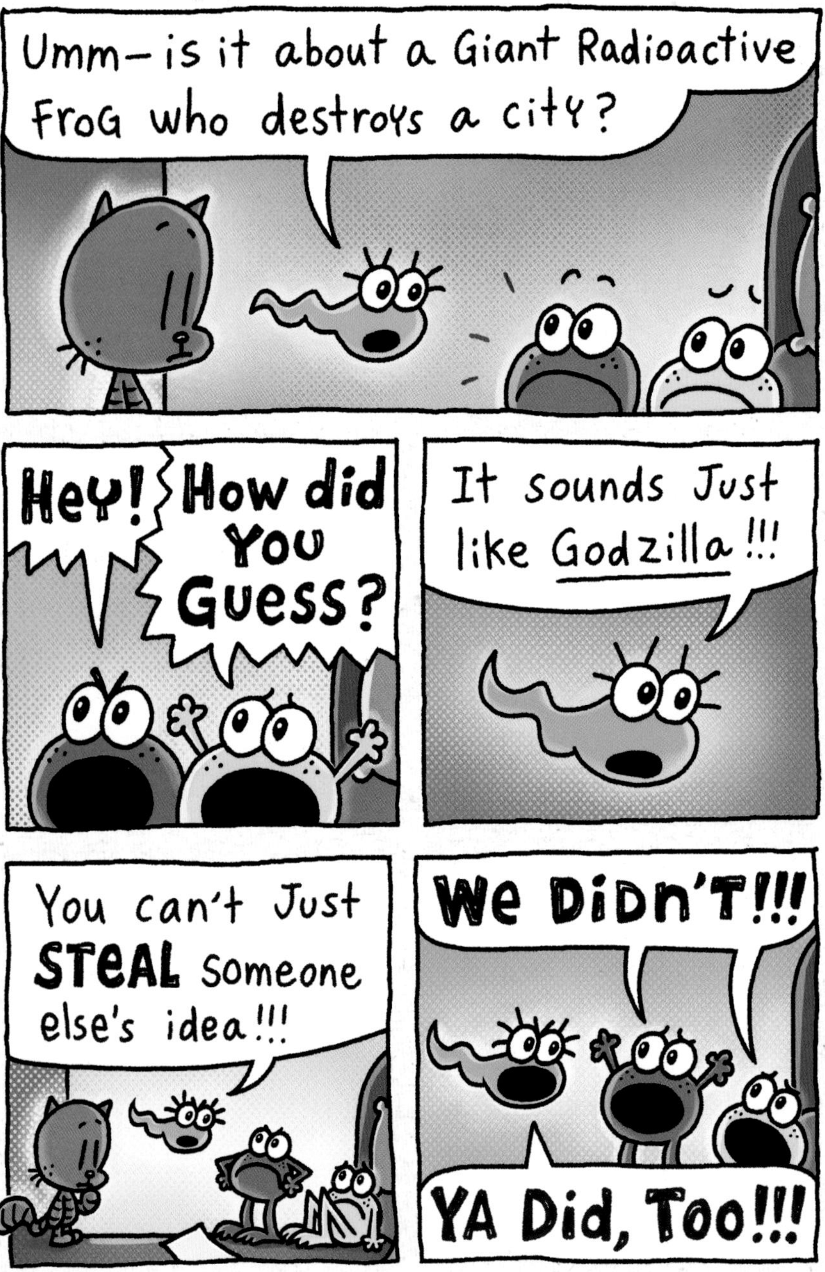
Umm—is it about a Giant Radioactive Frog who destroys a city?
Hey!
How did You Guess?
It sounds Just like Godzilla!!!
You can't Just STEAL someone else's idea!!!
We DIDN'T!!!
YA Did, Too!!!

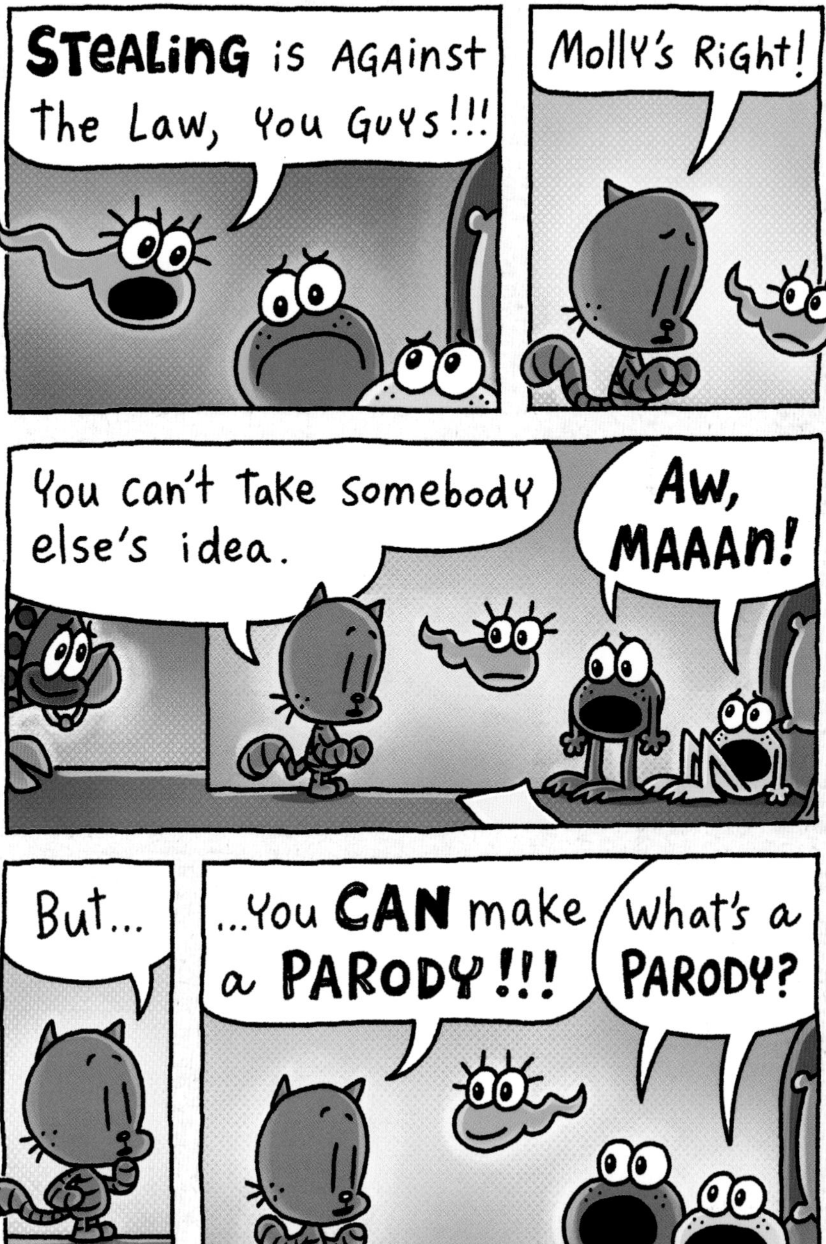
STEALING is AGAINST the LAW, YOU GUYS!!!
MOLLY'S RIGHT!
YOU CAN'T TAKE SOMEBODY ELSE'S IDEA.
AW, MAAAN!
BUT...
...YOU CAN MAKE A PARODY!!!
WHAT'S A PARODY?

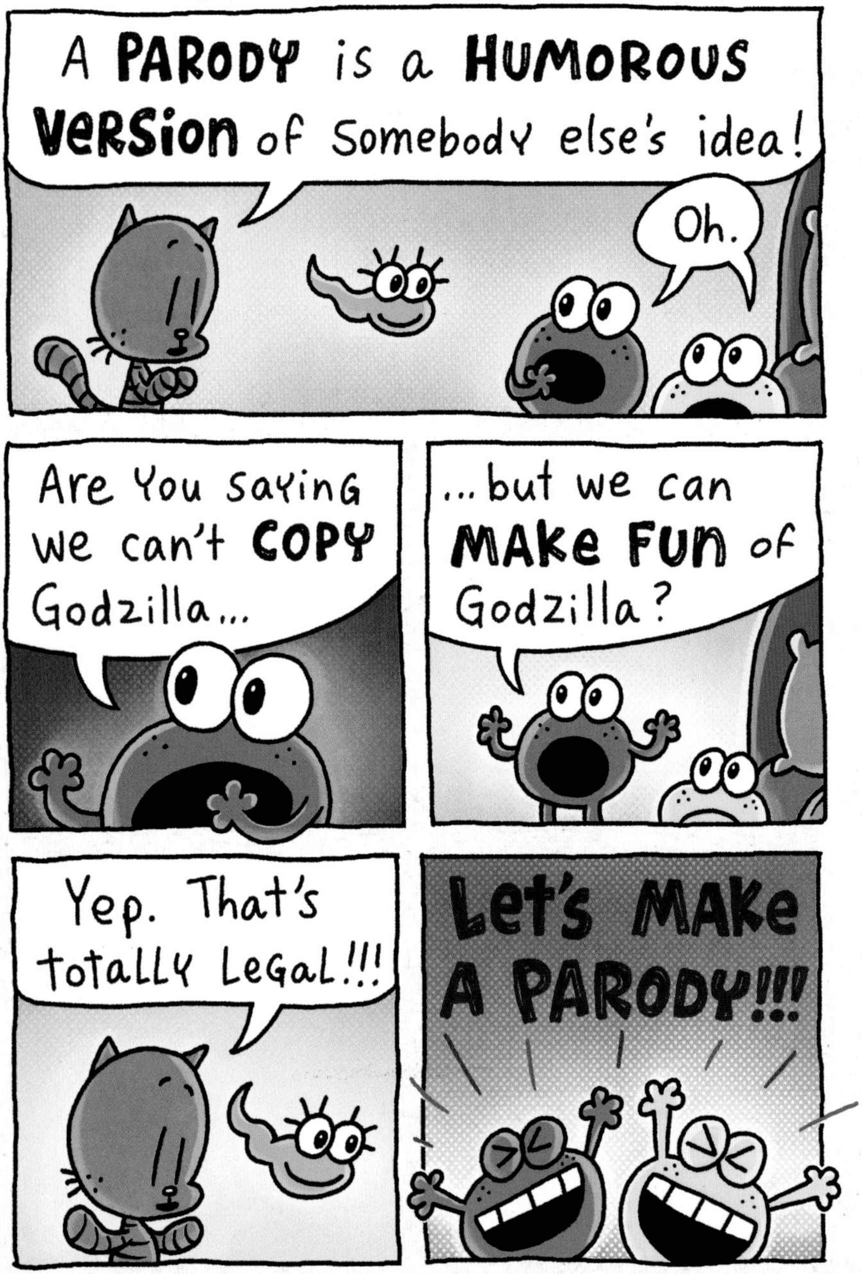
A PARODY is a HUMOROUS VERSION of Somebody else's idea!
Oh.
Are You saying we can't COPY Godzilla...
...but we can MAKE FUN of Godzilla?
Yep. That's totally LeGaL!!!
Let's MAKE A PARODY!!!

CHAPTER 5

The Parody That Relied Heavily on the Fair-Use Defense to Forestall Any Liability for Copyright Infringement

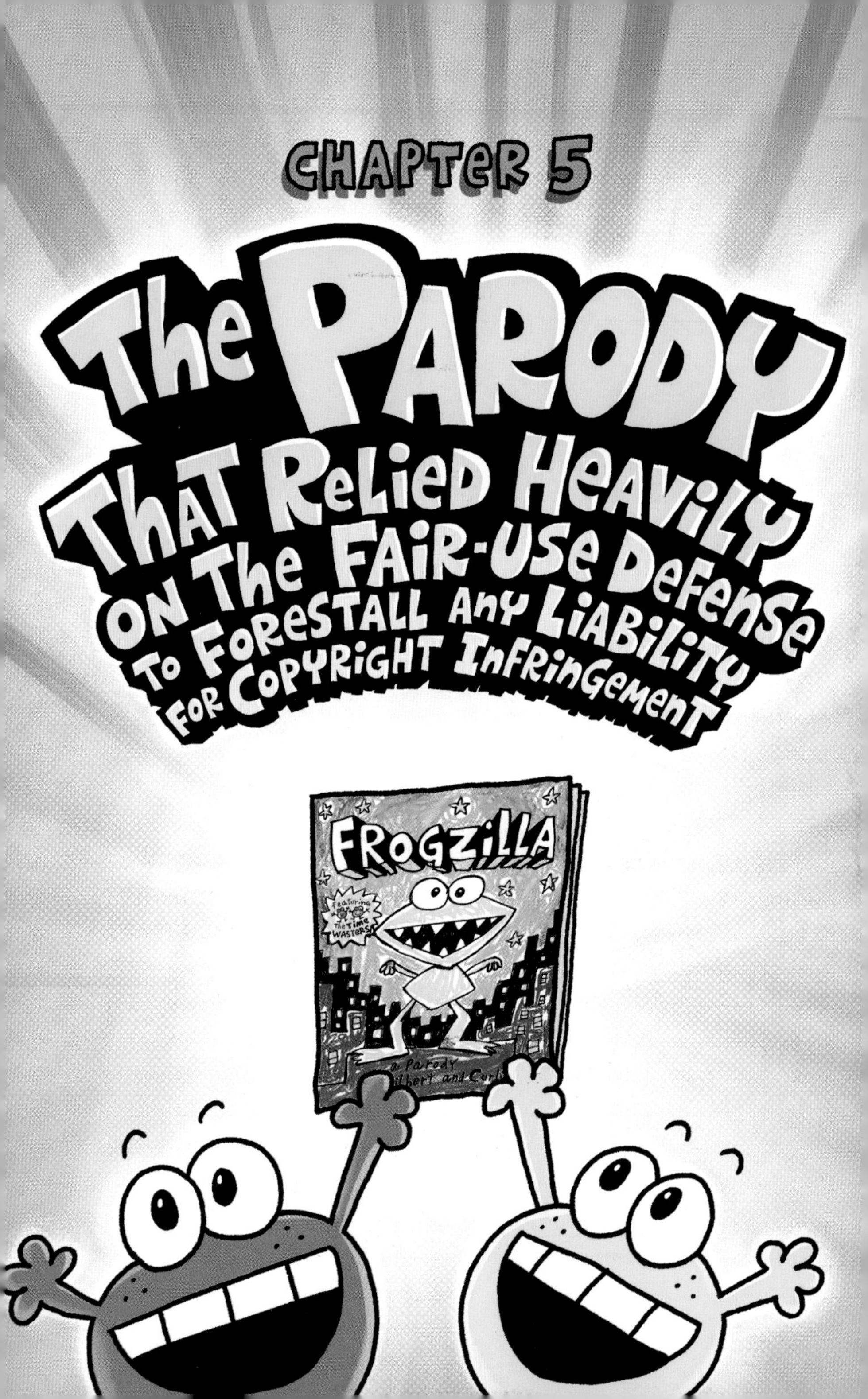
FROGZILLA

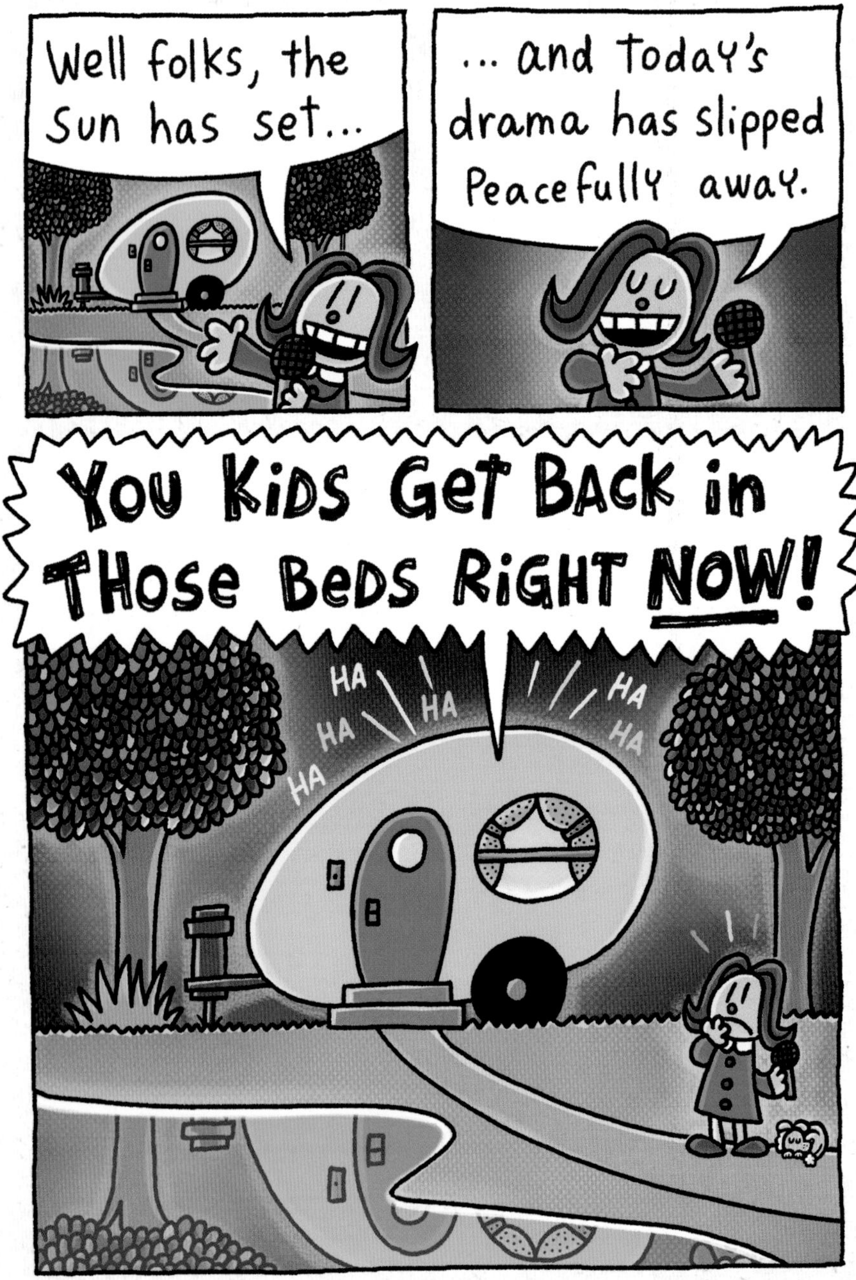
Well folks, the Sun has set...
... and Today's drama has slipped Peacefully away.
You Kids Get Back in Those Beds RiGHT NOW!
HA
HA
HA
HA
HA
HA

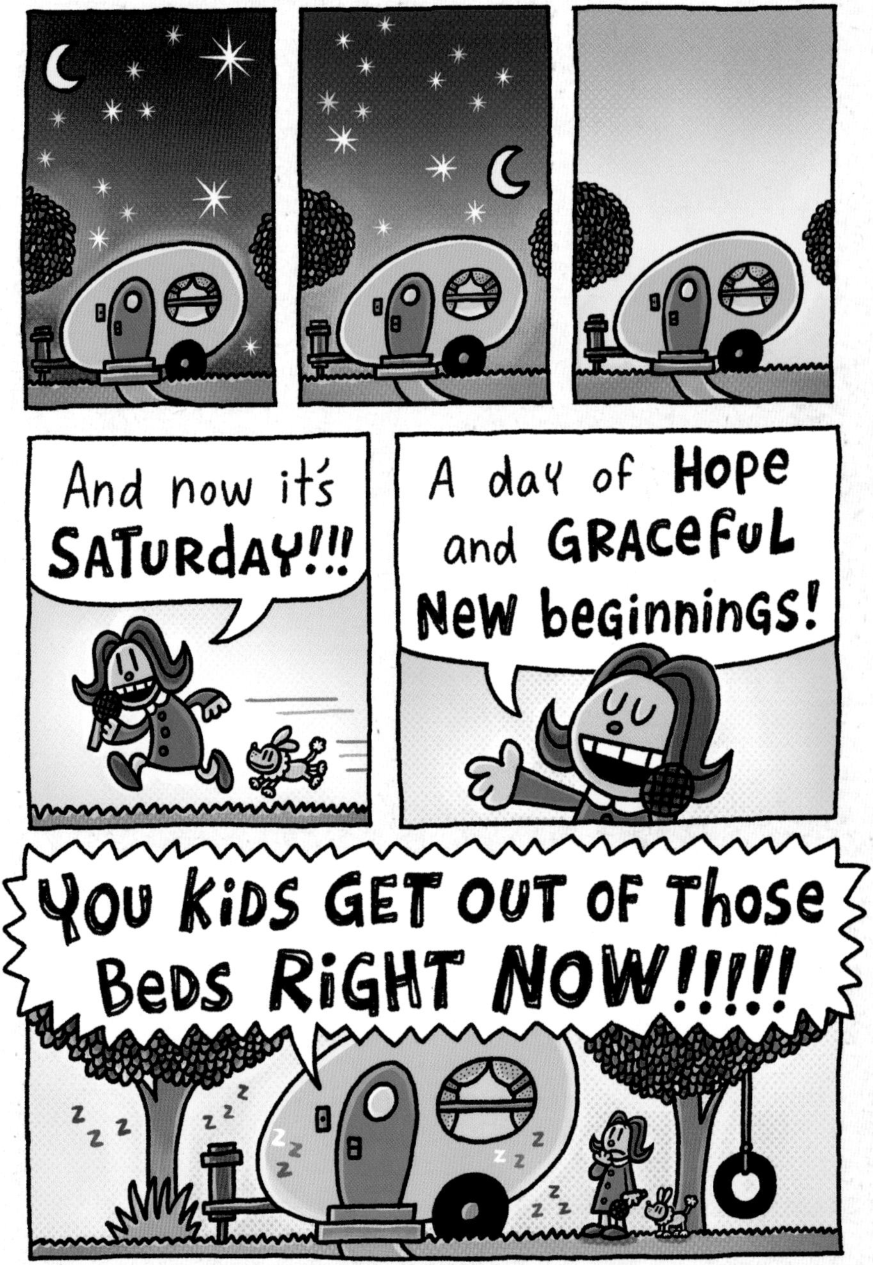
And now it's SATURDAY!!!
A day of HOPE and GRACEFUL NEW BEGINNINGS!
YOU KIDS GET OUT OF THOSE BEDS RIGHT NOW!!!!!
Z Z Z
Z Z Z
Z Z Z
Z Z Z
Z Z Z

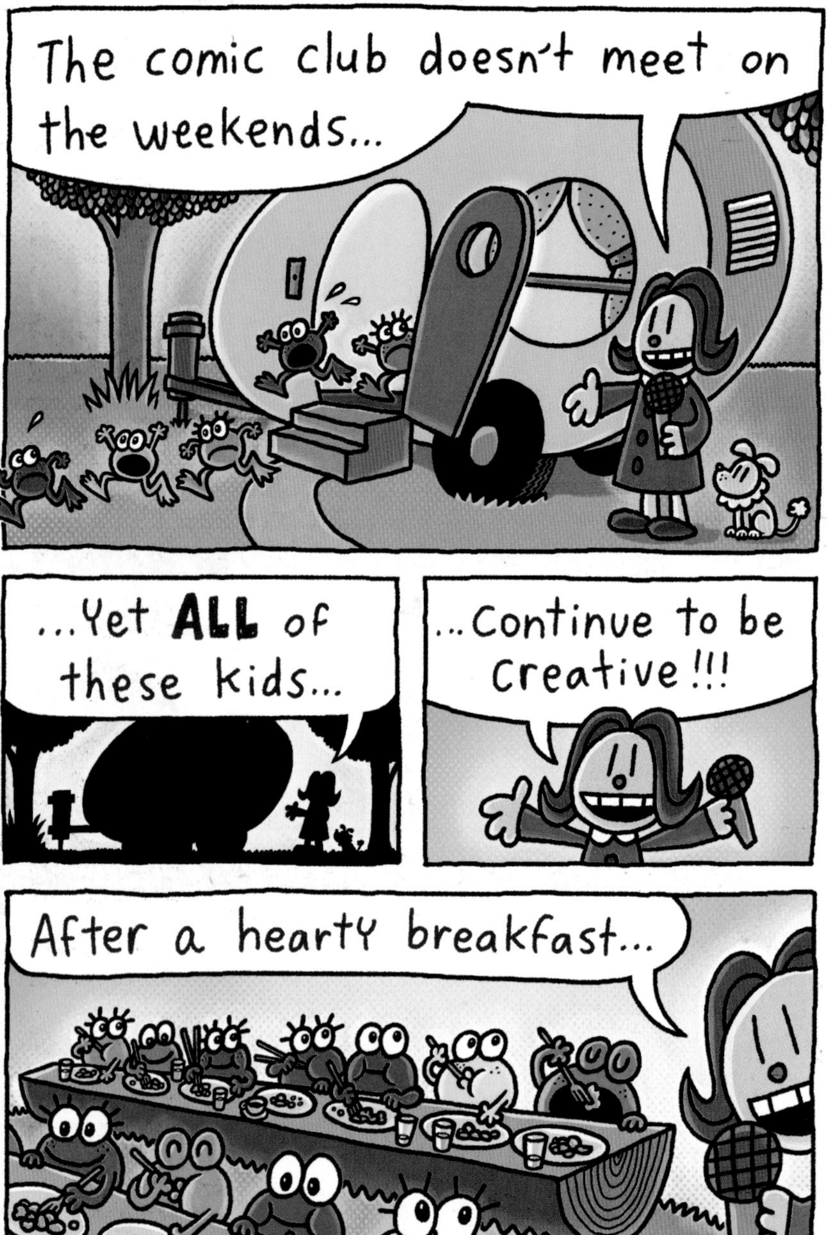
The comic club doesn't meet on the weekends...
...Yet ALL of these kids...
...Continue to be creative!!!
After a hearty breakfast...

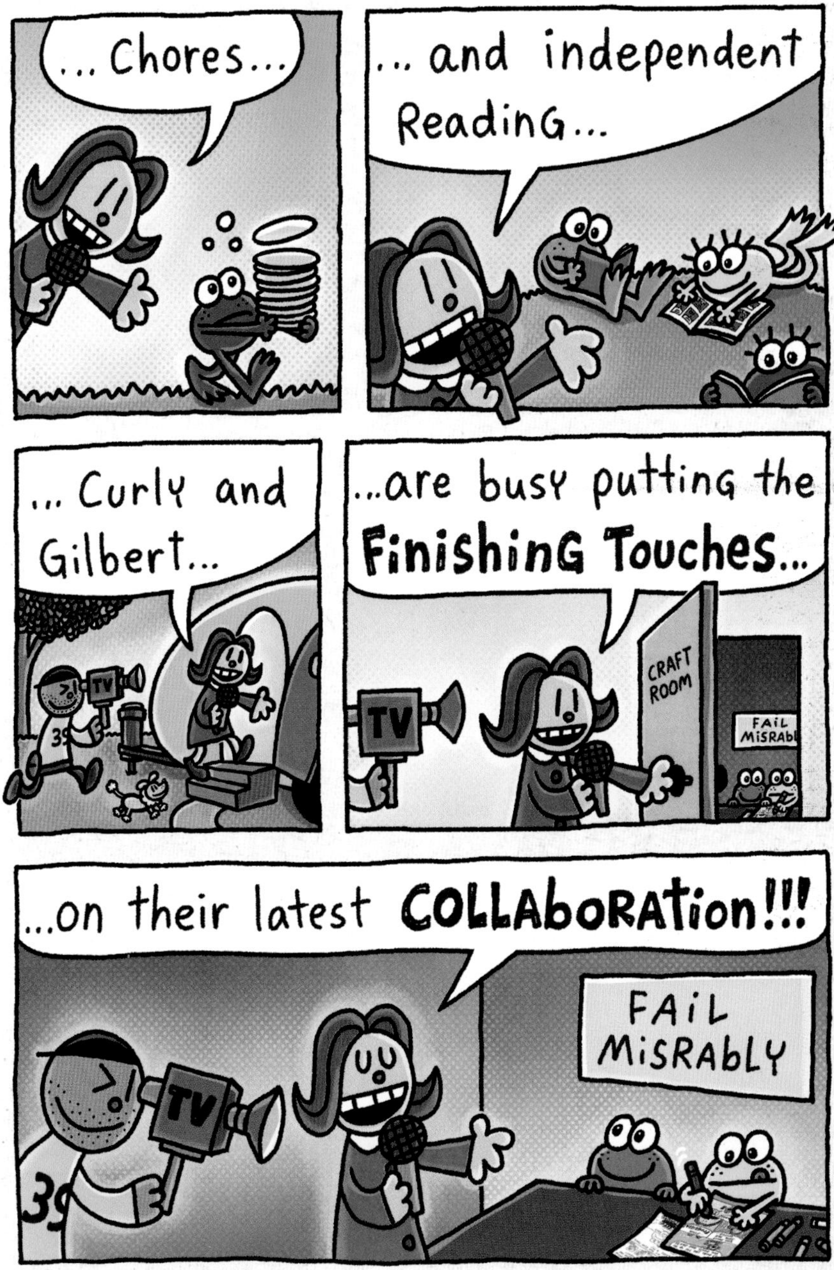
...Chores...
...and independent Reading...
...Curly and Gilbert...
TV
39
...are busy putting the Finishing Touches...
TV
CRAFT ROOM
FAIL MISRABLY
...on their latest COLLABORATION!!!
TV
39
FAIL MISRABLY

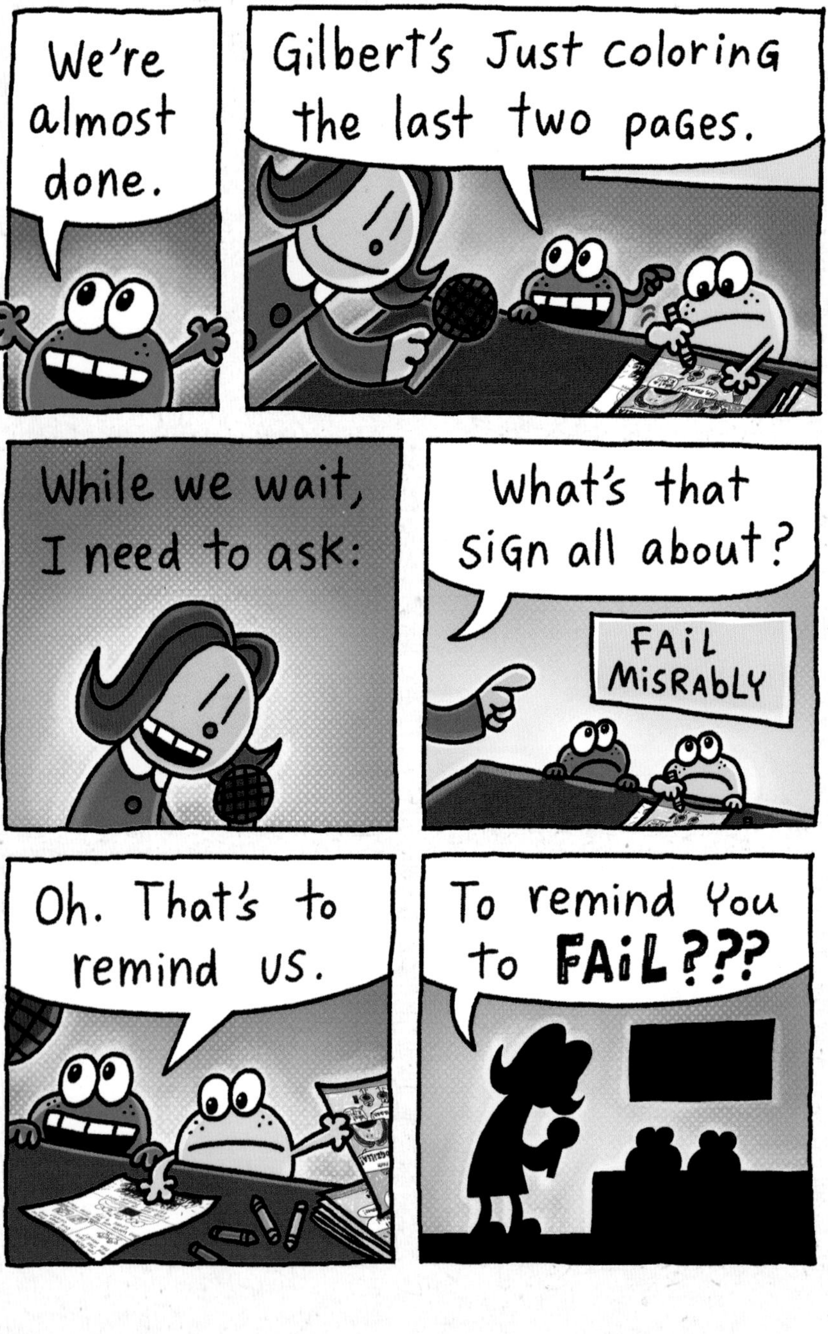
We're almost done.
Gilbert's Just coloring the last two pages.
While we wait, I need to ask:
What's that sign all about?
FAIL MISRABLY
Oh. That's to remind us.
To remind you to FAIL???

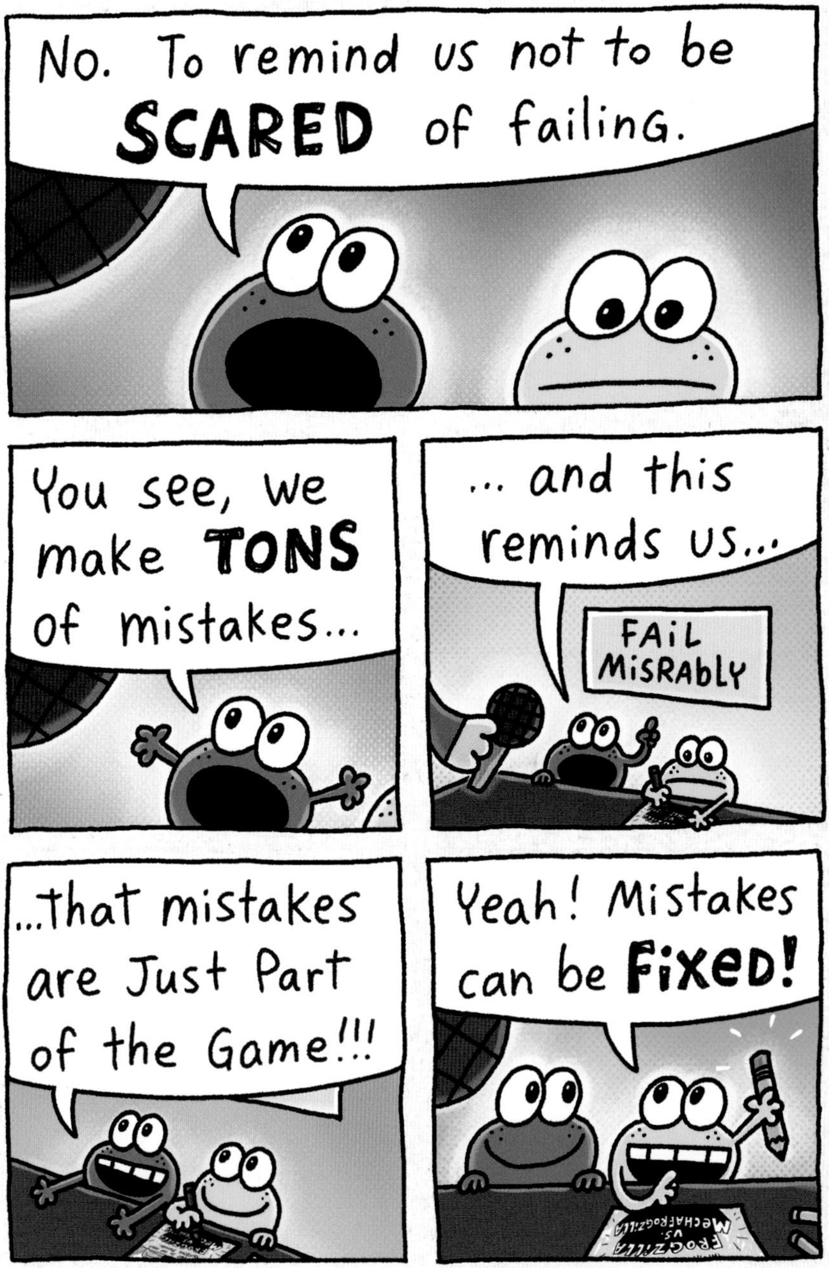
No. To remind us not to be SCARED of failing.
You see, we make TONS of mistakes...
... and this reminds us...
FAIL MISRABLY
...that mistakes are Just Part of the Game!!!
Yeah! Mistakes can be FIXED!
FROGZILLA VS. MECHAFROGZILLA

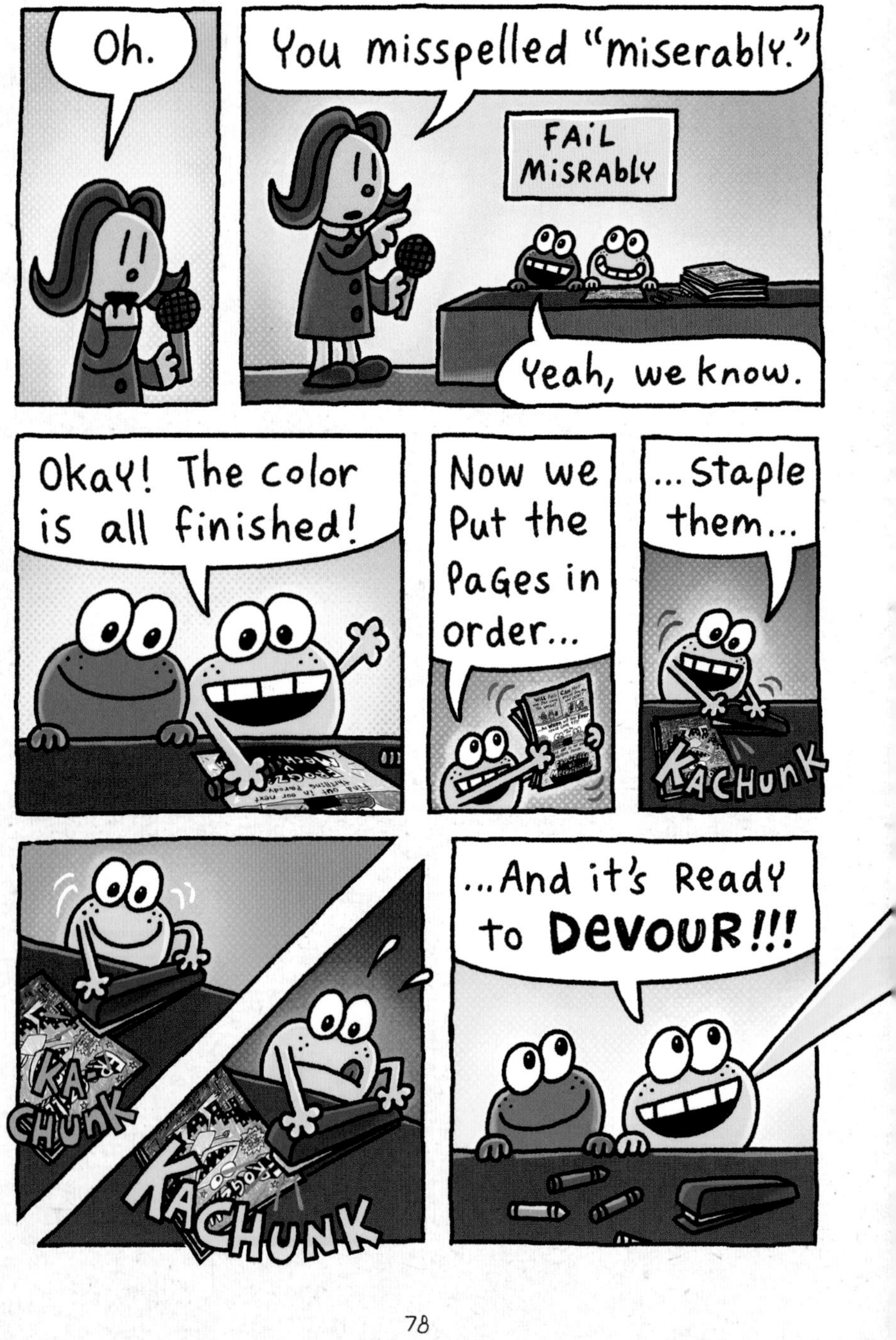
Oh.
You misspelled "miserably."
FAiL MiSRABLY
Yeah, we know.
Okay! The color is all finished!
Now we put the pages in order...
...Staple them...
KACHUNK
KA-CHUNK
KACHUNK
...And it's ready to DEVOUR!!!

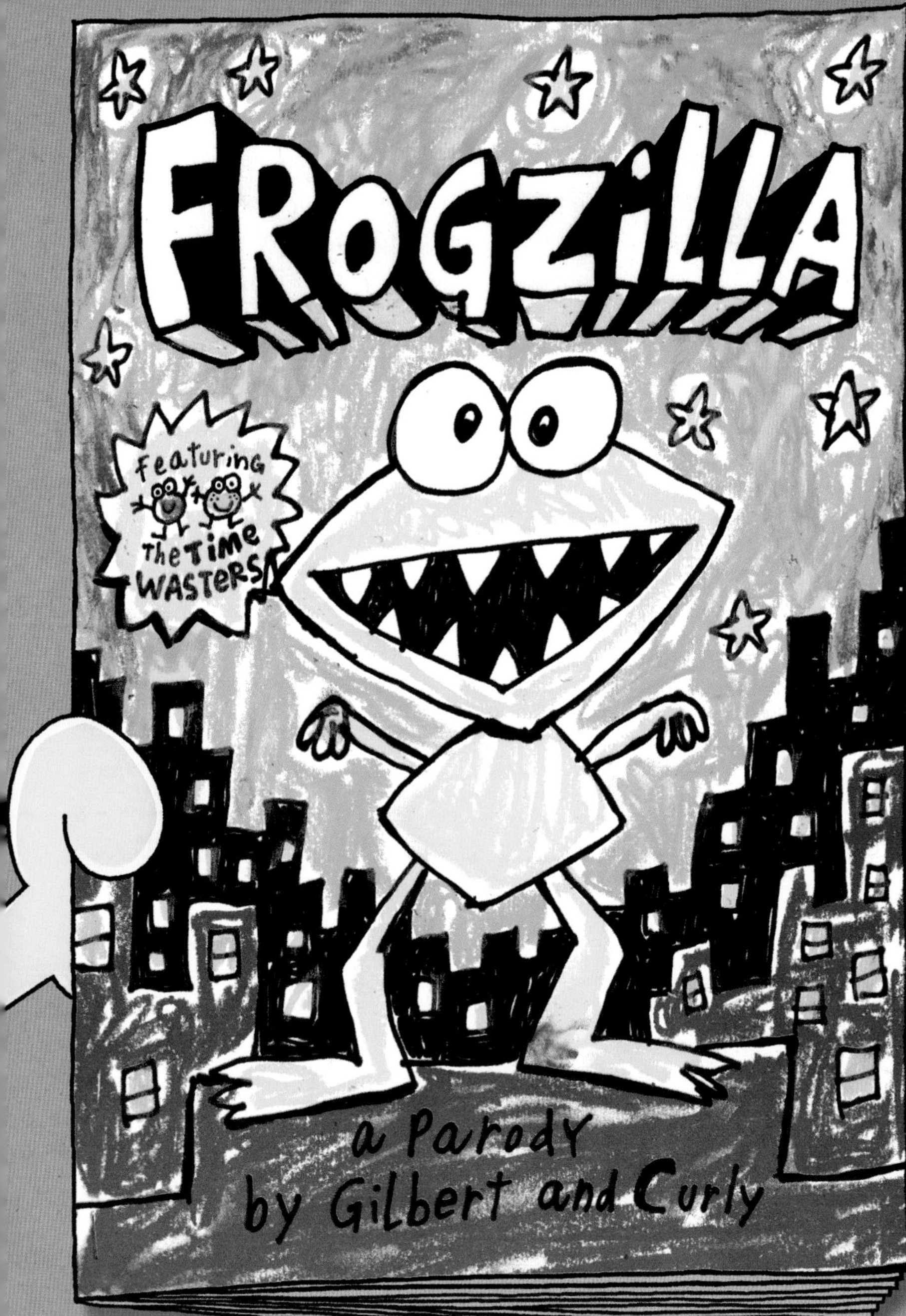
FROGZILLA
Featuring The TIME WASTERS
a Parody
by Gilbert and Curly

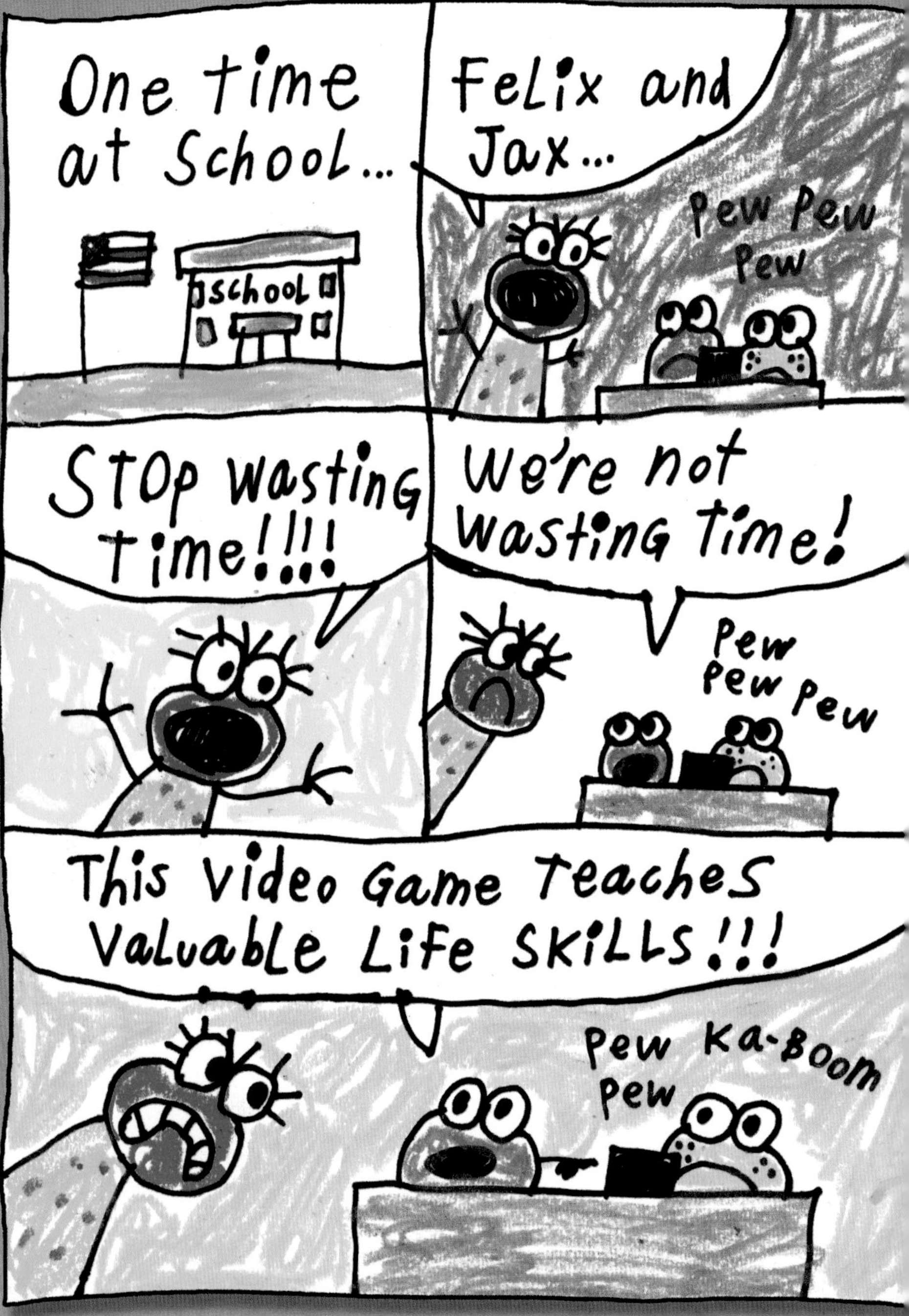

One time at School...
Felix and Jax...
Pew Pew Pew
SCHOOL
STOP wasting time!!!!
We're not wasting time!
Pew Pew Pew Pew
This video Game Teaches Valuable Life SKILLS!!!
Pew Ka-Boom Pew

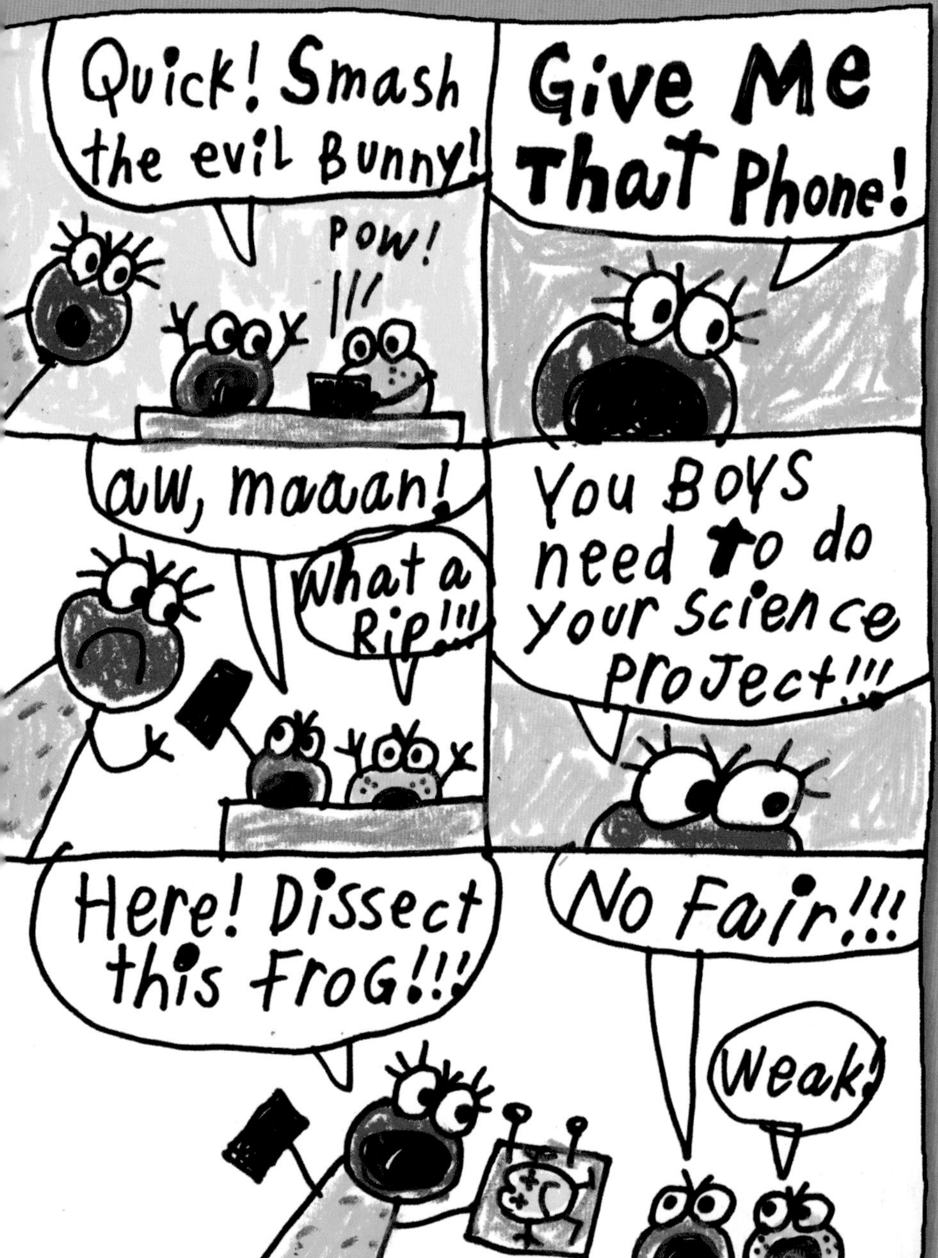
Quick! Smash the evil Bunny!
POW!
Give Me That Phone!
aw, maaan!
What a Rip!!!
You BOYS need to do your Science ProJect!!!
Here! Dissect this FroG!!!
No Fair!!!
Weak!

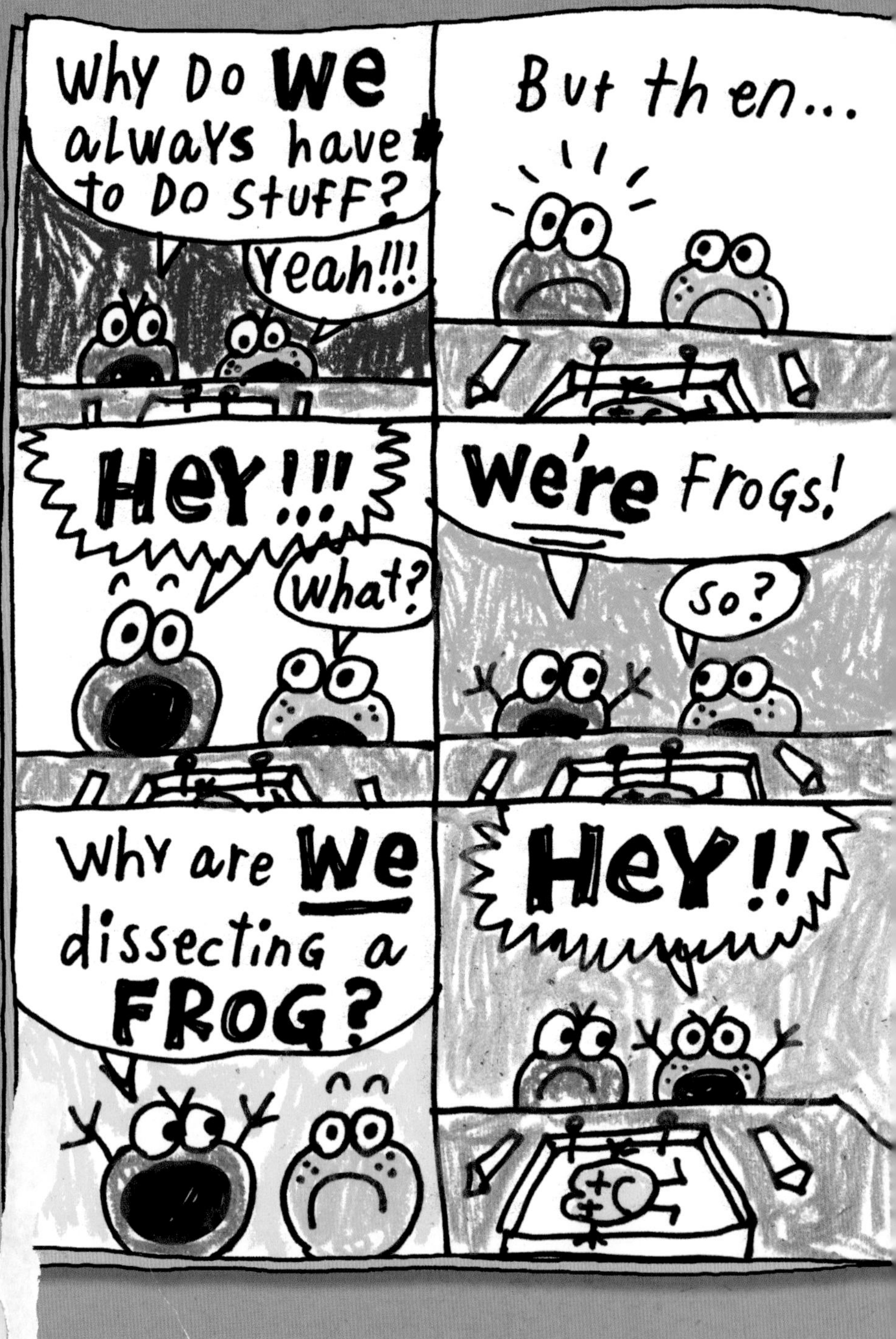
Why Do WE always have to DO STUFF?
Yeah!!!
But then...
HEY!!!
What?
We're Frogs!
So?
Why are WE dissecting a FROG?
HEY!!

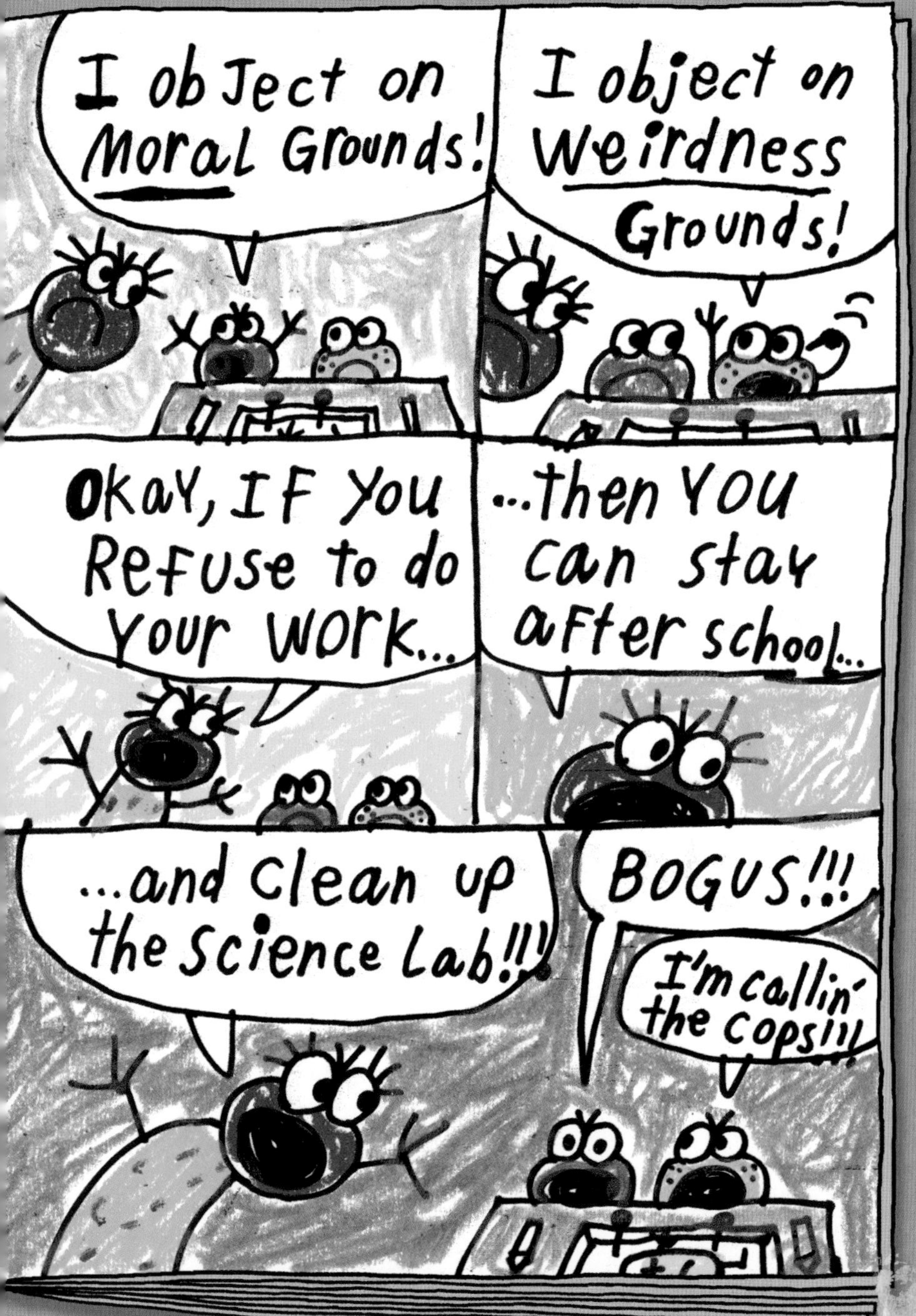
I obJect on Moral Grounds!
I object on Weirdness Grounds!
Okay, IF You Refuse to do your work...
...then YOU can stay after school...
...and Clean up the Science Lab!!!
BOGUS!!!
I'm callin' the cops!!!

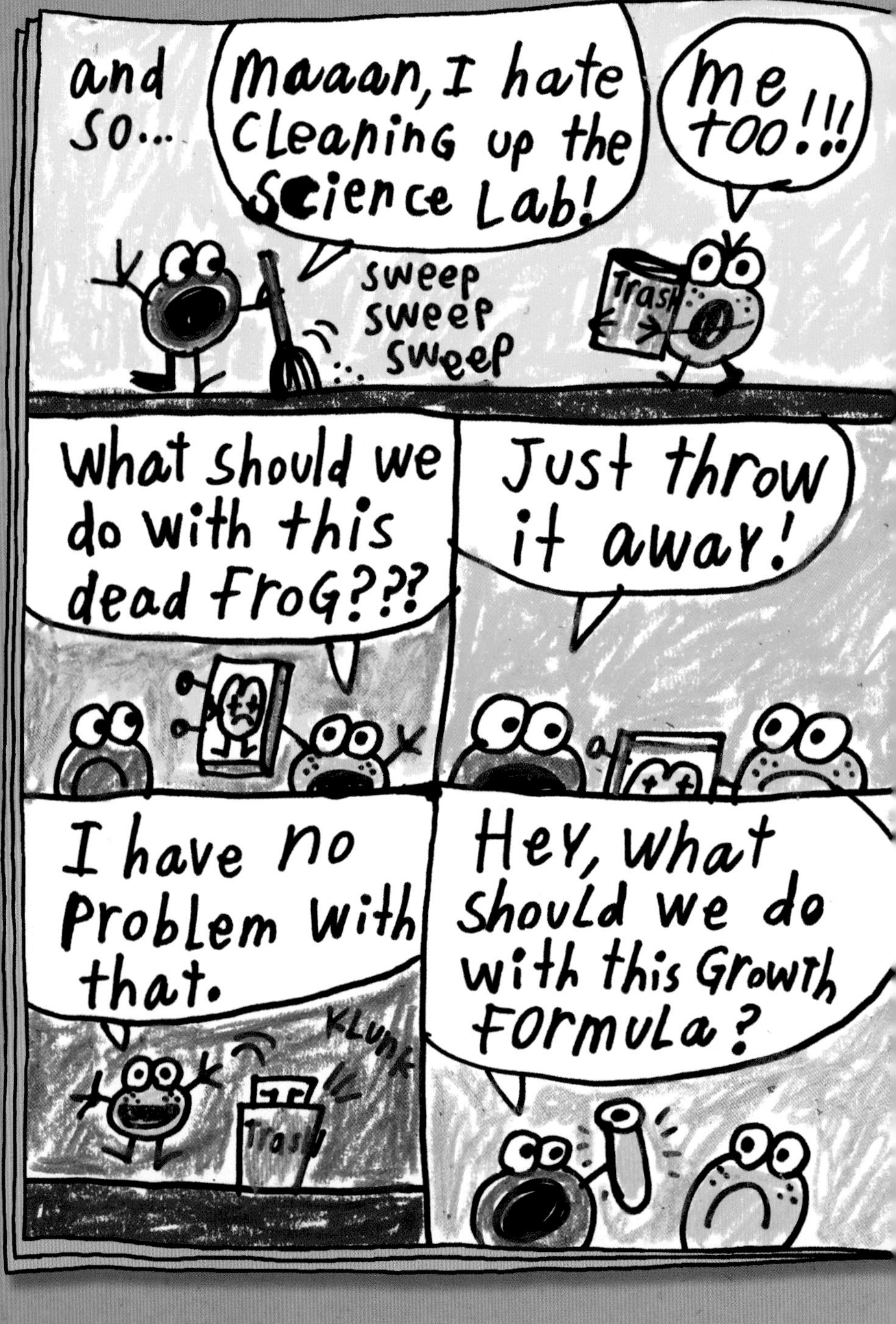
and so...
Maaan, I hate cleaning up the Science Lab!
Me too!!!
Trash
sweep sweep sweep
What should we do with this dead FroG???
Just throw it away!
I have no Problem with that.
KLUNK
Trash
Hey, what should we do with this Growth Formula?

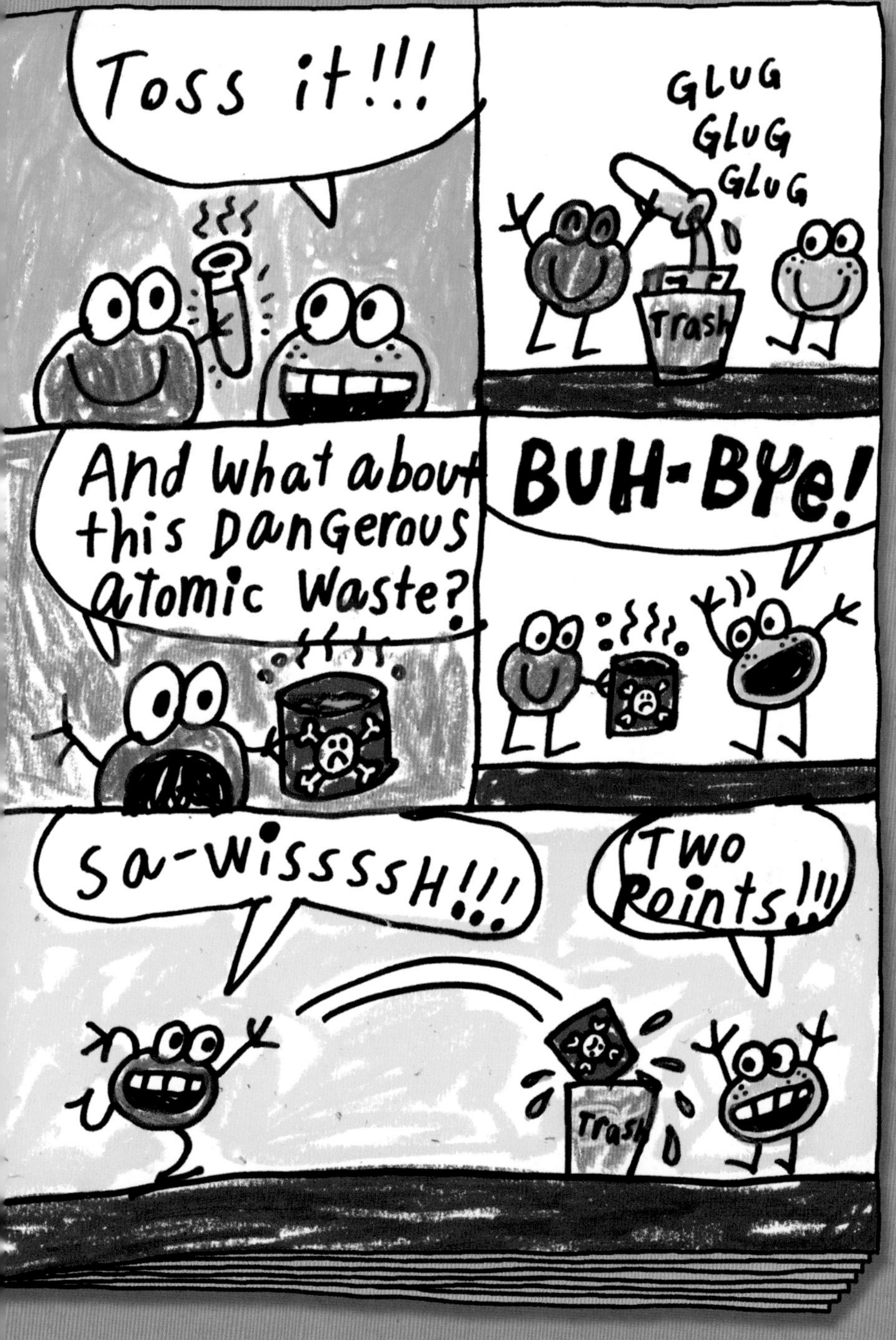
Toss it!!!
GLUG
GLUG
GLUG
Trash
And what about this DANGEROUS atomic Waste?
BUH-BYE!
SA-WISSSSSH!!!
TWO Points!!!
Trash

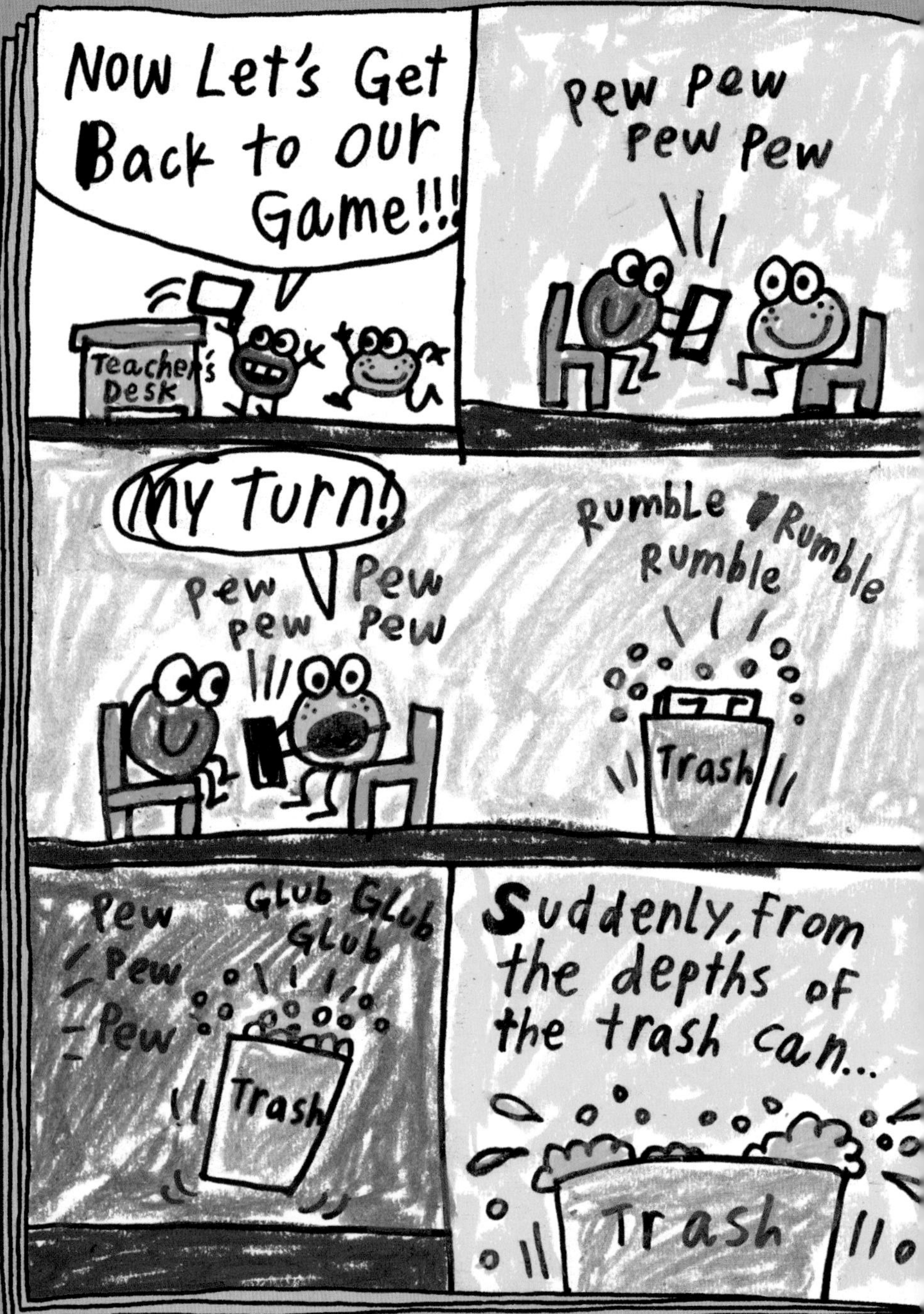
Now Let's Get Back to our Game!!!
Teacher's Desk
Pew Pew
Pew Pew
My Turn!
Pew Pew
Pew Pew
Rumble Rumble
Rumble
Trash
Pew
Pew
Pew
Glub Glub
Glub
Trash
Suddenly, from the depths of the trash can...
Trash

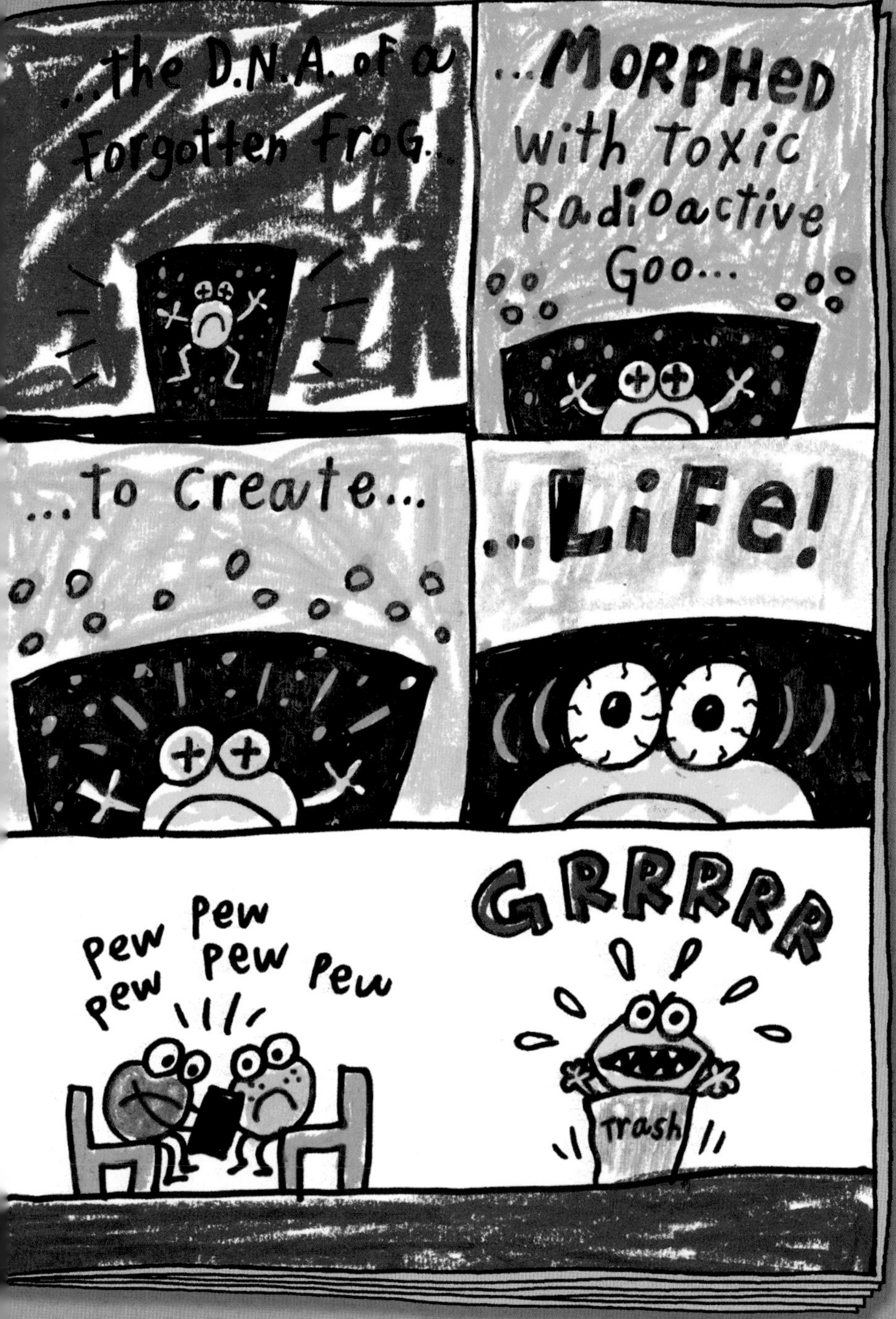
...the D.N.A. of a Forgotten Frog...
...Morphed with Toxic Radioactive Goo...
...To Create...
...Life!
pew pew pew pew pew
GRRRRR
Trash

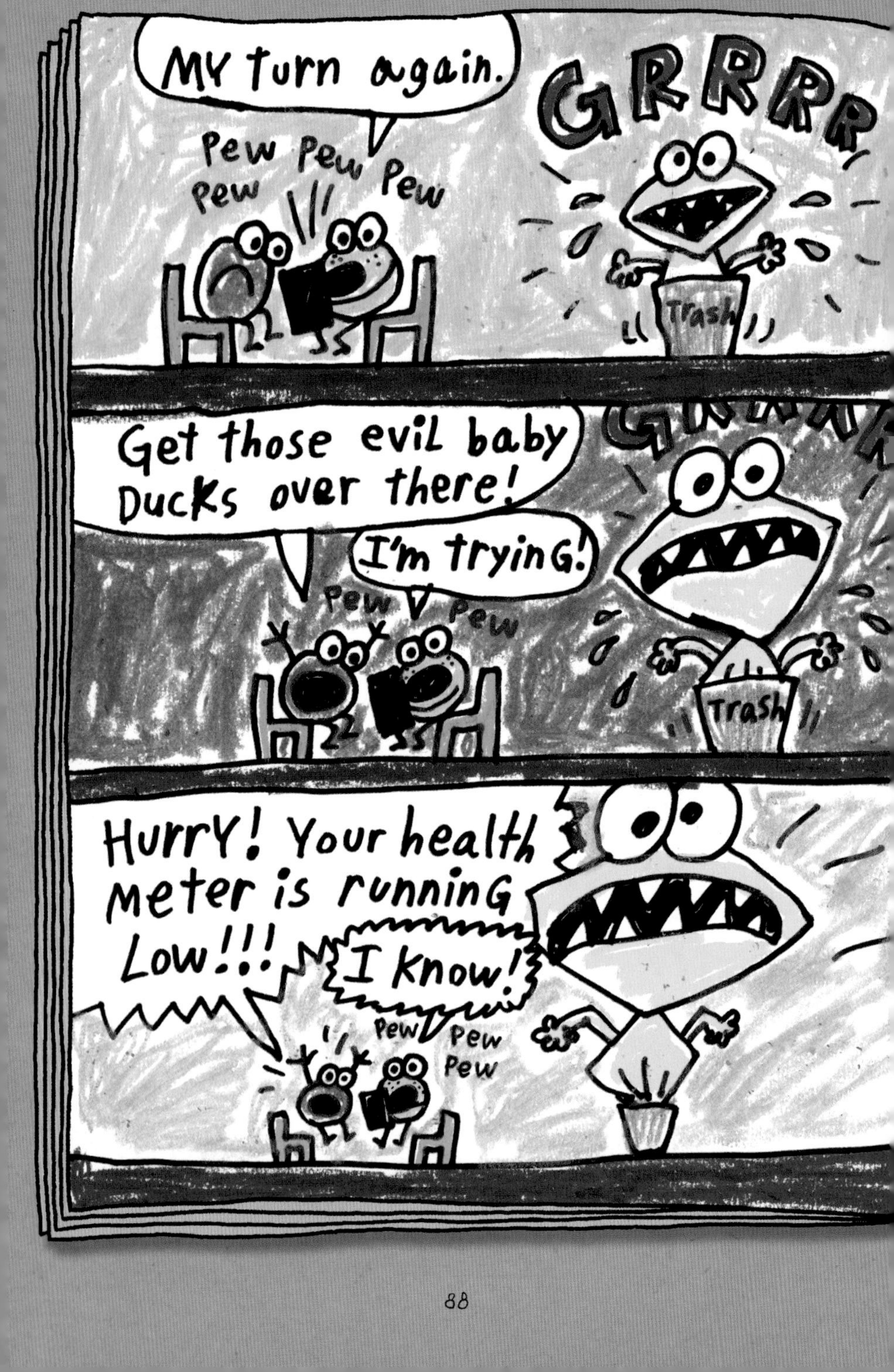
MY turn again.
Pew Pew Pew Pew
GRRRR
Trash
Get those evil baby Ducks over there!
I'm tryinG!
Pew Pew
Trash
HurrY! Your health meter is runninG Low!!!
I know!
Pew Pew Pew

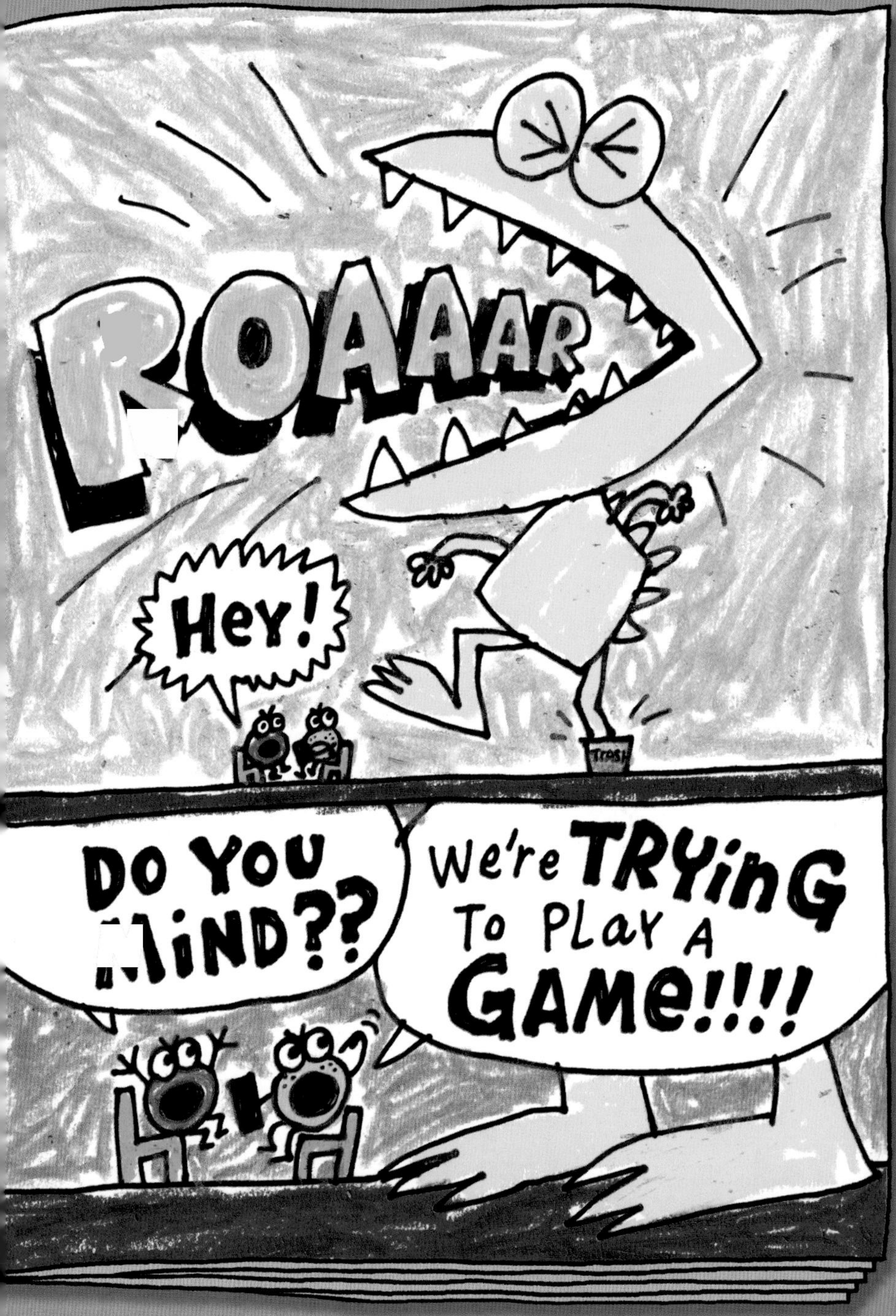
ROAAAR
Hey!
TRASH
DO YOU MIND??
We're TRYING TO PLAY A GAME!!!!

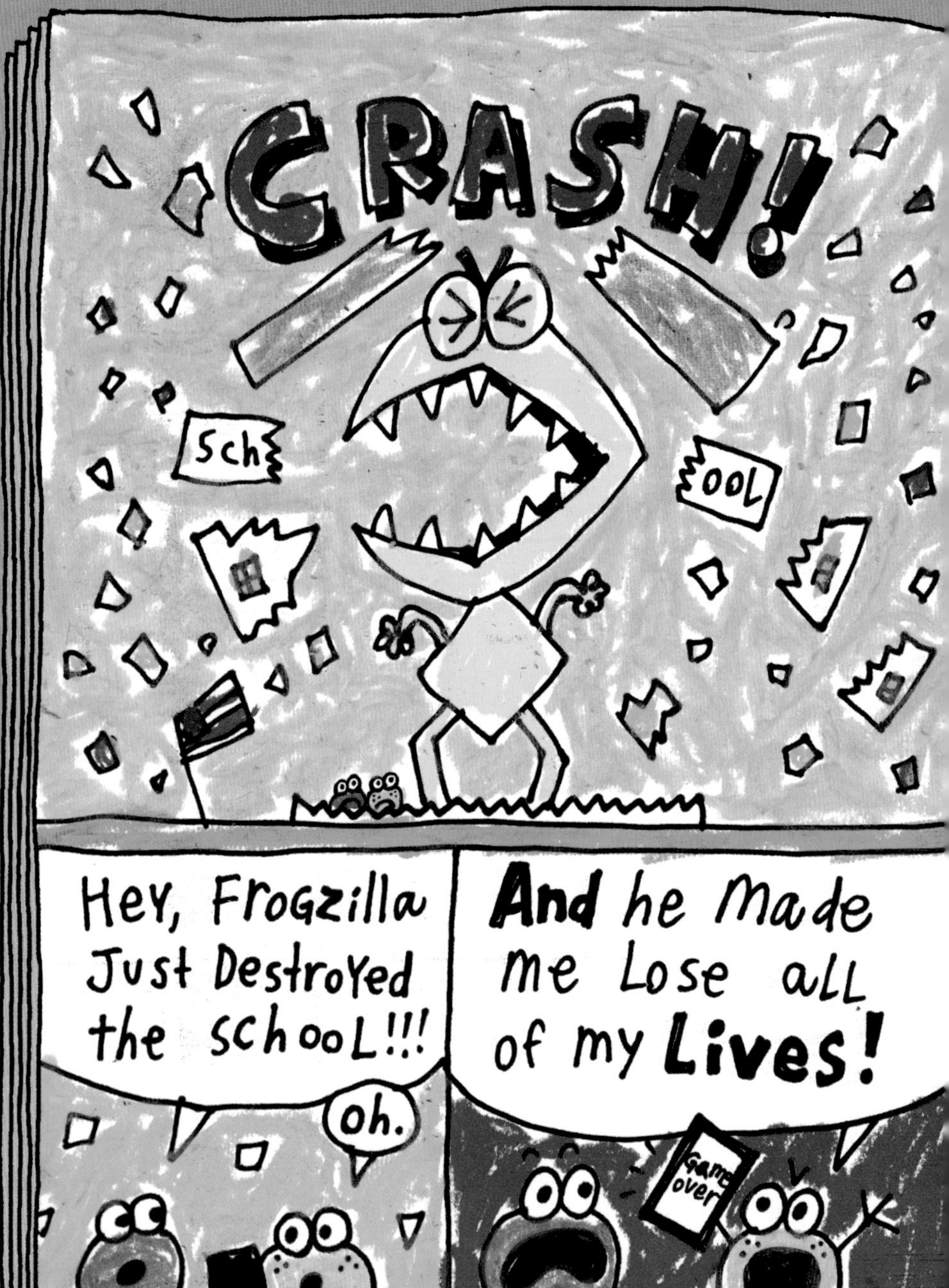
CRASH!
Sch
OOL
Hey, Frogzilla Just Destroyed the school!!!
oh.
And he made me Lose all of my Lives!
Game over

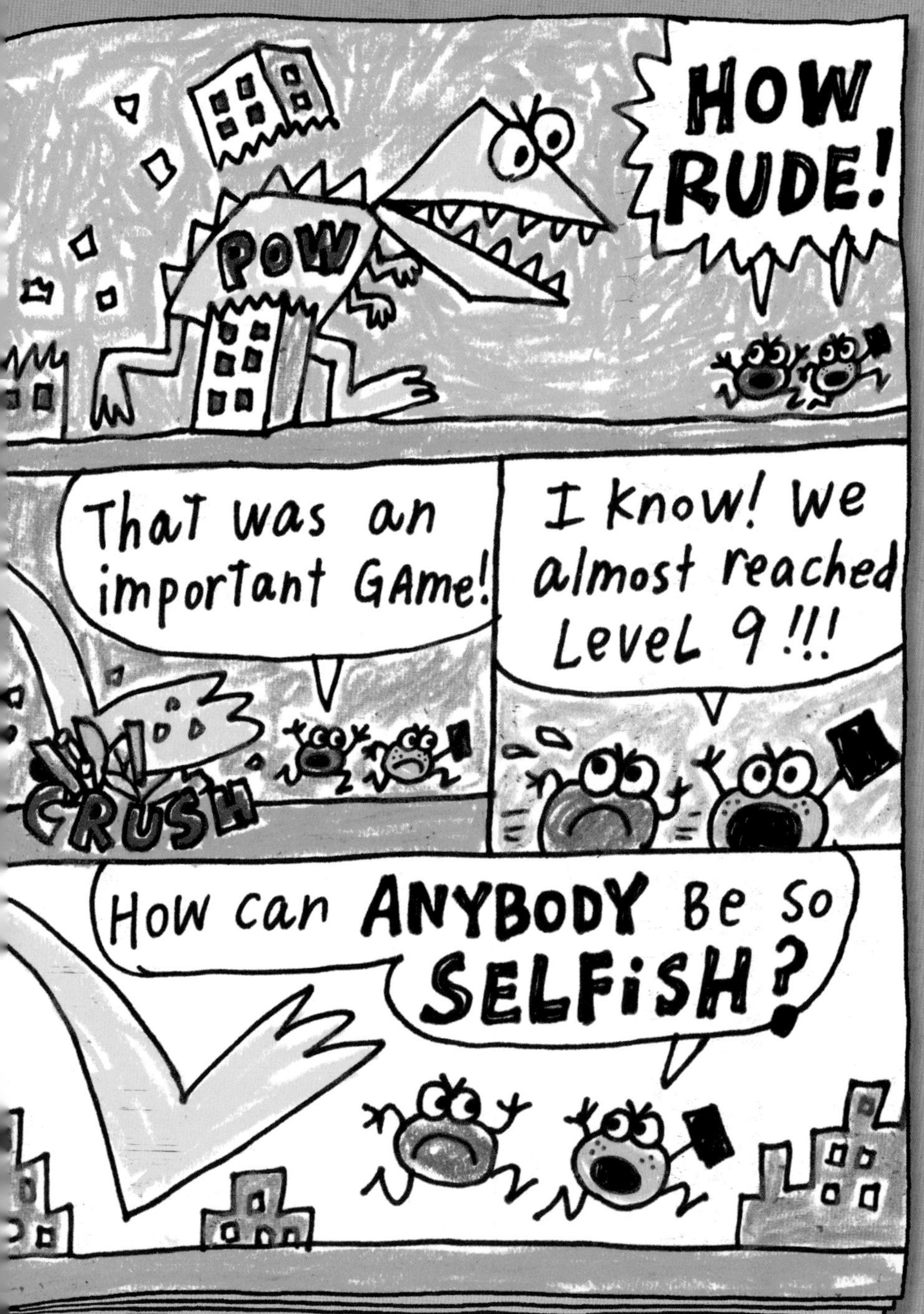
HOW RUDE!
POW
That was an important GAme!
CRUSH
I know! We almost reached LeveL 9!!!
How can ANYBODY Be so SELFiSH?

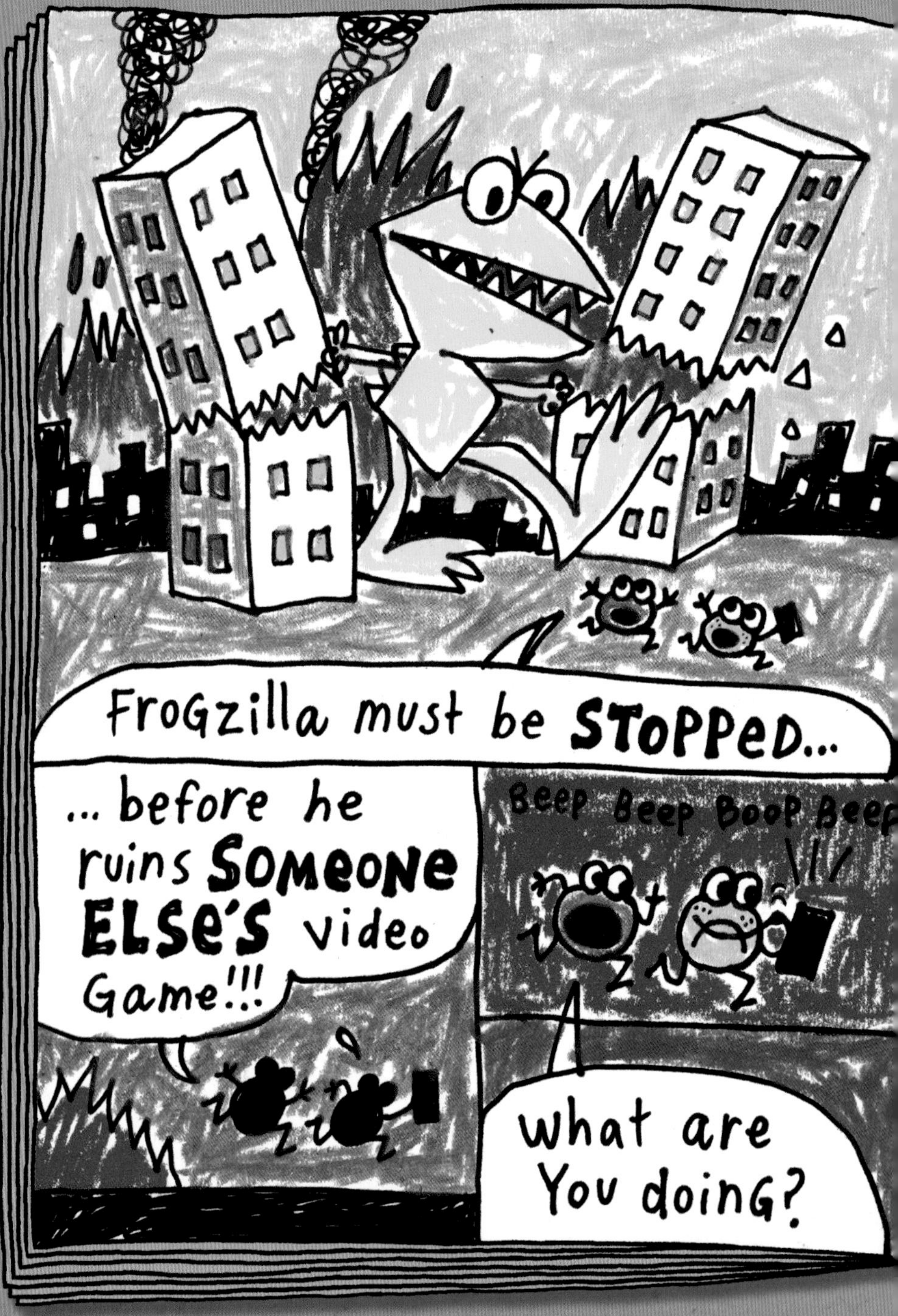
FroGzilla must be STOPPED...
... before he ruins SOMEONE ELSE'S video Game!!!
Beep Beep BooP Beep
What are You doinG?

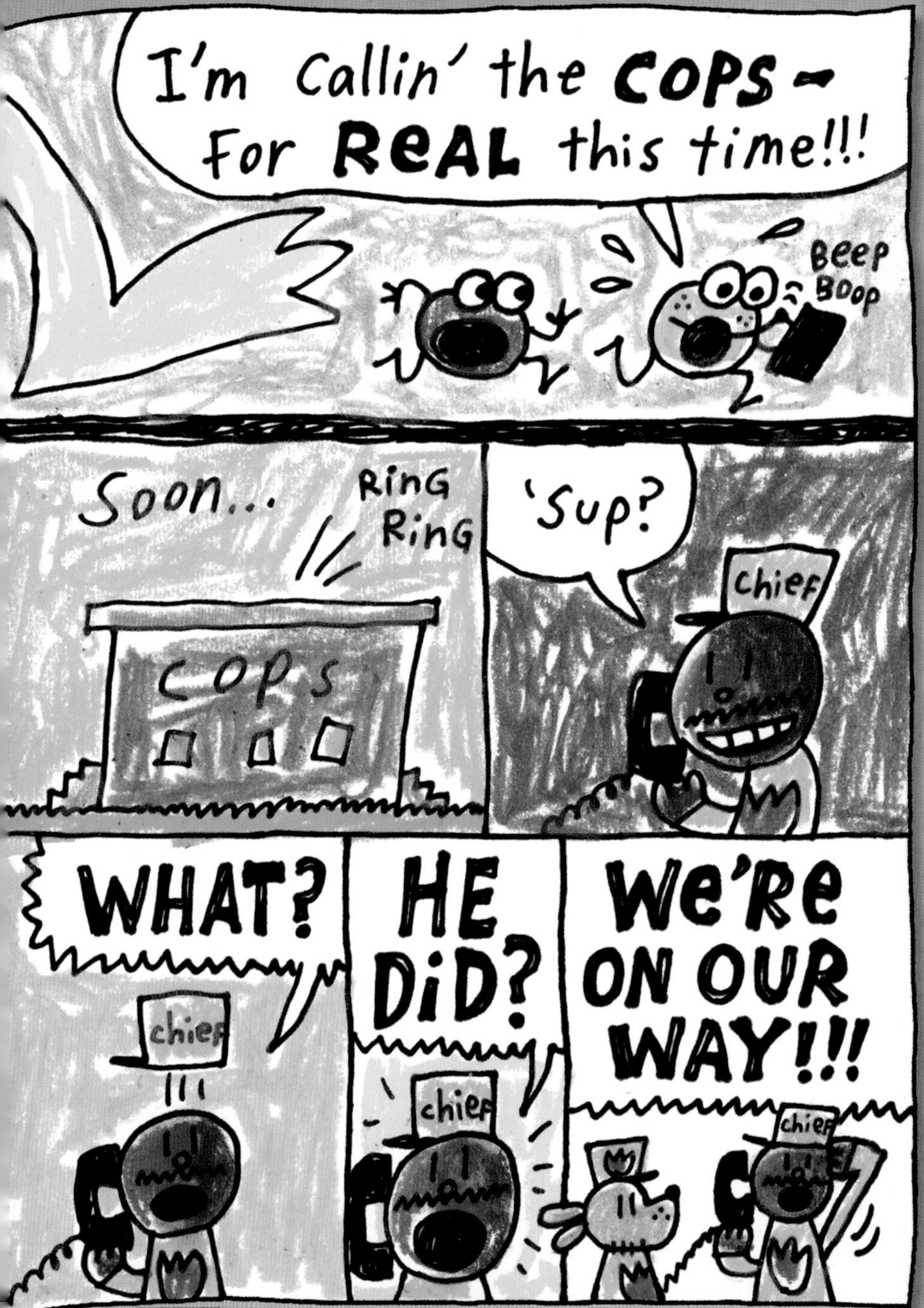
I'm Callin' the COPS - For REAL this time!!!
BEEP BOOP
Soon...
RING RING
COPS
'Sup?
Chief
WHAT?
chief
HE DiD?
chief
We're ON OUR WAY!!!
chief

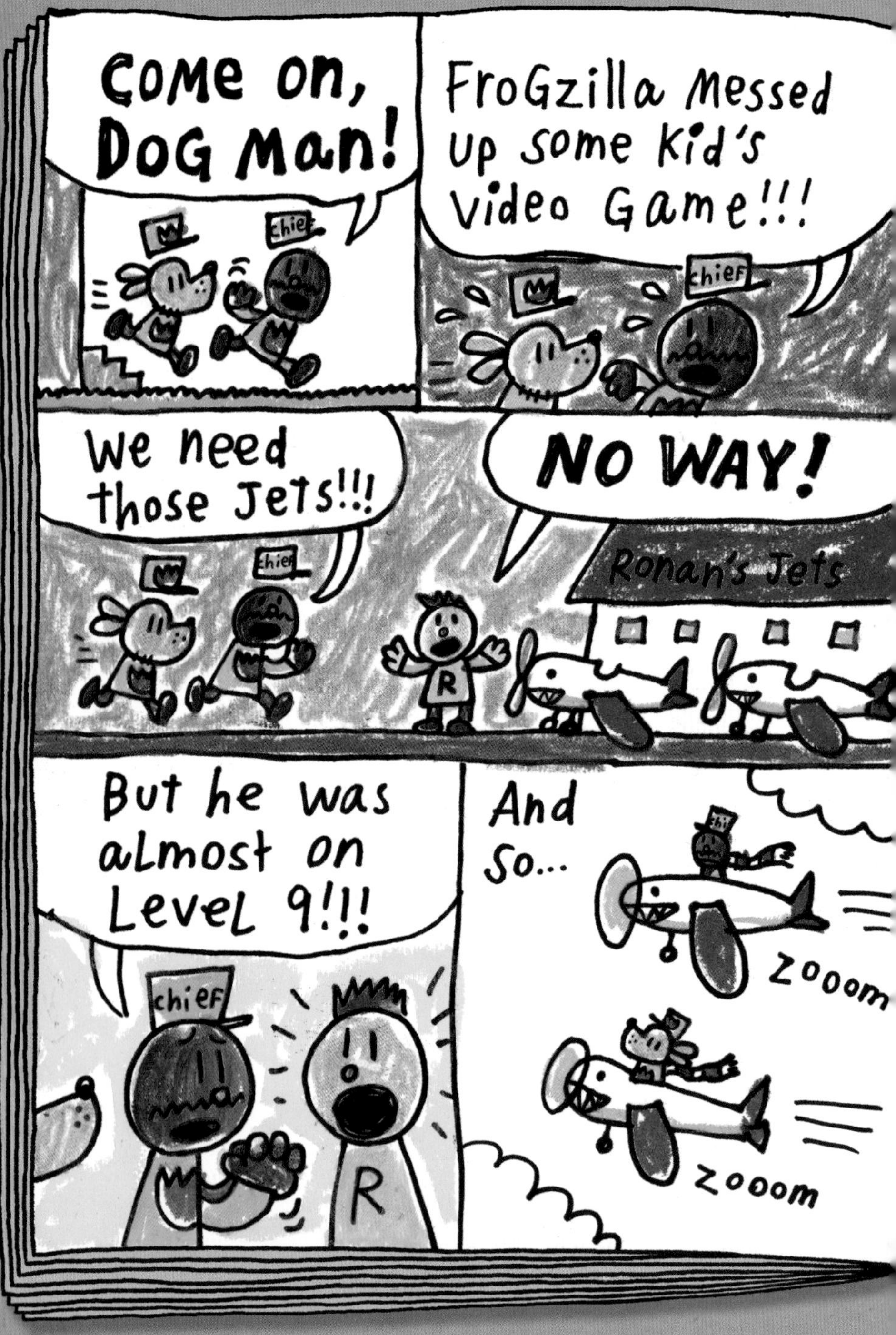
Come on, DOG Man!
FroGzilla Messed up some Kid's Video Game!!!
chief
We need those Jets!!!
NO WAY!
Ronan's Jets
R
But he was almost on LeveL 9!!!
chief
R
And so...
Zooom
Zooom

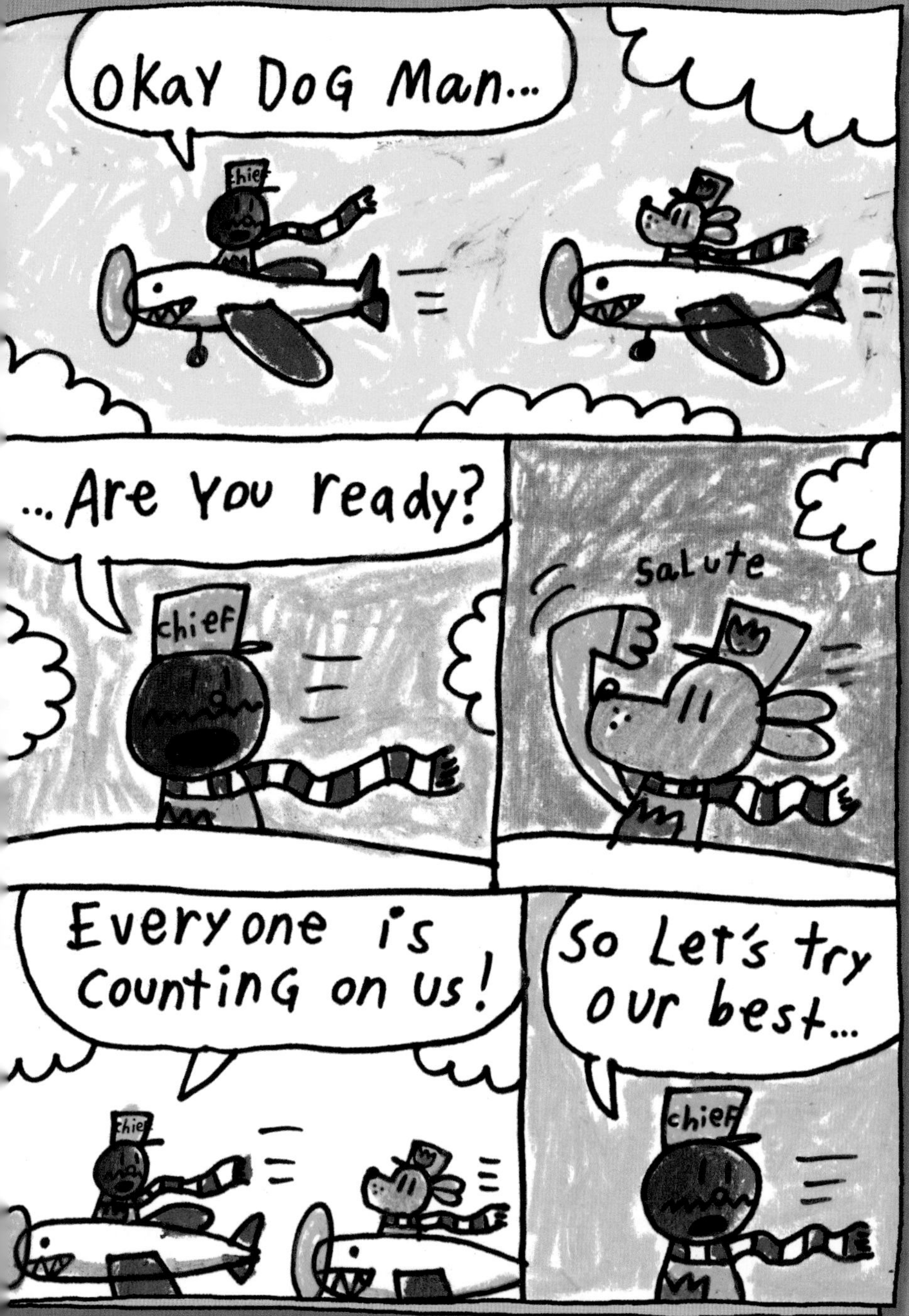
OKaY DoG Man...
...Are You ready?
Salute
Everyone is Counting on us!
So Let's try our best...
chief
chief

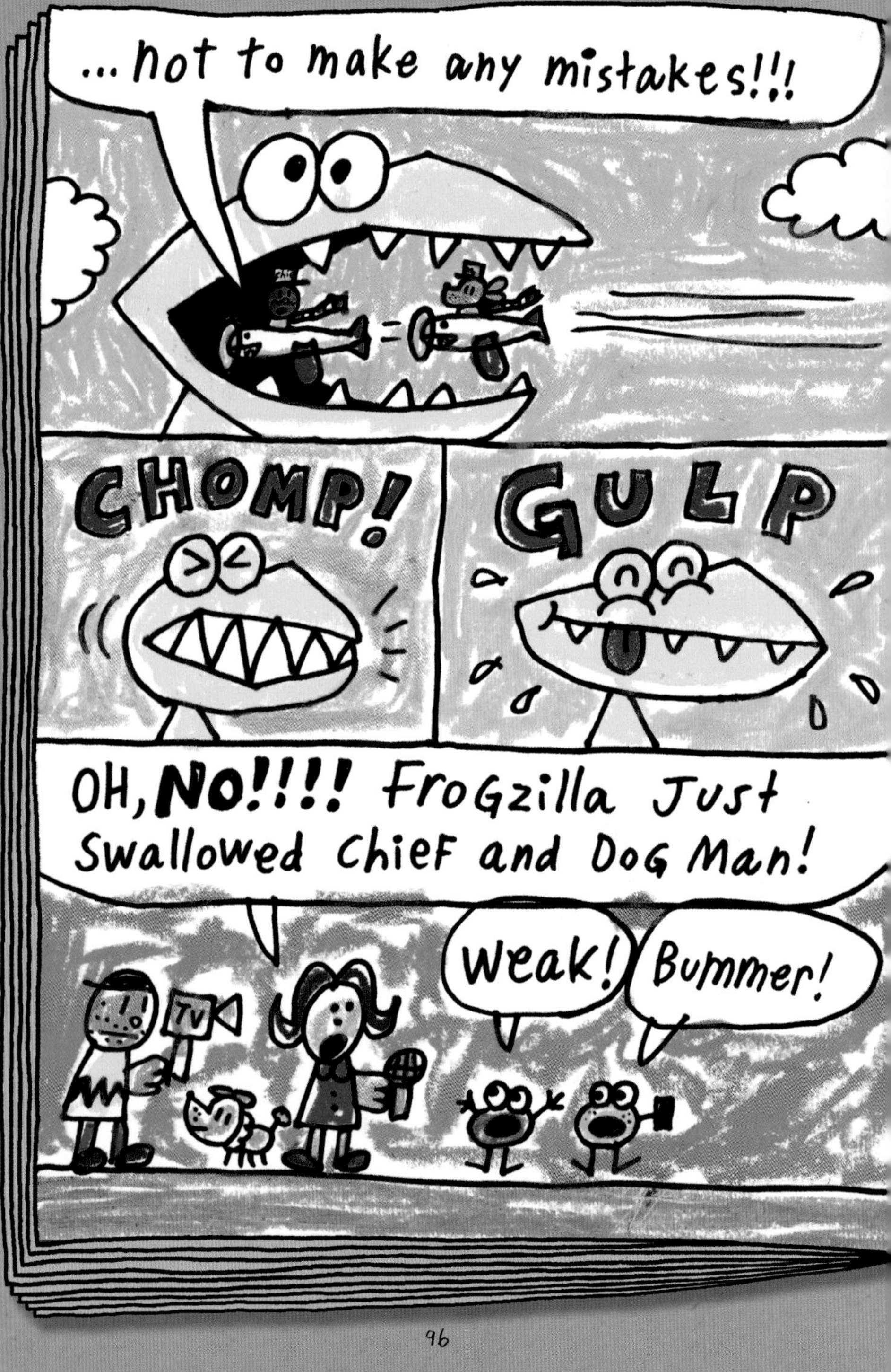
...not to make any mistakes!!!
CHOMP!
GULP
OH, NO!!!! FroGzilla Just Swallowed Chief and DoG Man!
Weak!
Bummer!

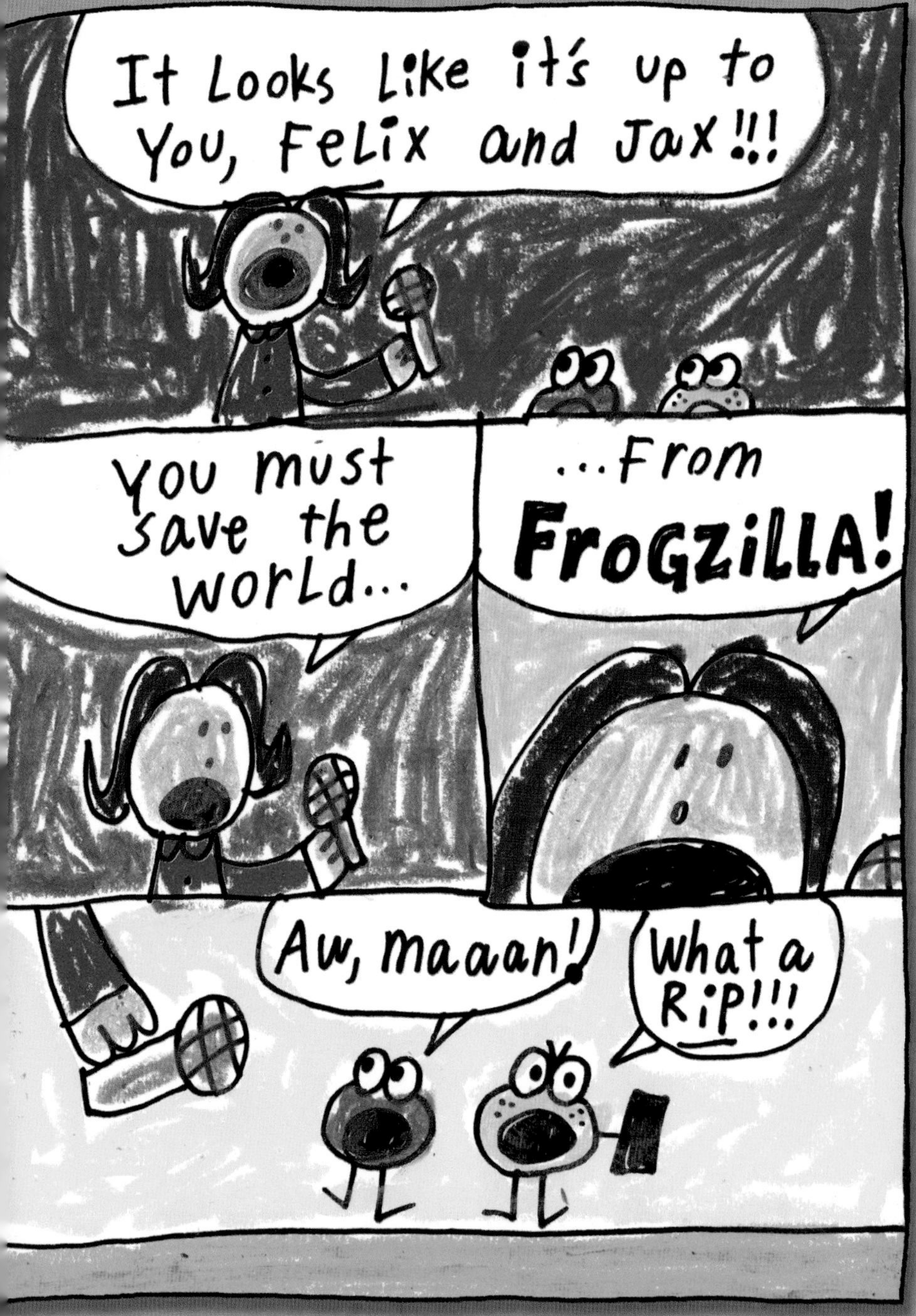
It Looks Like it's up to You, FeLix and Jax!!!
You must save the world...
...From FroGZiLLA!
Aw, maaan!
What a RiP!!!

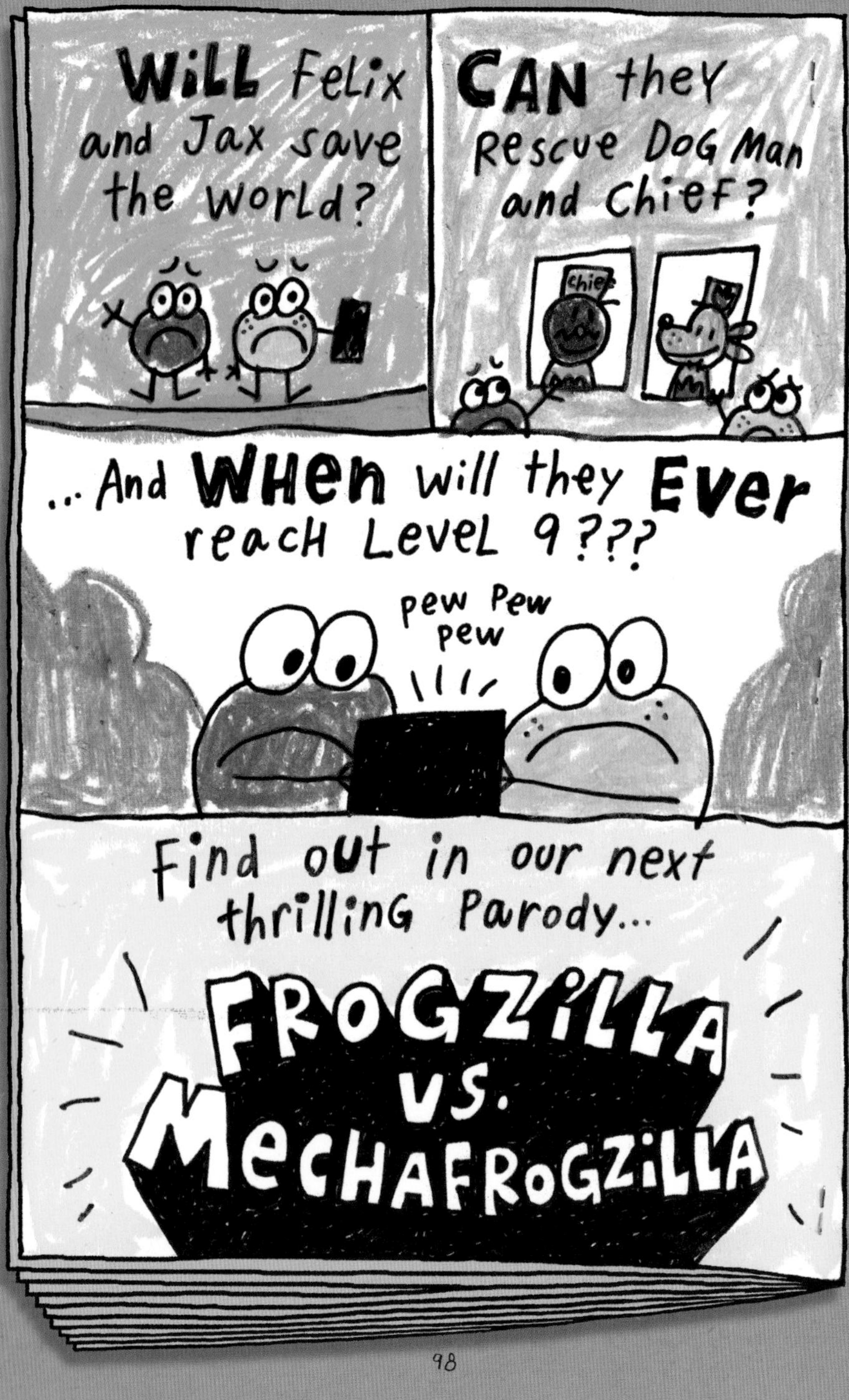
WiLL Felix and Jax save the WorLd?
CAN they Rescue DoG Man and ChieF?
chief
... And WHen will they Ever reach LeveL 9???
pew Pew pew
Find out in our next thrilling Parody...
FROGZiLLA VS. MECHAFROGZiLLA

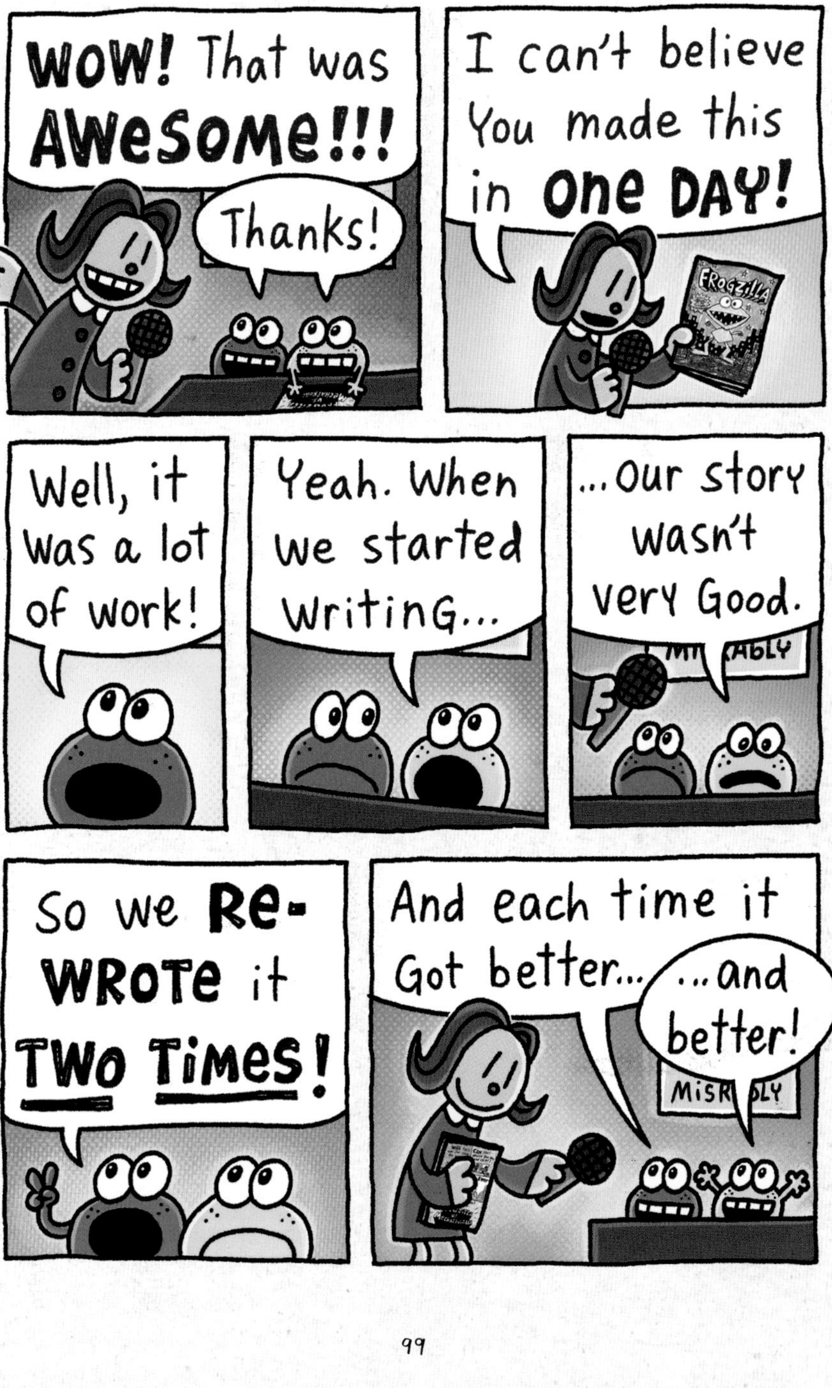
WOW! That was AWESOME!!!
Thanks!
I can't believe You made this in ONE DAY!
FROGZILLA
Well, it was a lot of work!
Yeah. When we started writinG...
...our story wasn't very Good.
So we RE-WROTE it TWO TIMES!
And each time it Got better...
...and better!

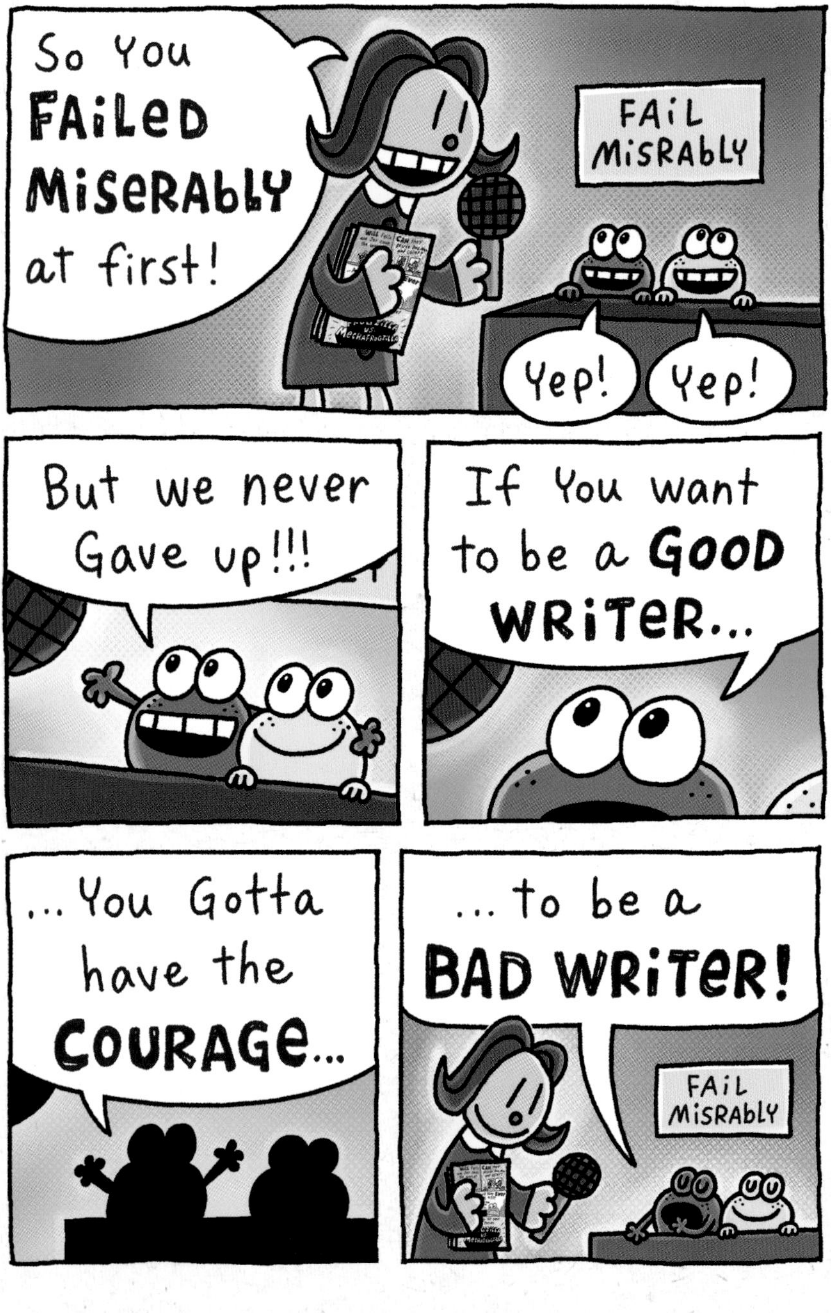
So you FAILED MISERABLY at first!
FAIL MISRABLY
Yep!
Yep!
But we never Gave up!!!
If you want to be a GOOD WRITER...
...You Gotta have the COURAGE...
...to be a BAD WRITER!
FAIL MISRABLY

CHAPTER 6

Business Partners

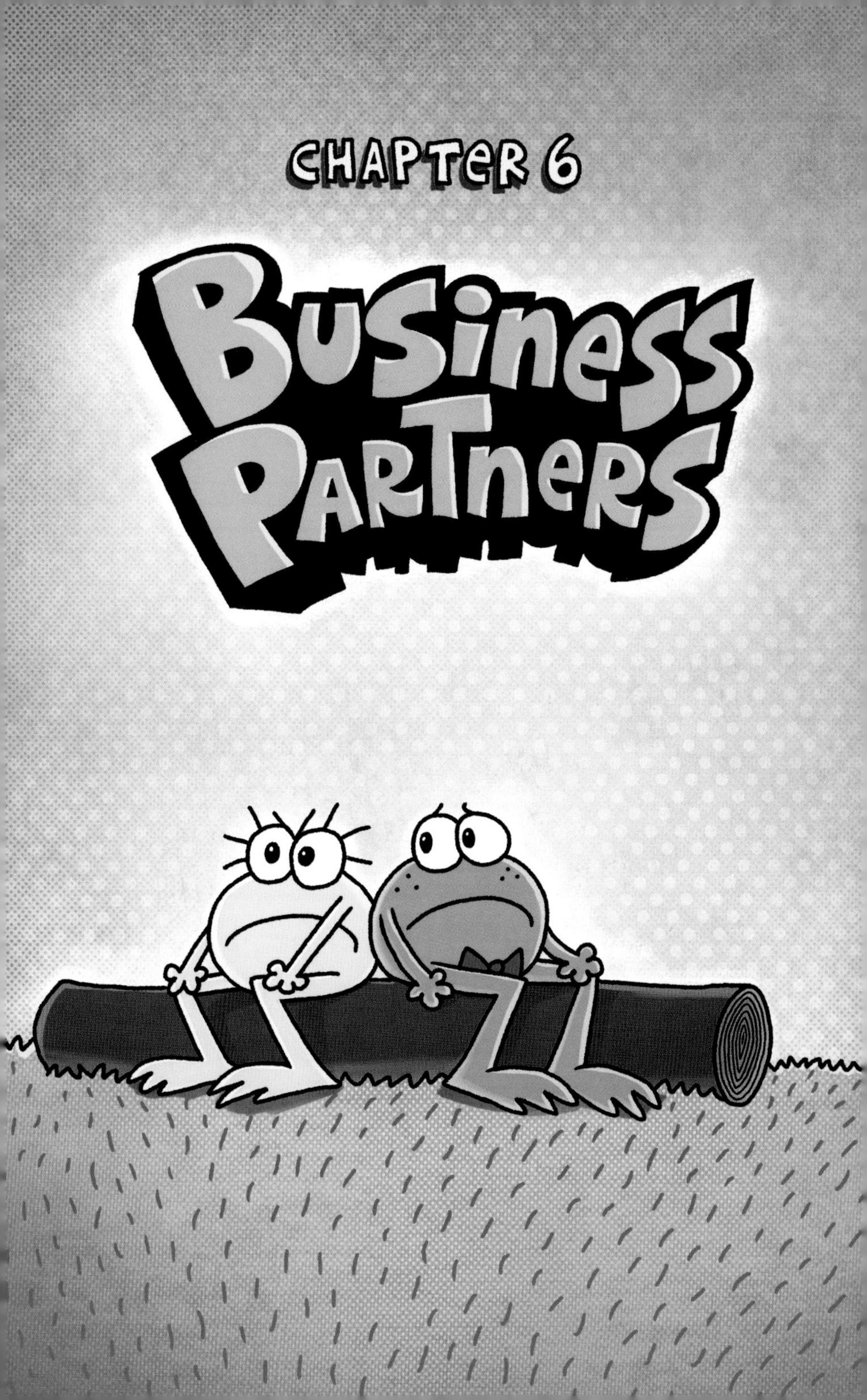

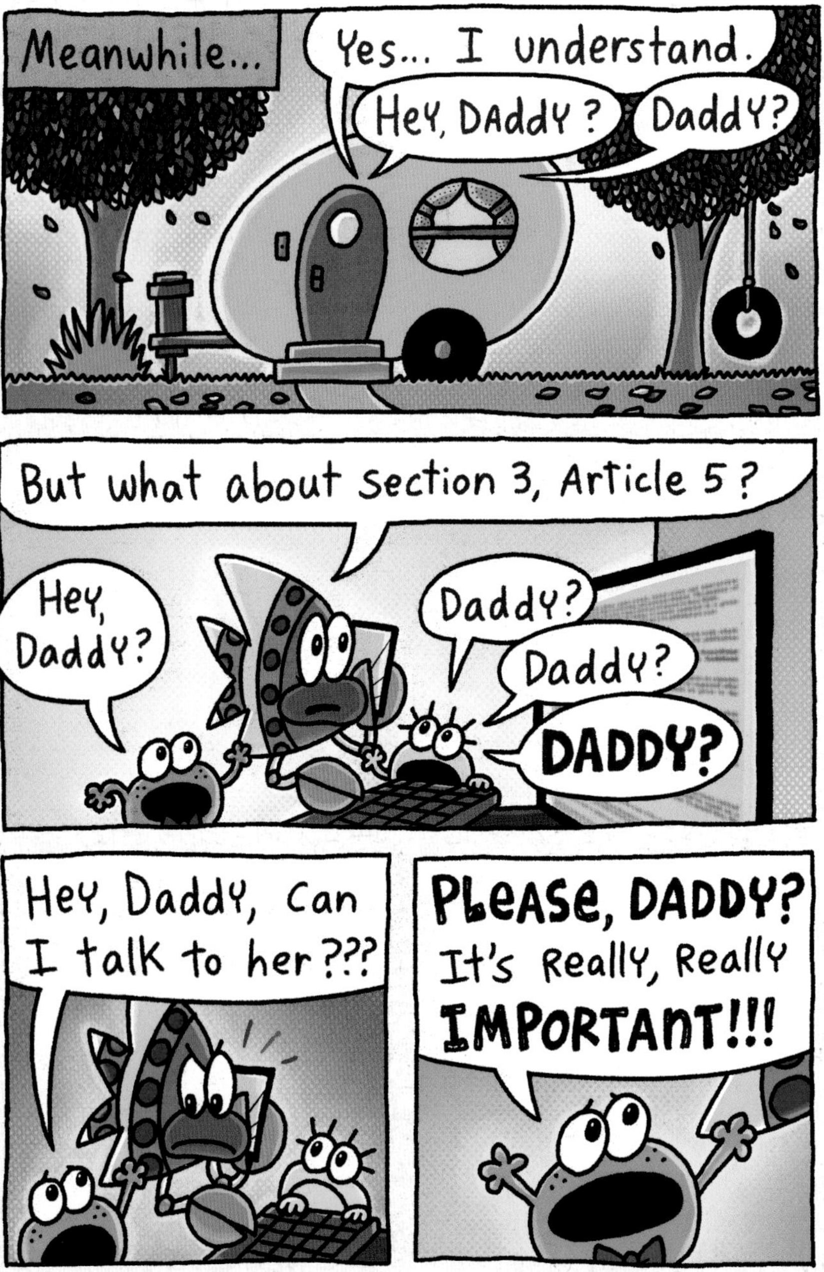
Meanwhile...
Yes... I understand.
Hey, DAddy?
Daddy?
But what about Section 3, Article 5?
Hey, Daddy?
Daddy?
Daddy?
DADDY?
Hey, Daddy, can I talk to her???
PLEASE, DADDY? It's Really, Really IMPORTANT!!!

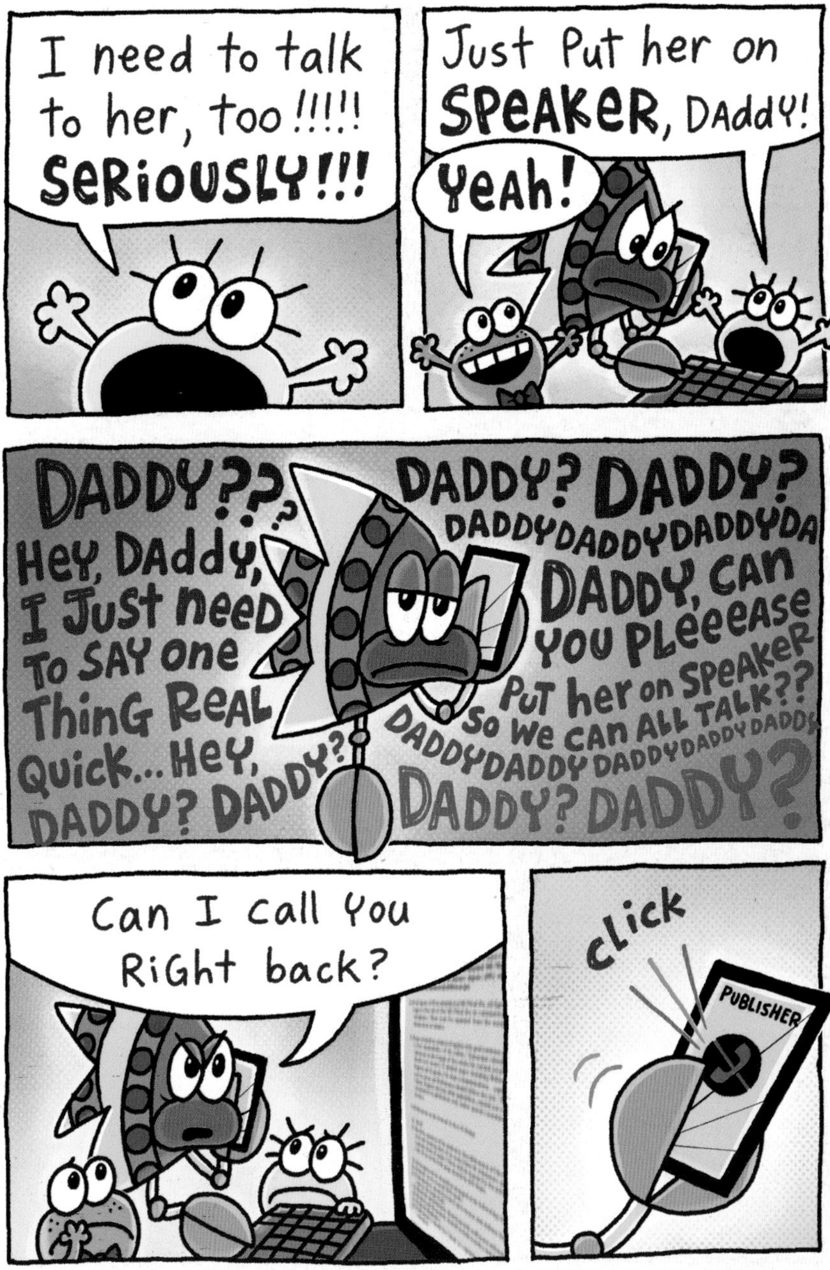
I need to talk to her, too!!!!! SERIOUSLY!!!
Just Put her on SPEAKER, DAddY!
Yeah!
DADDY???
DADDY? DADDY?
DADDYDADDYDADDYDA
Hey, DAddy, I Just need To SAY one Thing ReAL Quick... Hey, DADDY? DADDY?
DADDY, can you PLeeease PuT her on SPeaKeR So we can ALL TALK??
DADDYDADDY DADDYDADDY DADDY
DADDY? DADDY?
Can I call You RiGht back?
click
PUBLISHER

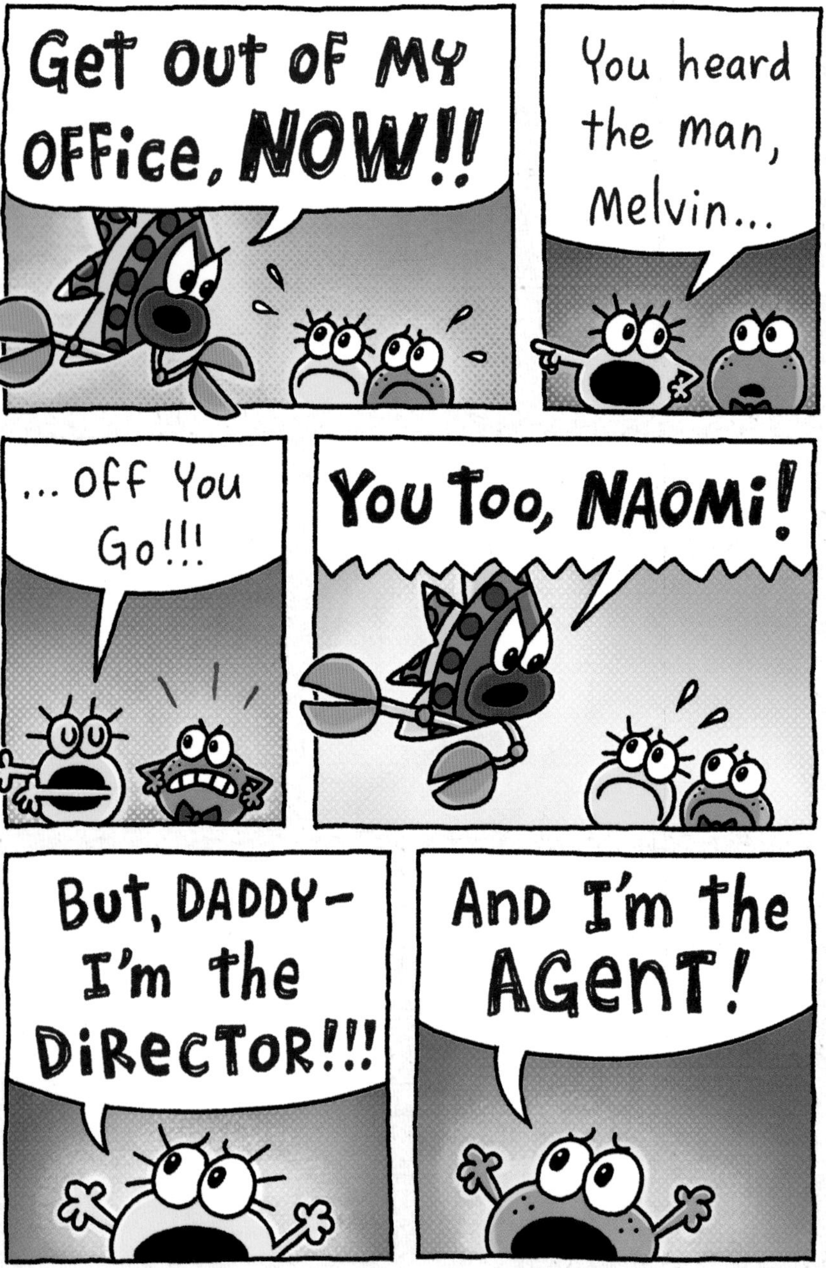
Get out of my office, NOW!!
You heard the man, Melvin...
...off you go!!!
You too, NAOMI!
But, DADDY- I'm the DIRECTOR!!!
And I'm the AGENT!

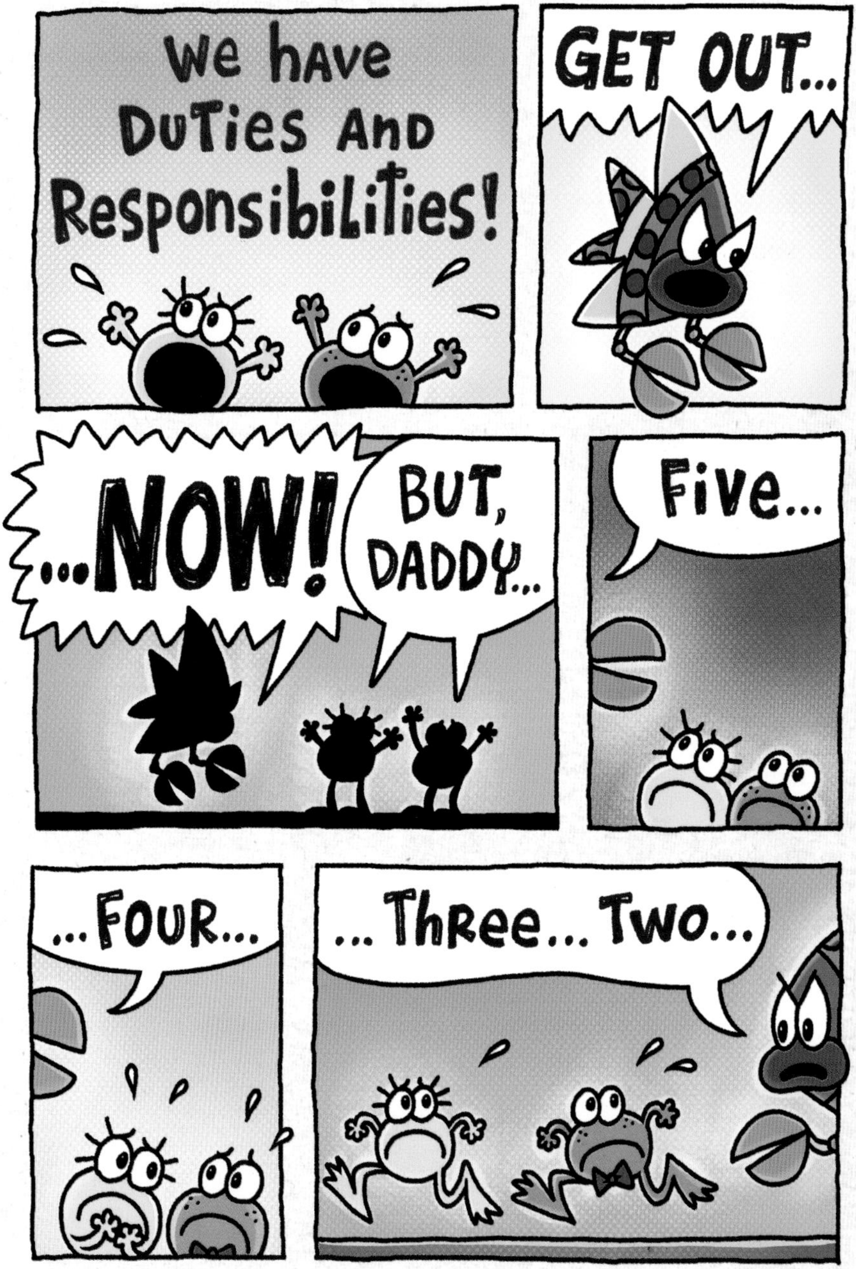
We have DuTies And Responsibilities!
GET OUT...
...NOW!
BUT, DADDY...
Five...
...FOUR...
...Three...Two...

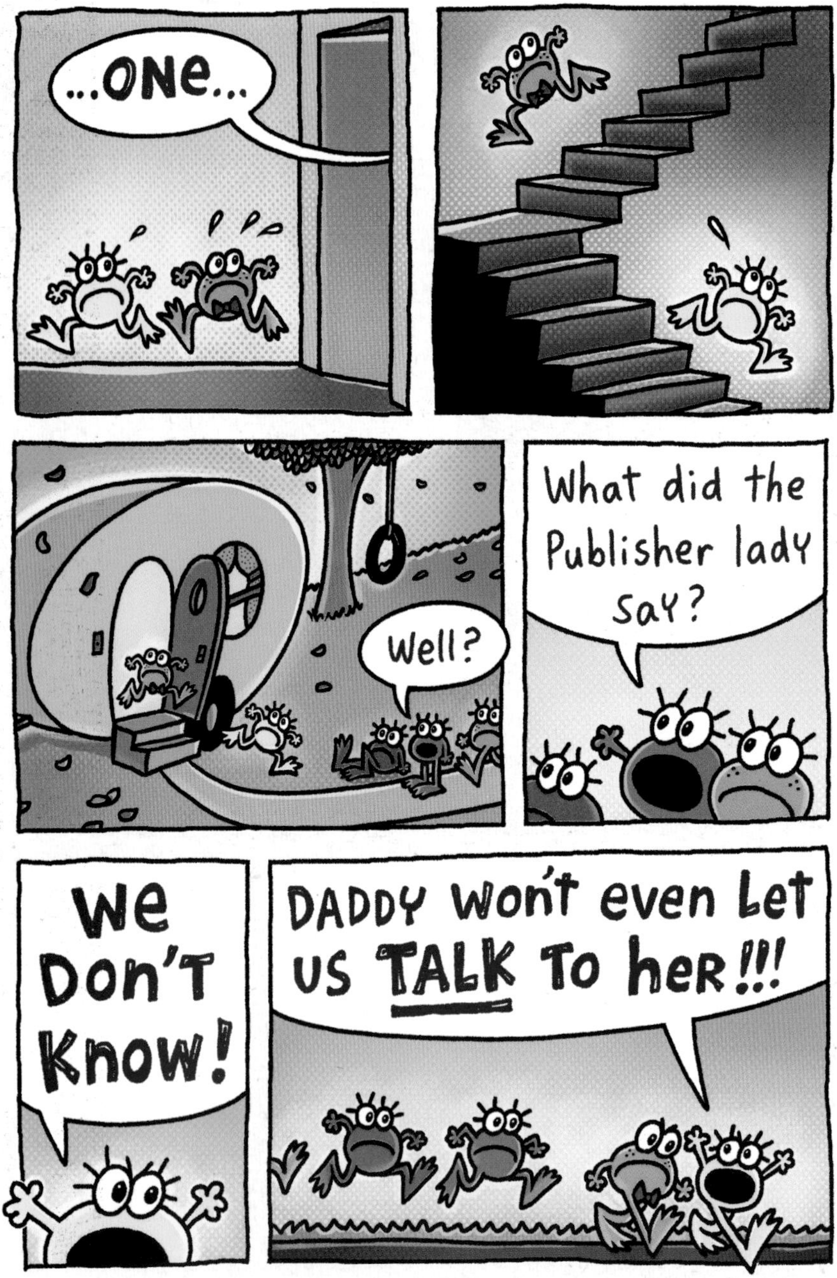
...ONE...
What did the Publisher lady say?
Well?
We Don't Know!
DADDY won't even Let us TALK To her!!!

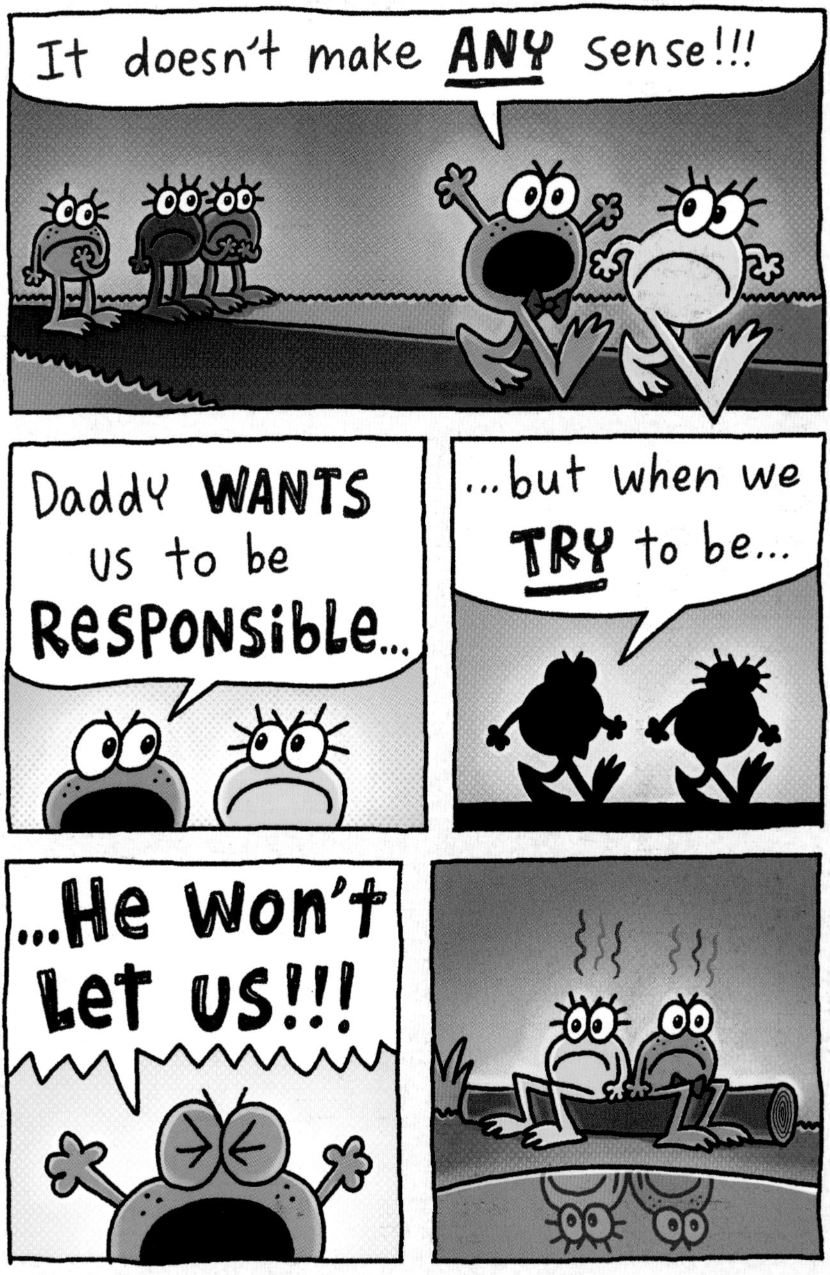
It doesn't make ANY sense!!!
Daddy WANTS us to be RESPONSIBLE...
...but when we TRY to be...
...He won't let us!!!

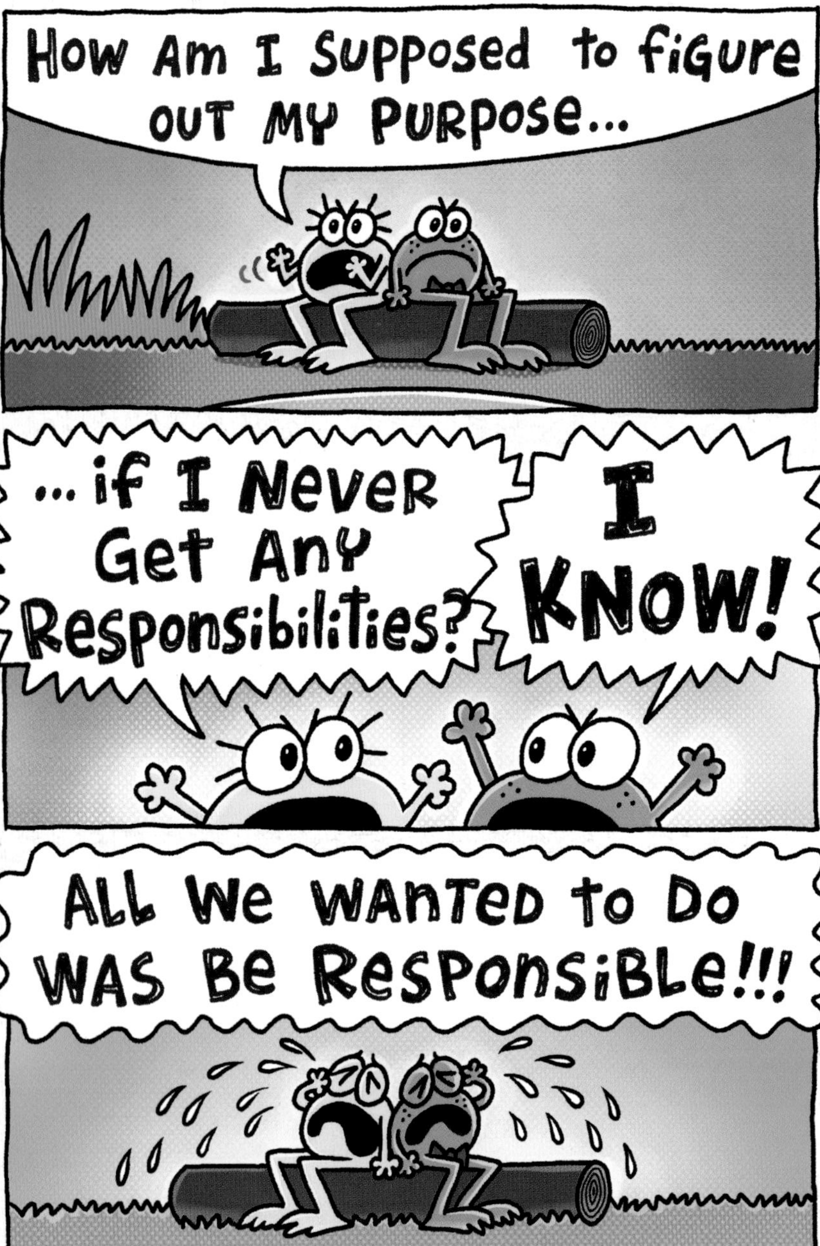
How Am I Supposed to figure out my purpose...
...if I Never Get Any Responsibilities?
I KNOW!
ALL We WANTED to Do WAS Be Responsible!!!

CHAPTER 7

Melvin and Naomi Get Their Chance

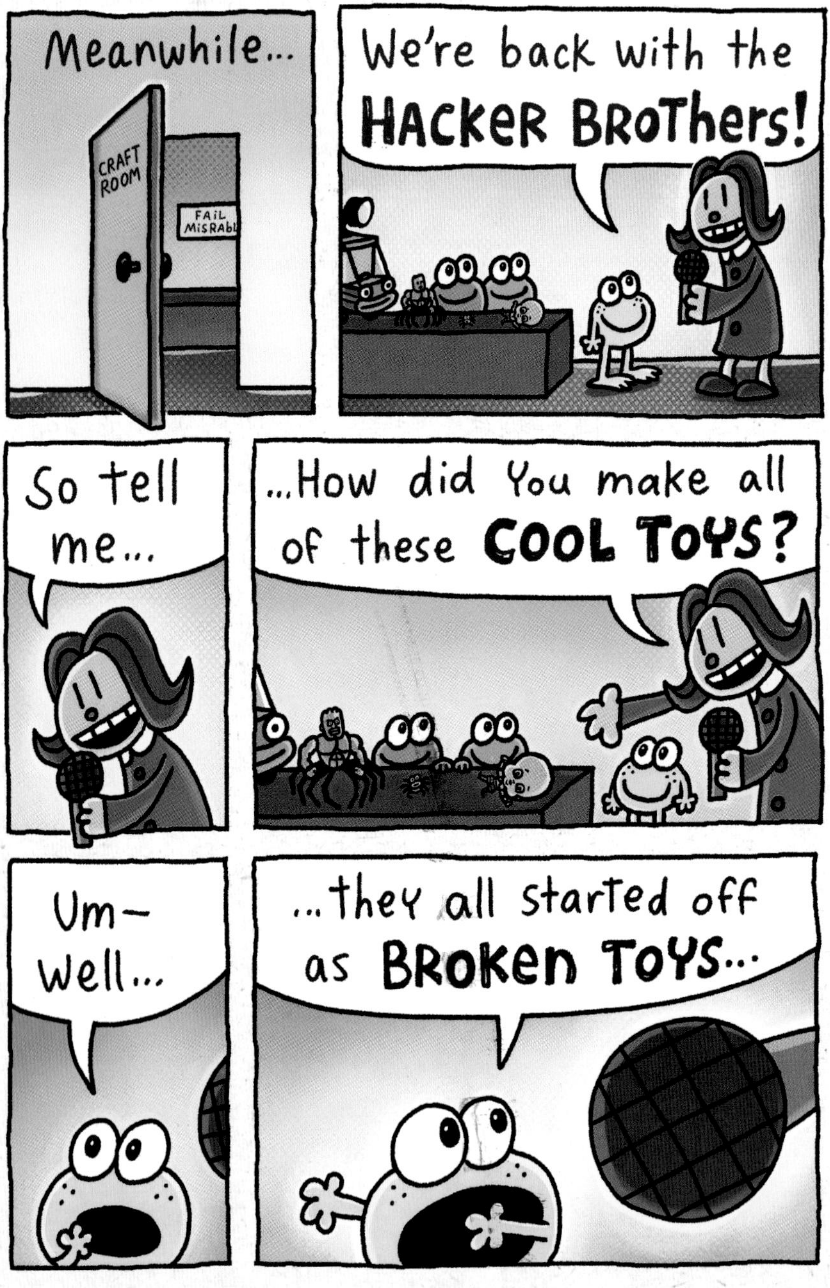
Meanwhile...
CRAFT ROOM
FAIL MISRABL
We're back with the HACKER BROThers!
So tell me...
...How did You make all of these COOL TOYS?
Um— Well...
...they all started off as BROKEN TOYS...

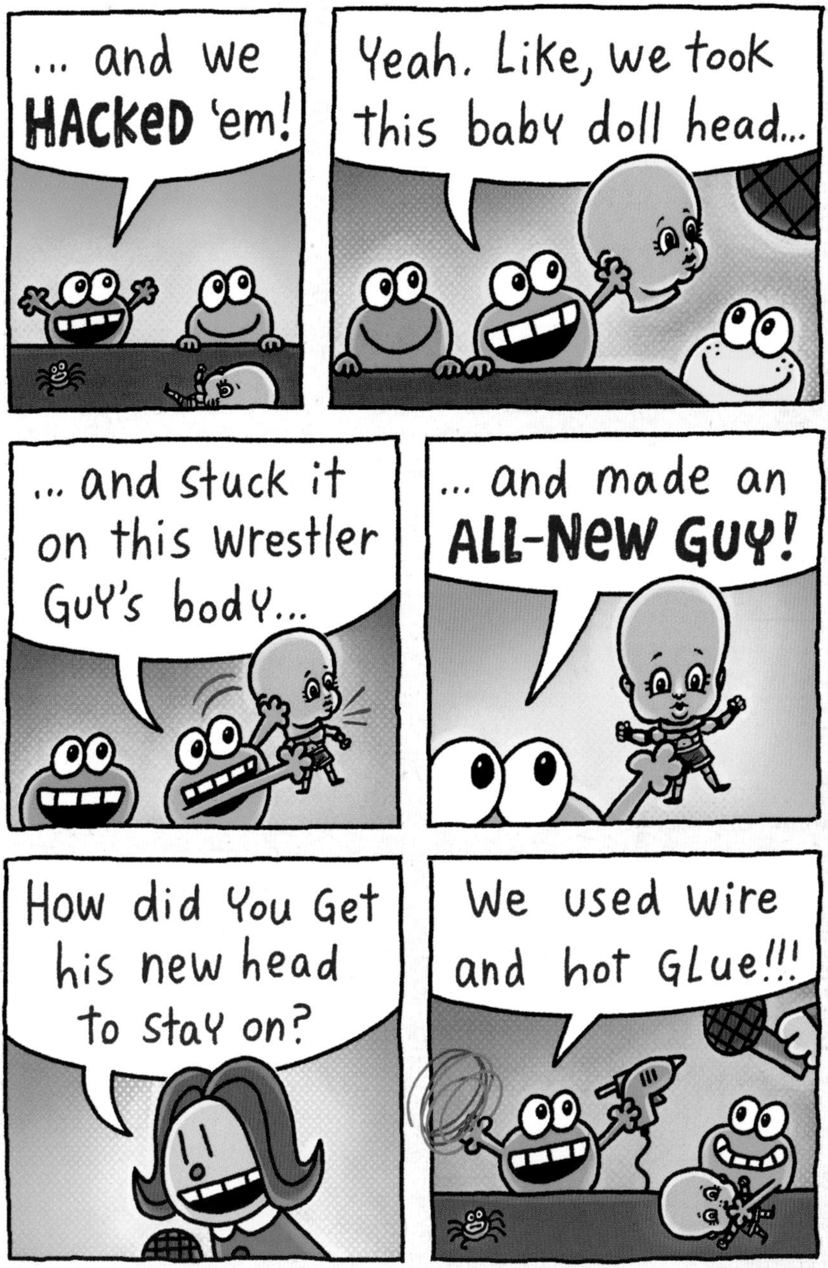
... and we HACKED 'em!
Yeah. Like, we took this baby doll head...
... and stuck it on this wrestler Guy's body...
... and made an ALL-NEW GUY!
How did You Get his new head to stay on?
We used wire and hot GLue!!!

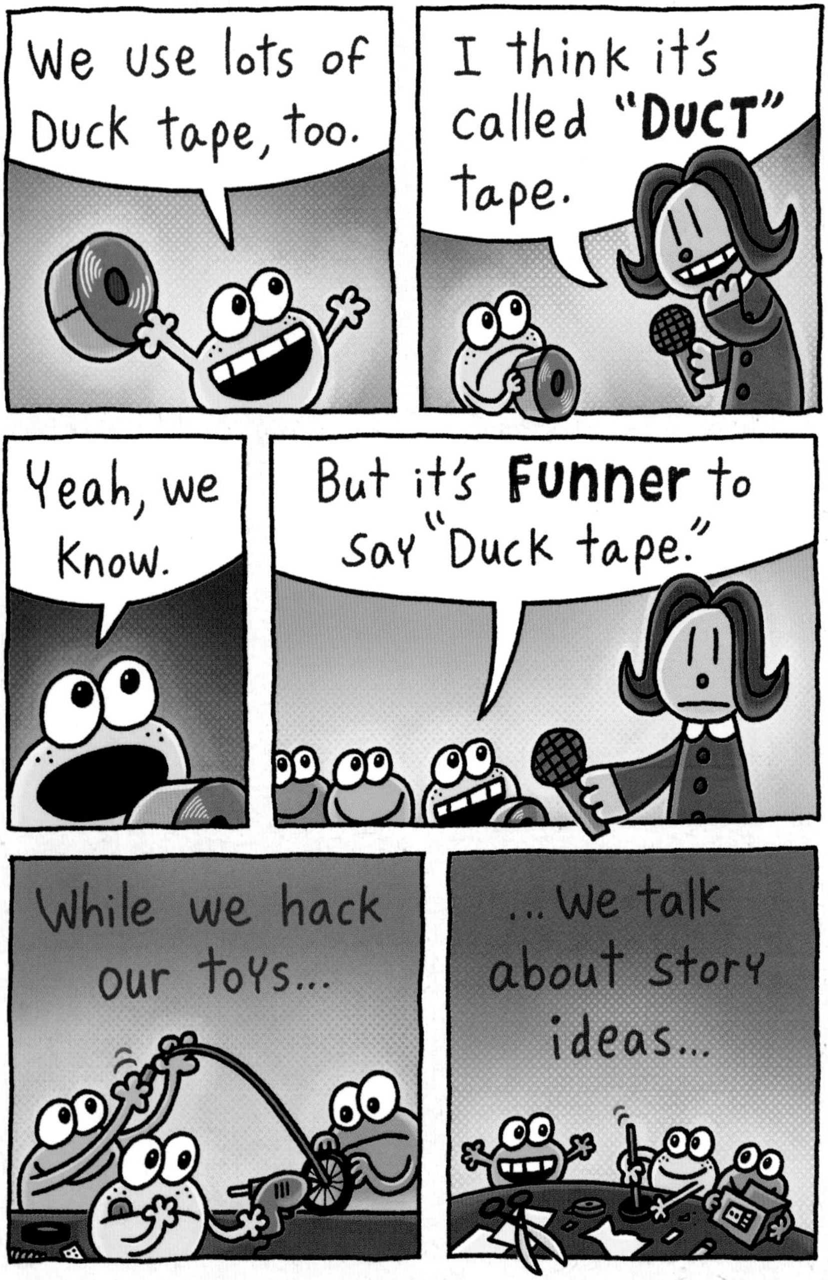
We use lots of Duck tape, too.
I think it's called "**DUCT**" tape.
Yeah, we Know.
But it's **FUNNER** to say "Duck tape."
While we hack our toys...
...we talk about story ideas...

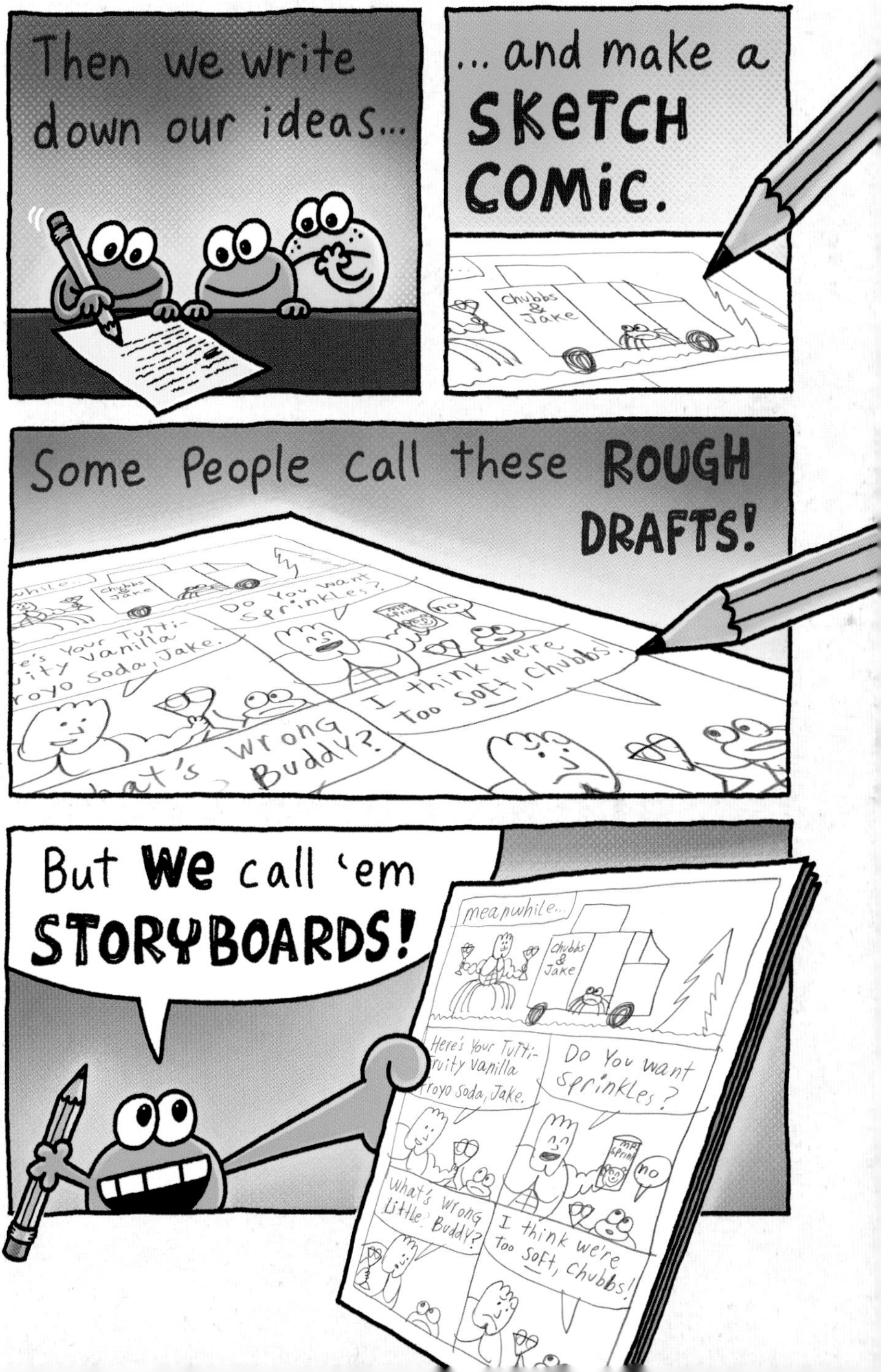

Then we write down our ideas...
... and make a SKETCH COMIC.
Chubbs & Jake
Some People call these ROUGH DRAFTS!
But WE call 'em STORYBOARDS!
meanwhile...
Chubbs & Jake
Here's Your Tutti-Fruity Vanilla Froyo Soda, Jake.
Do You want Sprinkles?
no
What's wrong Little Buddy?
I think we're too SOFT, Chubbs!

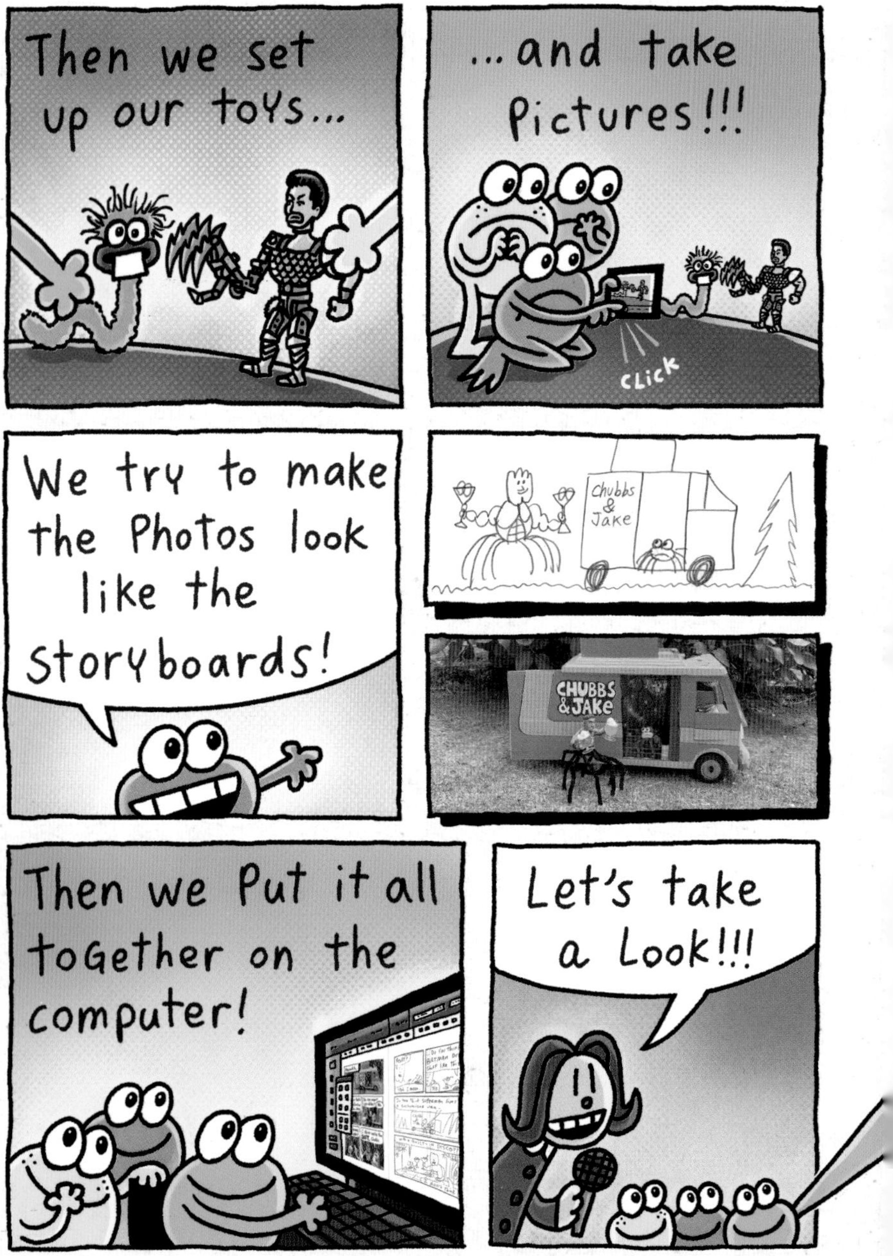
Then we set up our toys...
...and take pictures!!!
CLICK
We try to make the photos look like the storyboards!
Chubbs & Jake
CHUBBS & JAKE
Then we put it all together on the computer!
Let's take a look!!!

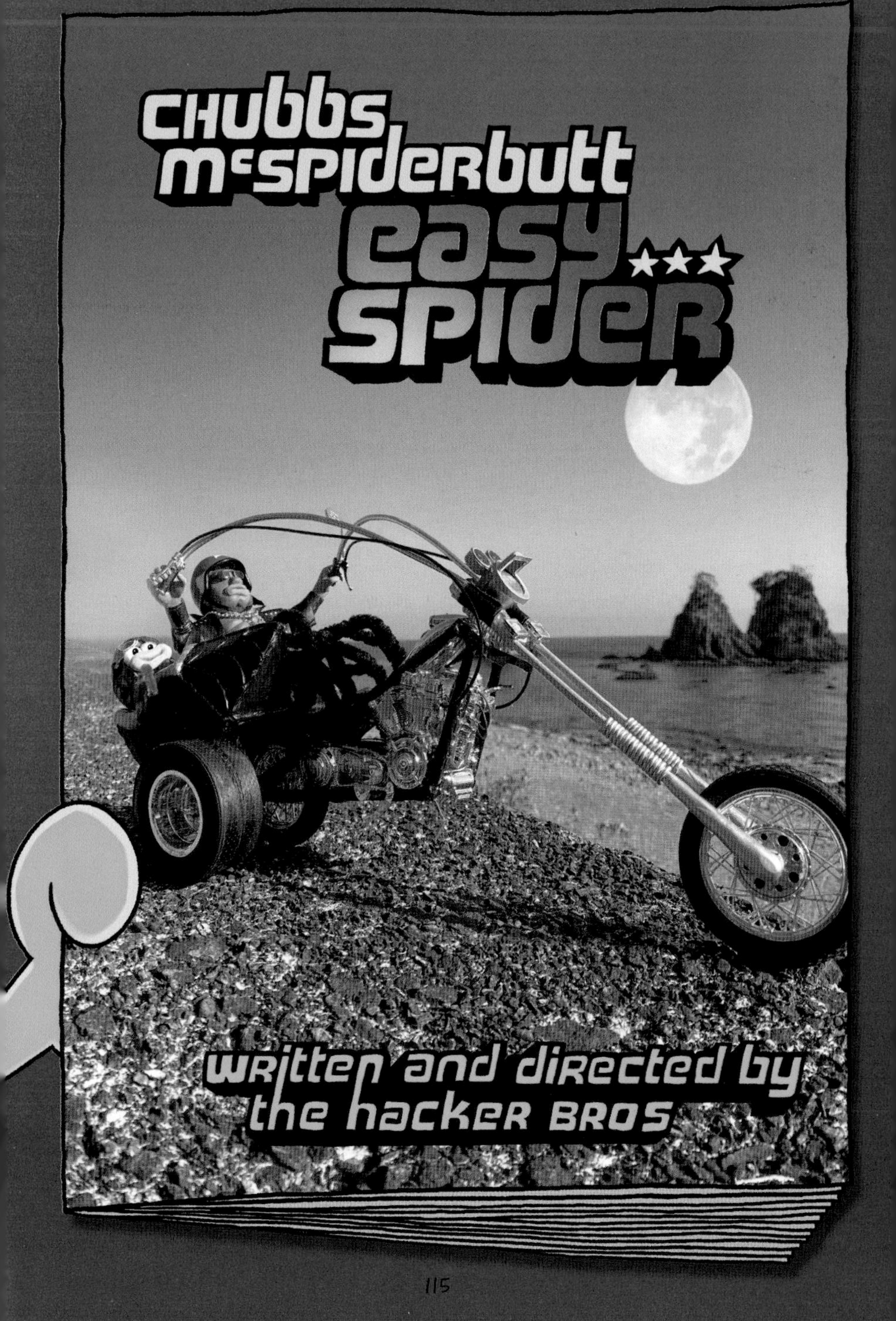
CHUBBS McSPIDERBUTT
EASY SPIDER
WRITTEN AND DIRECTED BY
THE HACKER BROS

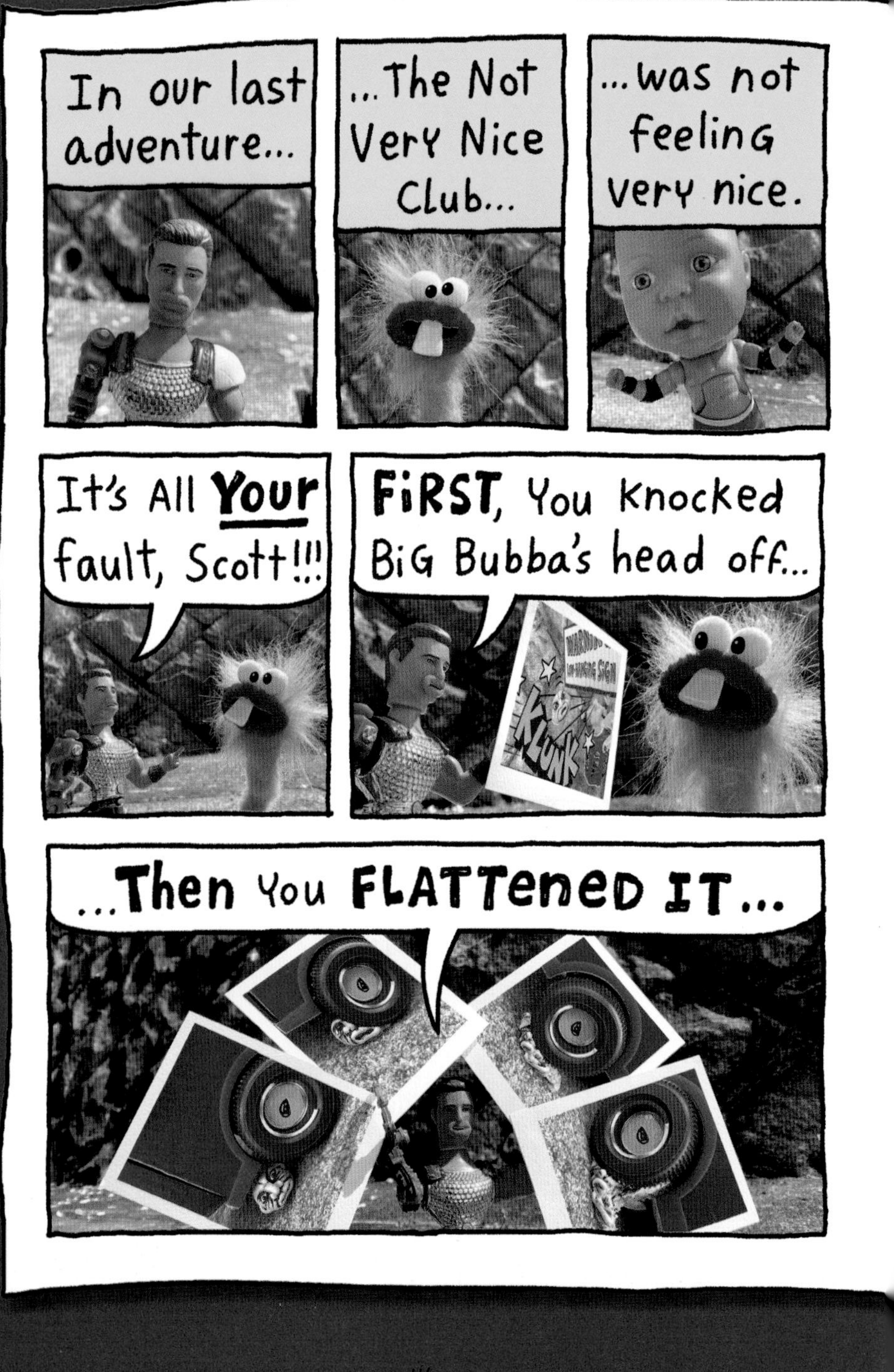
In our last adventure...
...The Not Very Nice Club...
...was not feeling very nice.
It's All **Your** fault, Scott!!!
FiRST, You knocked BiG Bubba's head off...
KLUNK
...**Then** You **FLATTENED IT**...

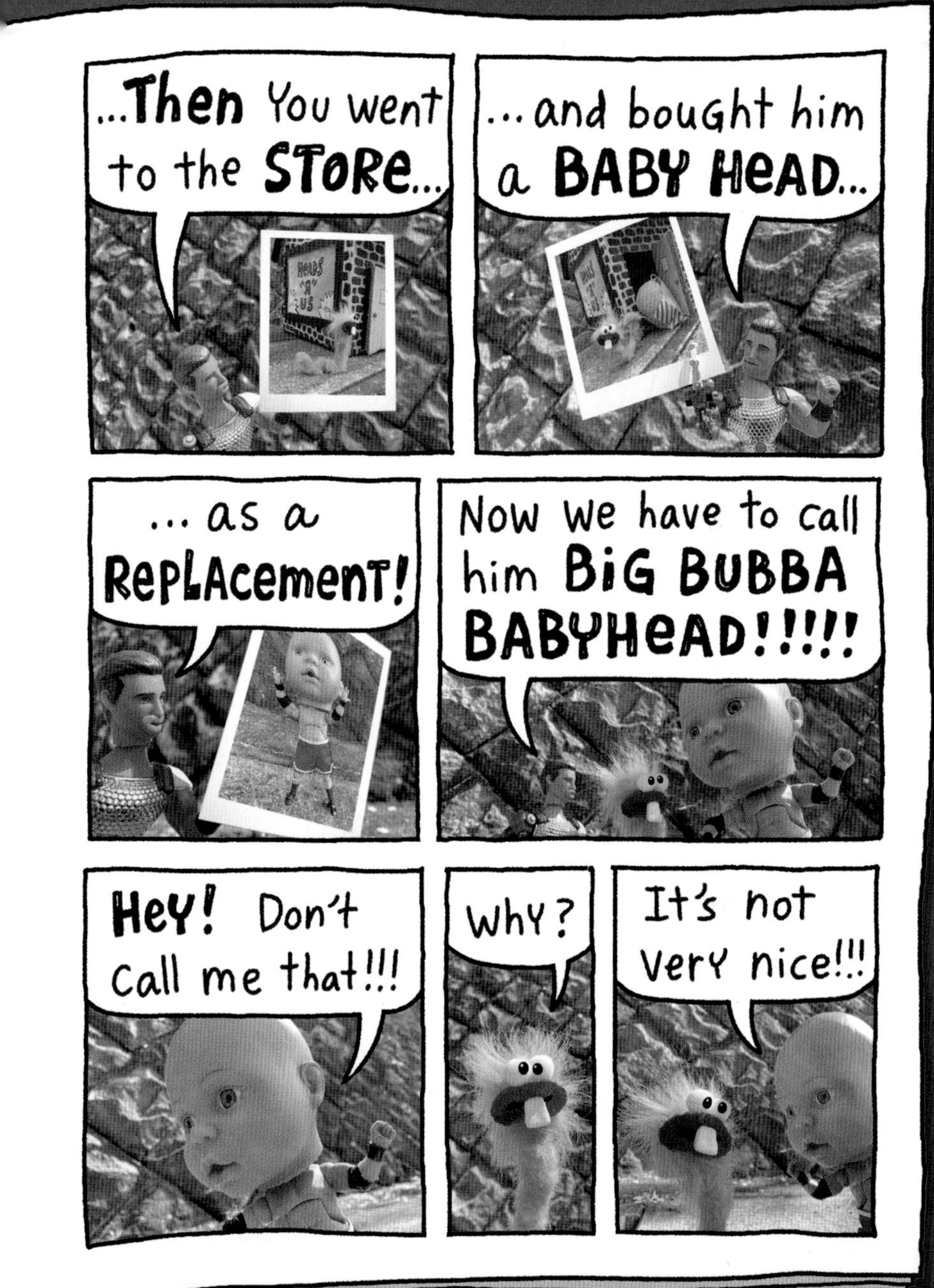
...Then You went to the STORE...
...and bought him a BABY HEAD...
... as a REPLACEMENT!
Now we have to call him BIG BUBBA BABYHEAD!!!!!
HEY! Don't call me that!!!
WHY?
It's not very nice!!!

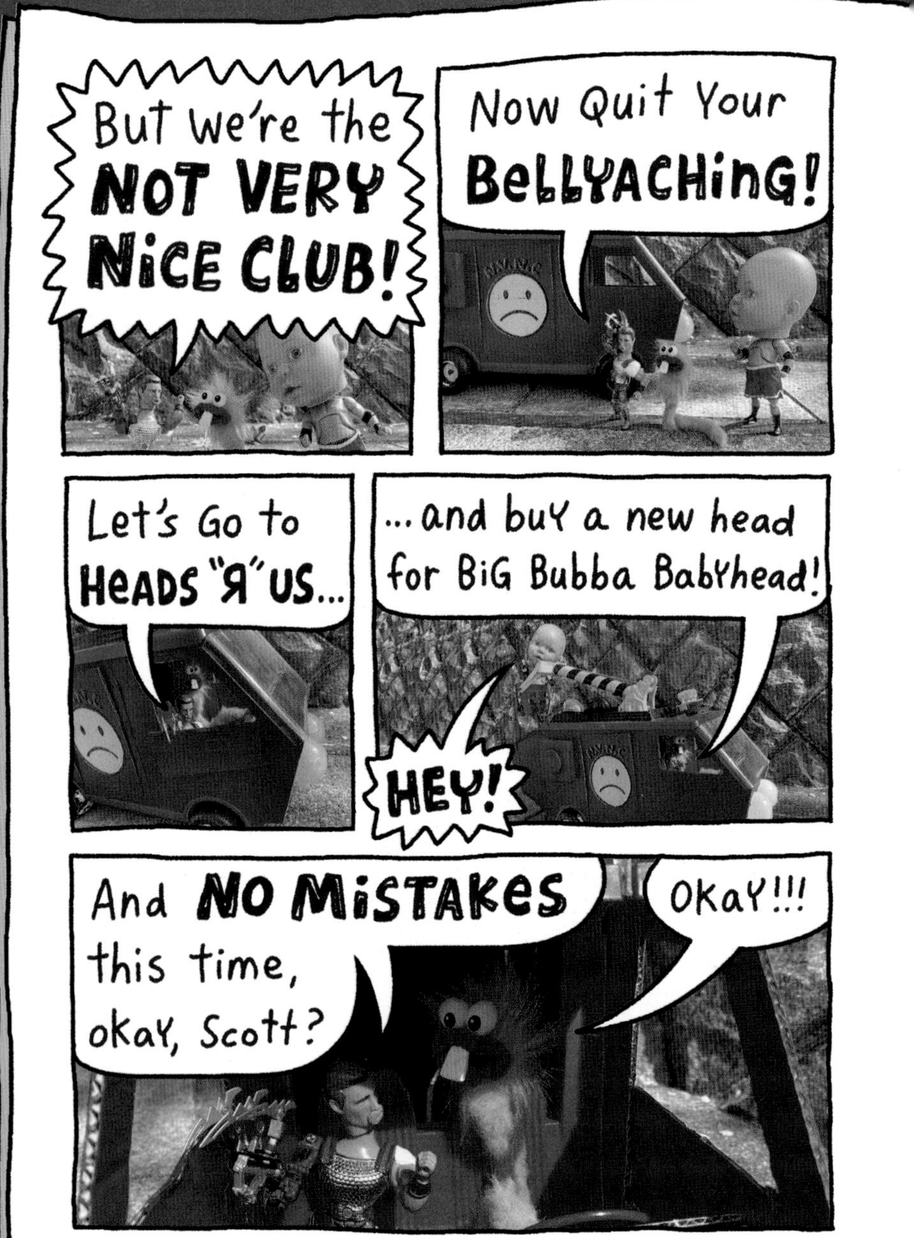
But we're the NOT VERY NiCE CLUB!
Now Quit Your BeLLYACHinG!
Let's Go to HeADS "Я" US...
...and buy a new head for BiG Bubba Babyhead!
HEY!
And NO MiSTAKes this time, okay, Scott?
OKaY!!!

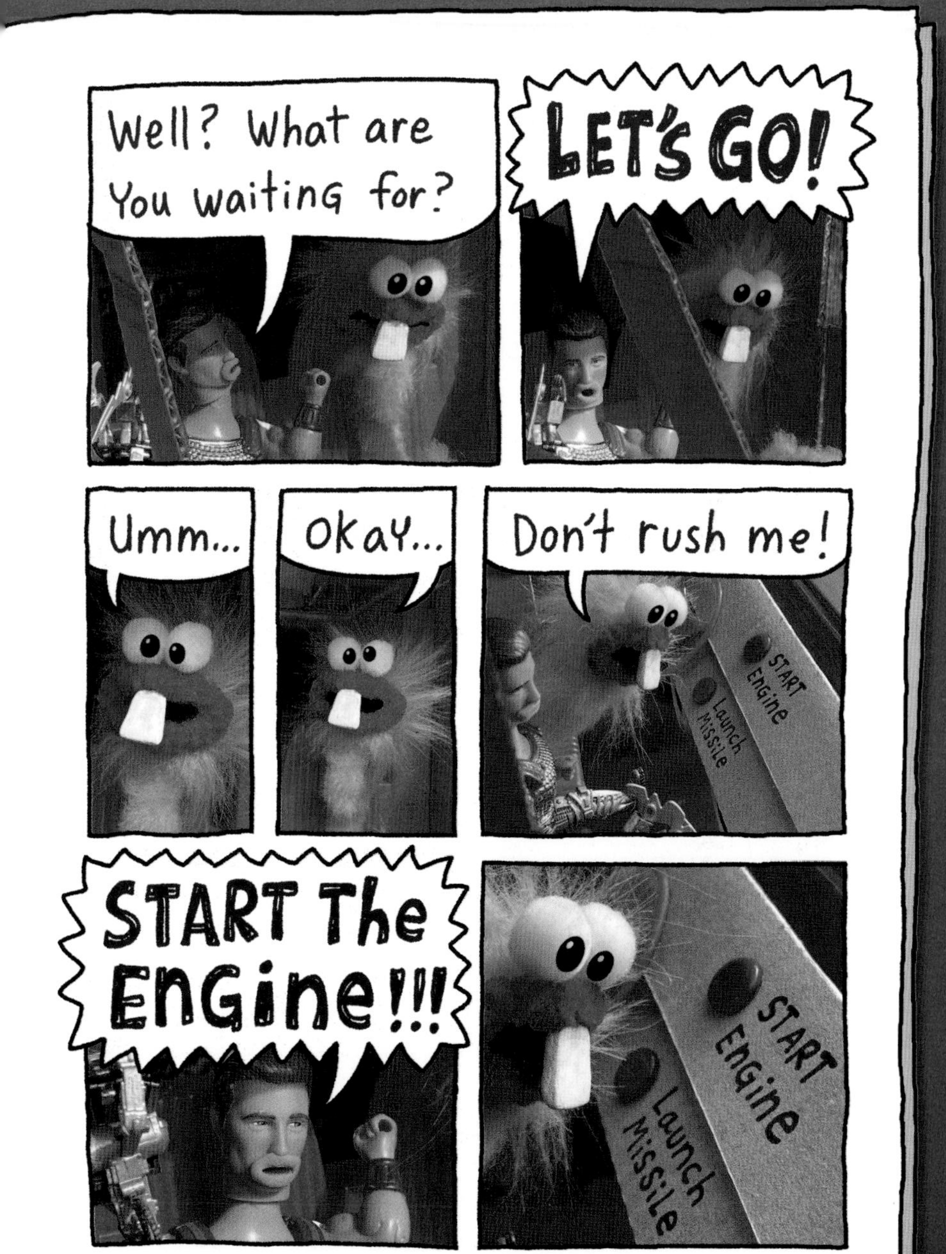

Well? What are You waiting for?
LET'S GO!
Umm...
OkaY...
Don't rush me!
START Engine
Launch Missile
START The EnGine!!!
START Engine
Launch Missile

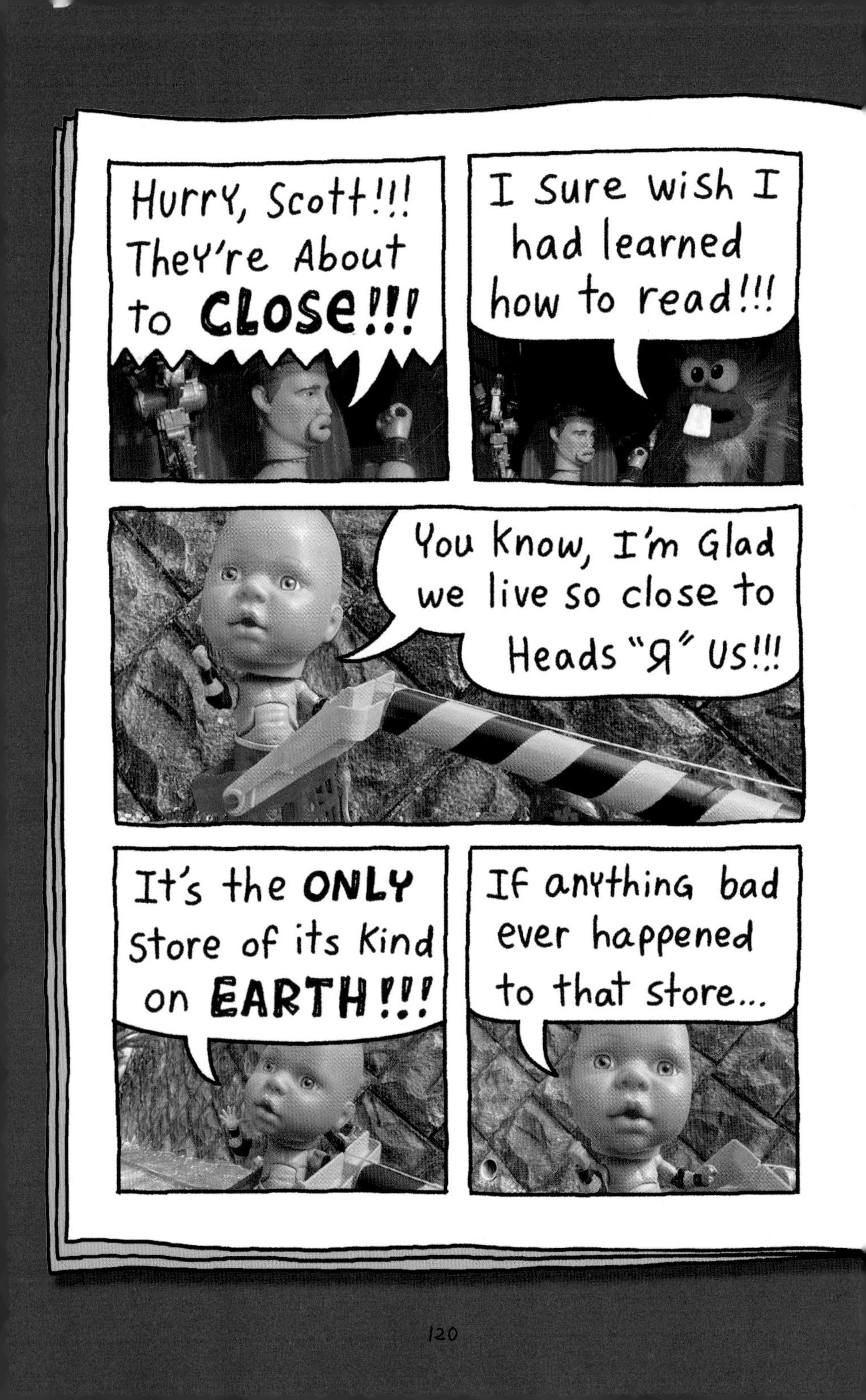
Hurry, Scott!!! They're About to CLOSE!!!
I sure wish I had learned how to read!!!
You know, I'm Glad we live so close to Heads "R" Us!!!
It's the ONLY store of its kind on EARTH!!!
If anything bad ever happened to that store...

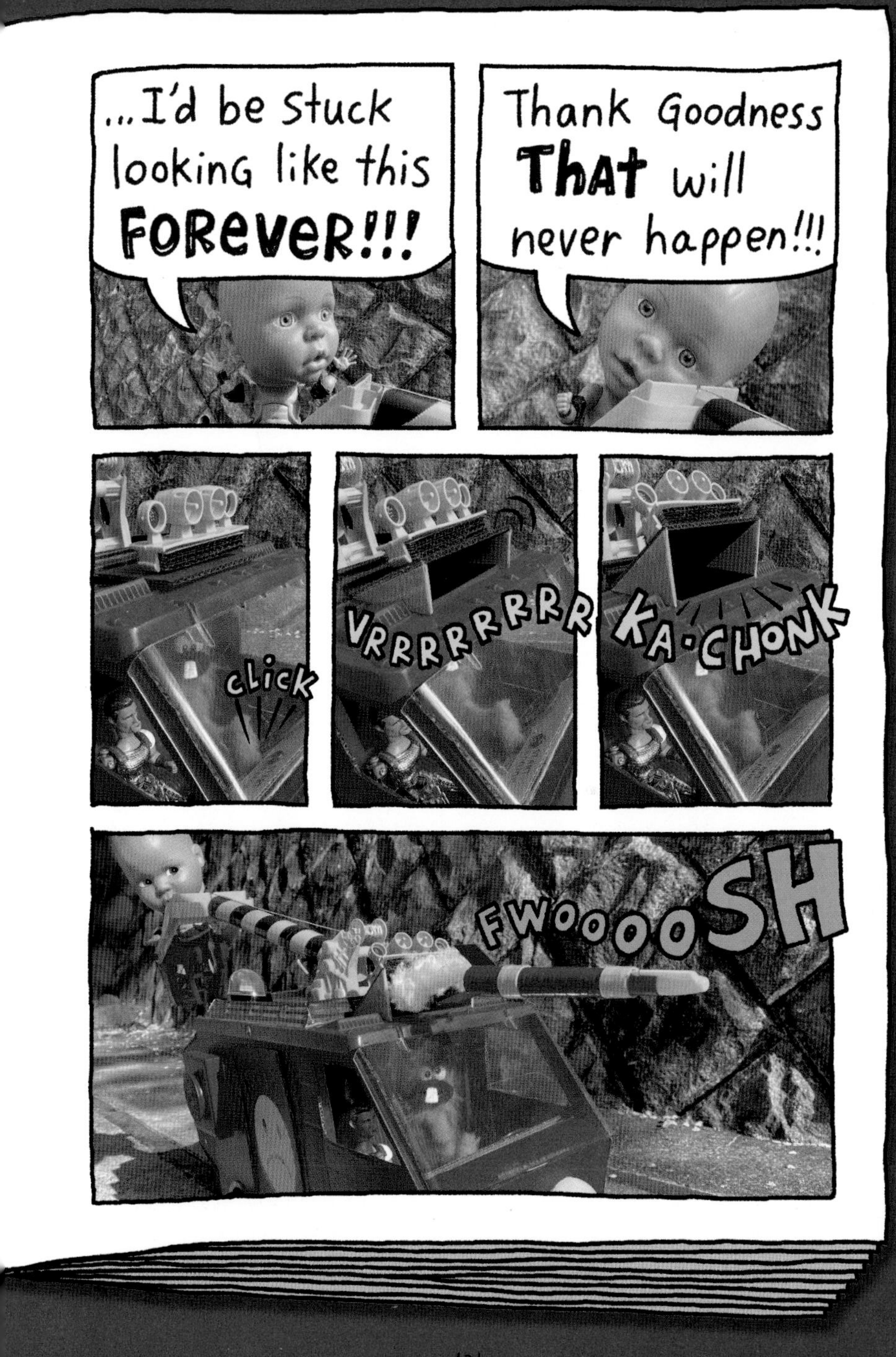
...I'd be Stuck looking like this FOREVER!!!
Thank Goodness THAT will never happen!!!
CLICK
VRRRRRRRR
KA-CHONK
FWOOOOOSH

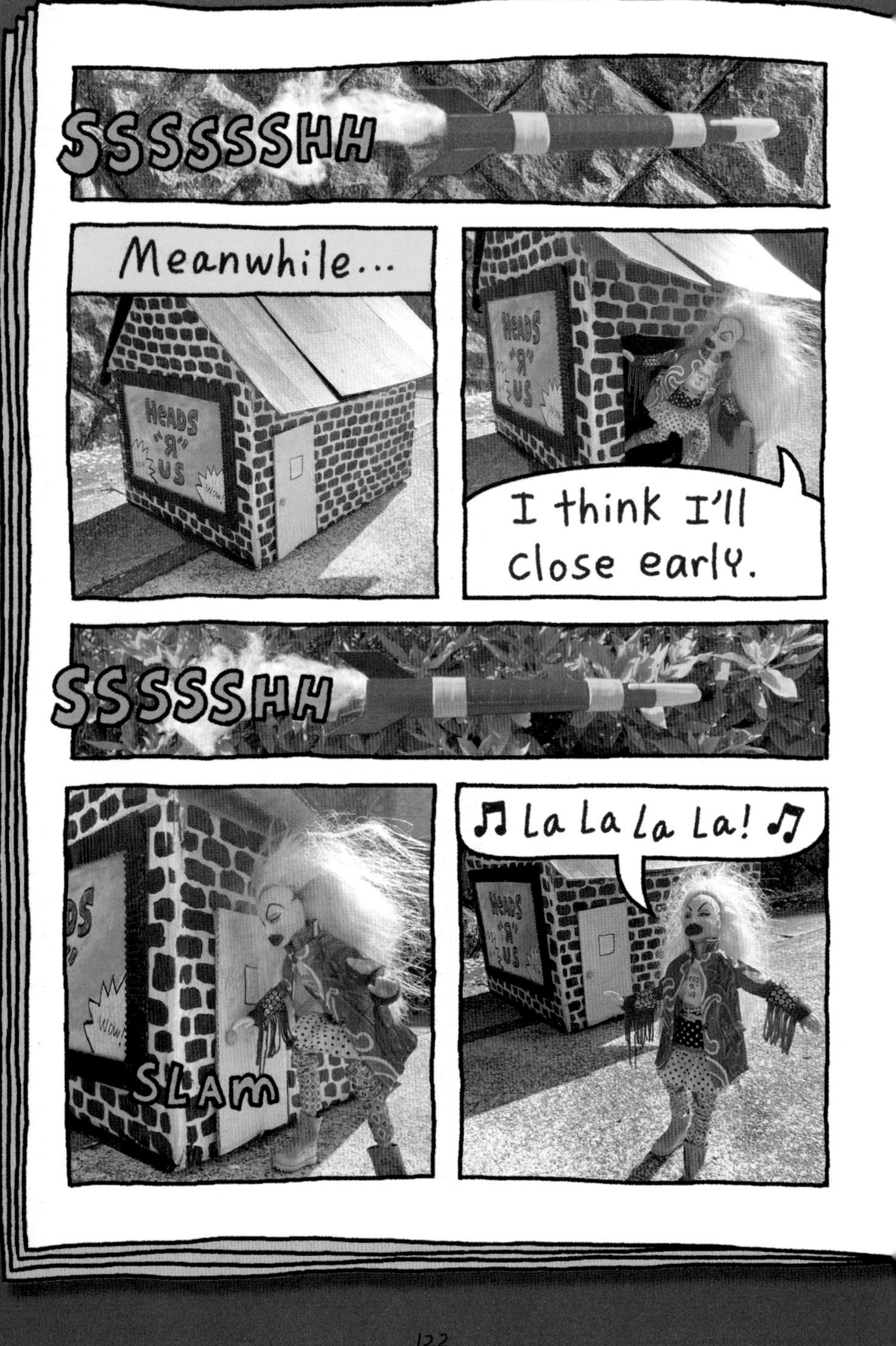
SSSSSSHH
Meanwhile...
HEADS "R" US
I think I'll close early.
SSSSSHH
SLAM
♫ La La La La! ♫

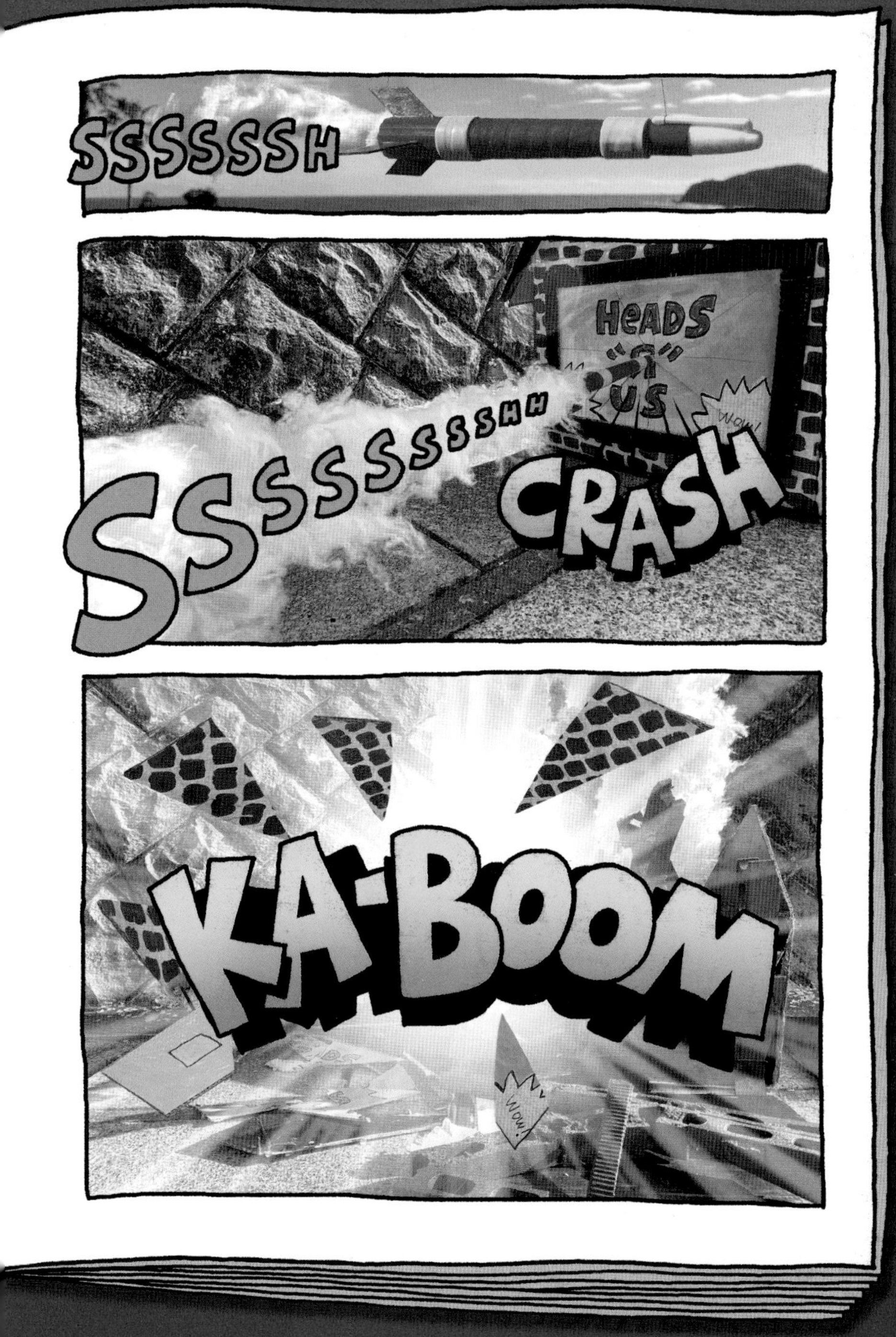
SSSSSSH
HEADS "R" US
SSSSSSSSSHH
WOW!
CRASH
KA-BOOM
WOW!

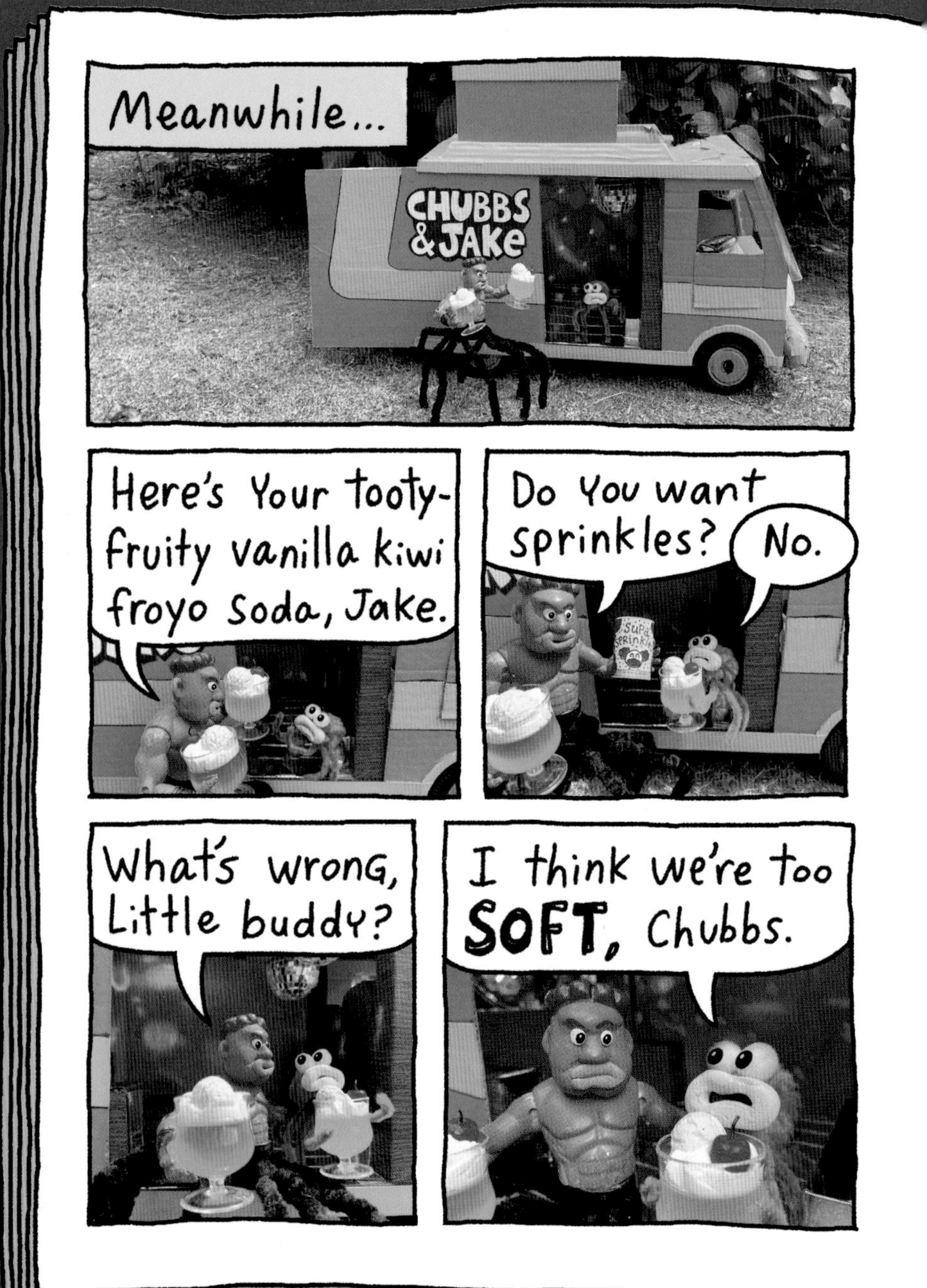
Meanwhile...
CHUBBS & JAKE
Here's your tooty-fruity vanilla kiwi froyo soda, Jake.
Do you want sprinkles?
No.
What's wrong, little buddy?
I think we're too **SOFT**, Chubbs.

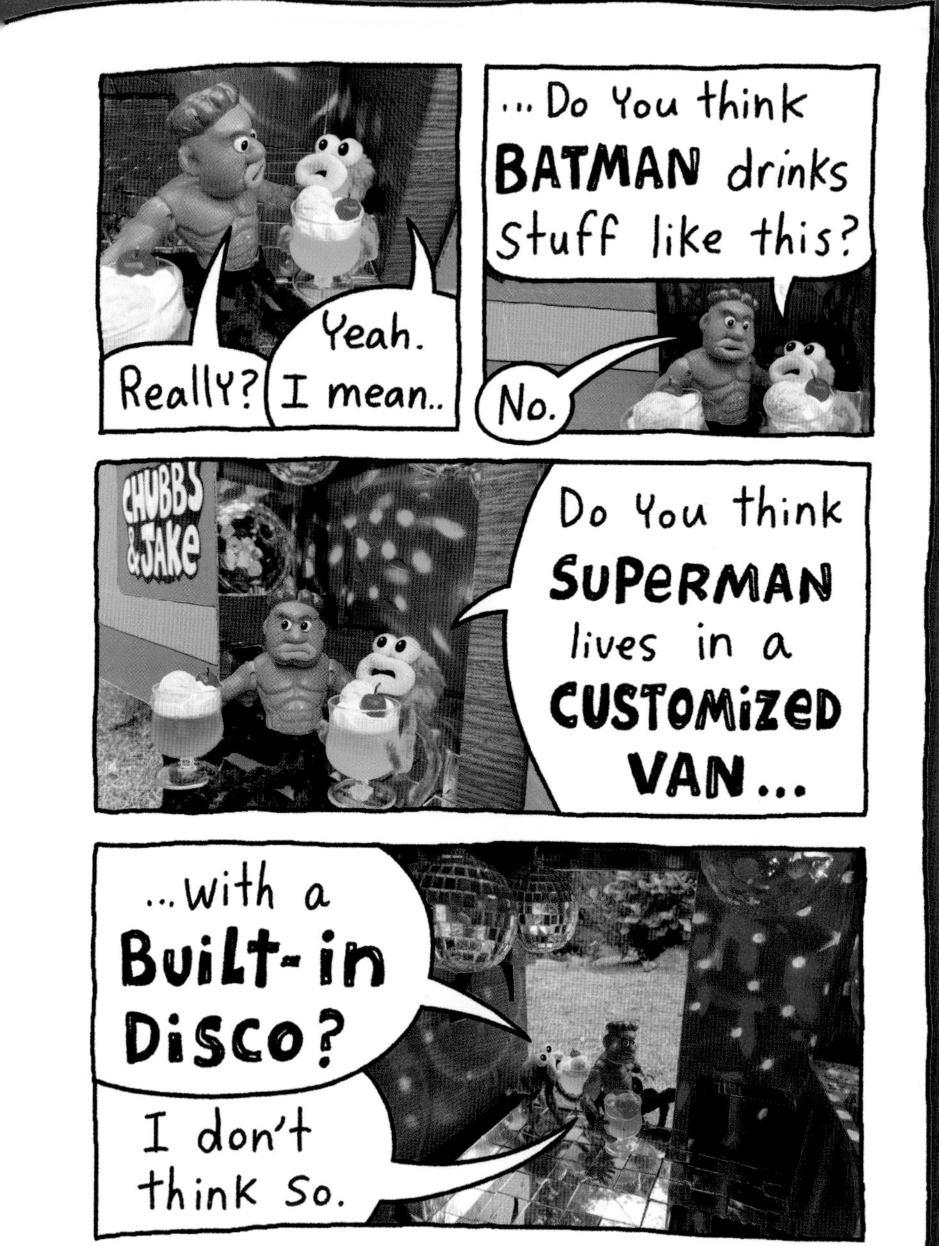
Really?
Yeah. I mean..
...Do You think BATMAN drinks Stuff like this?
No.
CHUBBS &JAKE
Do You think SUPERMAN lives in a CUSTOMIZED VAN...
...with a Built-in Disco?
I don't think So.

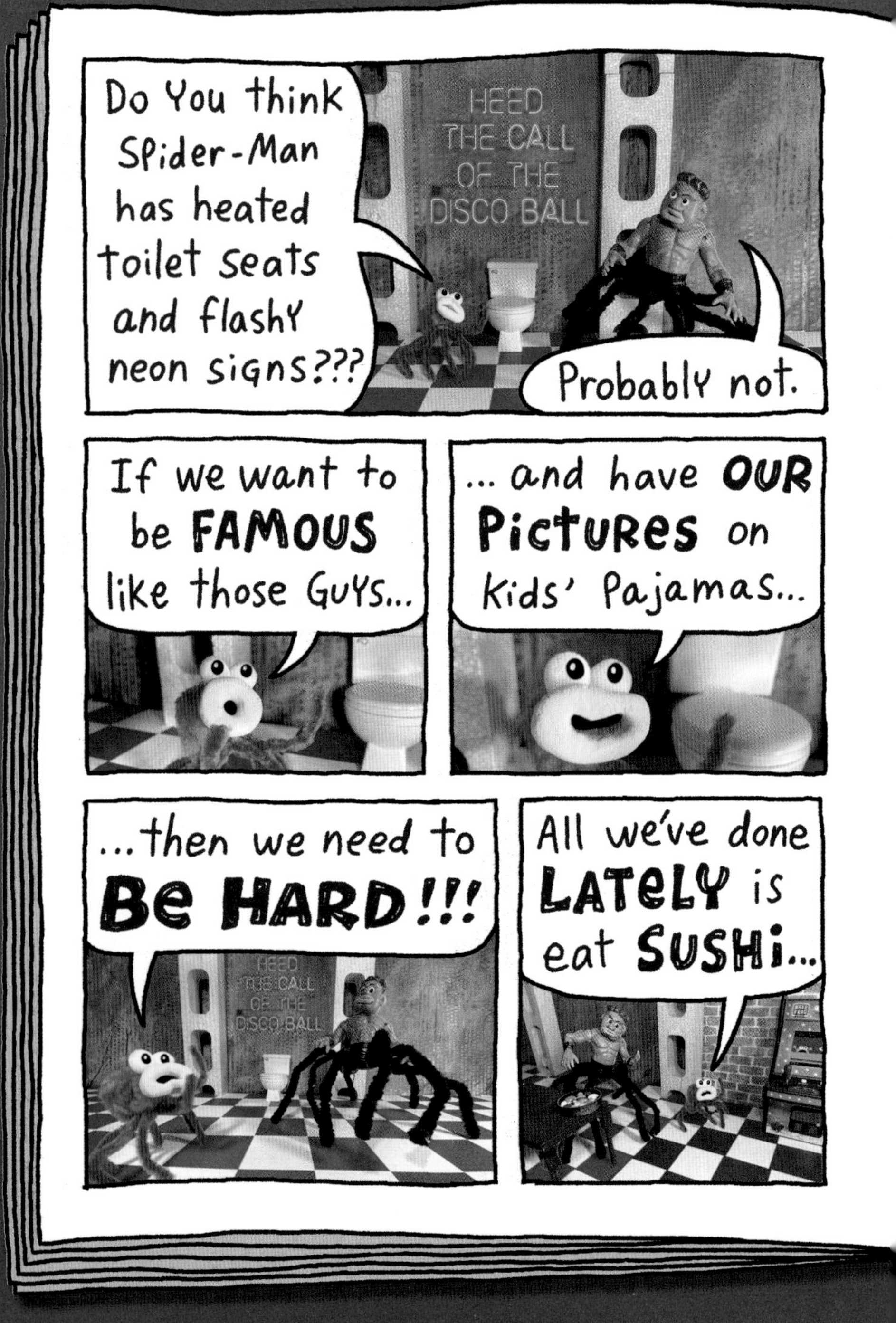
Do You think Spider-Man has heated toilet seats and flashy neon signs???
HEED THE CALL OF THE DISCO BALL
Probably not.
If we want to be FAMOUS like those Guys...
... and have OUR Pictures on Kids' Pajamas...
... then we need to Be HARD!!!
HEED THE CALL OF THE DISCO BALL
All we've done LATELY is eat SUSHI...

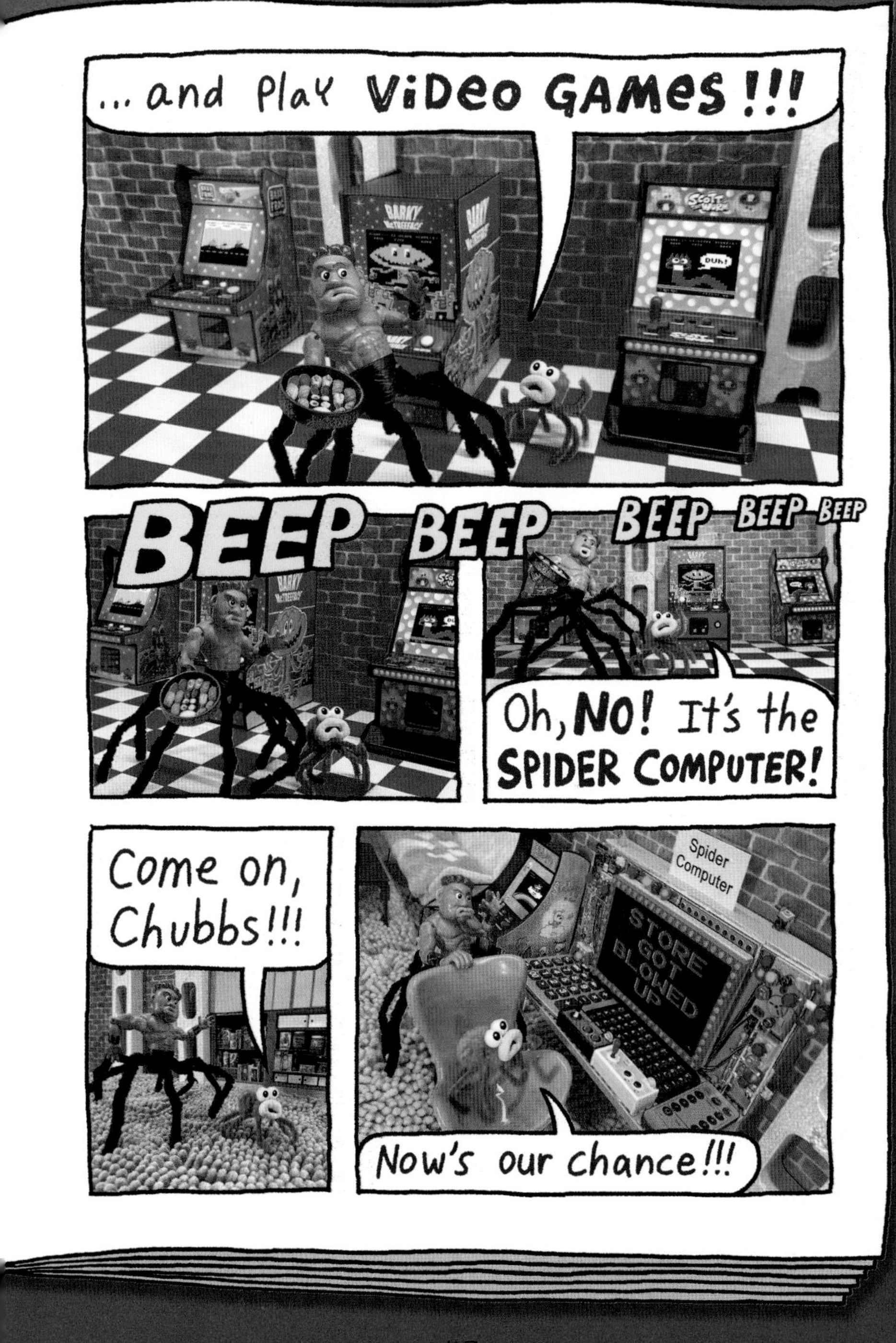
...and Play VIDEO GAMES!!!
BEEP BEEP BEEP BEEP BEEP
Oh, NO! It's the SPIDER COMPUTER!
Come on, Chubbs!!!
Spider Computer
STORE GOT BLOWED UP
Now's our chance!!!

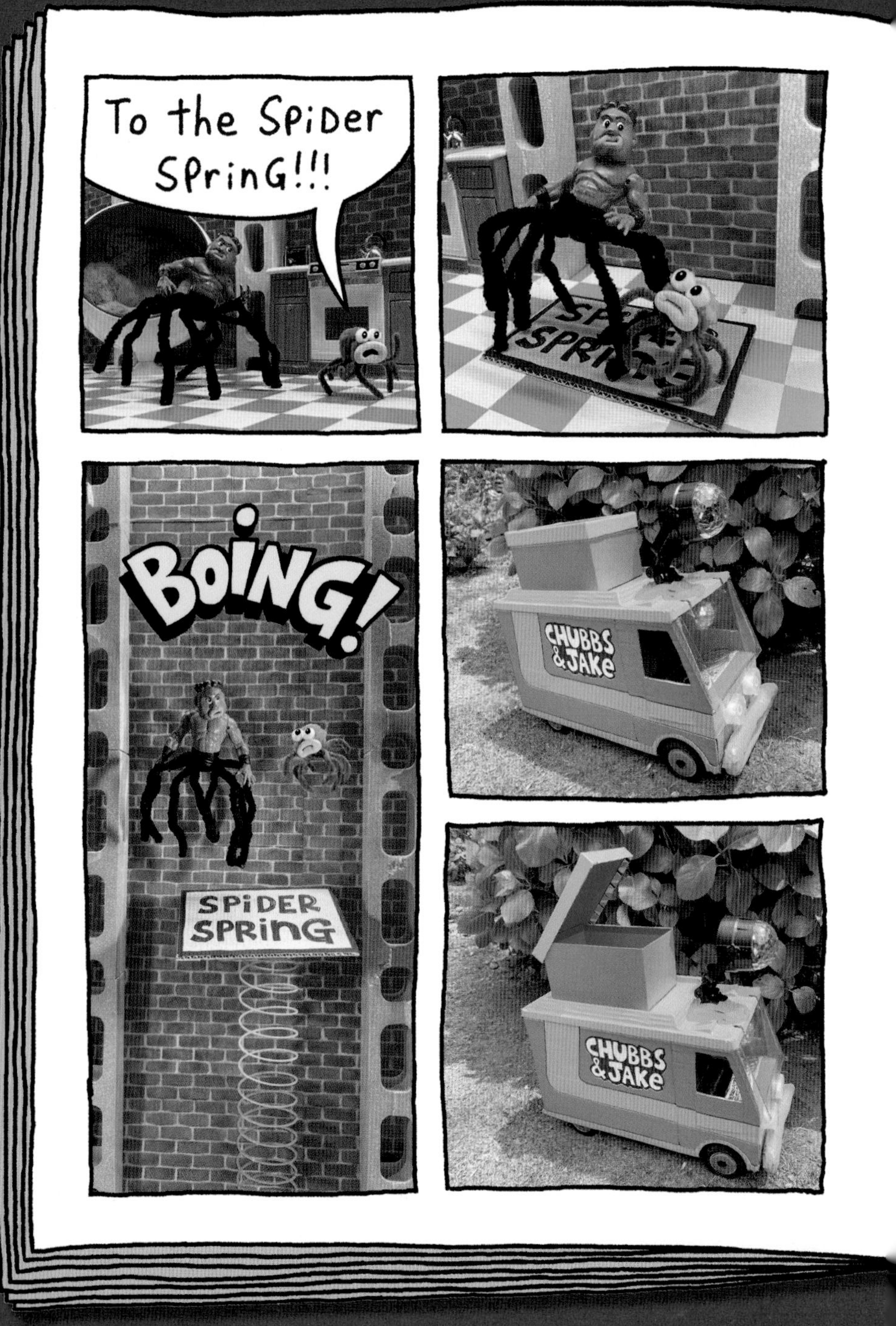
To the SPiDer SPrinG!!!
SP
SPRI
BOiNG!
SPiDER SPRinG
CHUBBS & JAKE
CHUBBS & JAKE

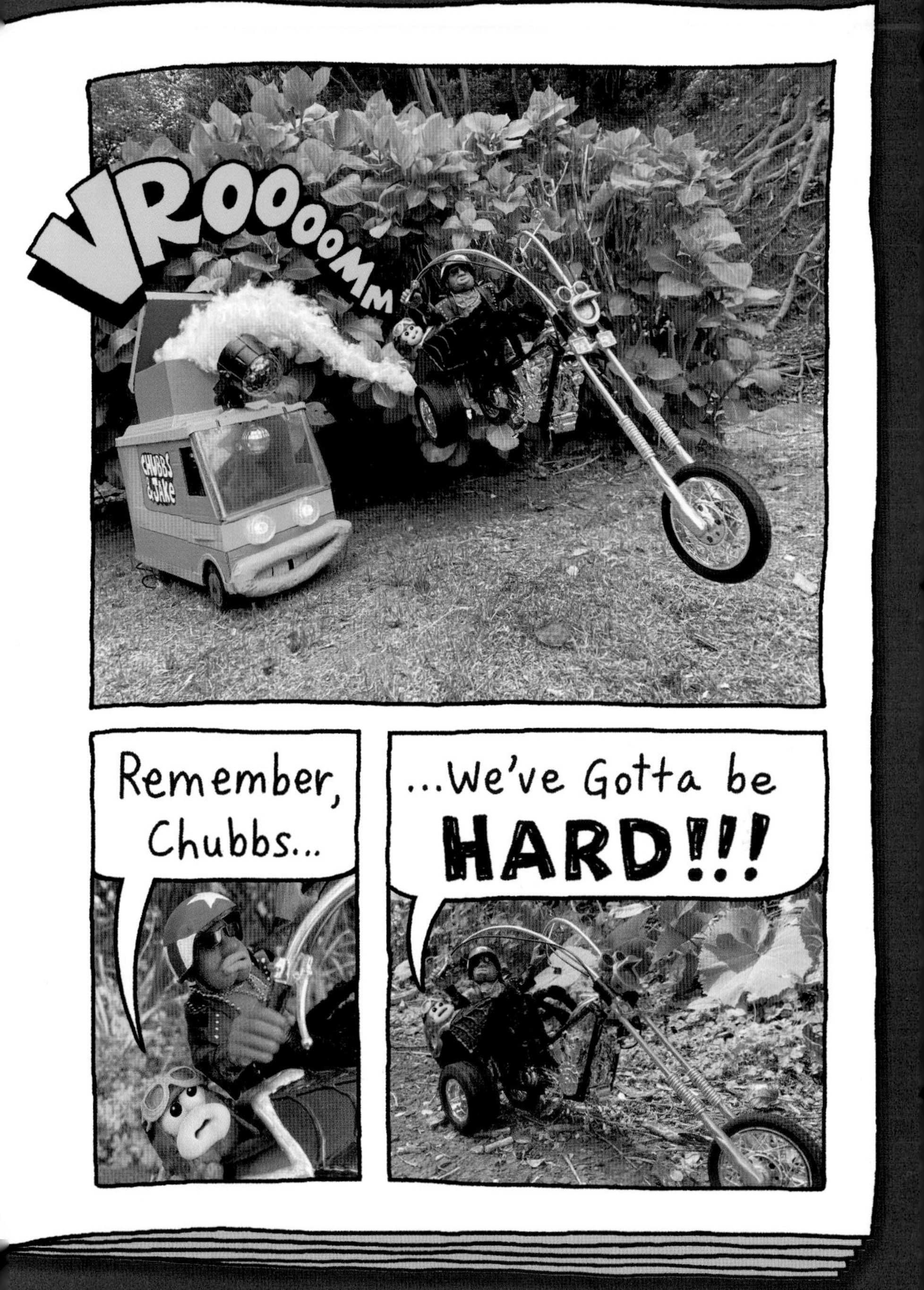
VROOOOOMM
CHUBBS & JAKE
Remember, Chubbs...
...We've Gotta be HARD!!!

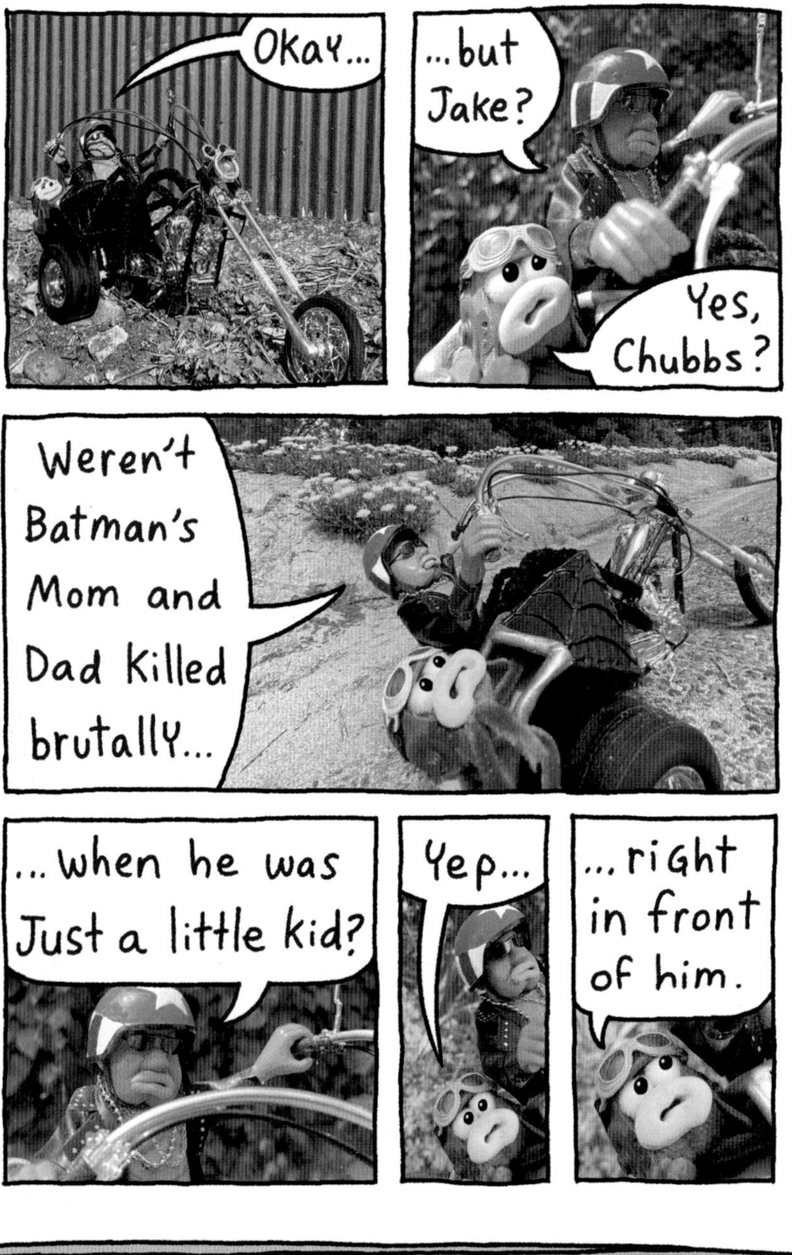
OKAY...
...but Jake?
Yes, Chubbs?
Weren't Batman's Mom and Dad Killed brutally...
...when he was Just a little kid?
Yep...
...right in front of him.

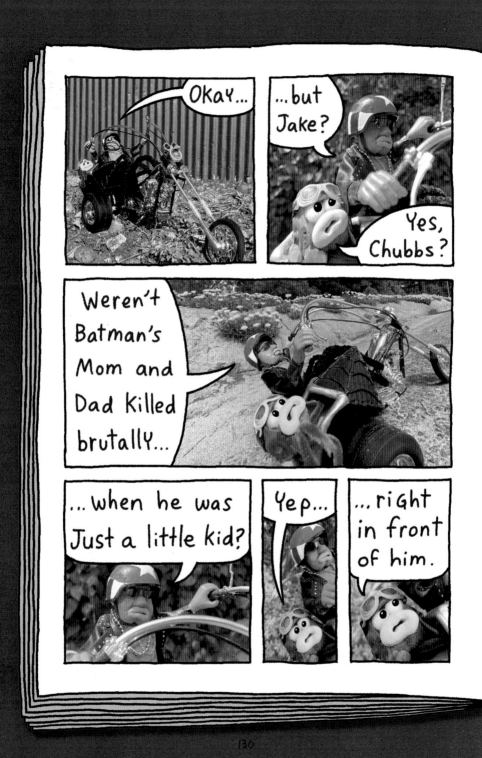

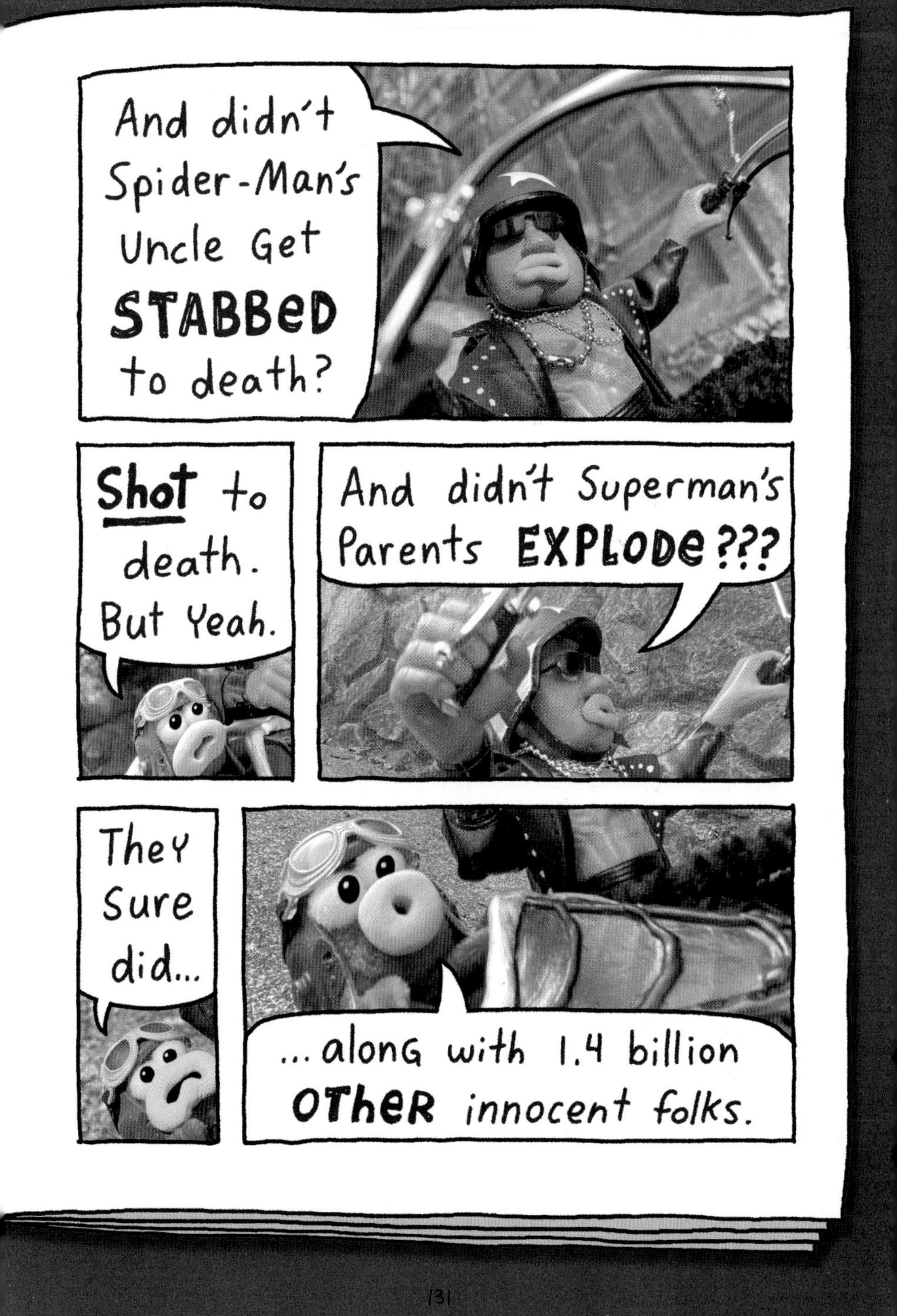
And didn't Spider-Man's Uncle Get STABBED to death?
Shot to death. But Yeah.
And didn't Superman's Parents EXPLODE???
They Sure did...
...along with 1.4 billion OTHER innocent folks.

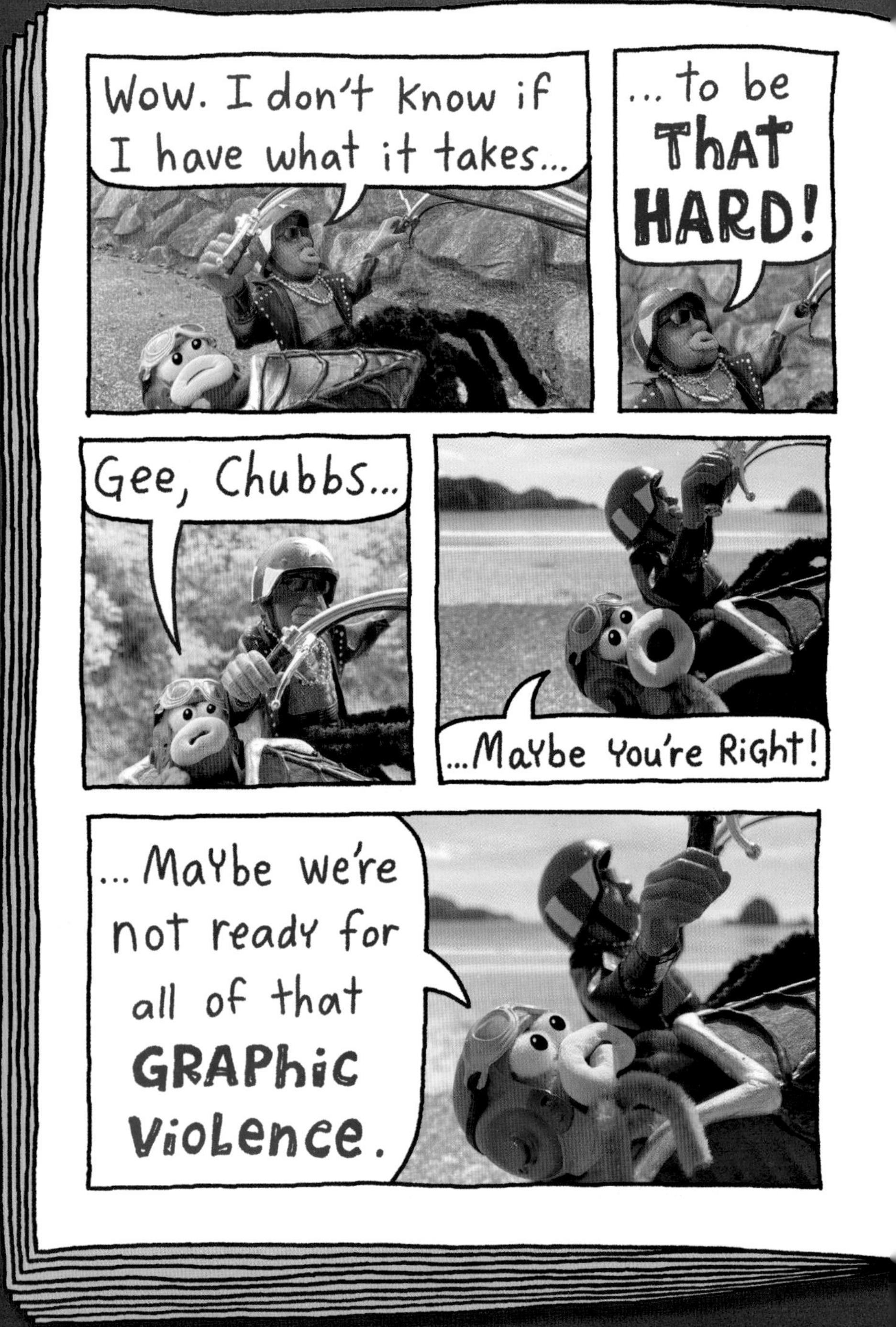
Wow. I don't know if I have what it takes...
... to be THAT HARD!
Gee, Chubbs...
...Maybe You're Right!
... Maybe we're not ready for all of that GRAPHic VioLence.

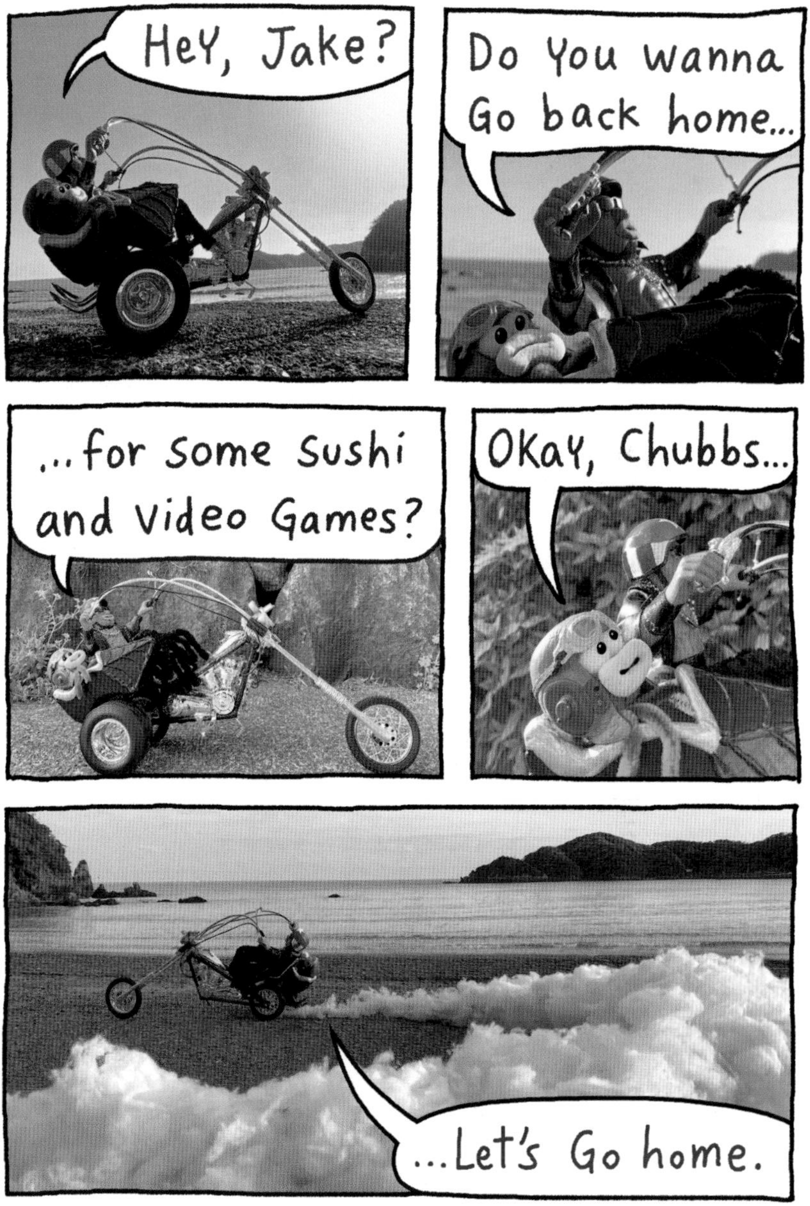
Hey, Jake?
Do you wanna Go back home...
...for some Sushi and Video Games?
OKay, Chubbs...
...Let's Go home.

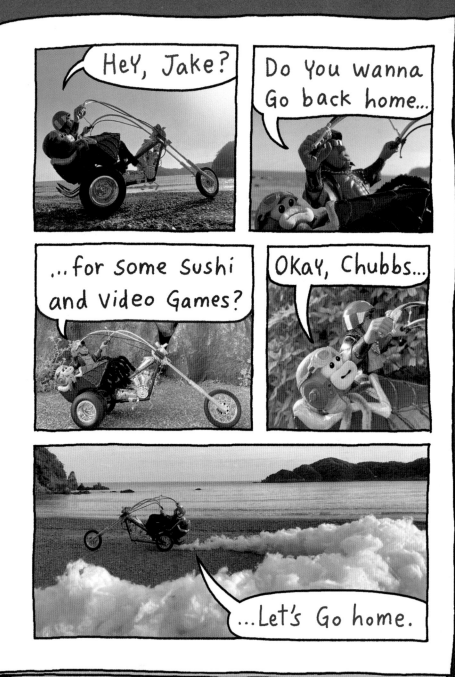

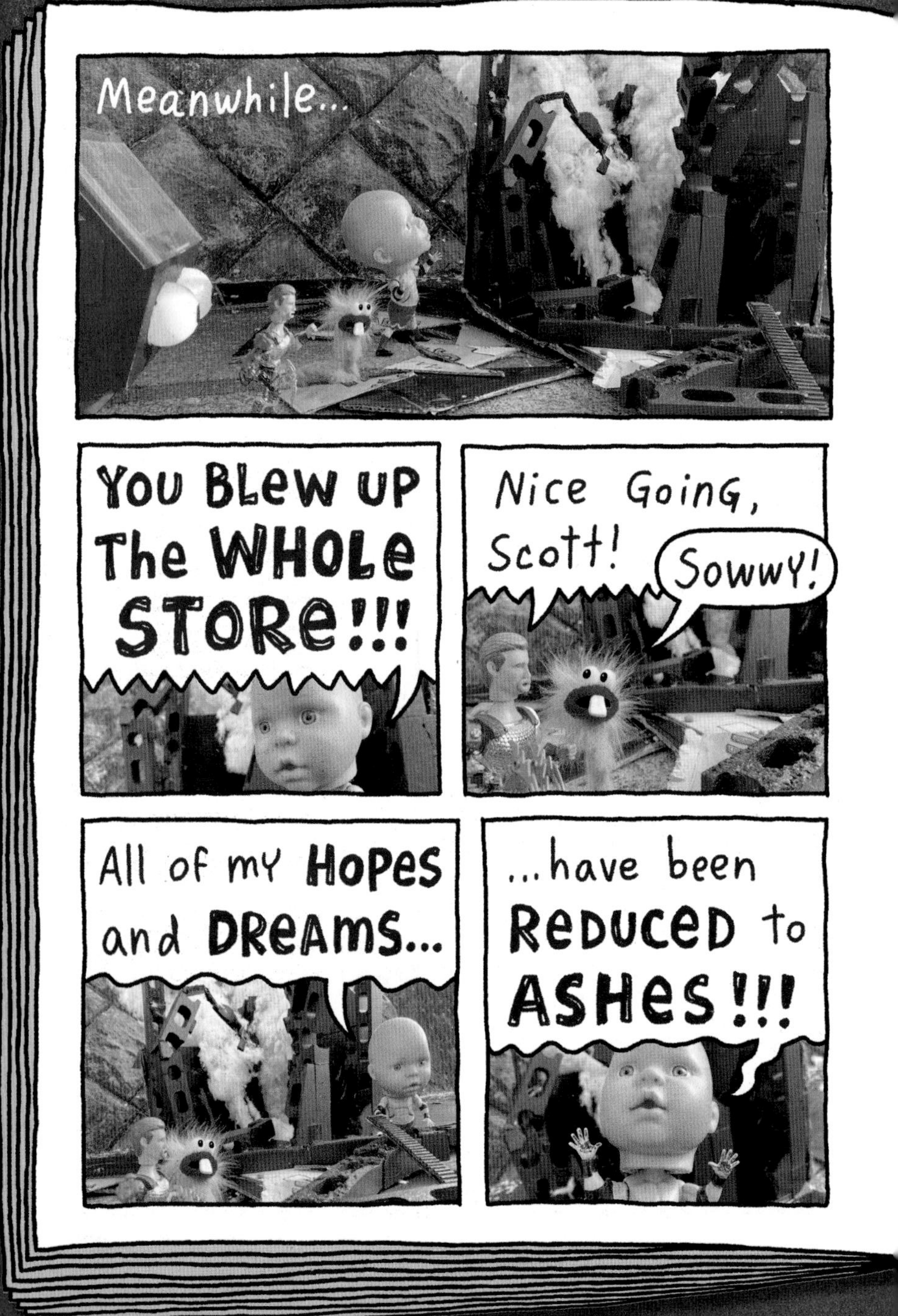
Meanwhile...
YOU BLEW UP The WHOLE STORE!!!
Nice Going, Scott!
Sowwy!
All of my HOPES and DREAMS...
...have been REDUCED to ASHES!!!

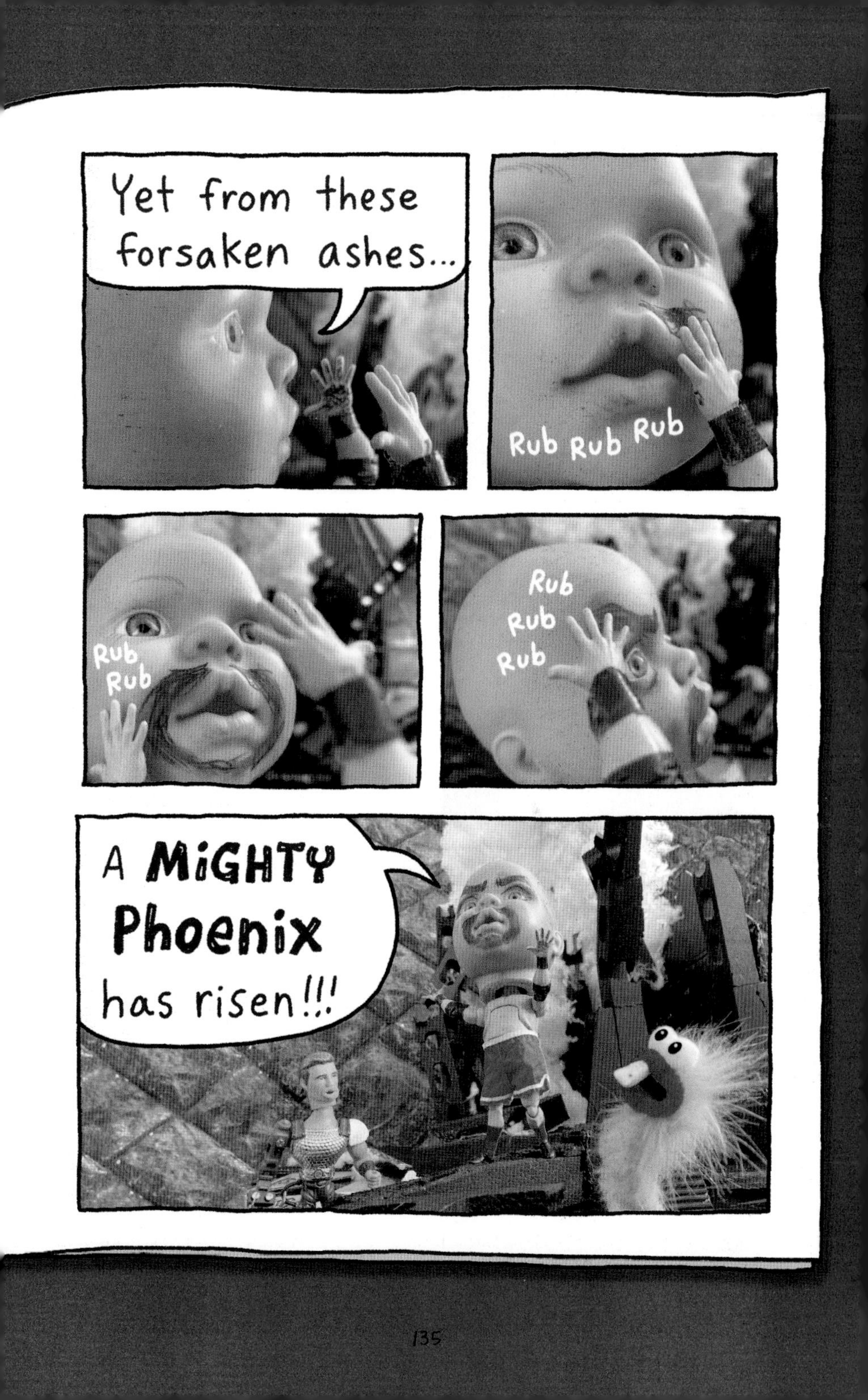
Yet from these forsaken ashes...
Rub Rub Rub
Rub Rub
Rub Rub Rub
A MiGHTY Phoenix has risen!!!

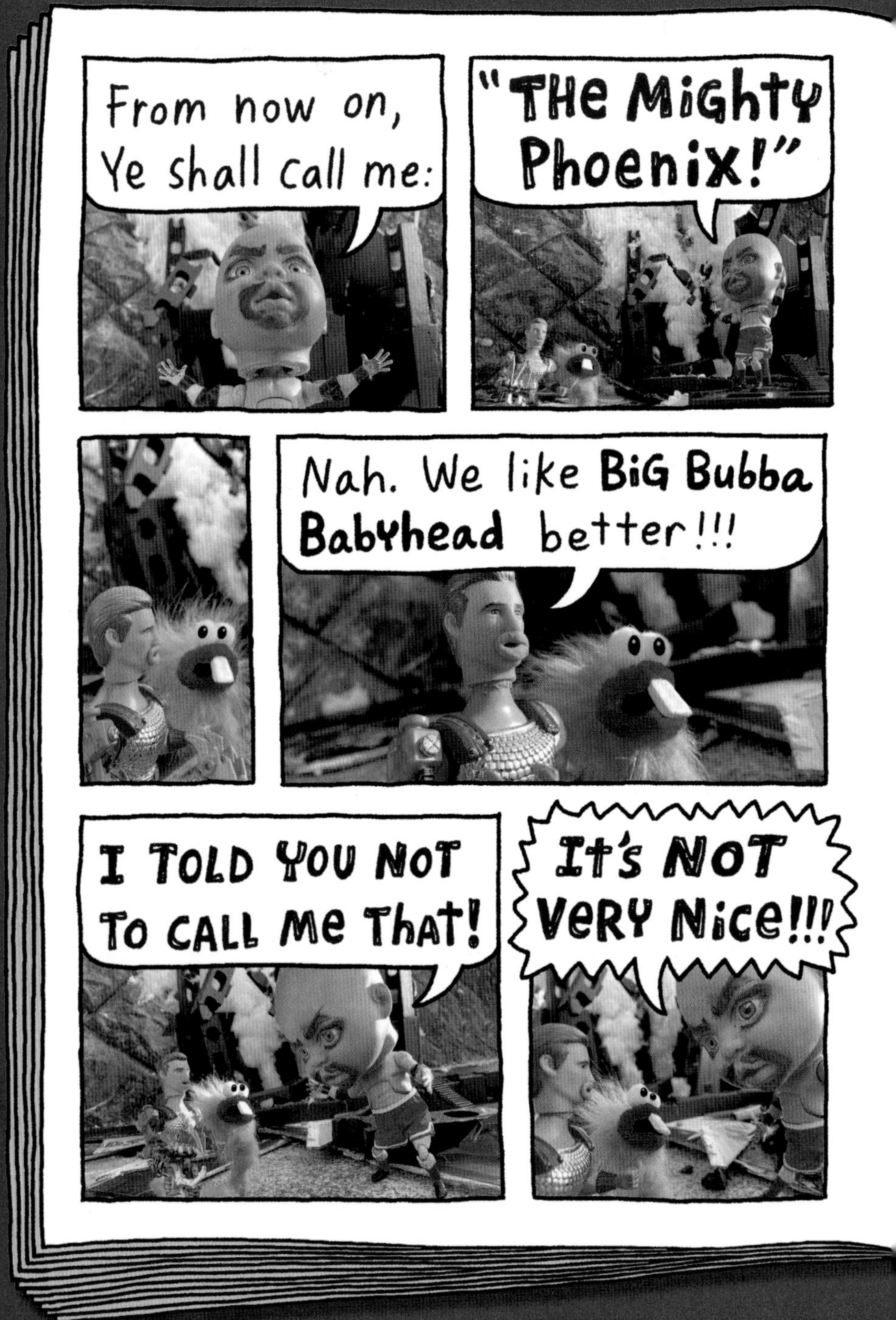
From now on, Ye shall call me:
"THE MIGHTY Phoenix!"
Nah. We like BIG Bubba Babyhead better!!!
I TOLD YOU NOT TO CALL ME THAT!
It's NOT VERY Nice!!!

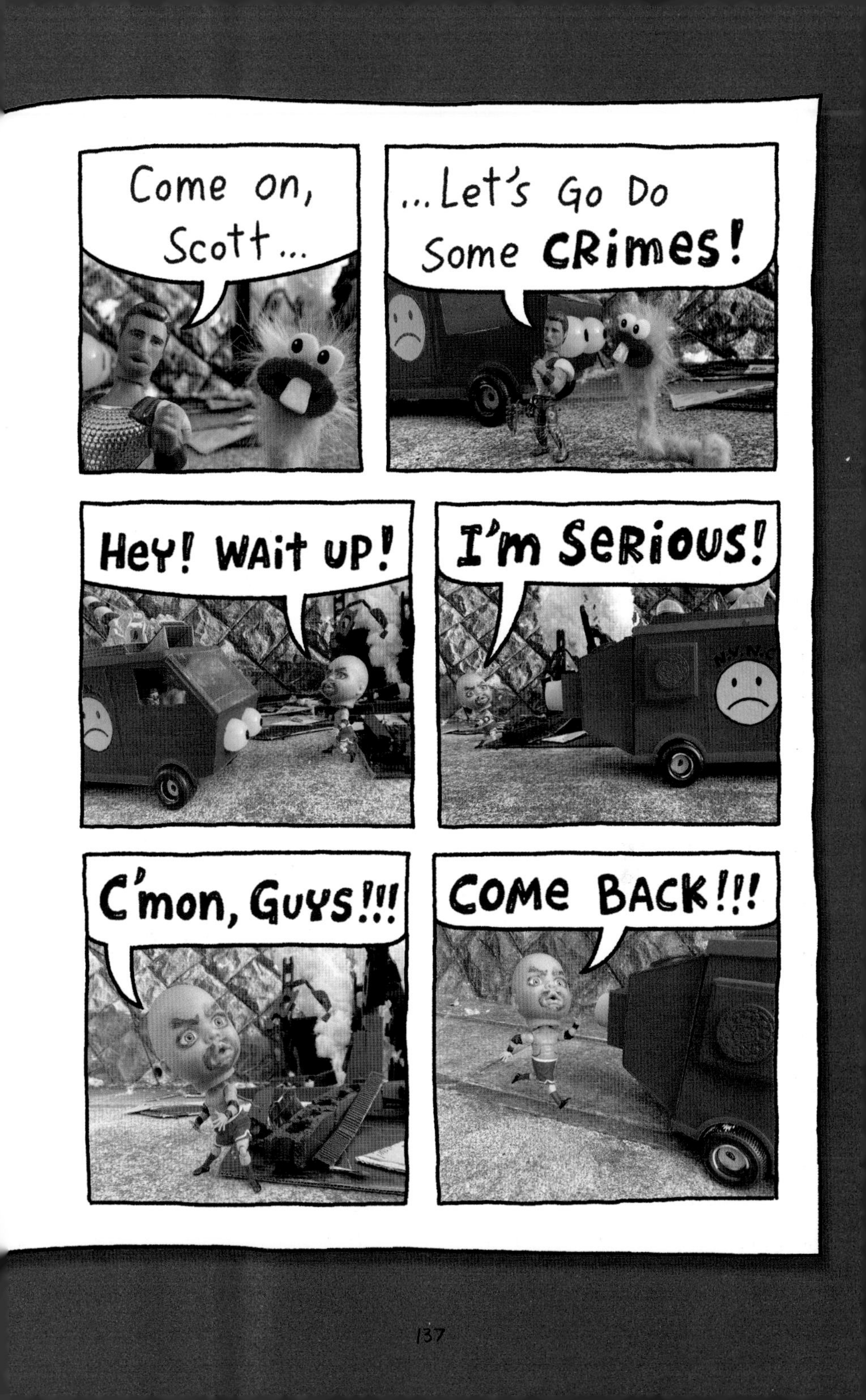
Come on, Scott...
...Let's Go Do Some CRimes!
Hey! WAit up!
I'm SeRiOUS!
C'mon, Guys!!!
COMe BACK!!!

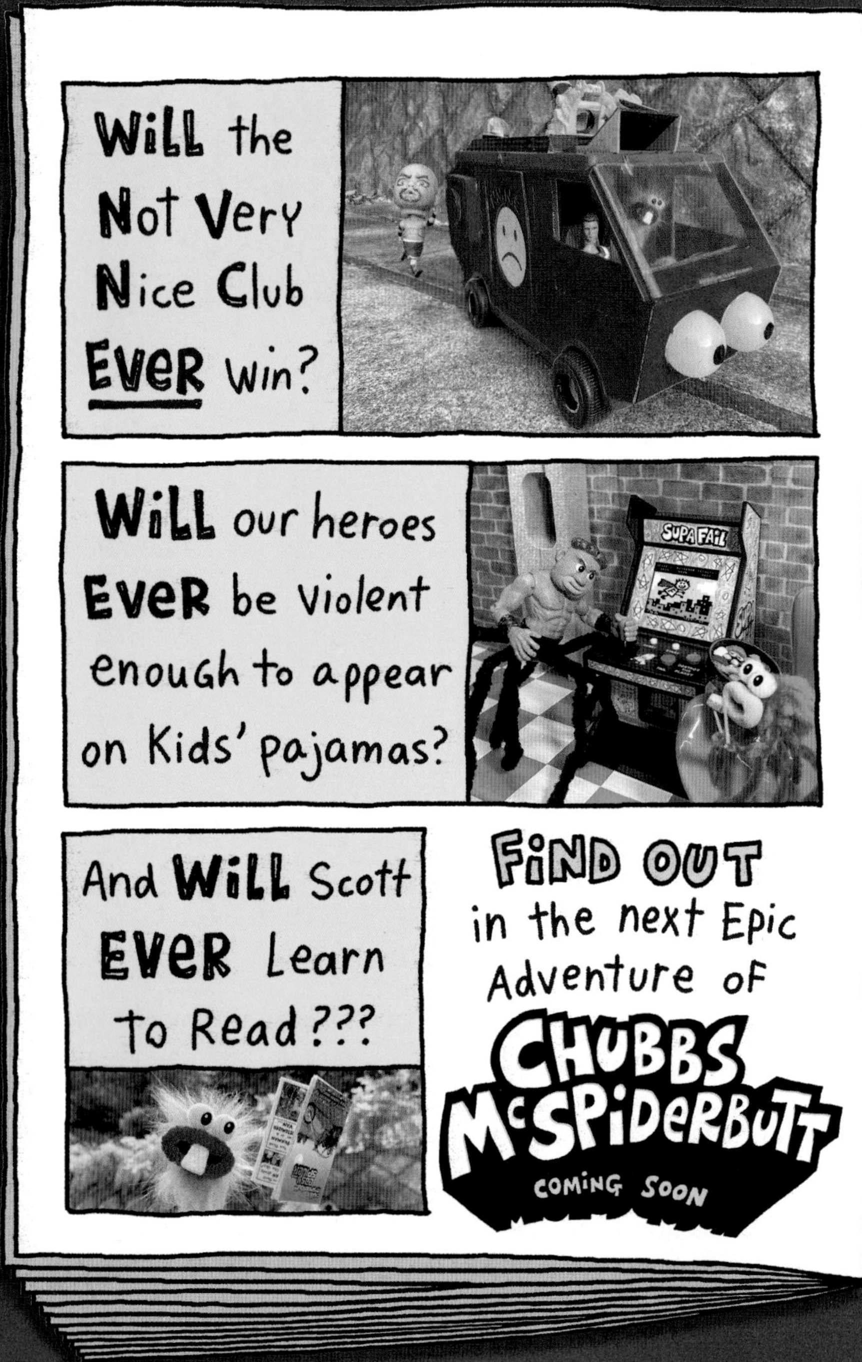
Will the Not Very Nice Club EVER win?
Will our heroes EVER be violent enough to appear on Kids' pajamas?
SUPA FAIL
And Will Scott EVER Learn to Read???
FIND OUT in the next Epic Adventure of
CHUBBS McSPIDERBUTT
COMING SOON

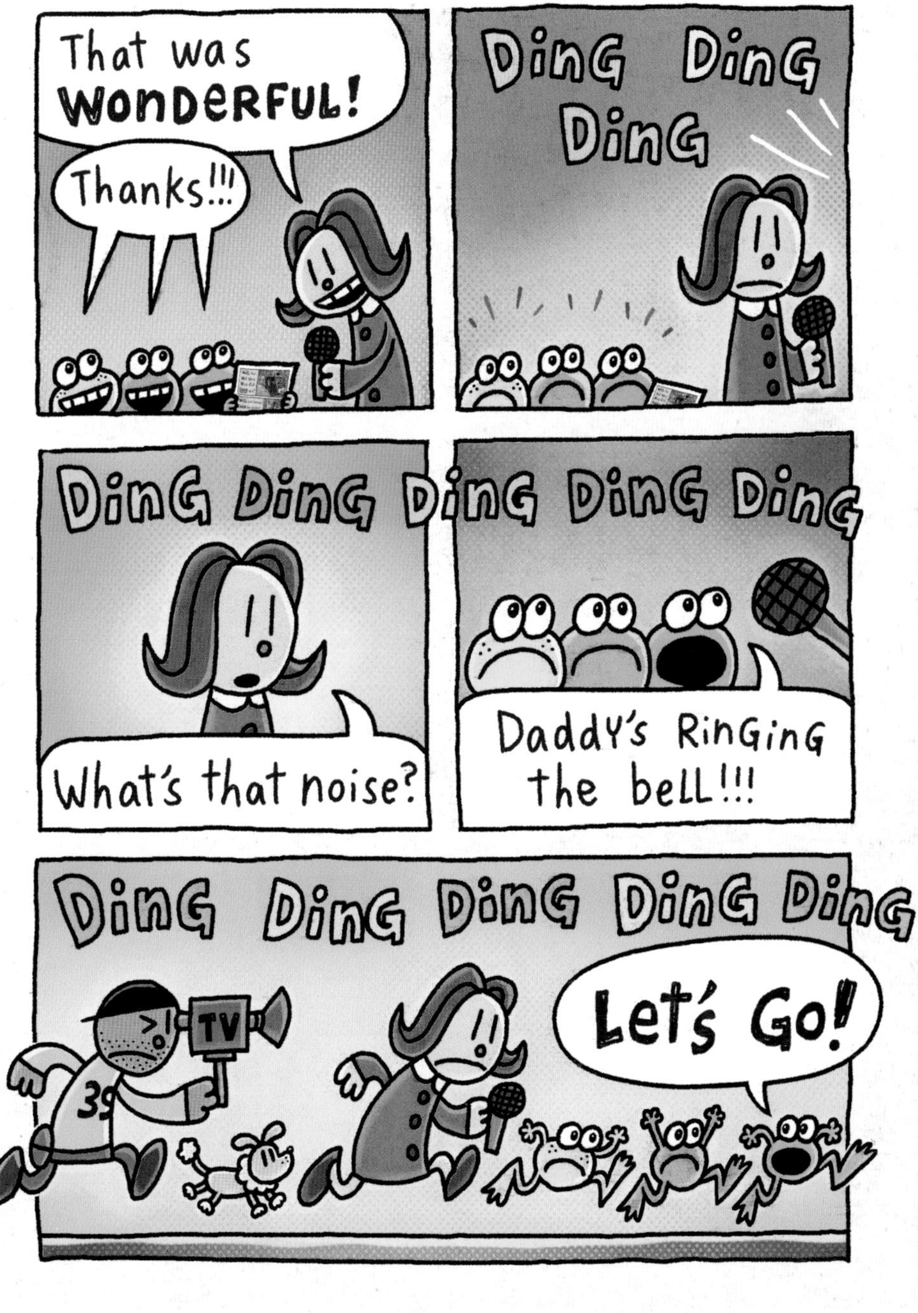
That was WONDERFUL!
Thanks!!!
DinG DinG DinG
DinG DinG DinG DinG DinG
What's that noise?
Daddy's RinGinG the beLL!!!
DinG DinG DinG DinG DinG
TV
39
Let's Go!

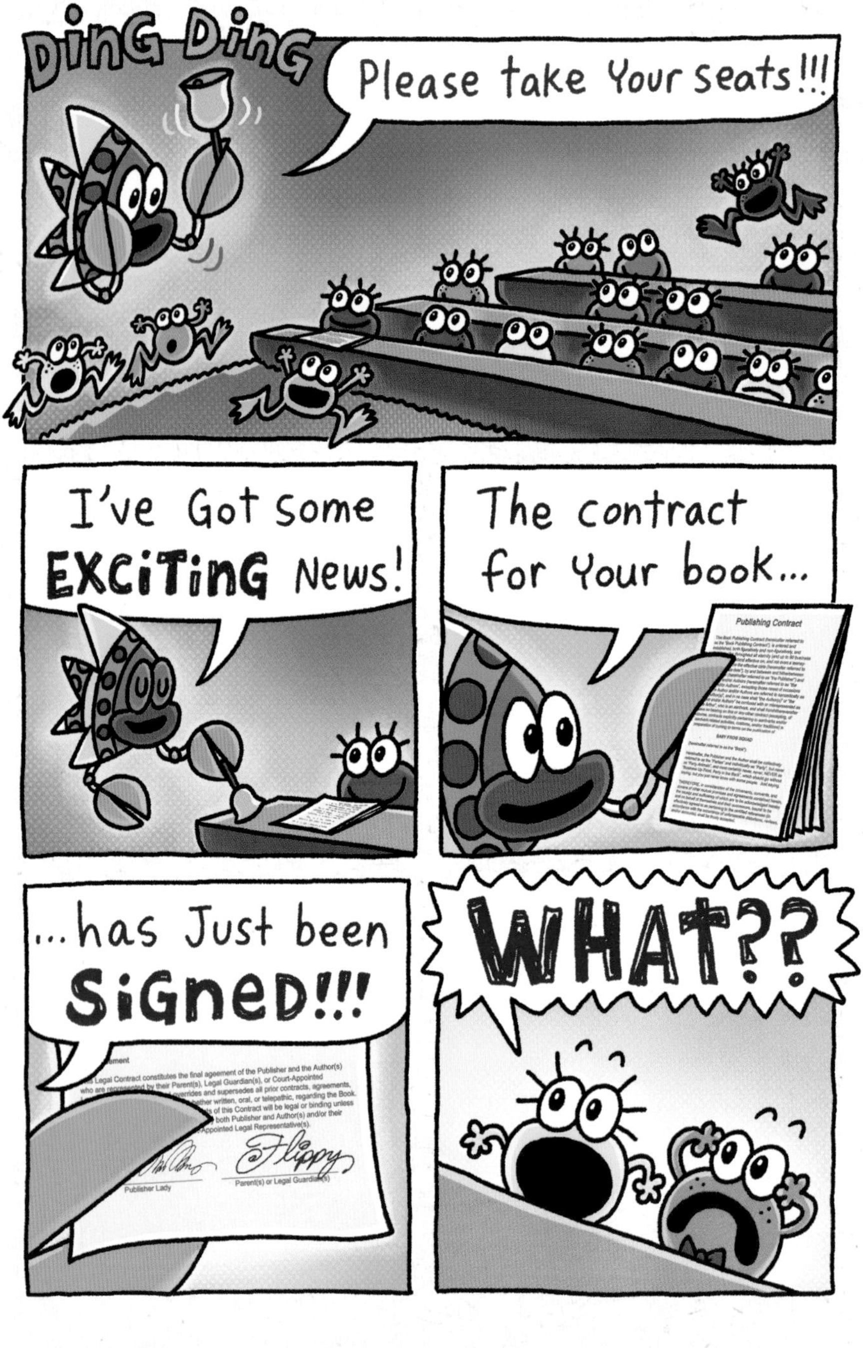
DING DING
Please take Your seats!!!
I've Got some EXCITING News!
The contract for Your book...
Publishing Contract
...has Just been SIGNED!!!
Publisher Lady
WHAT??

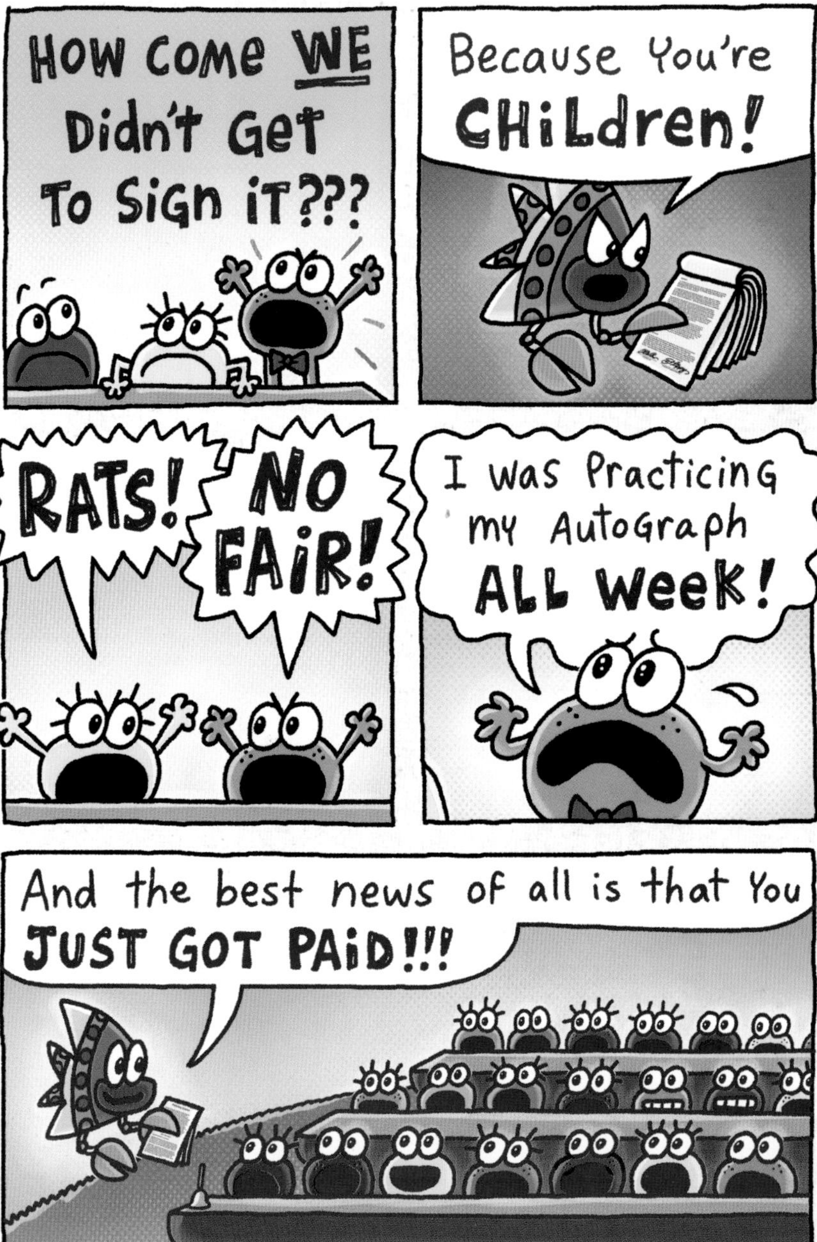
HOW COME WE Didn't Get To SiGn iT???
Because You're CHiLdren!
RATS!
NO FAiR!
I was Practicing my AutoGraph ALL Week!
And the best news of all is that You JUST GOT PAiD!!!

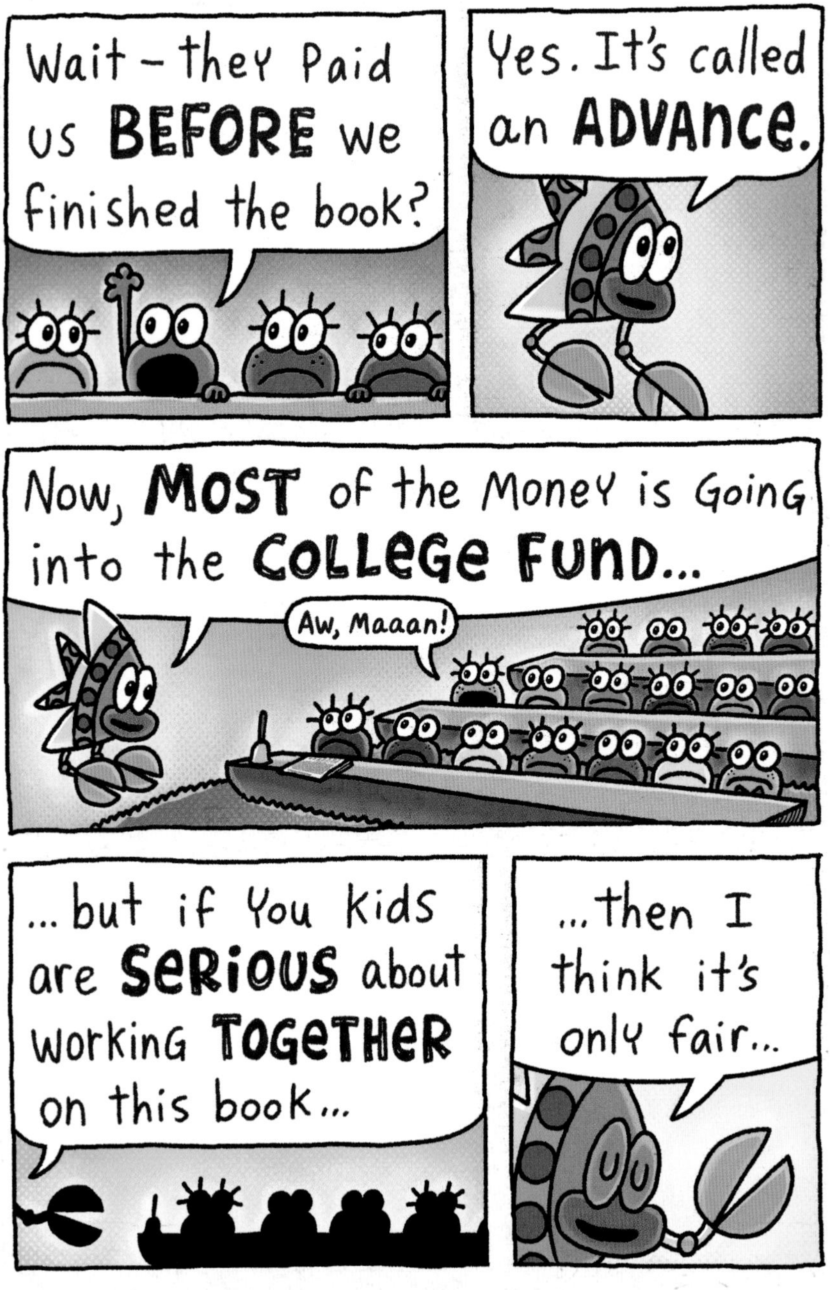
Wait – they paid us BEFORE we finished the book?
Yes. It's called an ADVANCE.
Now, MOST of the money is going into the COLLEGE FUND...
Aw, Maaan!
...but if you kids are SERIOUS about working TOGETHER on this book...
...then I think it's only fair...

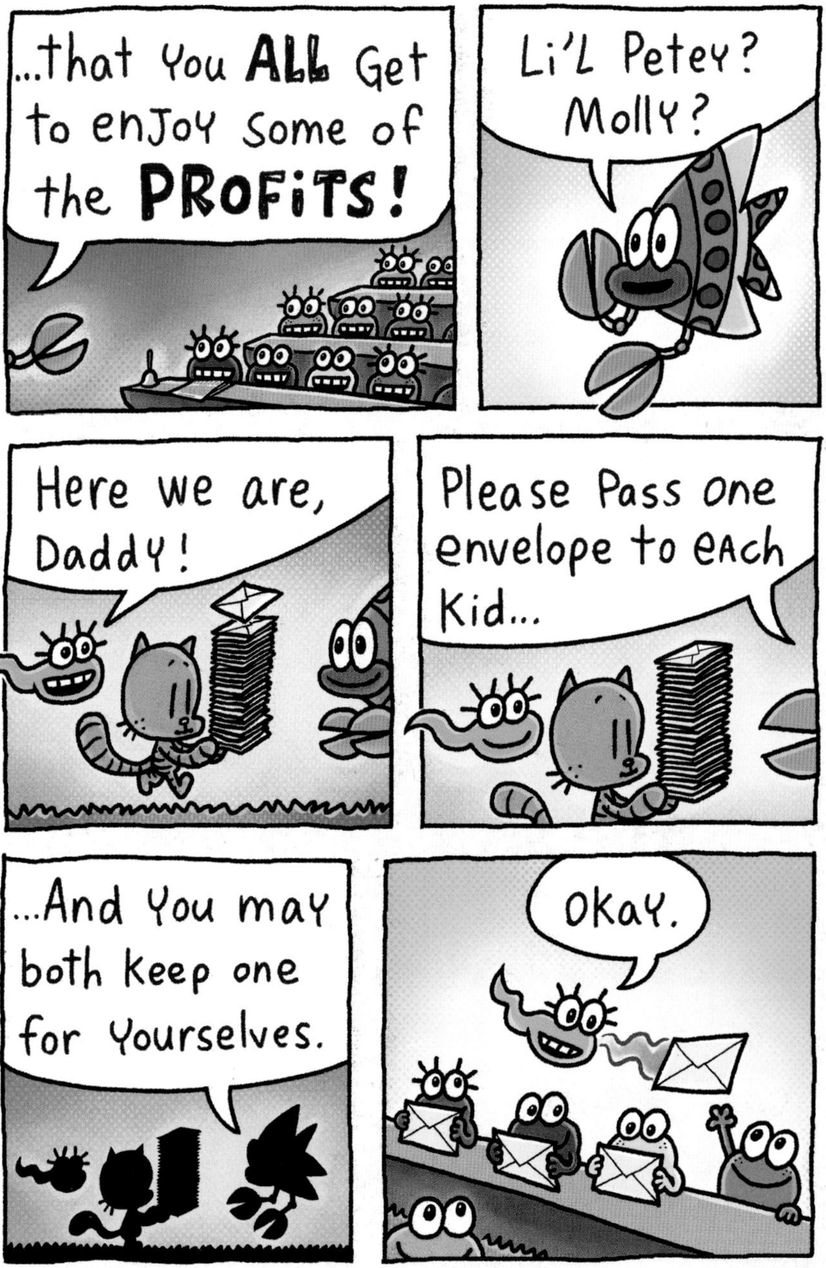

...that You ALL Get to enJoy some of the PROFITS!
Li'L Petey? Molly?
Here we are, Daddy!
Please Pass one envelope to eACh Kid...
...And You may both keep one for Yourselves.
OKay.

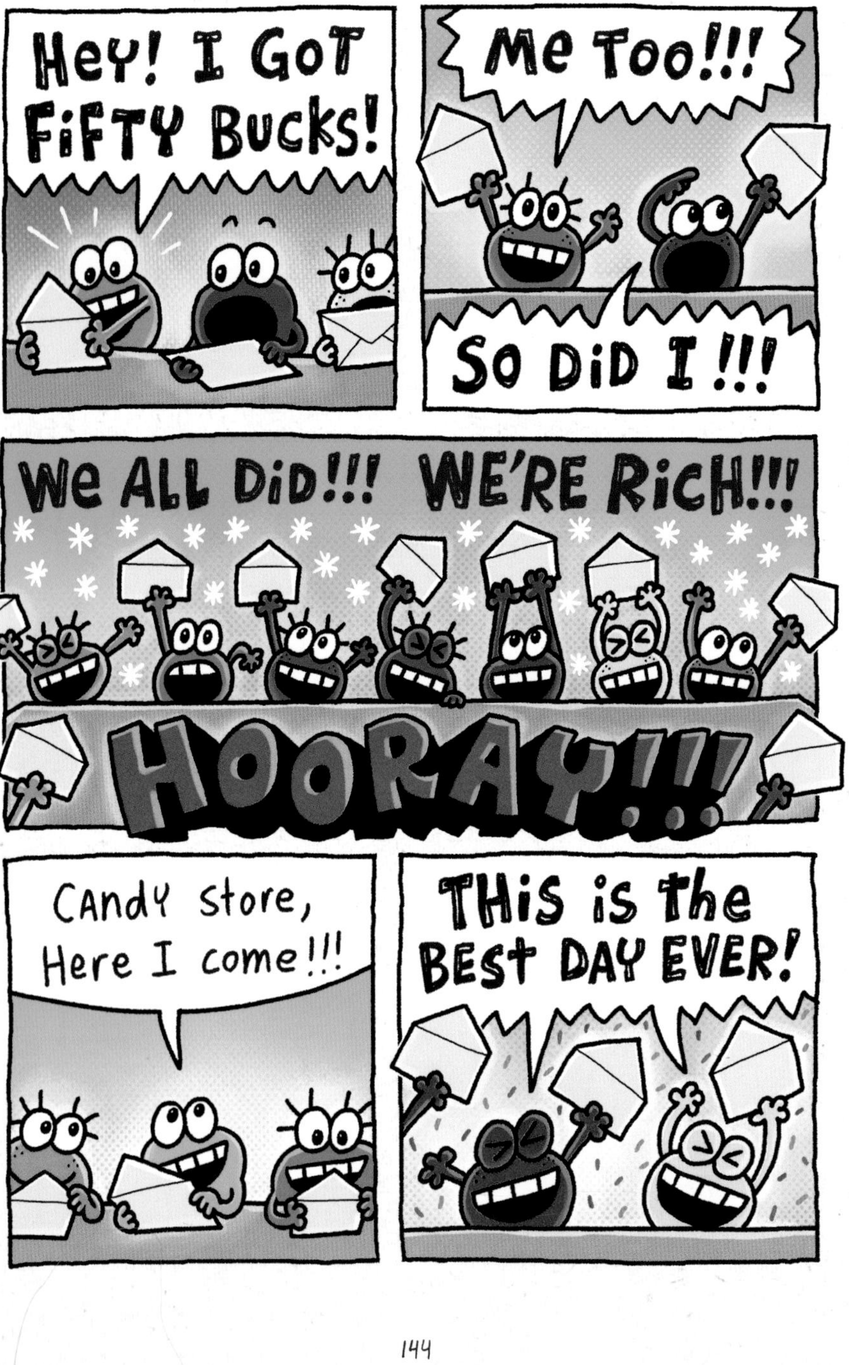
Hey! I GoT FiFTY BUCKS!
Me Too!!!
So DiD I!!!
We ALL DiD!!! WE'RE RiCH!!!
HOORAY!!!
Candy store, Here I come!!!
THIS is the BEST DAY EVER!

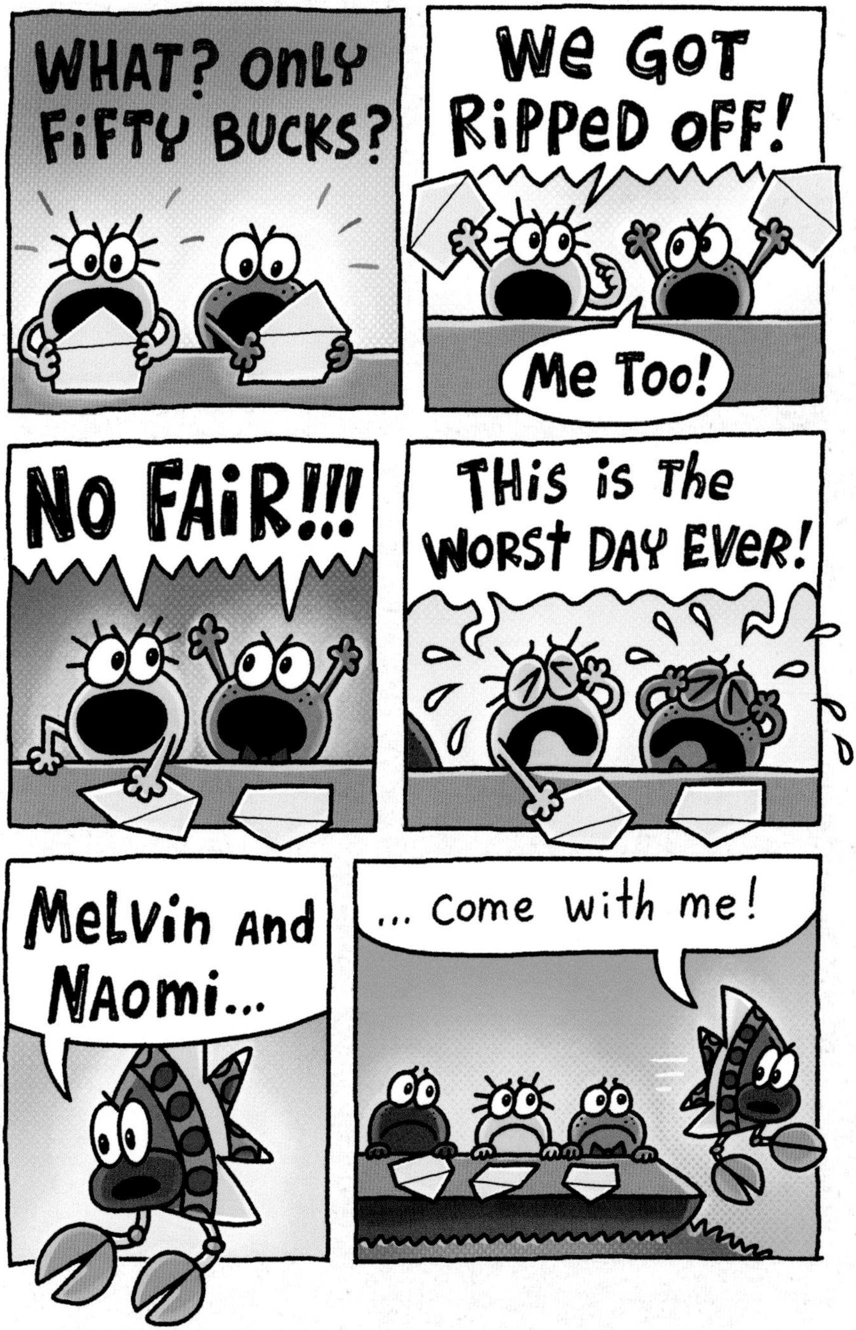
WHAT? ONLY FIFTY BUCKS?
WE GOT RIPPED OFF!
Me Too!
NO FAIR!!!
THIS is The WORST DAY EVER!
MELVIN AND NAOMI...
... come with me!

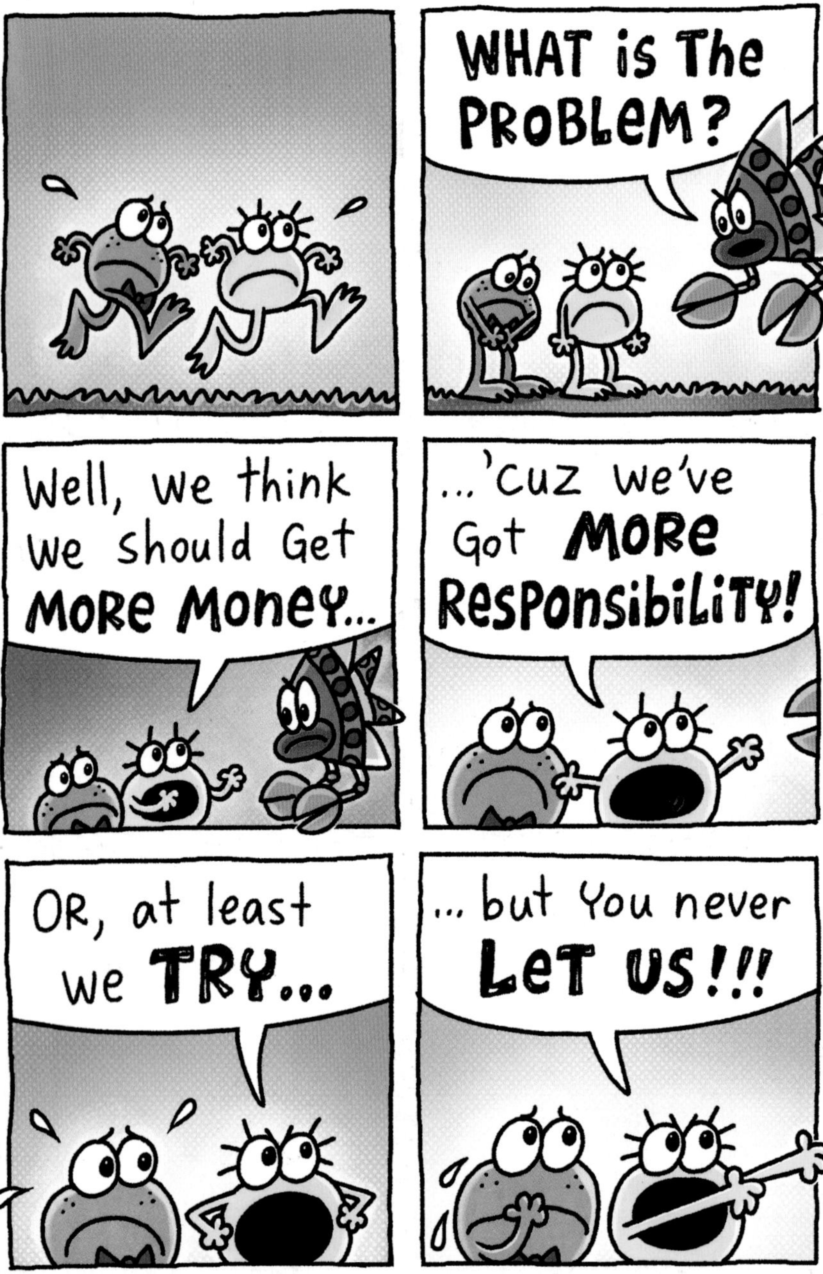
WHAT is The PROBLEM?
Well, we think we should Get MORE MONEY...
...'cuz we've Got MORE RESPONSIBILITY!
OR, at least we TRY...
...but You never LET US!!!

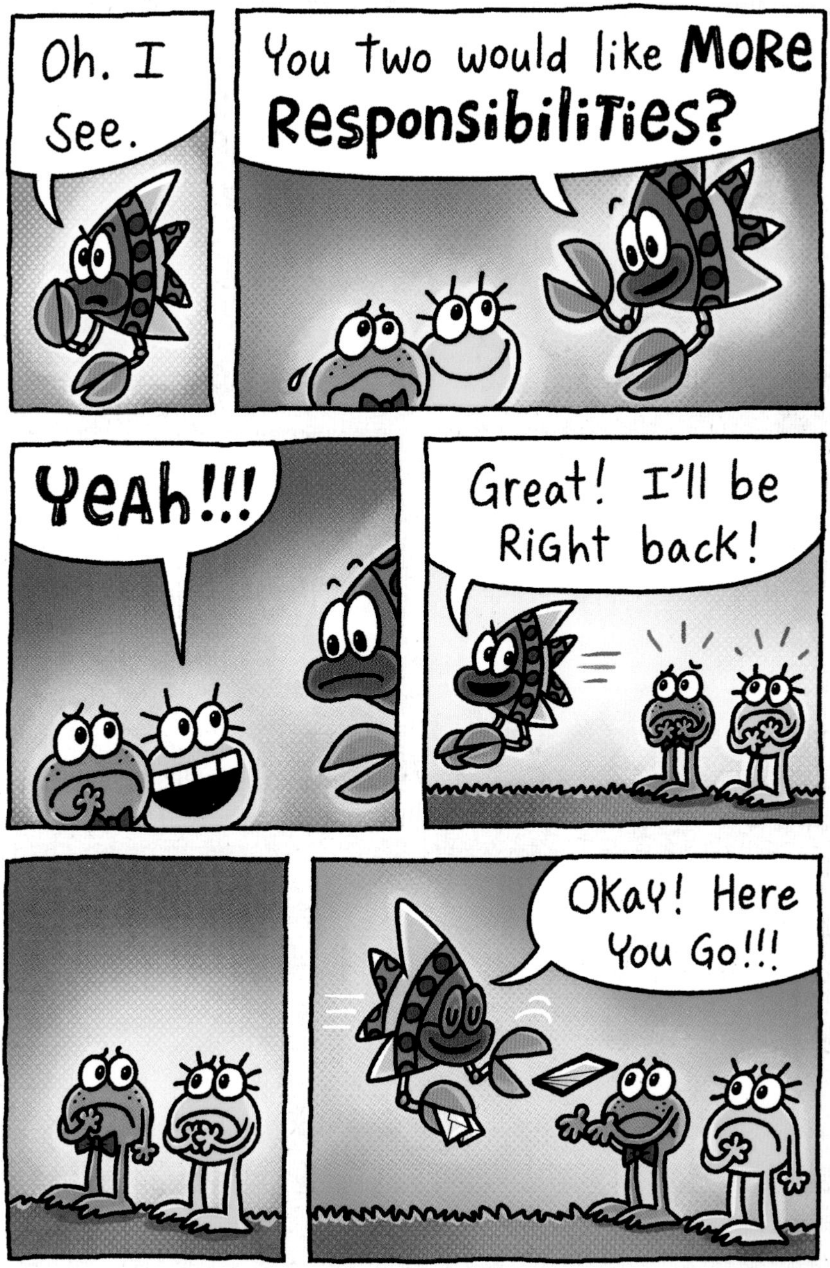
Oh. I See.
You two would like MORE RESPONSIBILITIES?
YEAH!!!
Great! I'll be Right back!
OKAY! Here You Go!!!

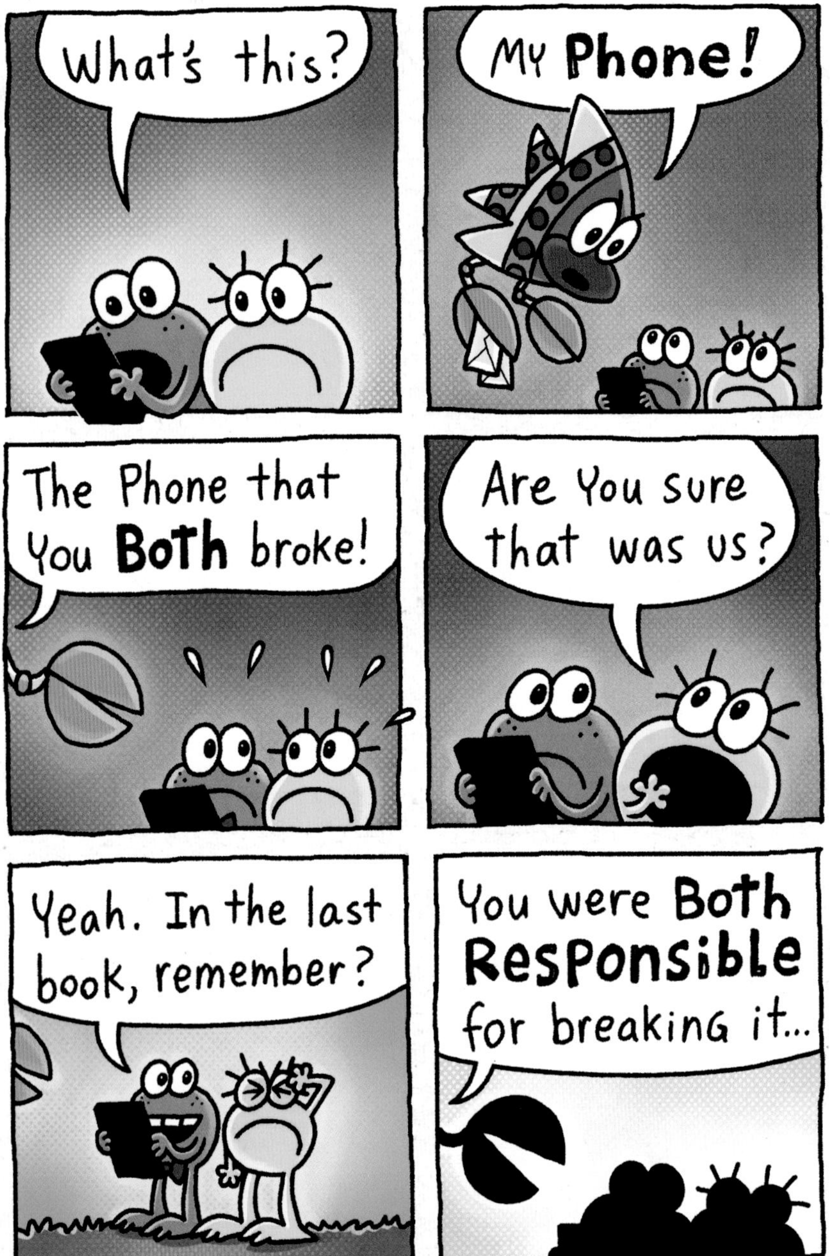
What's this?
My Phone!
The Phone that You Both broke!
Are You sure that was us?
Yeah. In the last book, remember?
You were Both Responsible for breaking it...

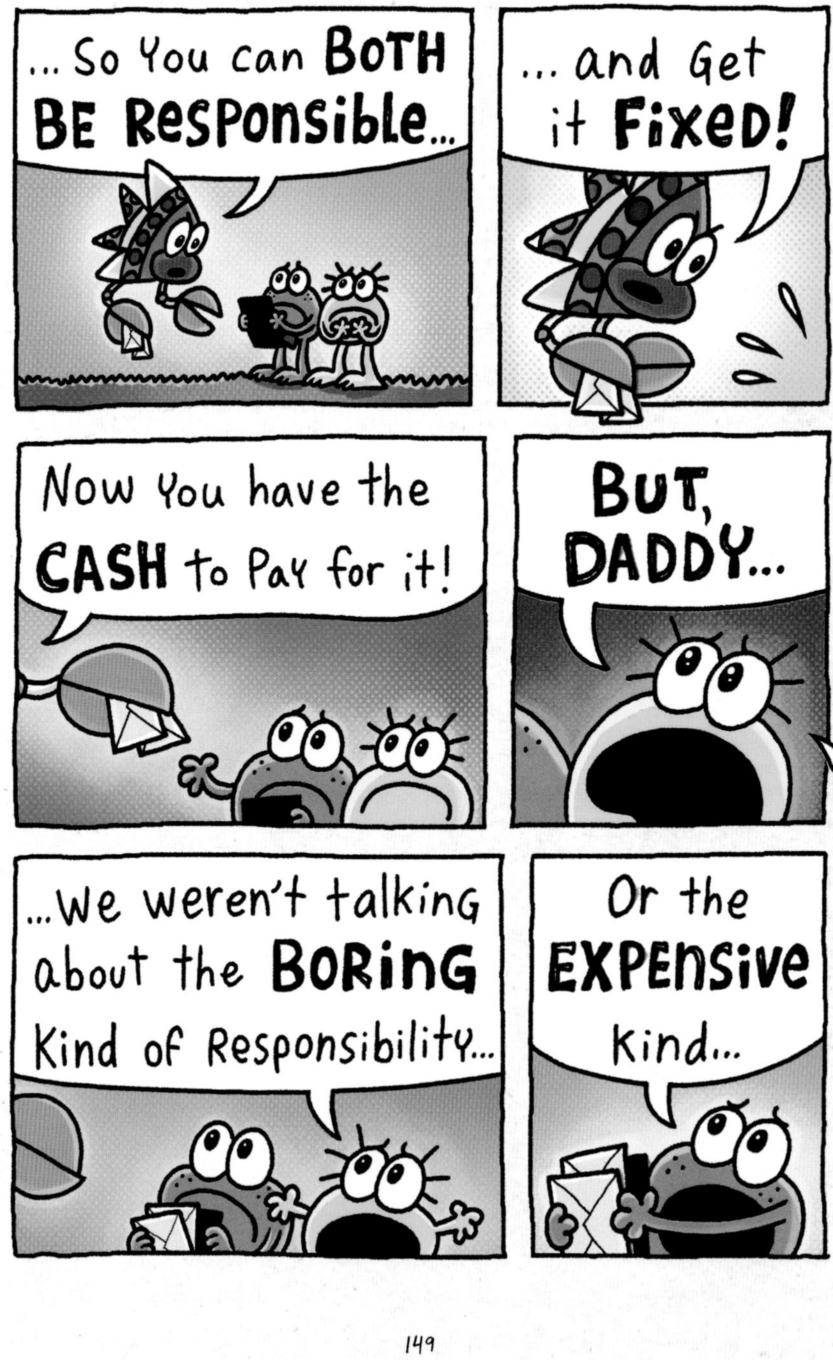
... So You can BOTH BE RESPONSIBLE...
... and Get it FIXED!
Now You have the CASH to Pay for it!
BUT, DADDY...
...We weren't talking about the BORING Kind of Responsibility...
Or the EXPENSIVE Kind...

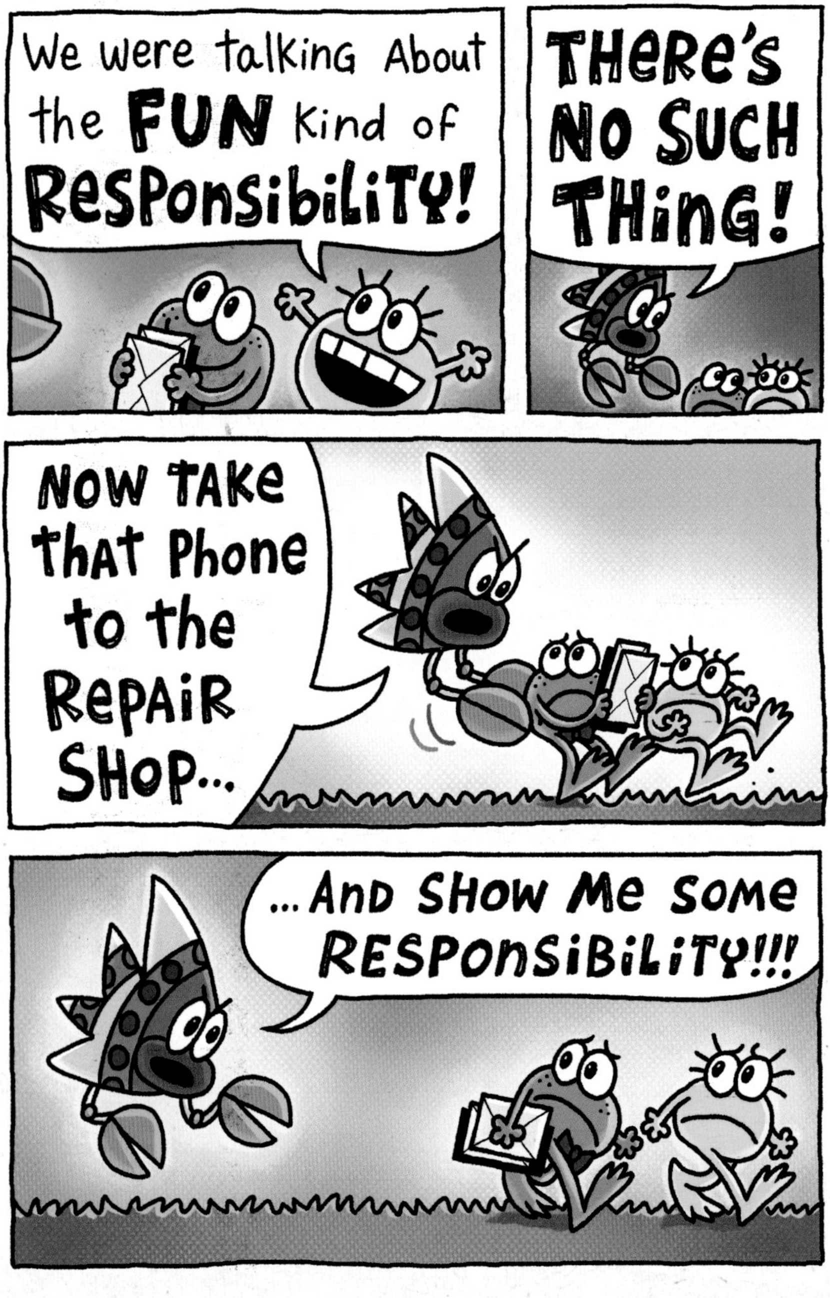
We were talking About the FUN Kind of RESPONSIBILITY!
THERE'S NO SUCH THING!
NOW TAKE that Phone to the REPAIR SHOP...
...AND SHOW Me SOME RESPONSIBILITY!!!

CHAPTER 8

The Smallest Act of Kindness

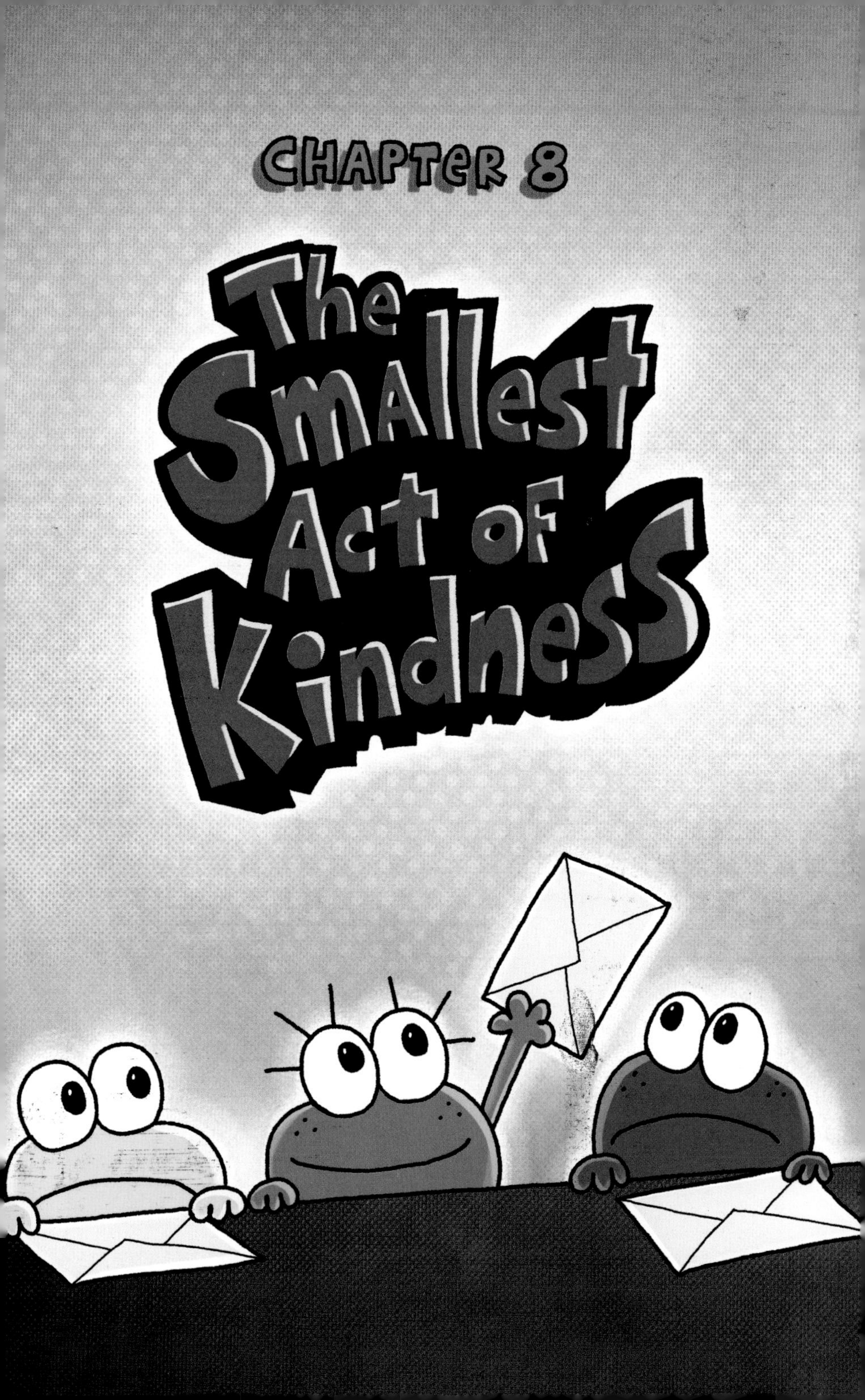

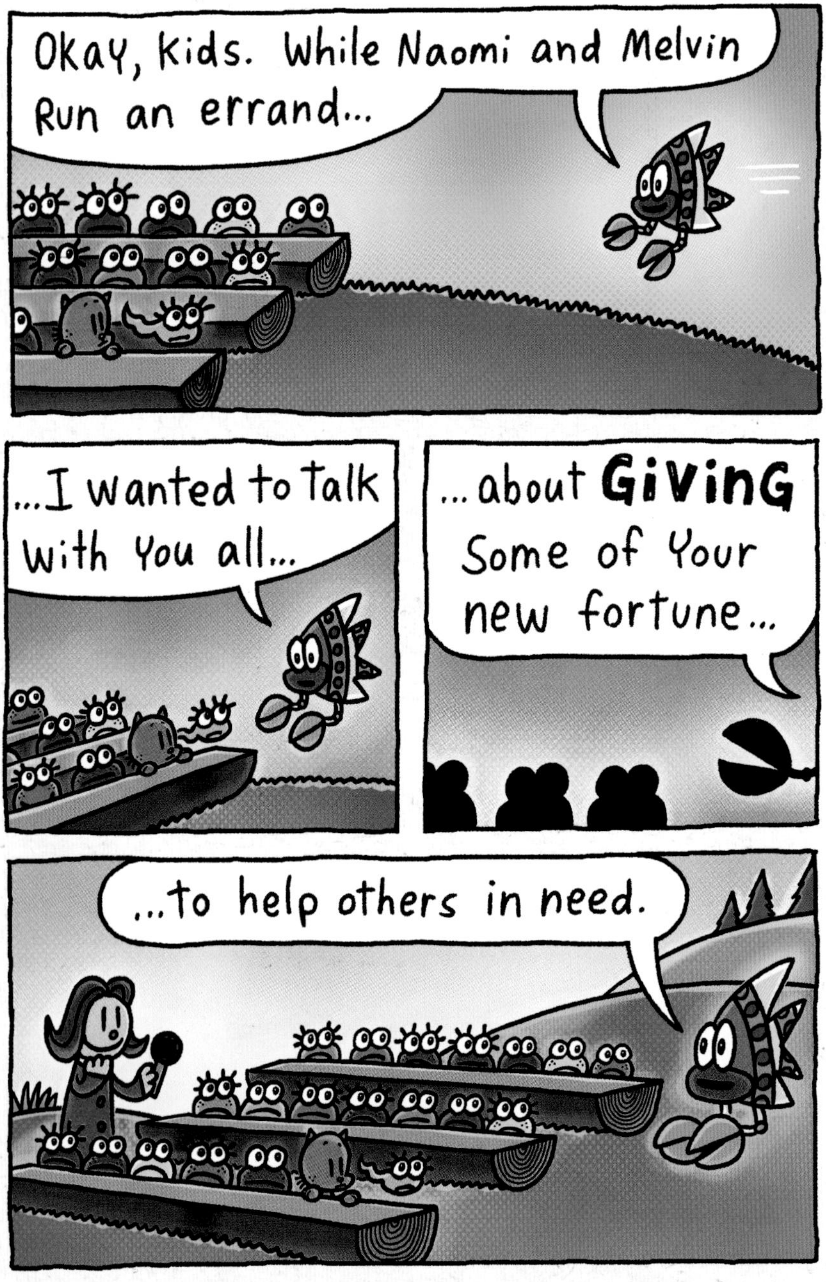
OKAY, KIDS. WHILE NAOMI AND MELVIN RUN AN ERRAND...
...I WANTED TO TALK WITH YOU ALL...
...ABOUT **GIVING** SOME OF YOUR NEW FORTUNE...
...TO HELP OTHERS IN NEED.

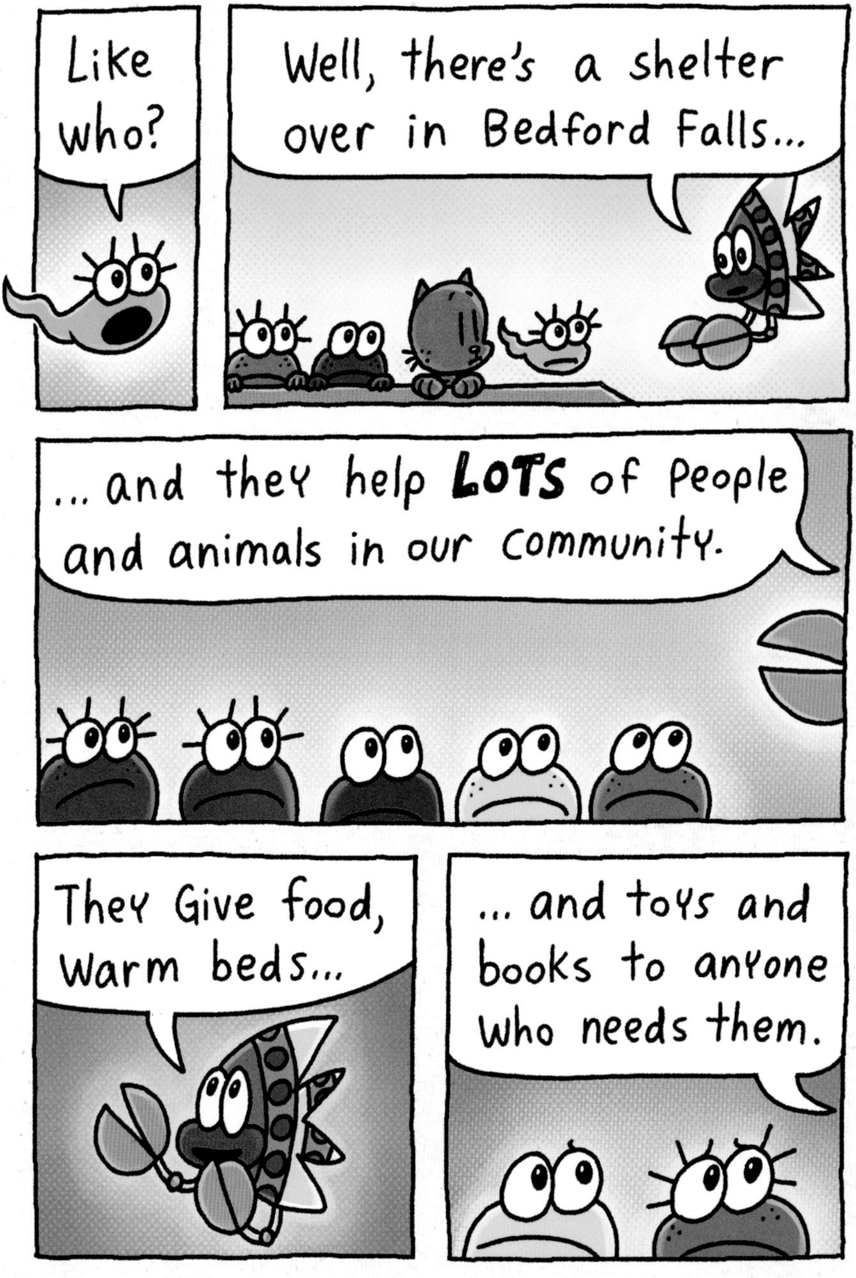
Like who?
Well, there's a shelter over in Bedford Falls...
... and they help LOTS of people and animals in our community.
They give food, warm beds...
... and toys and books to anyone who needs them.

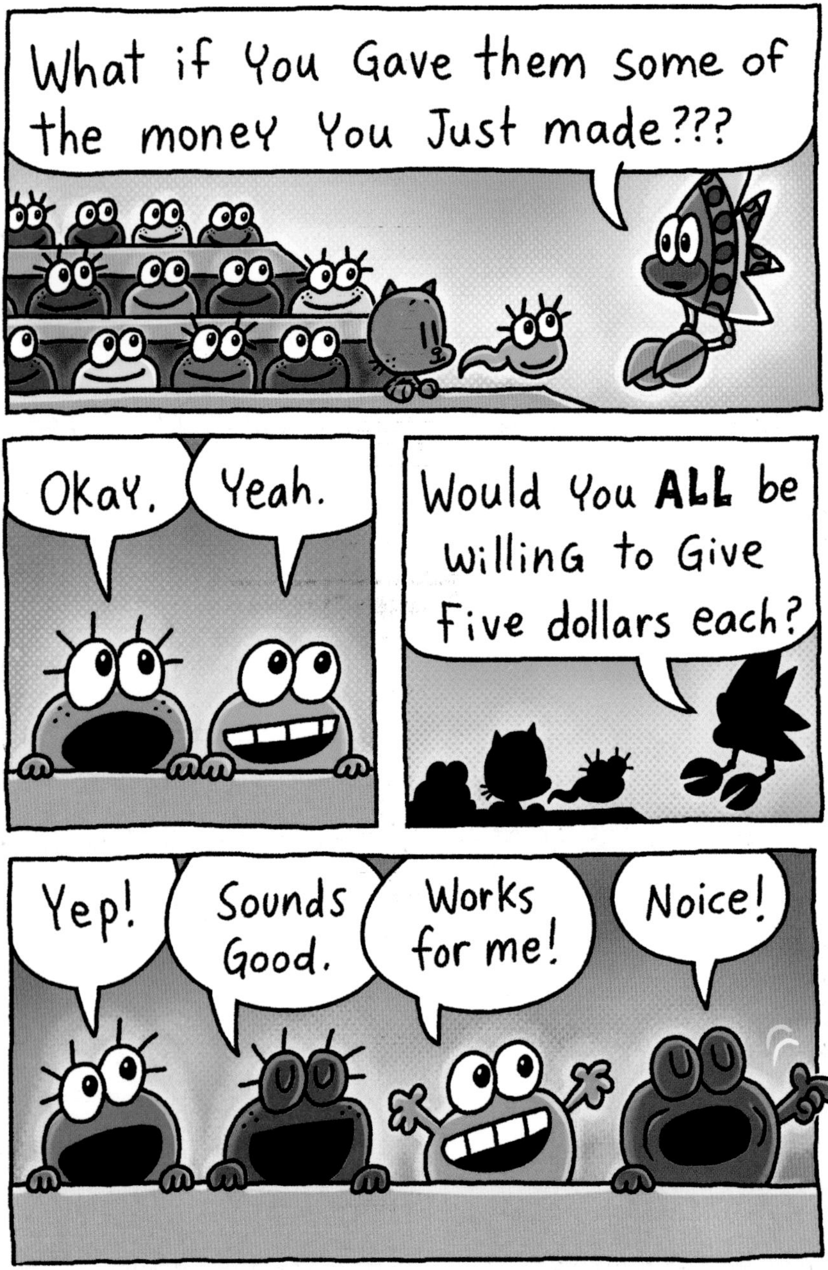
What if You Gave them some of the money You Just made???
OKay.
Yeah.
Would You **ALL** be willinG to Give Five dollars each?
Yep!
Sounds Good.
Works for me!
Noice!

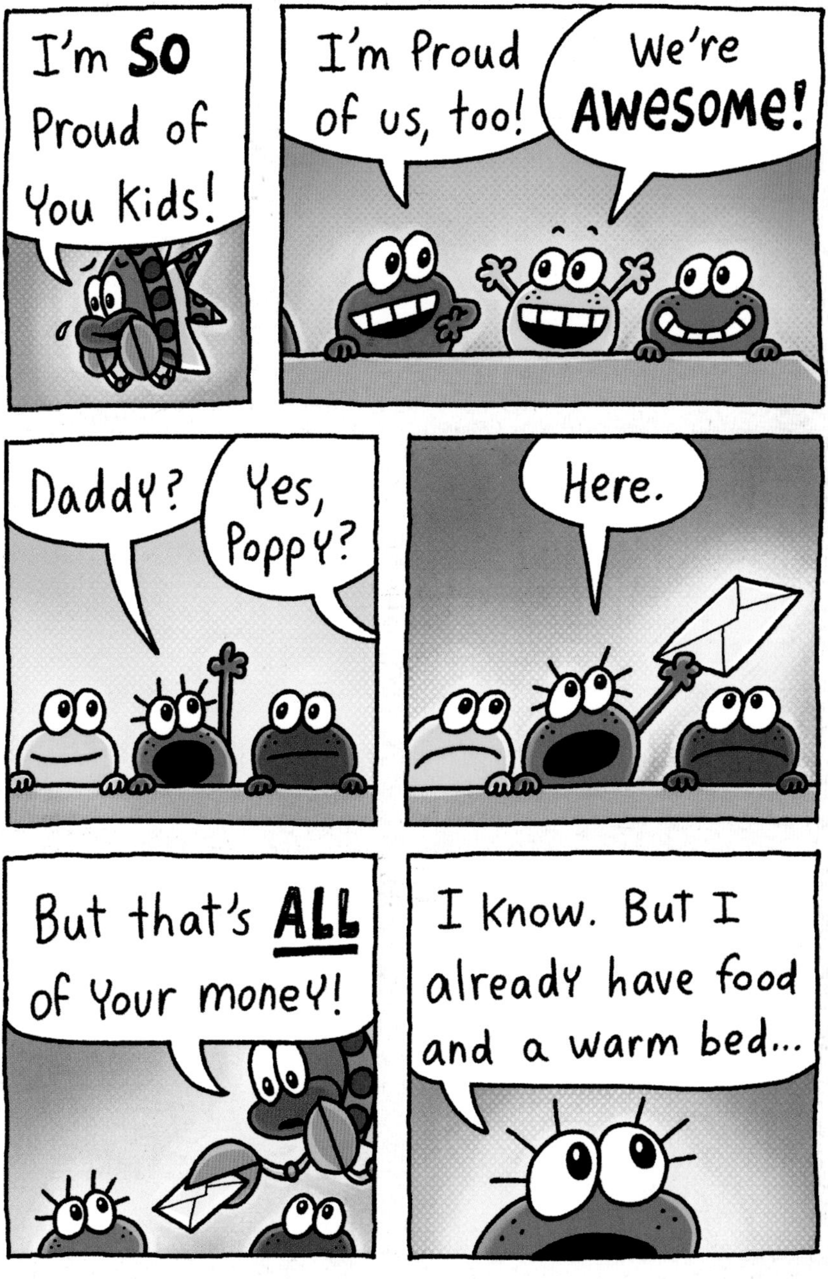
I'm **SO** Proud of You Kids!
I'm Proud of us, too!
We're **AWESOME!**
Daddy?
Yes, Poppy?
Here.
But that's **ALL** of your money!
I know. But I already have food and a warm bed...

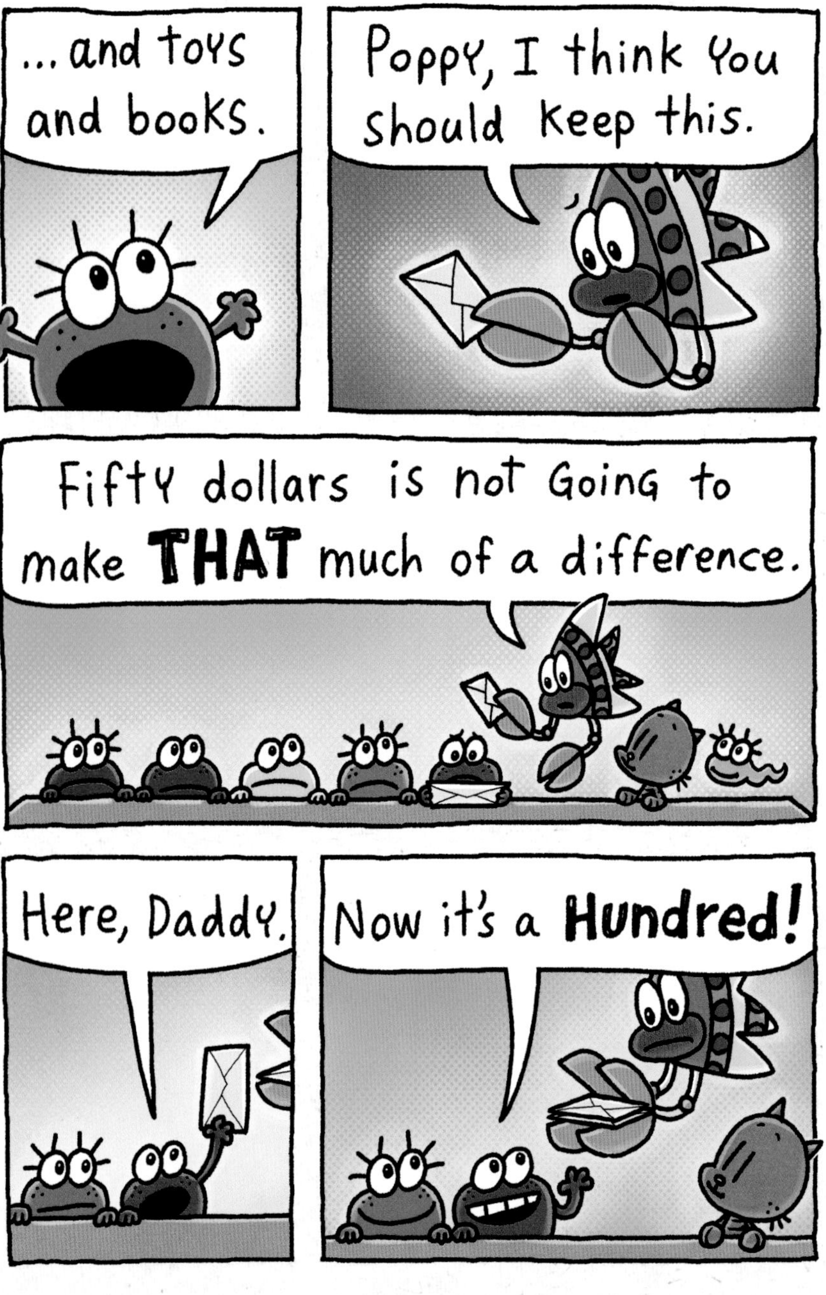
...and toys and books.
Poppy, I think you should keep this.
Fifty dollars is not going to make **THAT** much of a difference.
Here, Daddy.
Now it's a **Hundred!**

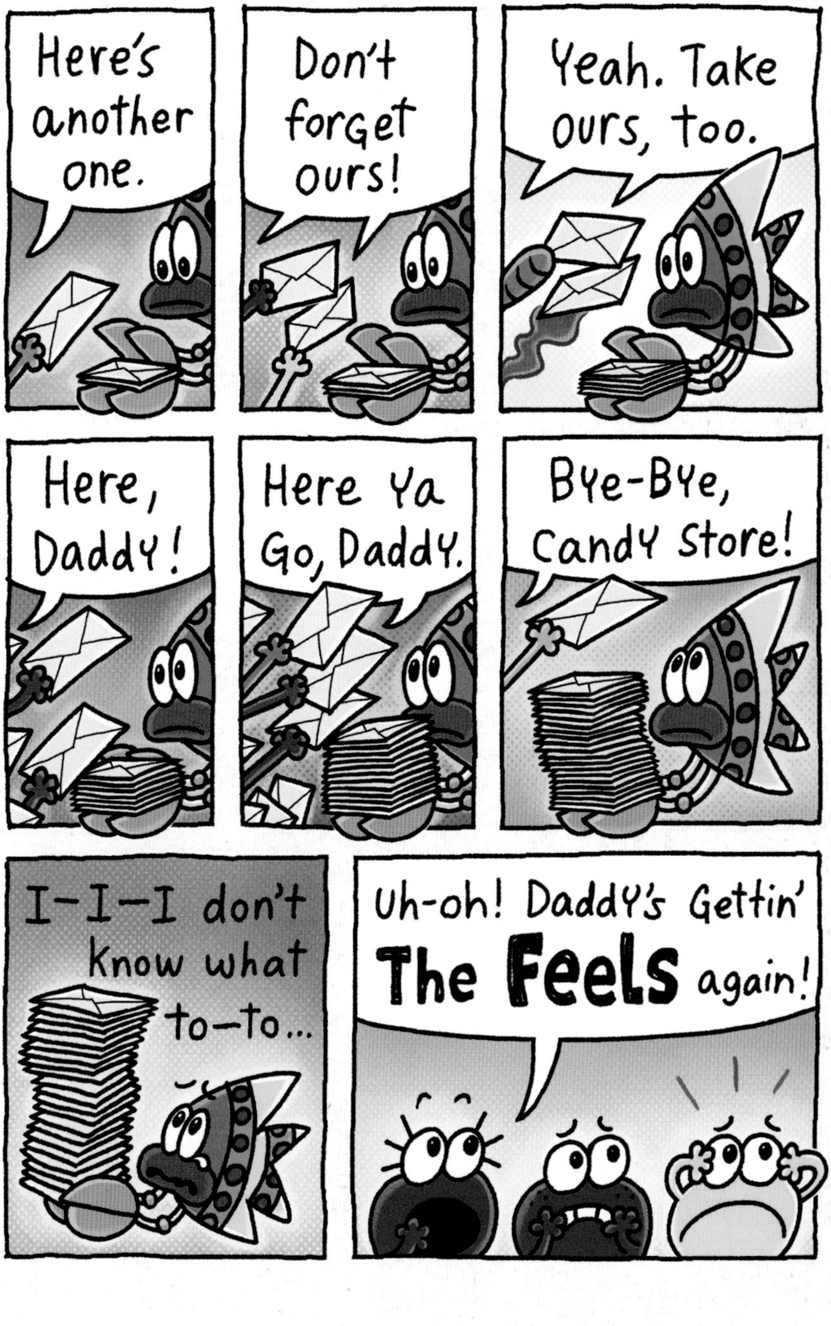
Here's another one.
Don't forget ours!
Yeah. Take ours, too.
Here, Daddy!
Here ya go, Daddy.
Bye-bye, candy store!
I-I-I don't know what to-to...
Uh-oh! Daddy's gettin' The Feels again!

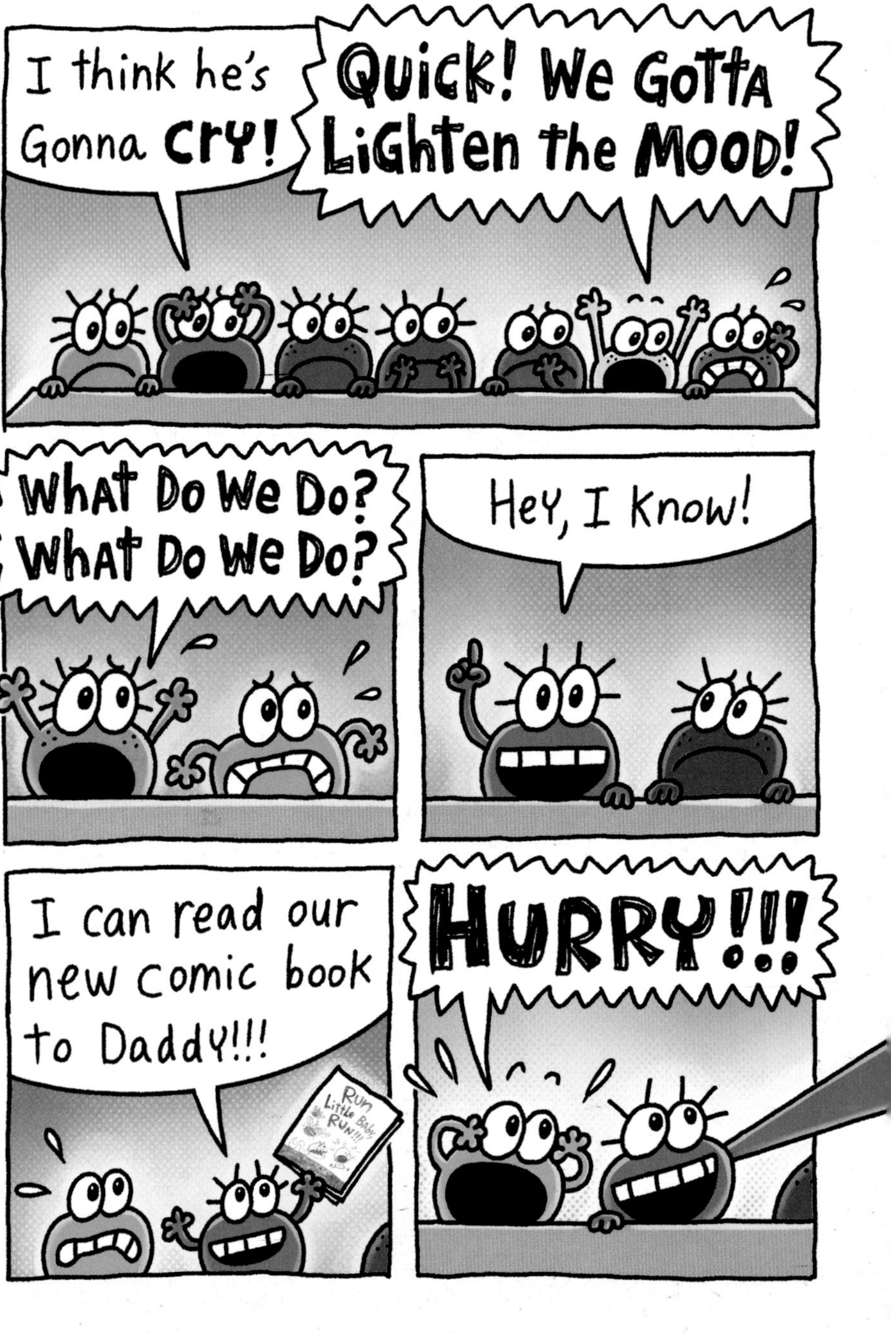
I think he's Gonna CRY!
QUICK! WE GOTTA LIGHTEN THE MOOD!
WHAT DO WE DO? WHAT DO WE DO?
Hey, I know!
I can read our new comic book to Daddy!!!
RUN Little Baby RUN!!!
HURRY!!!

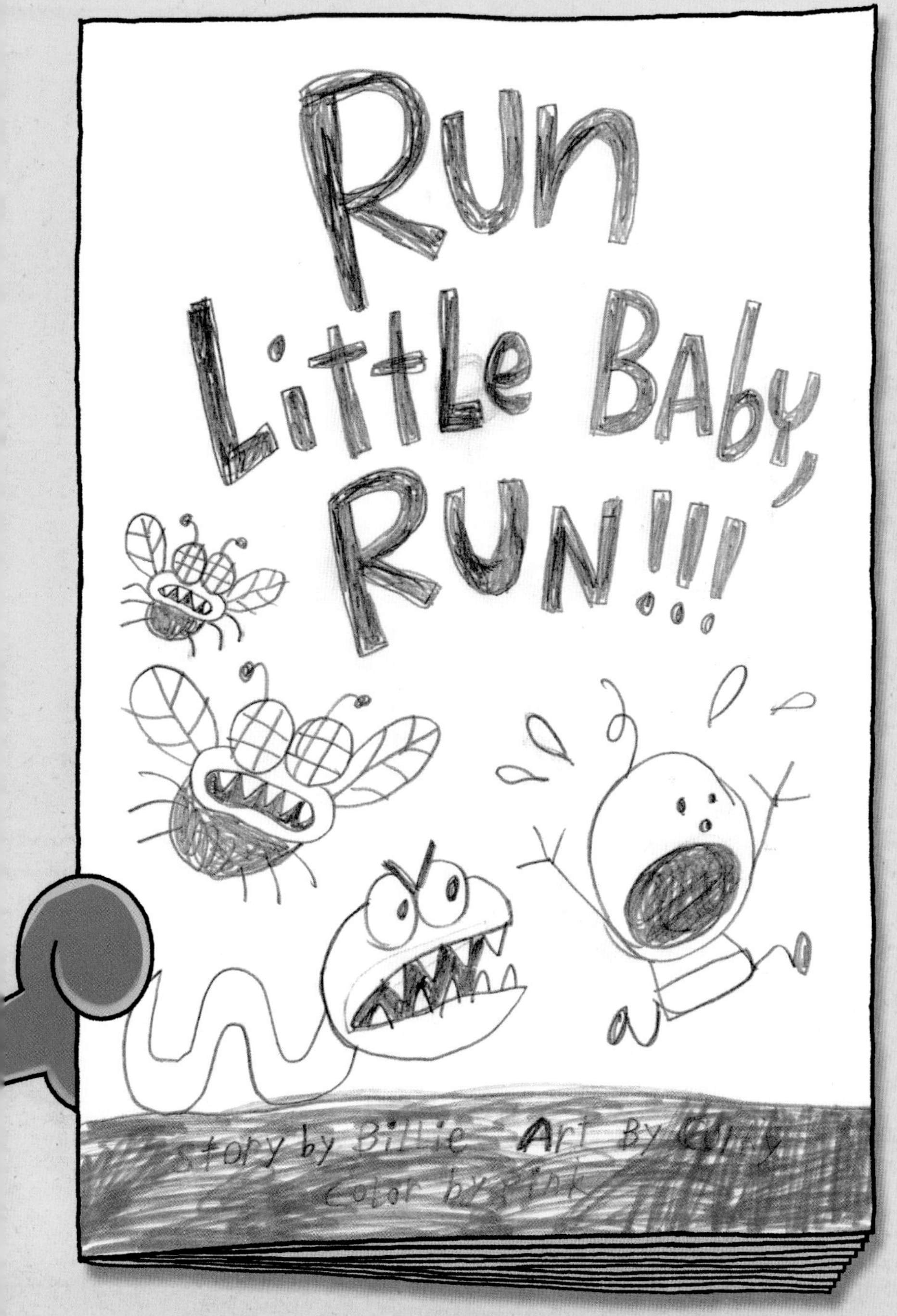
Run Little Baby, RUN!!!
story by Billie Art By
color by pink

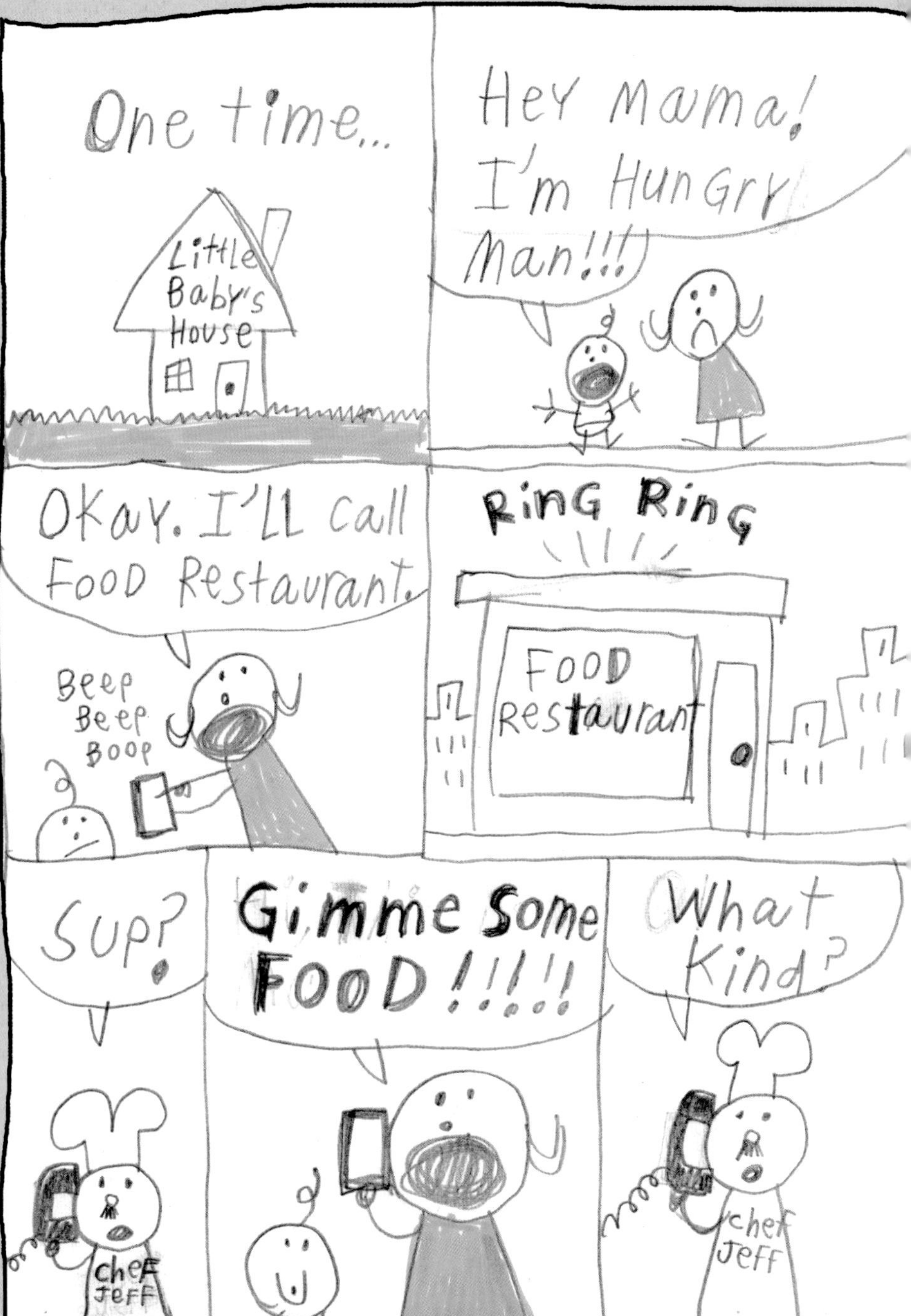
One time...
Little Baby's House
Hey Mama! I'm Hungry Man!!!
Okay. I'LL call Food Restaurant.
Beep Beep Boop
RinG Ring
FOOD Restaurant
Sup?
Gimme Some FOOD!!!!!
What Kind?
Chef Jeff
Chef Jeff

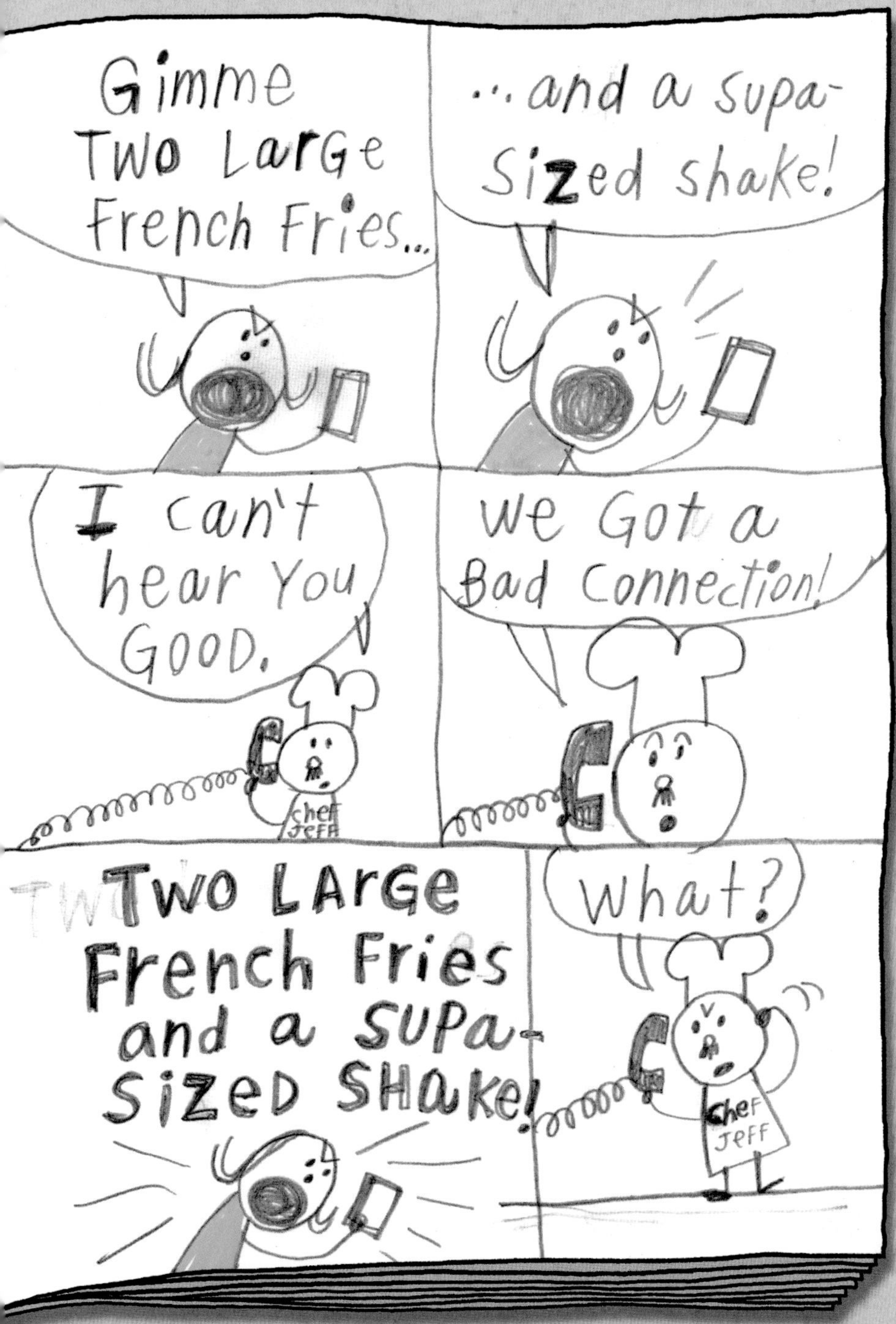
Gimme Two Large French Fries...
...and a supa-Sized shake!
I can't hear You GOOD.
We Got a Bad Connection!
TWO LARGE French Fries and a SUPA-SIZED SHAKE!
What?
Chef Jeff
Chef Jeff

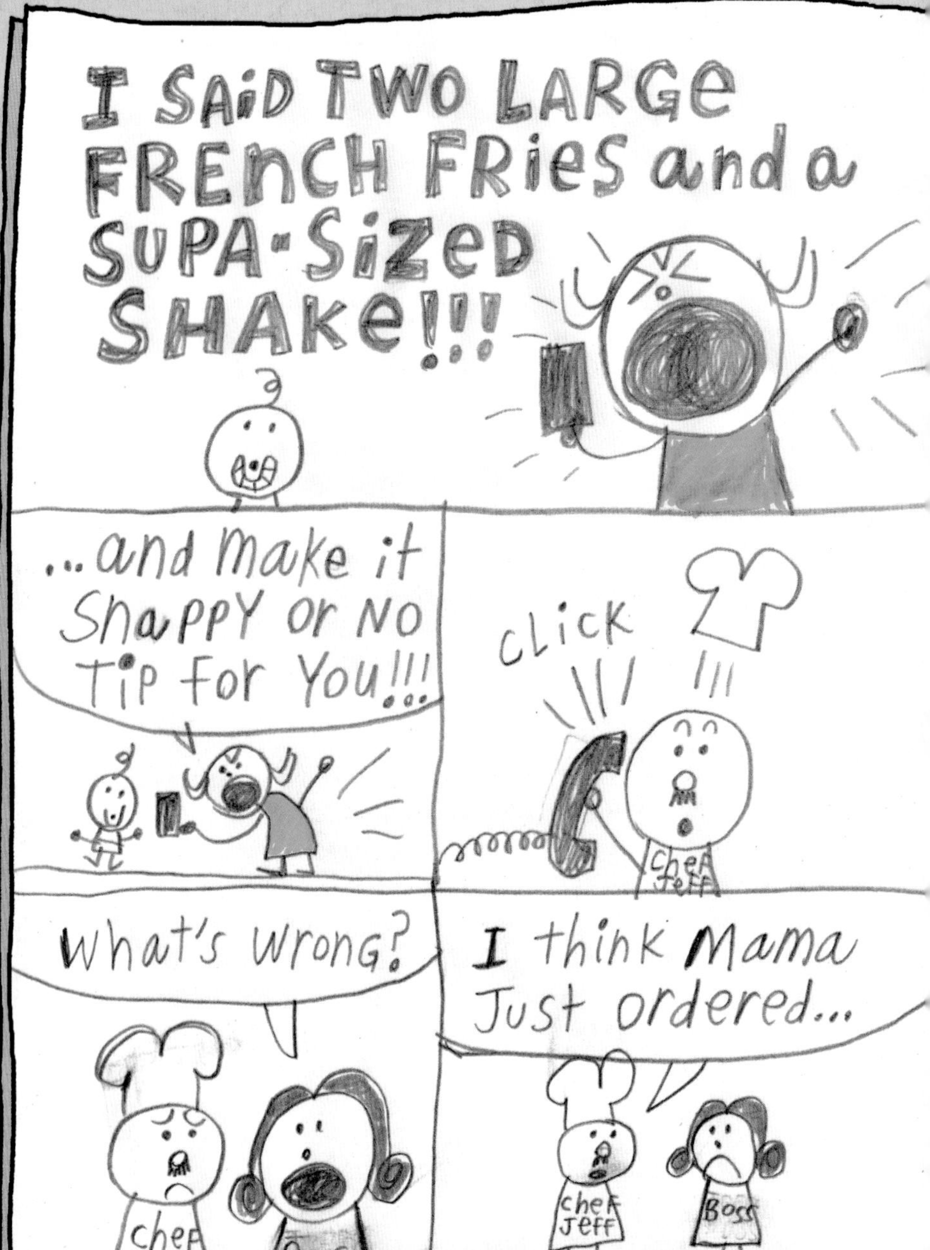
I SAID TWO LARGE FRENCH FRIES and a SUPA-SIZED SHAKE!!!
...and make it snappy or no tip for you!!!
CLICK
CHEF JEFF
What's wrong?
CHEF JEFF
BOSS
I think Mama just ordered...
CHEF JEFF
BOSS

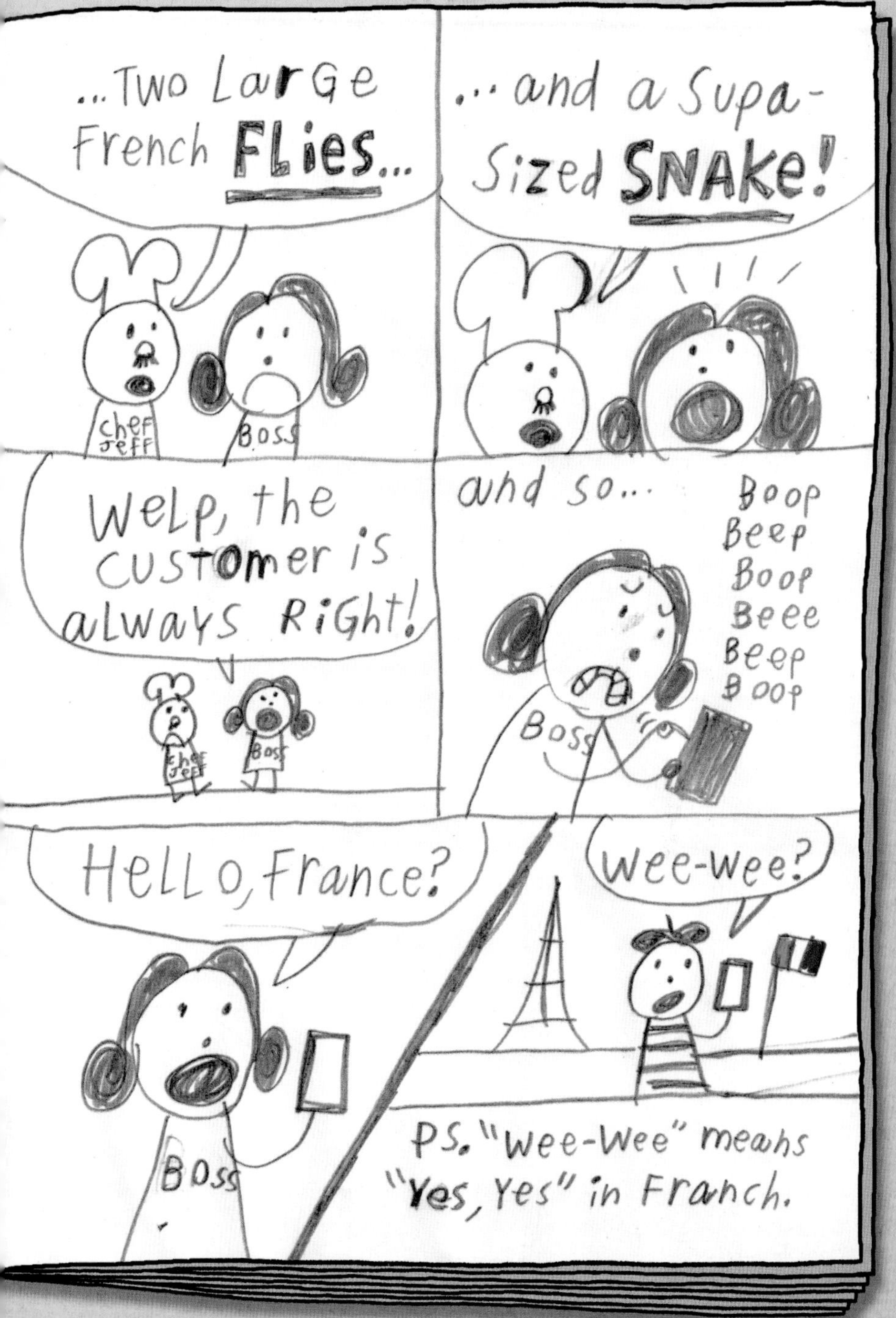
...Two Large French Flies...
...and a Supa-Sized SNAKE!
Chef Jeff
Boss
Welp, the customer is always Right!
Chef Jeff
Boss
and so...
Boop Beep Boop Beee Beep Boop
Boss
Hello, France?
Boss
Wee-Wee?
P.S. "Wee-Wee" means "Yes, Yes" in Franch.

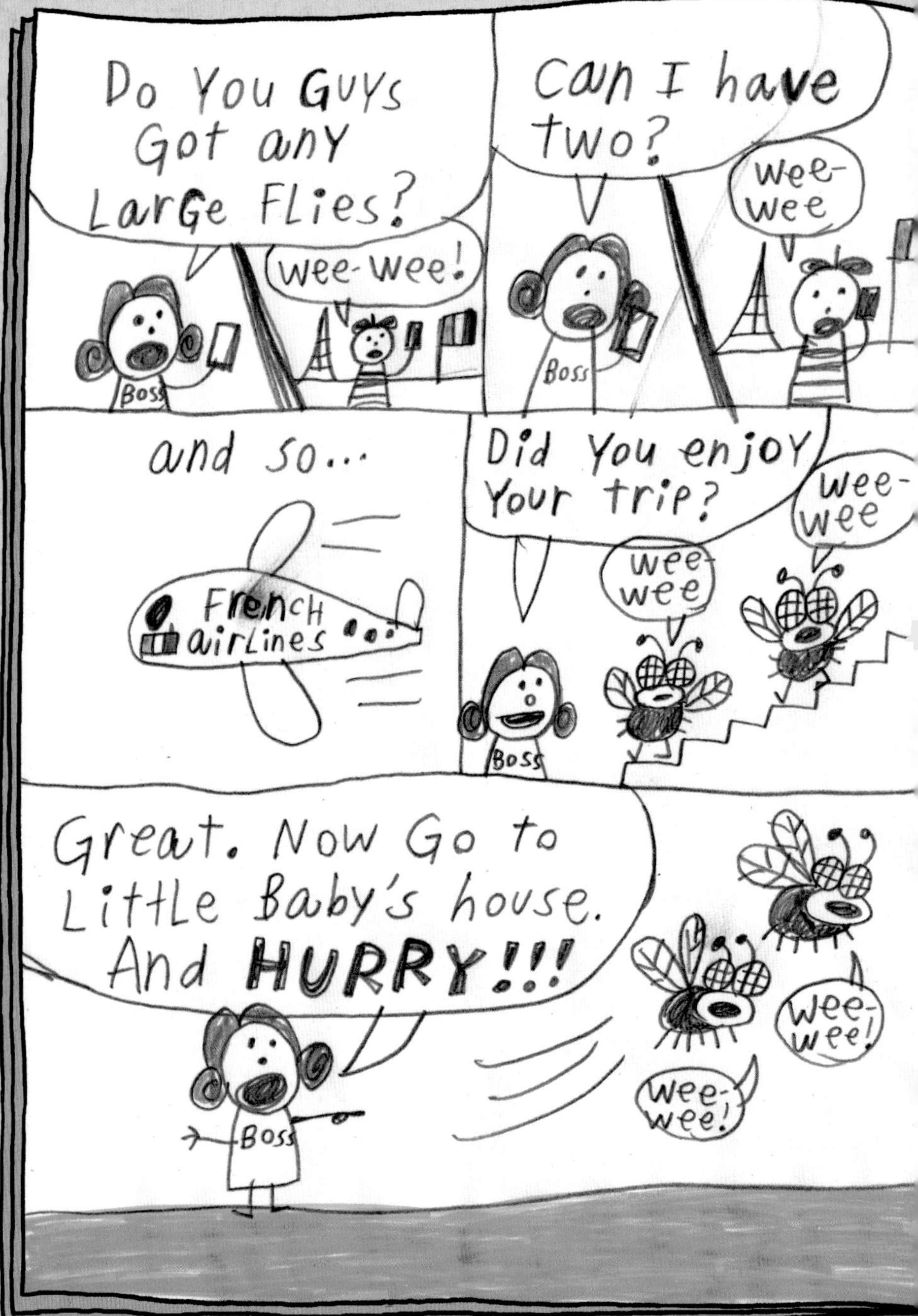
Do You Guys Got any Large Flies?
wee-wee!
Can I have two?
wee-wee
and so...
French airLines
Did You enjoy Your trip?
wee-wee
wee-wee
Boss
Great. Now Go to Little Baby's house. And HURRY!!!
wee-wee!
wee-wee!

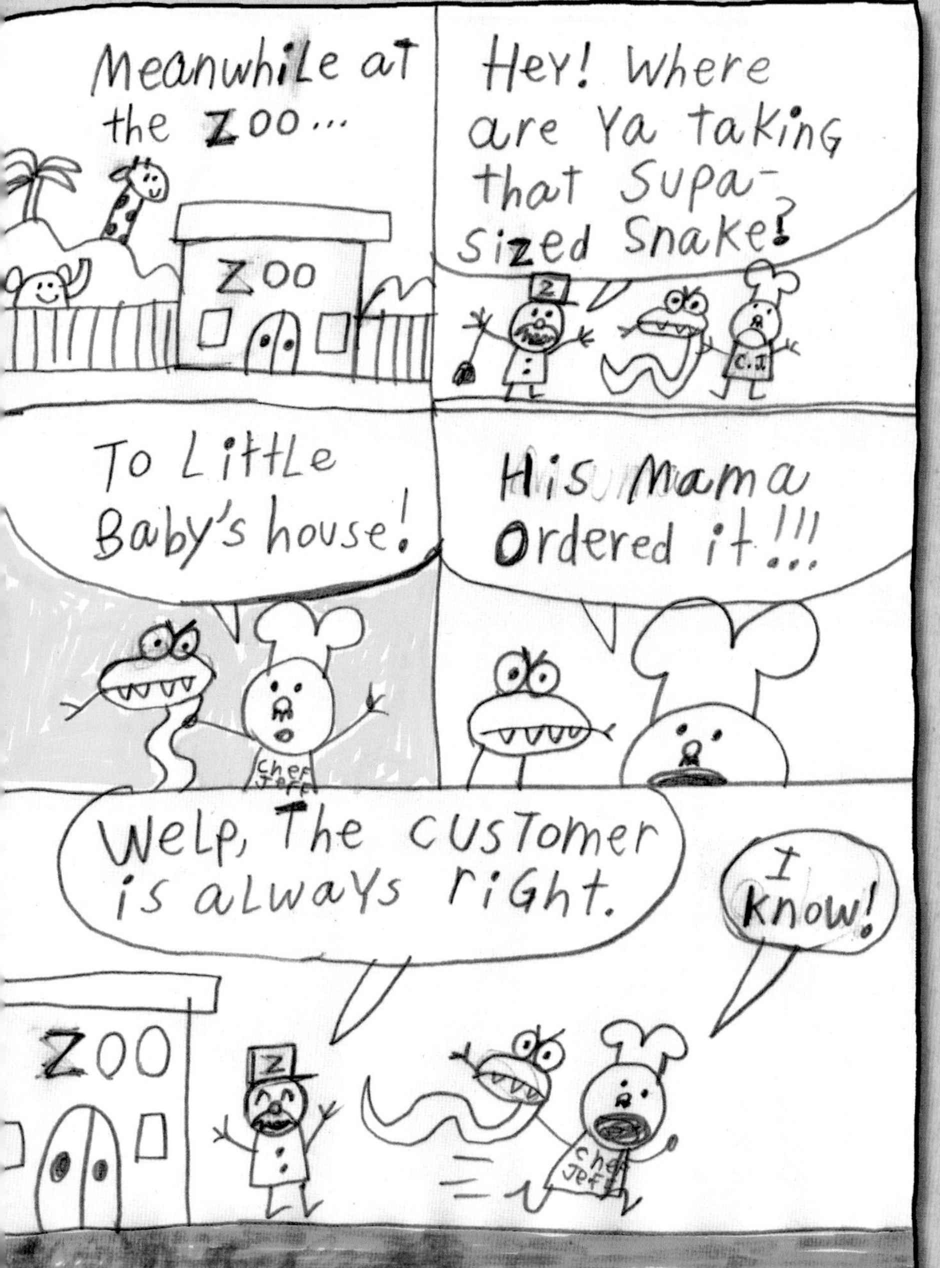
Meanwhile at the Zoo...
ZOO
Hey! Where are ya taking that Supa-sized Snake?
Z
C.J
To Little Baby's house!
His Mama Ordered it!!!
Chef Jeff
Welp, The customer is always right.
I know!
ZOO
Z
Chef Jeff

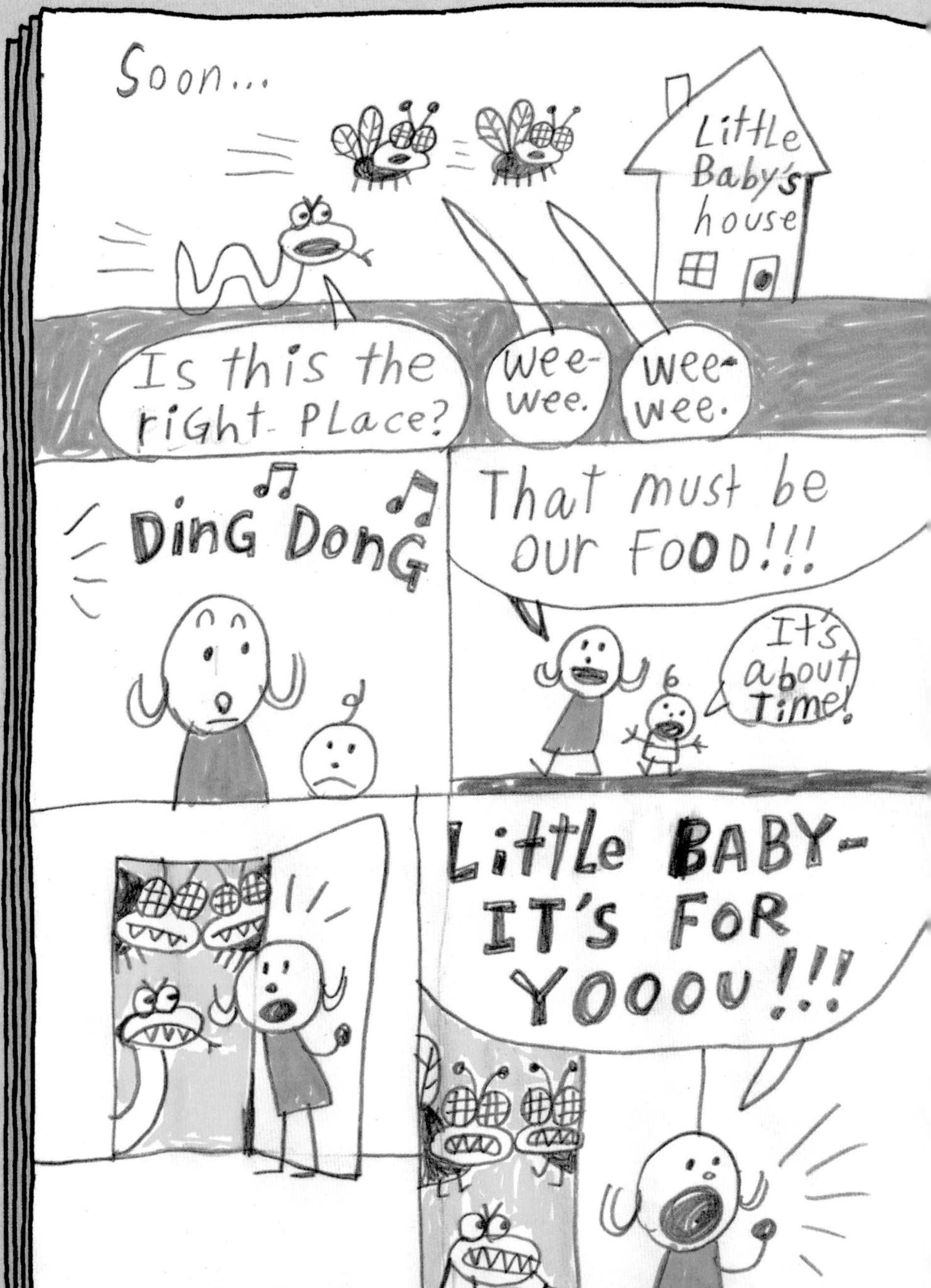
Soon...
Little Baby's house
Is this the right Place?
wee-wee.
wee-wee.
DING DONG
That must be our FOOD!!!
It's about Time!
Little BABY-IT'S FOR YOOOU!!!

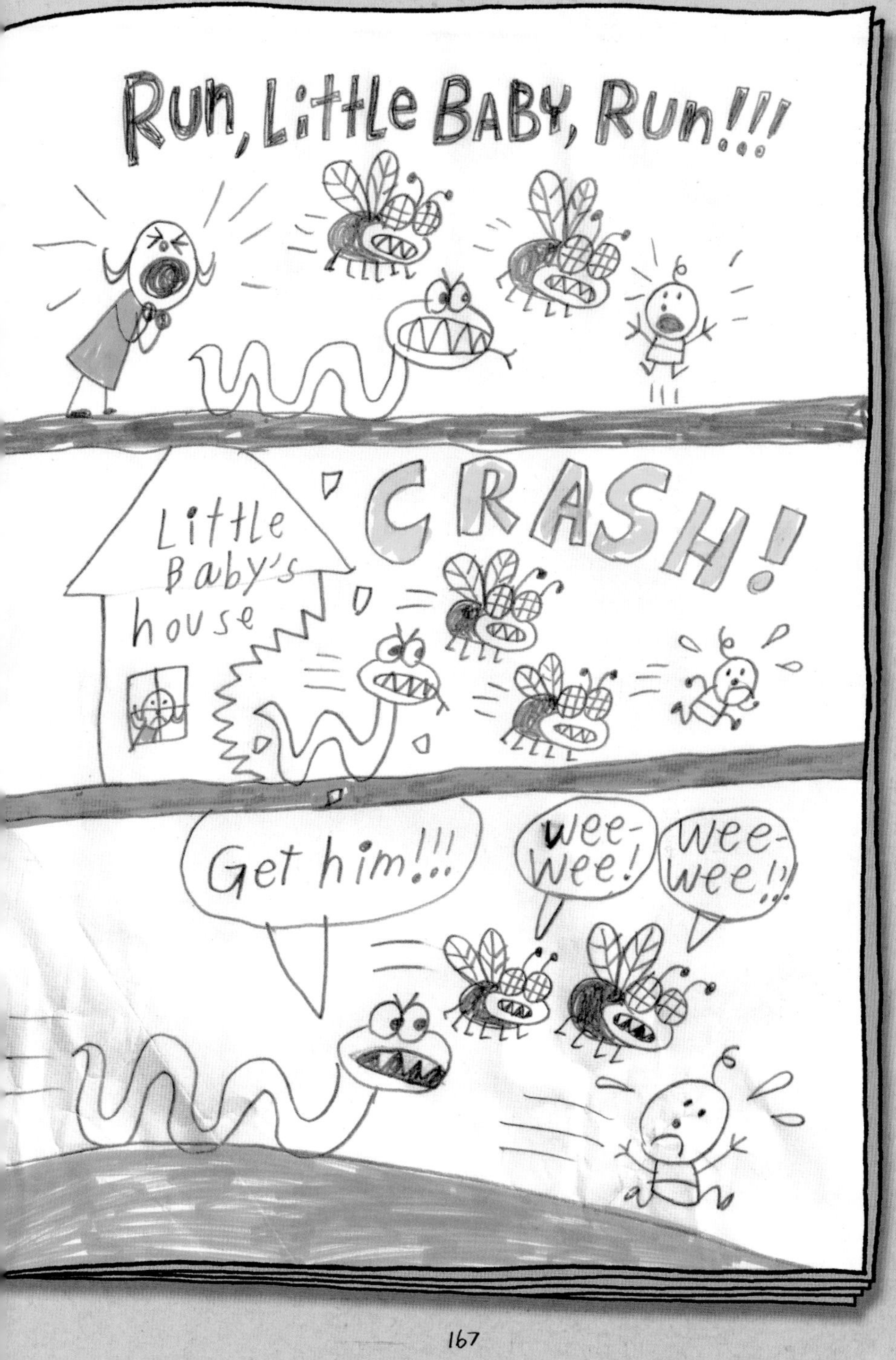
Run, Little Baby, Run!!!
Little Baby's house
CRASH!
Get him!!!
wee-wee!
wee-wee!!!

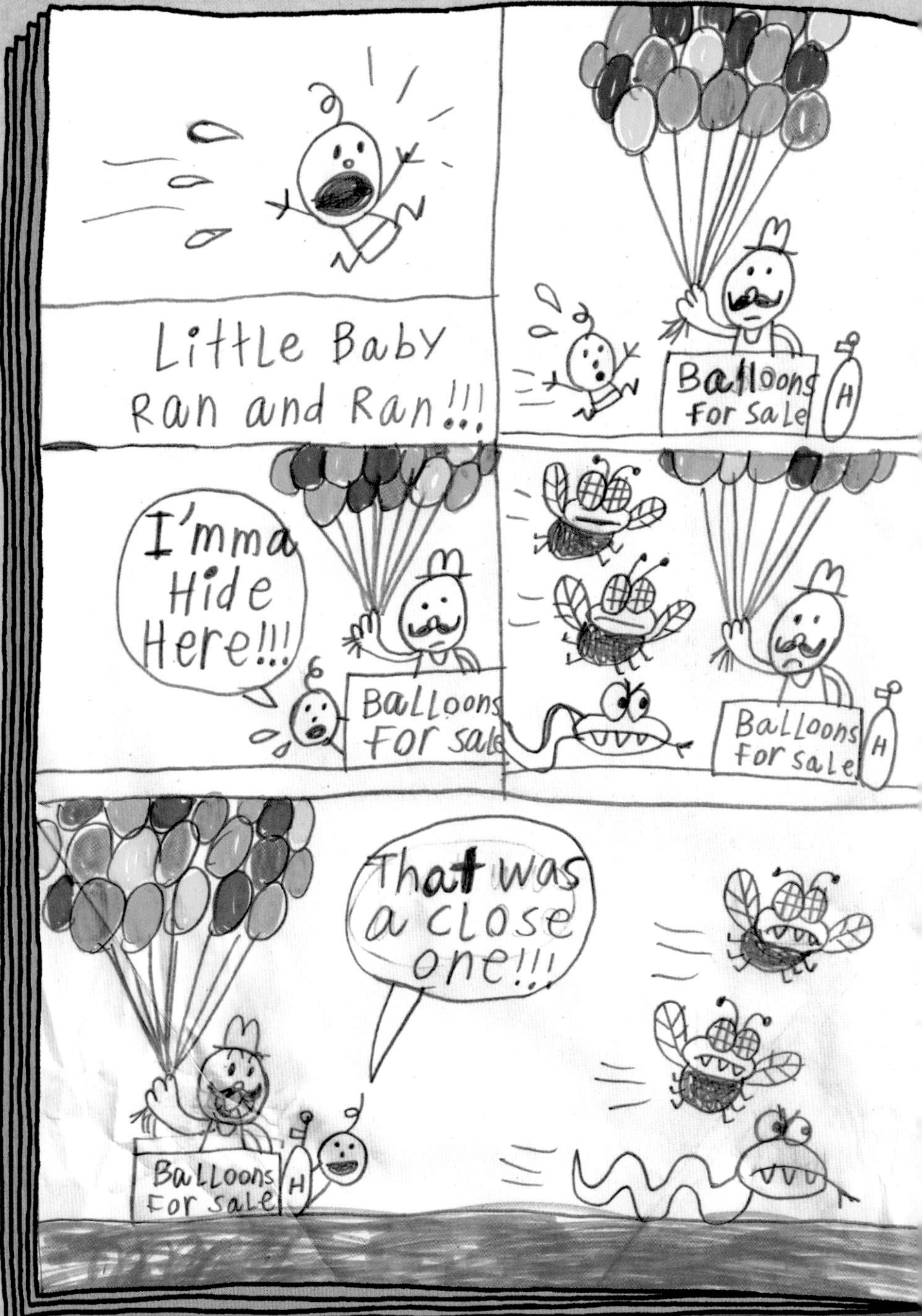
Little Baby
Ran and Ran!!!
Balloons For Sale
H
I'mma Hide Here!!!
Balloons For sale
Balloons For sale
H
That was a close one!!!
Balloons For sale
H

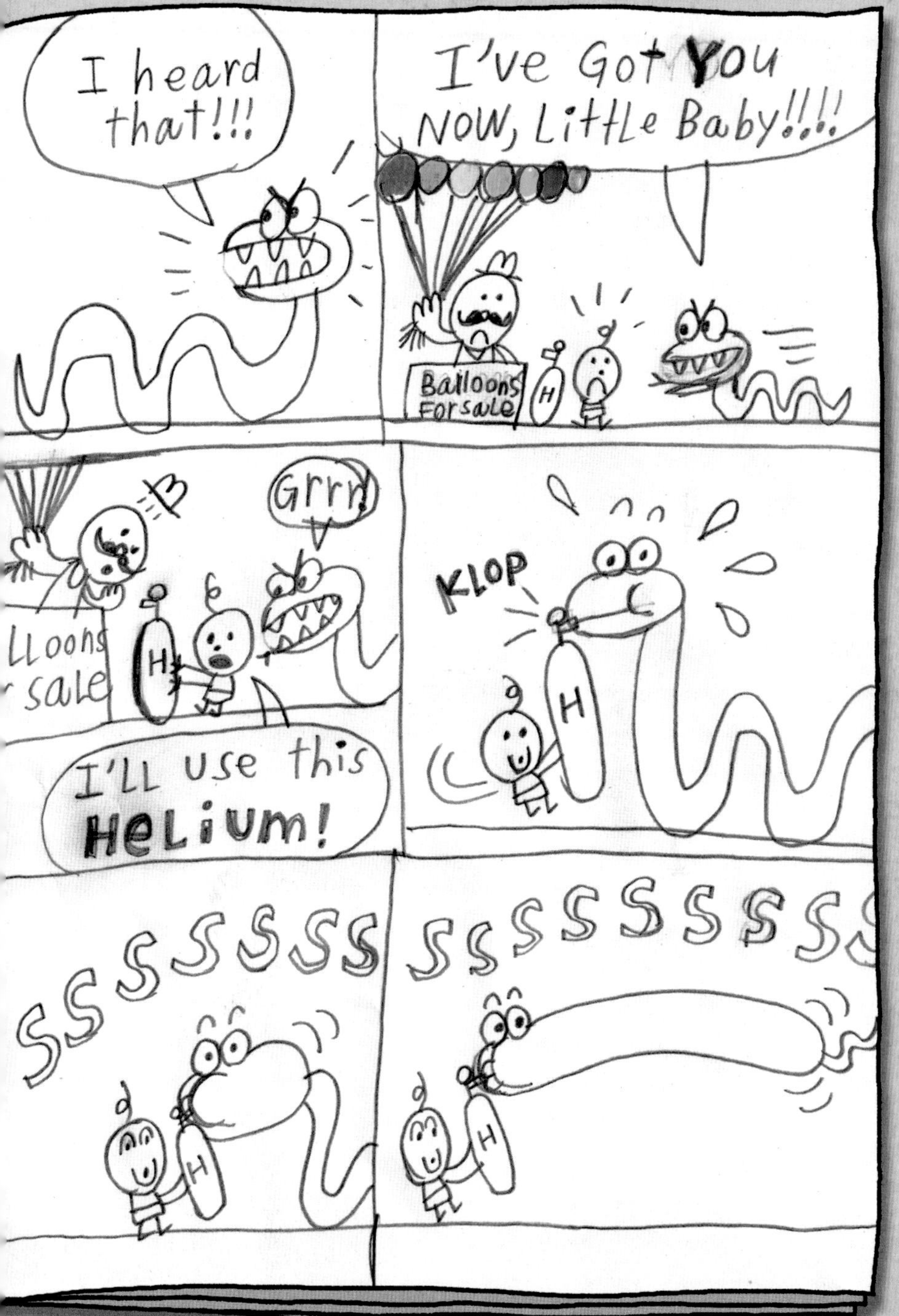
I heard that!!!
I've Got YOU NOW, Little Baby!!!!
Balloons For sale
H
B
Grrr!
I'll use this HELIUM!
KLOP
SSSSSSSS
SSSSSSSSSS

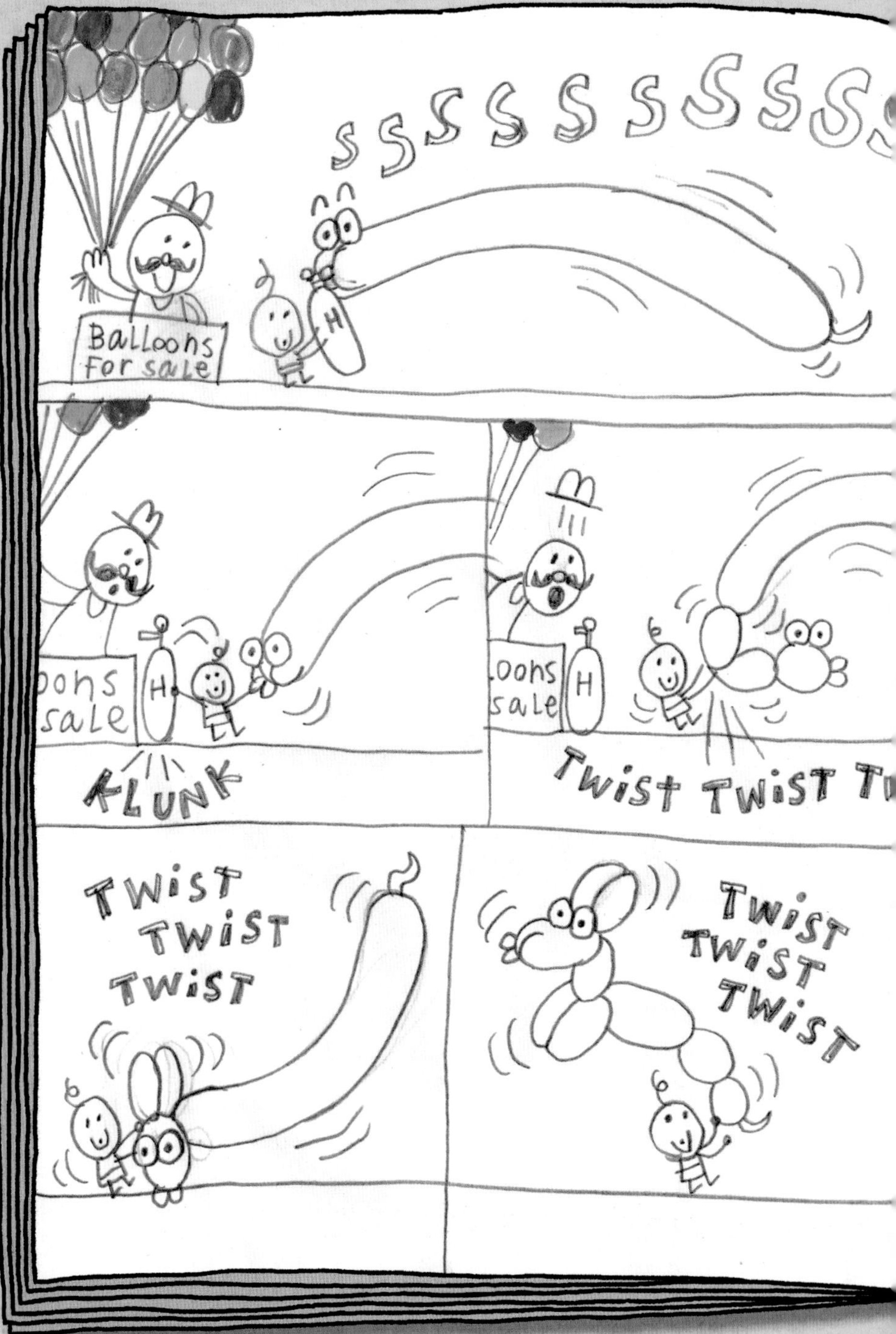
Balloons For sale
SSSSSSSSSSS
H
oons sale
H
KLUNK
oons sale
H
TWIST TWIST TW
TWIST TWIST TWIST
TWIST TWIST TWIST

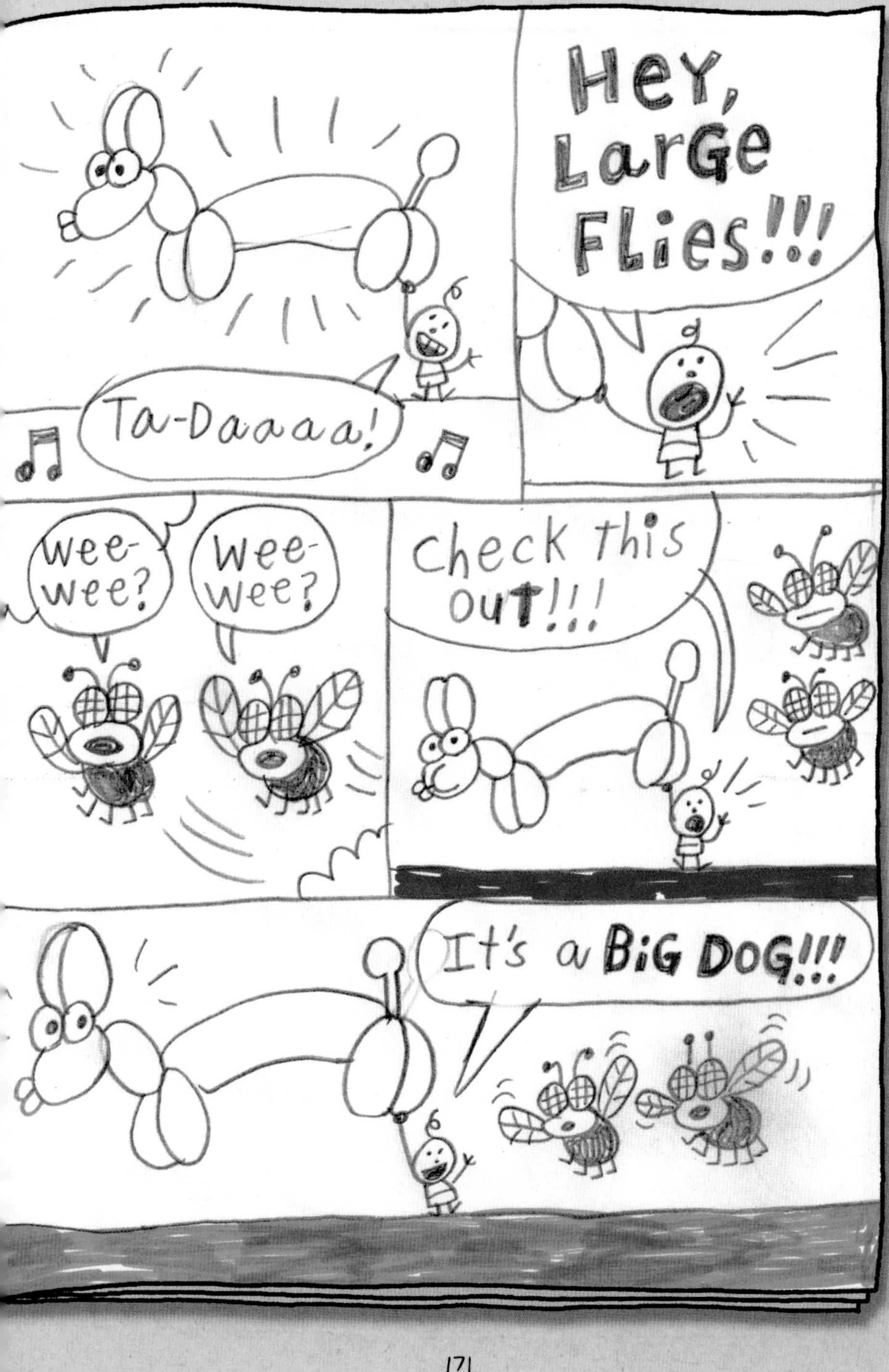
Ta-Daaaa!
Hey, Large Flies!!!
Wee-wee?
Wee-wee?
Check this out!!!
It's a BIG DOG!!!

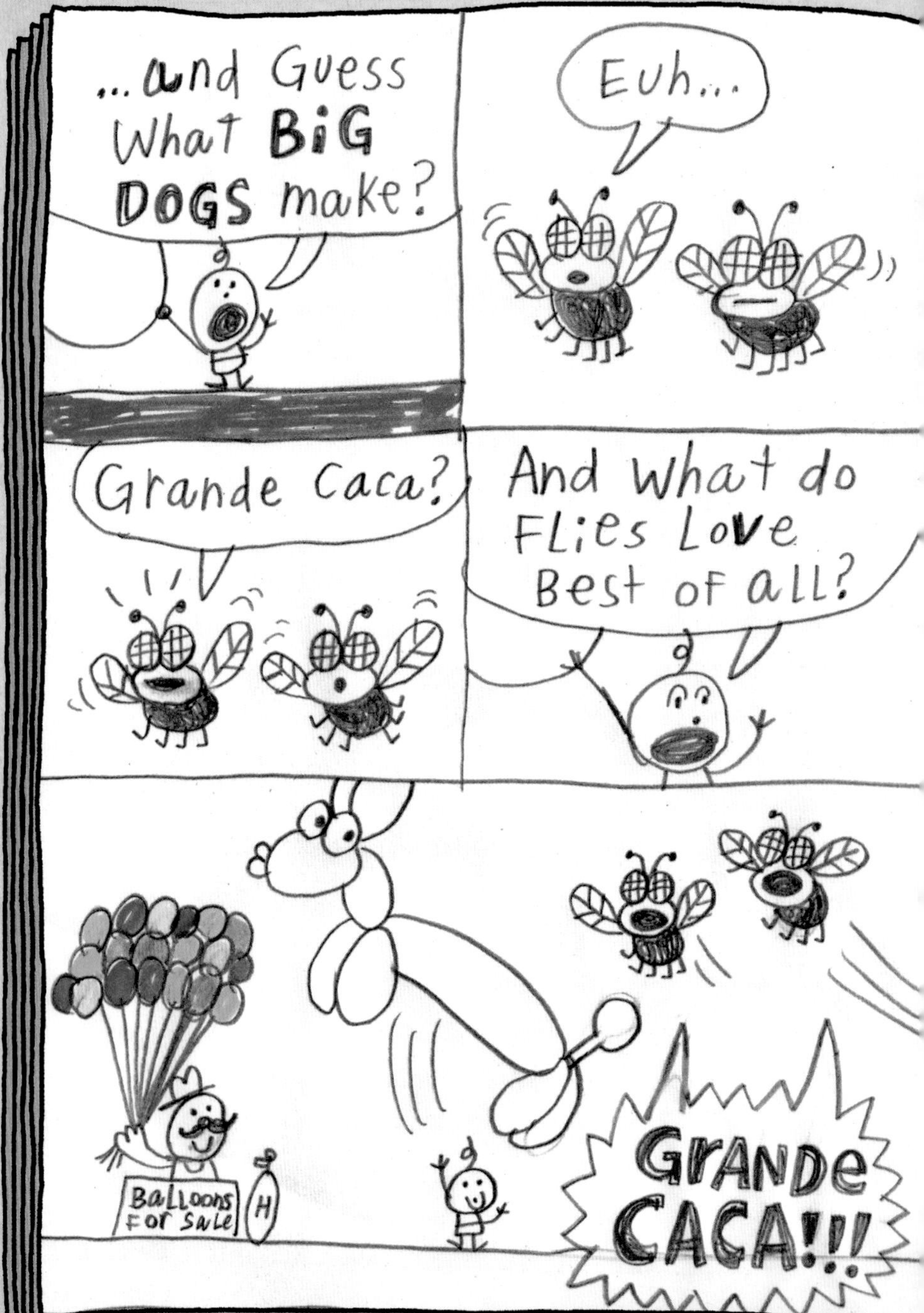
...and Guess What BiG DOGS make?
Euh...
Grande Caca?
And What do FLies Love Best of all?
Balloons For Sale
H
GRANDE CACA!!!

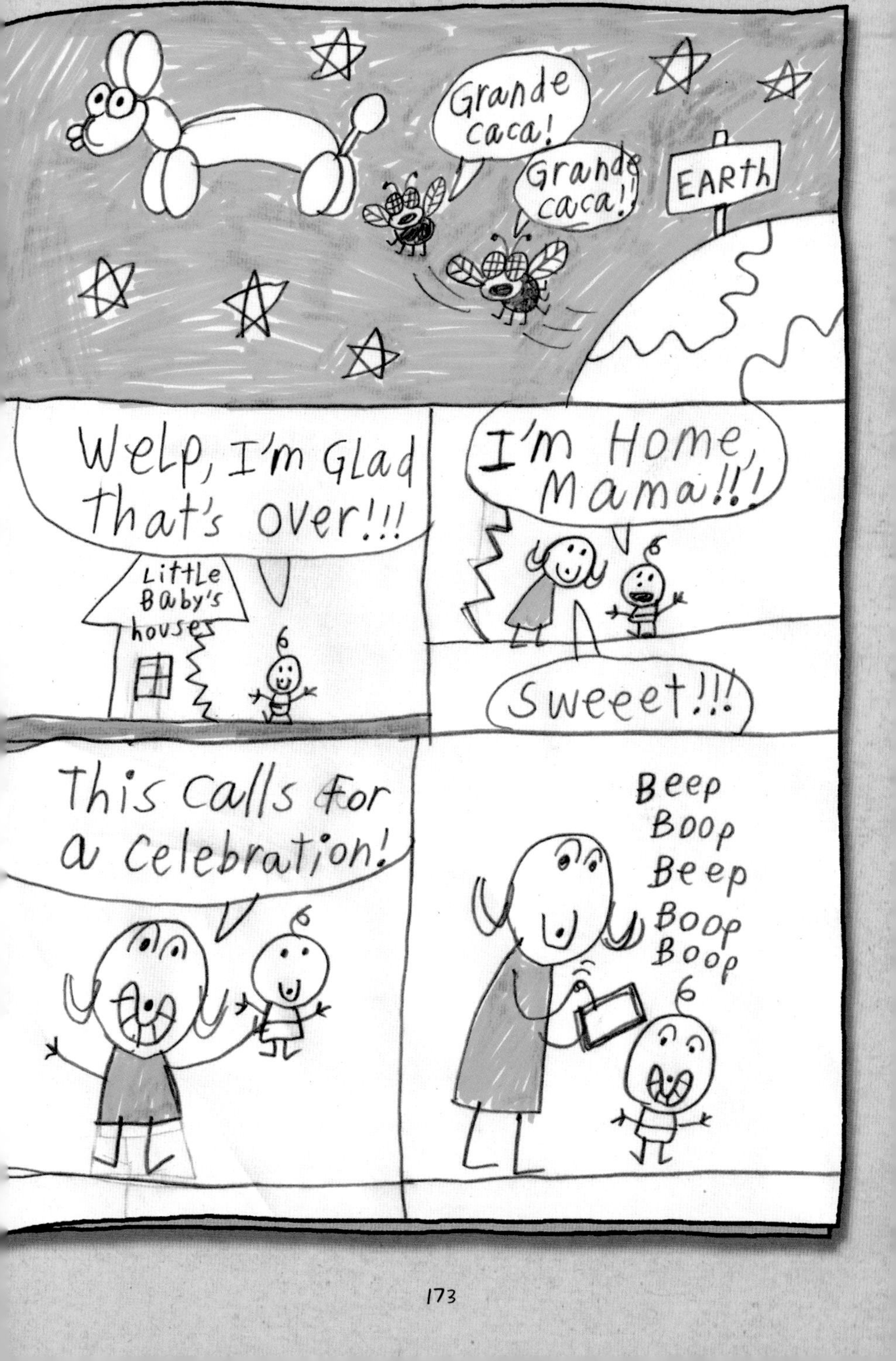
Grande caca!
Grande caca!!
EARTH
Welp, I'm Glad that's over!!!
Little Baby's house
I'm Home, Mama!!!
Sweeet!!!
This calls for a celebration!
Beep Boop Beep Boop Boop

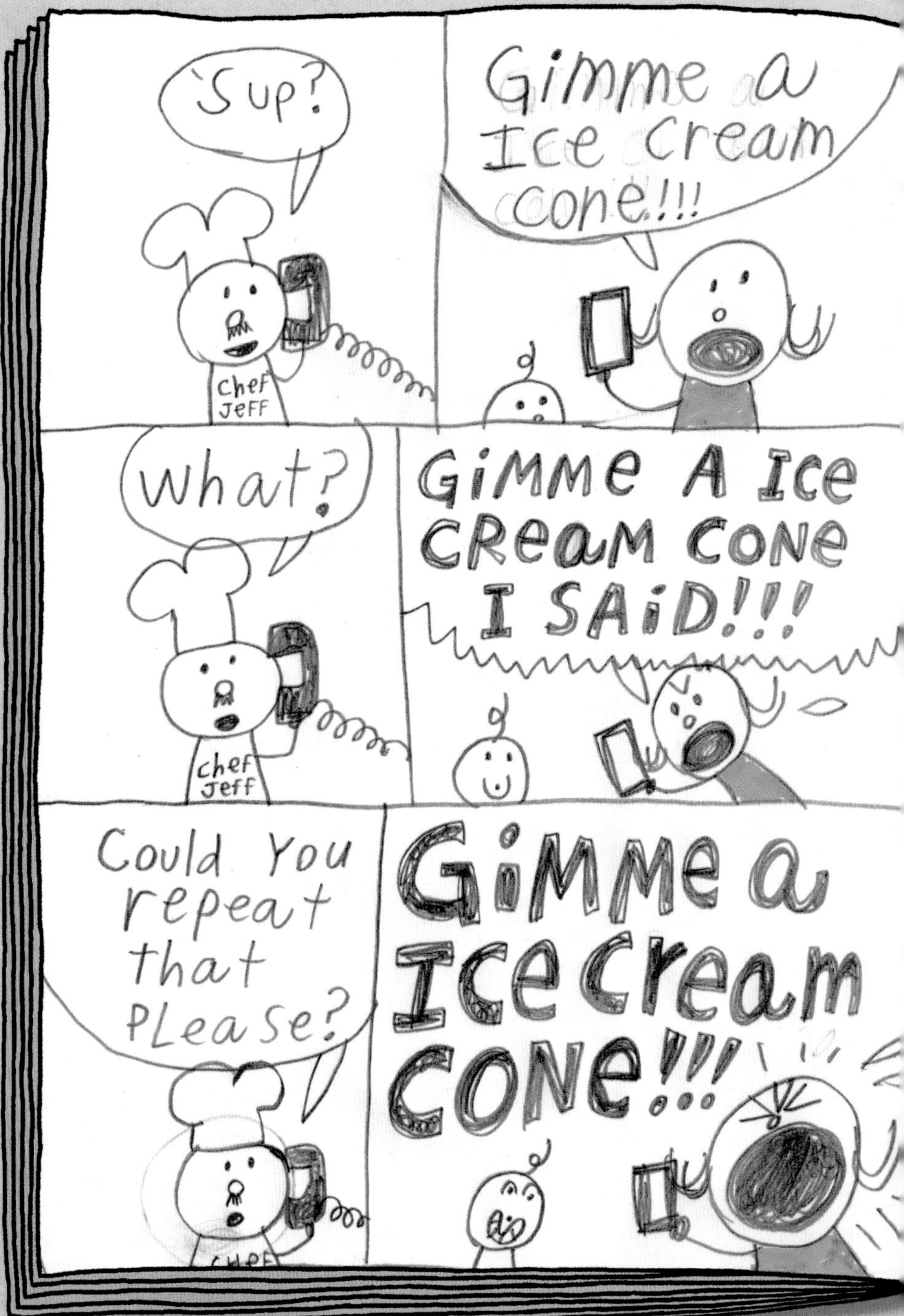
'Sup?
Gimme a Ice cream cone!!!
chef Jeff
What?
GiMMe A Ice CReaM CONe I SAiD!!!
chef Jeff
Could You repeat that PLease?
GiMMe a IceCream CONe!!!

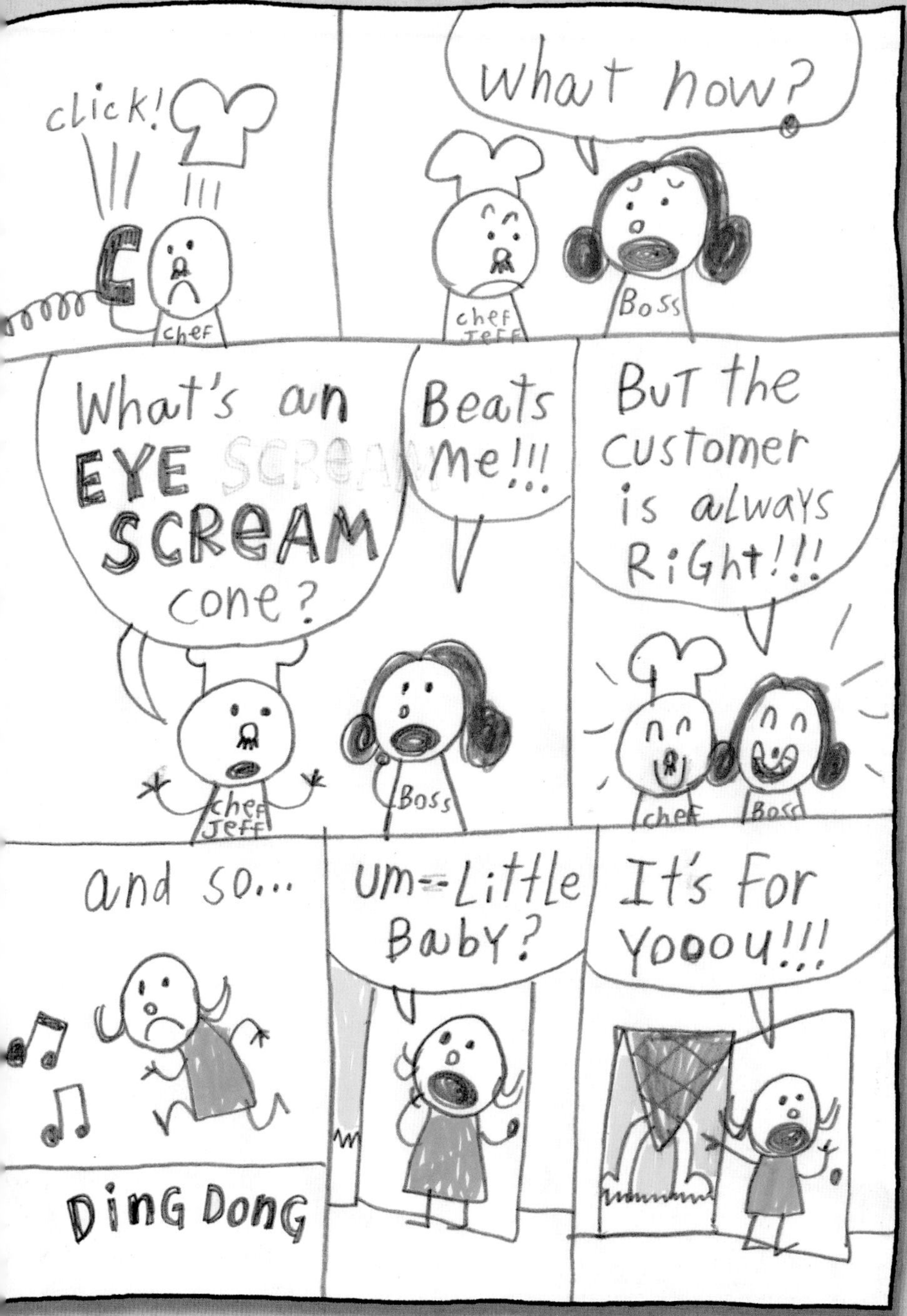
click!
chef
what now?
chef Jeff
Boss
What's an EYE SCREAM cone?
chef Jeff
Beats me!!!
Boss
But the customer is always Right!!!
chef
Boss
and so...
DinG DonG
um--Little Baby?
It's For Yooou!!!

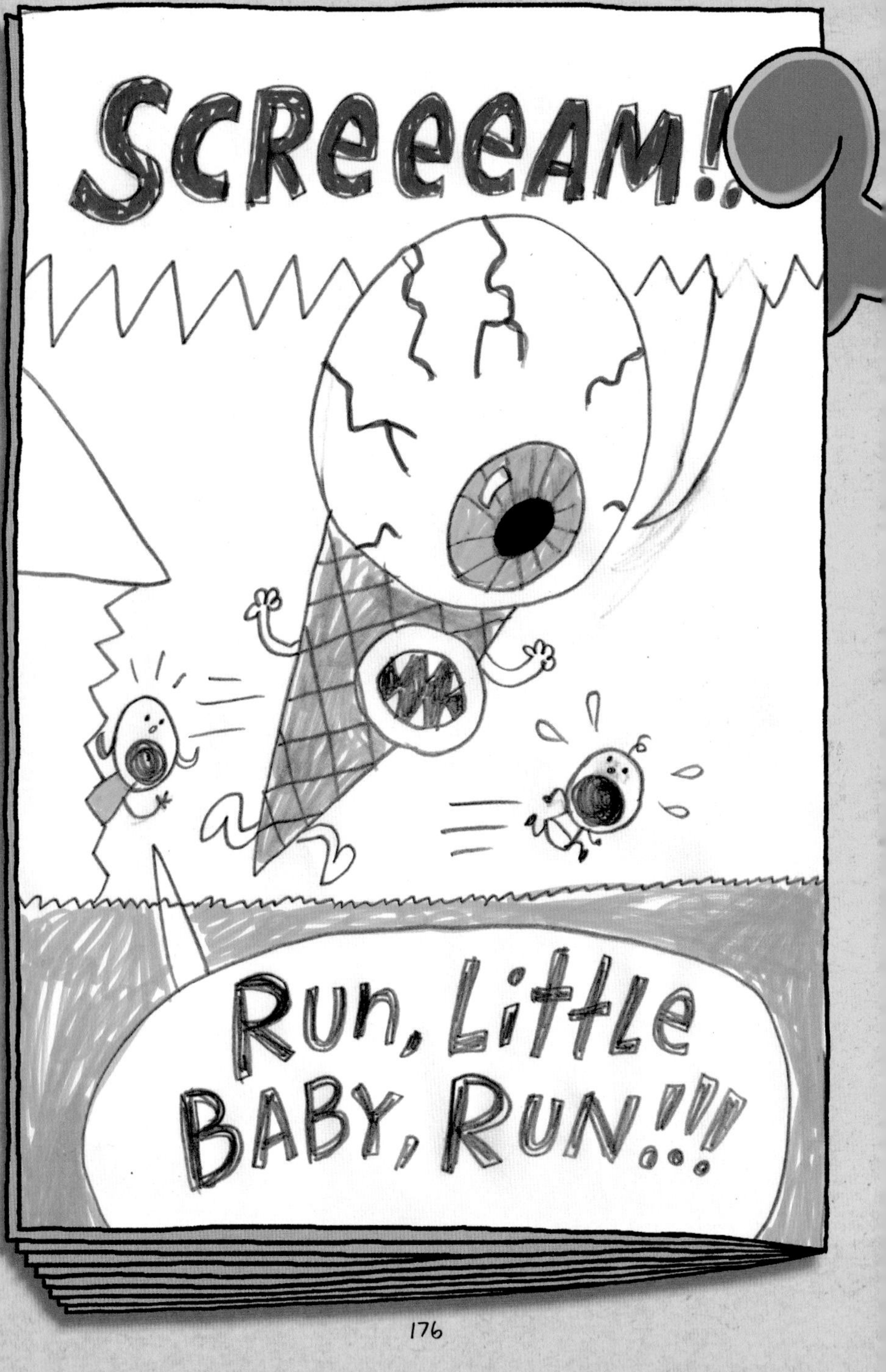
SCREEEAM!!
Run, Little BABY, RUN!!!

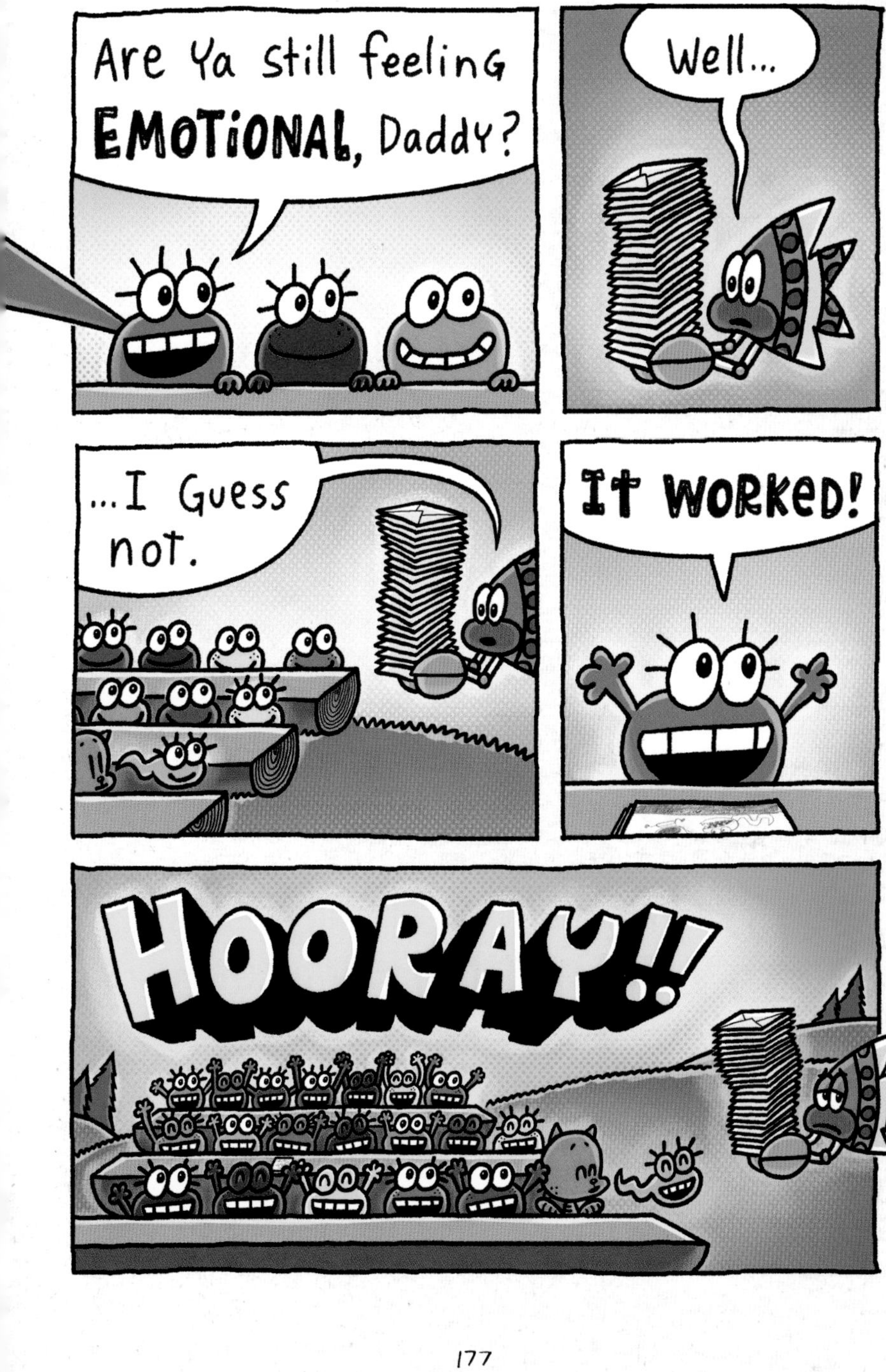
Are Ya still feeling EMOTIONAL, Daddy?
Well...
...I Guess not.
It WORKED!
HOORAY!!

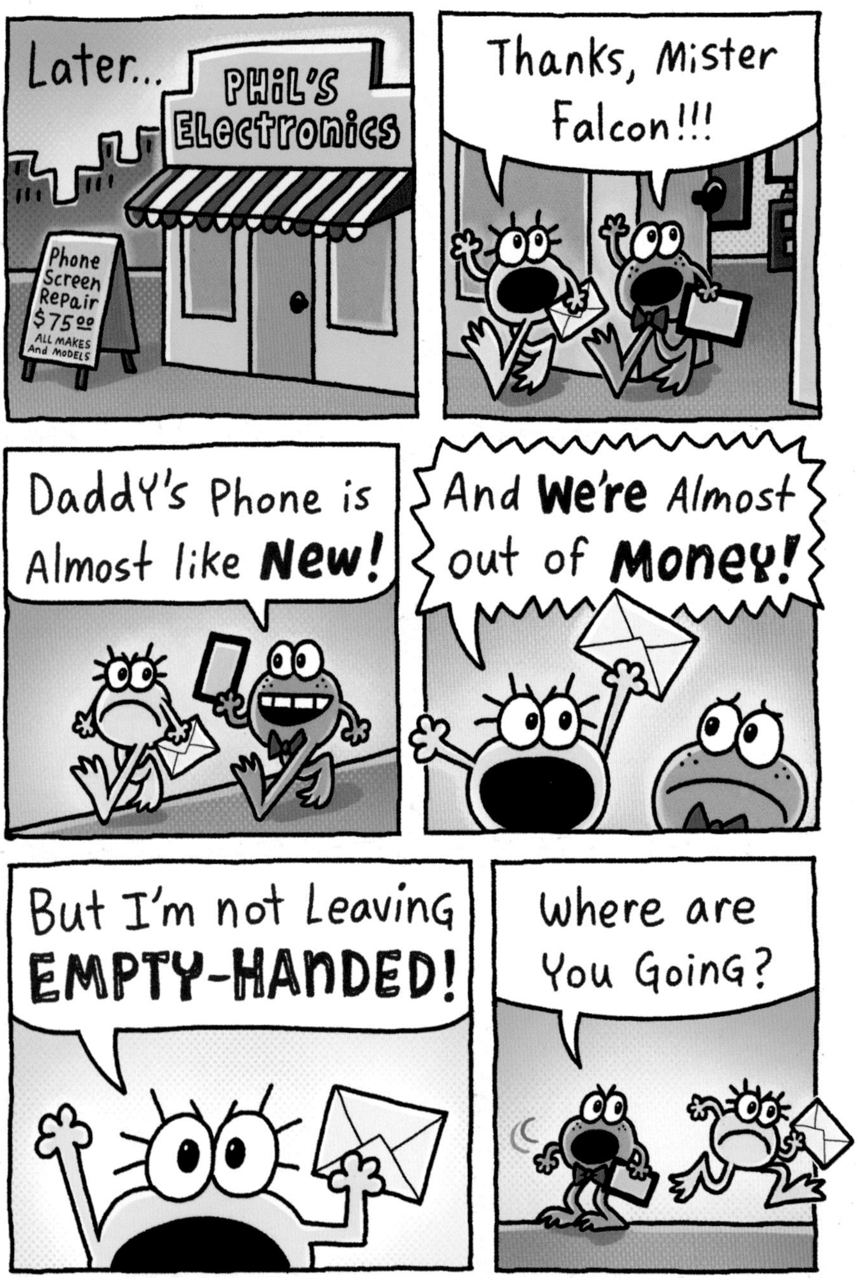
Later...
PHiL'S Electronics
Phone Screen Repair $75.00 ALL MAKES And MODELS
Thanks, Mister Falcon!!!
DaddY's Phone is Almost like **New!**
And **We're** Almost out of **Money!**
But I'm not Leaving **EMPTY-HANDED!**
Where are You GoinG?

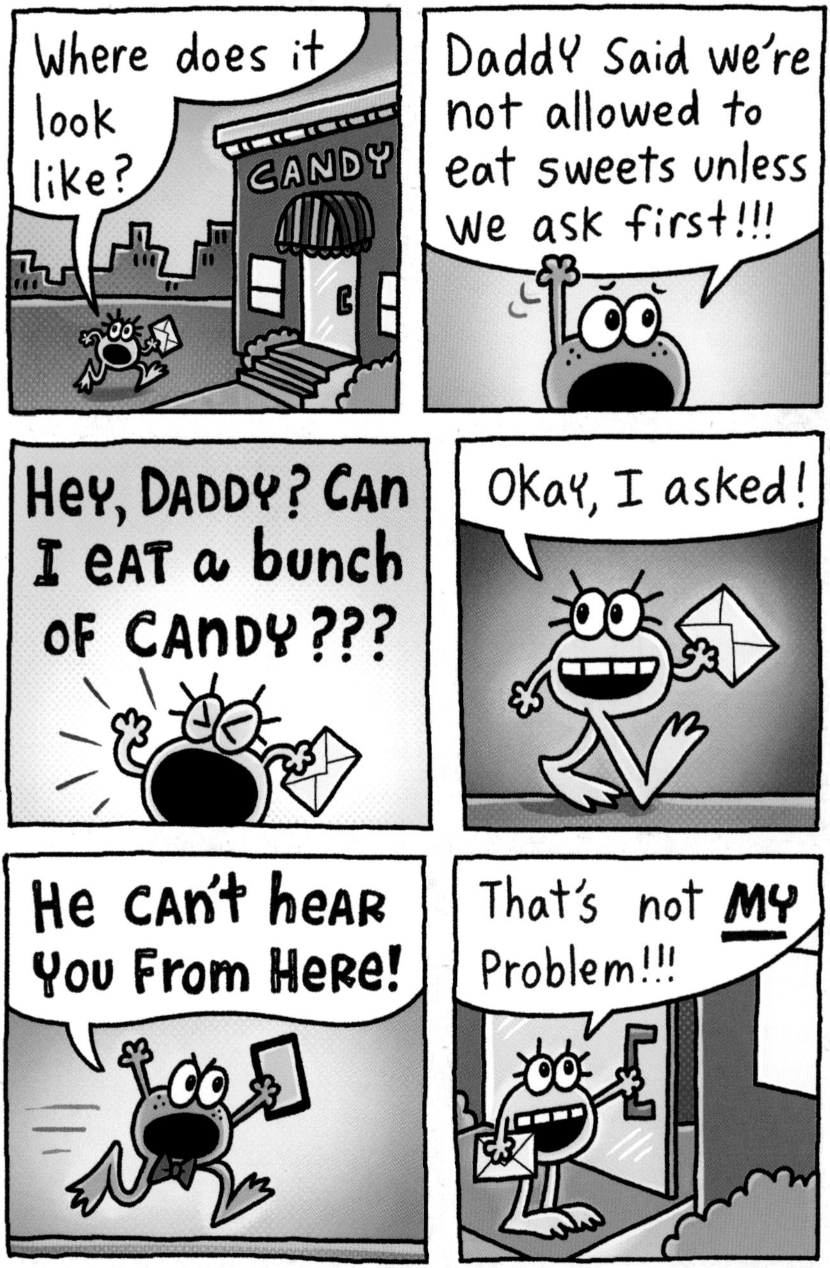
Where does it look like?
CANDY
Daddy Said we're not allowed to eat sweets unless we ask first!!!
Hey, DADDY? CAN I EAT a bunch of CANDY???
OKay, I asked!
He CAN'T hEAR You From HERE!
That's not MY Problem!!!

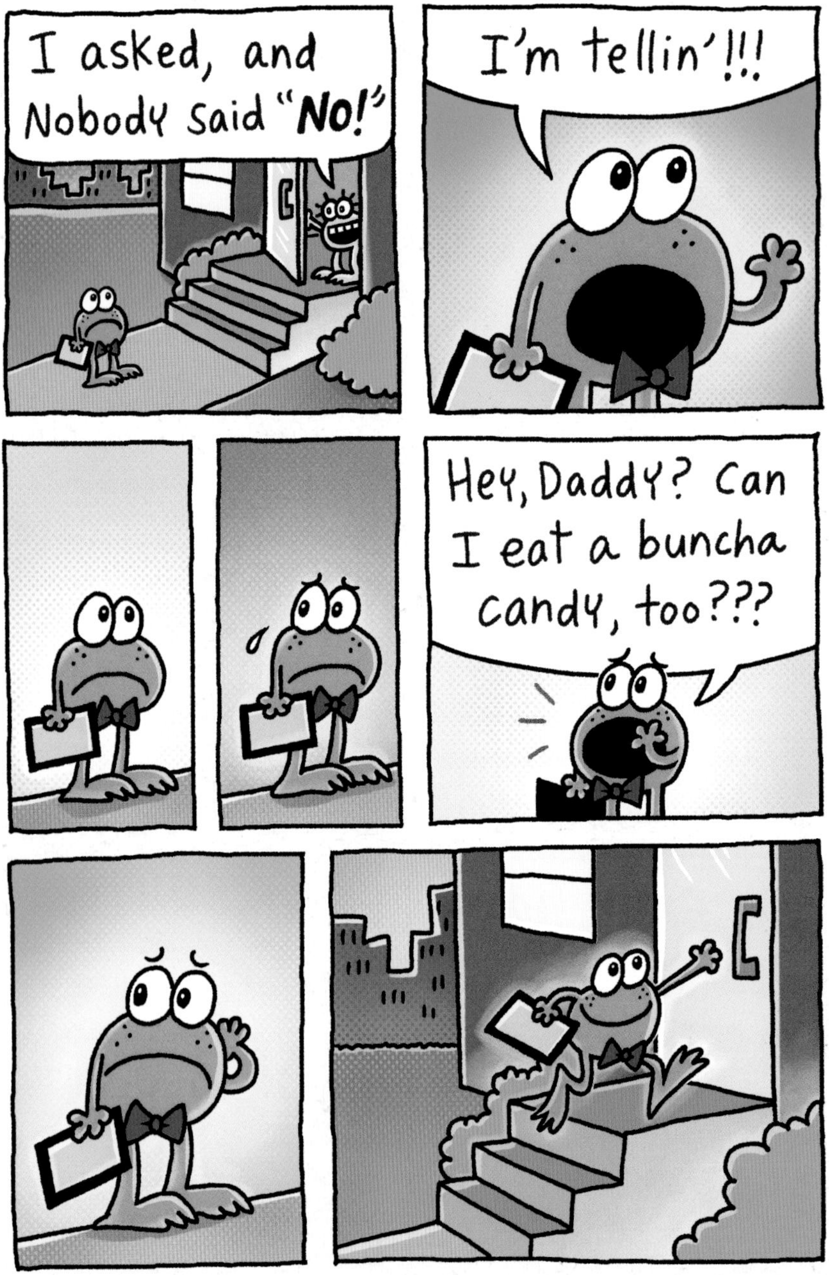
I asked, and Nobody said "NO!"
I'm tellin'!!!
Hey, Daddy? Can I eat a buncha candy, too???

CHAPTER 9

Regrets

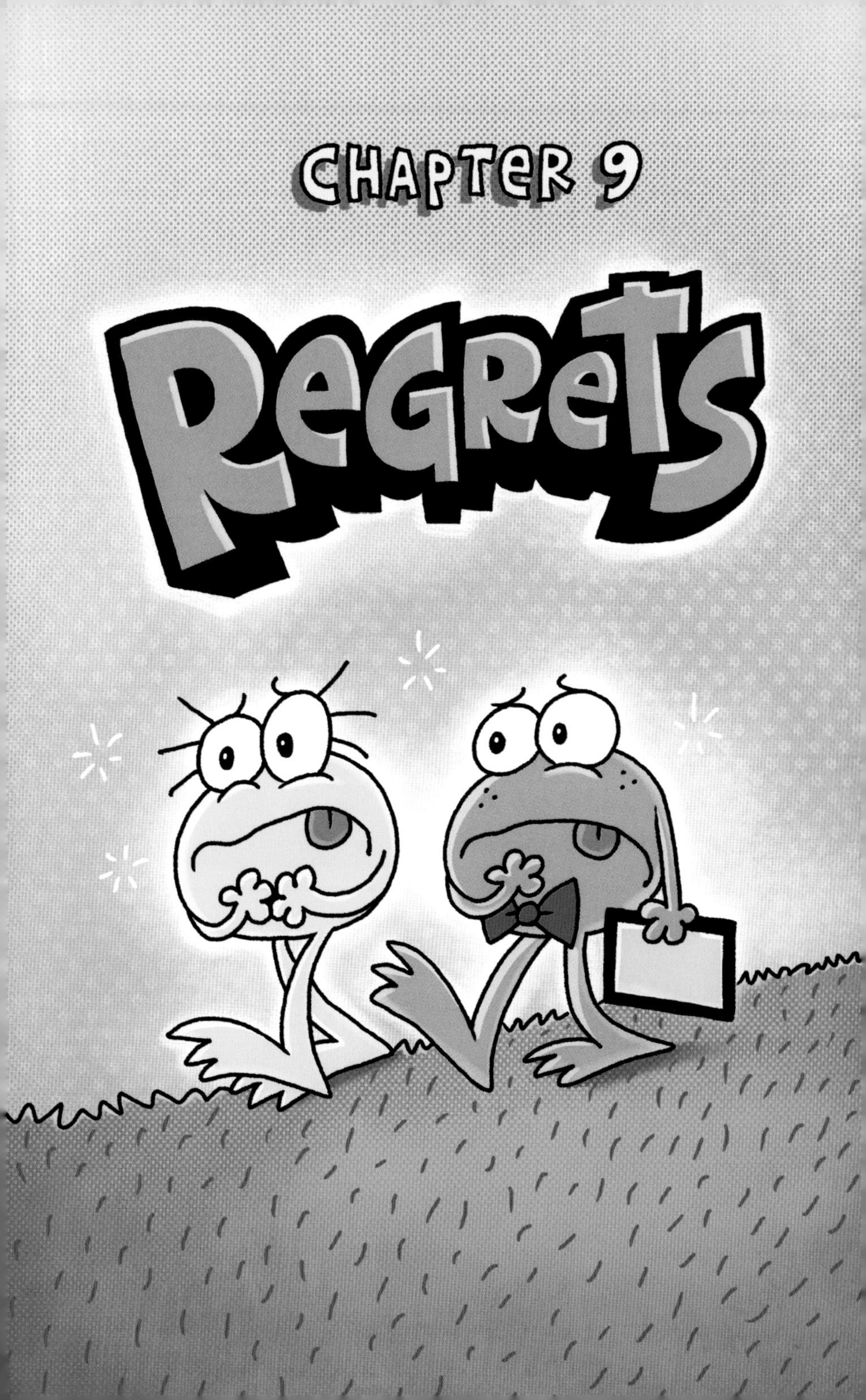

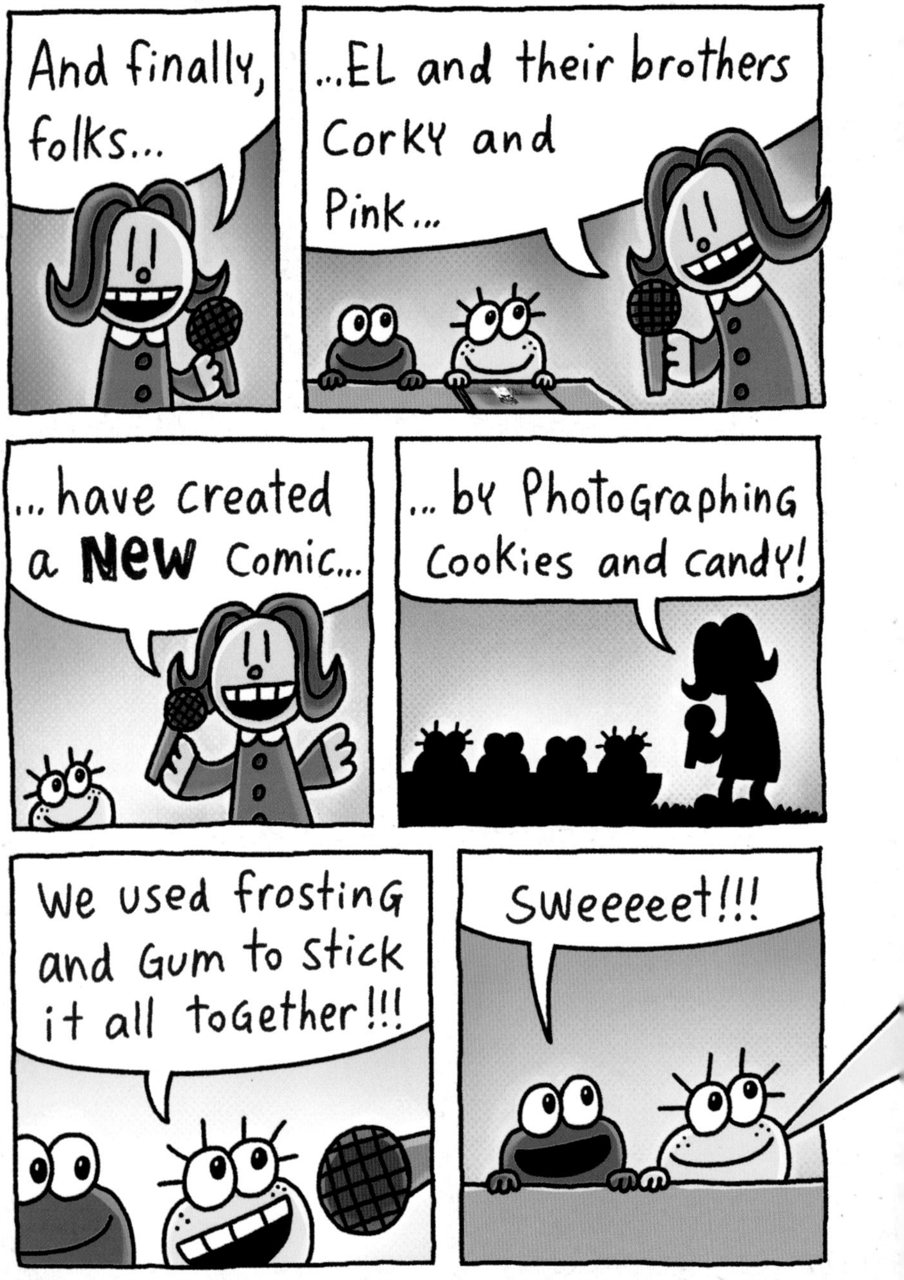
And finally, folks...
...EL and their brothers Corky and Pink...
...have created a NEW Comic...
...by Photographing Cookies and candy!
We used frosting and Gum to stick it all together!!!
Sweeeeet!!!

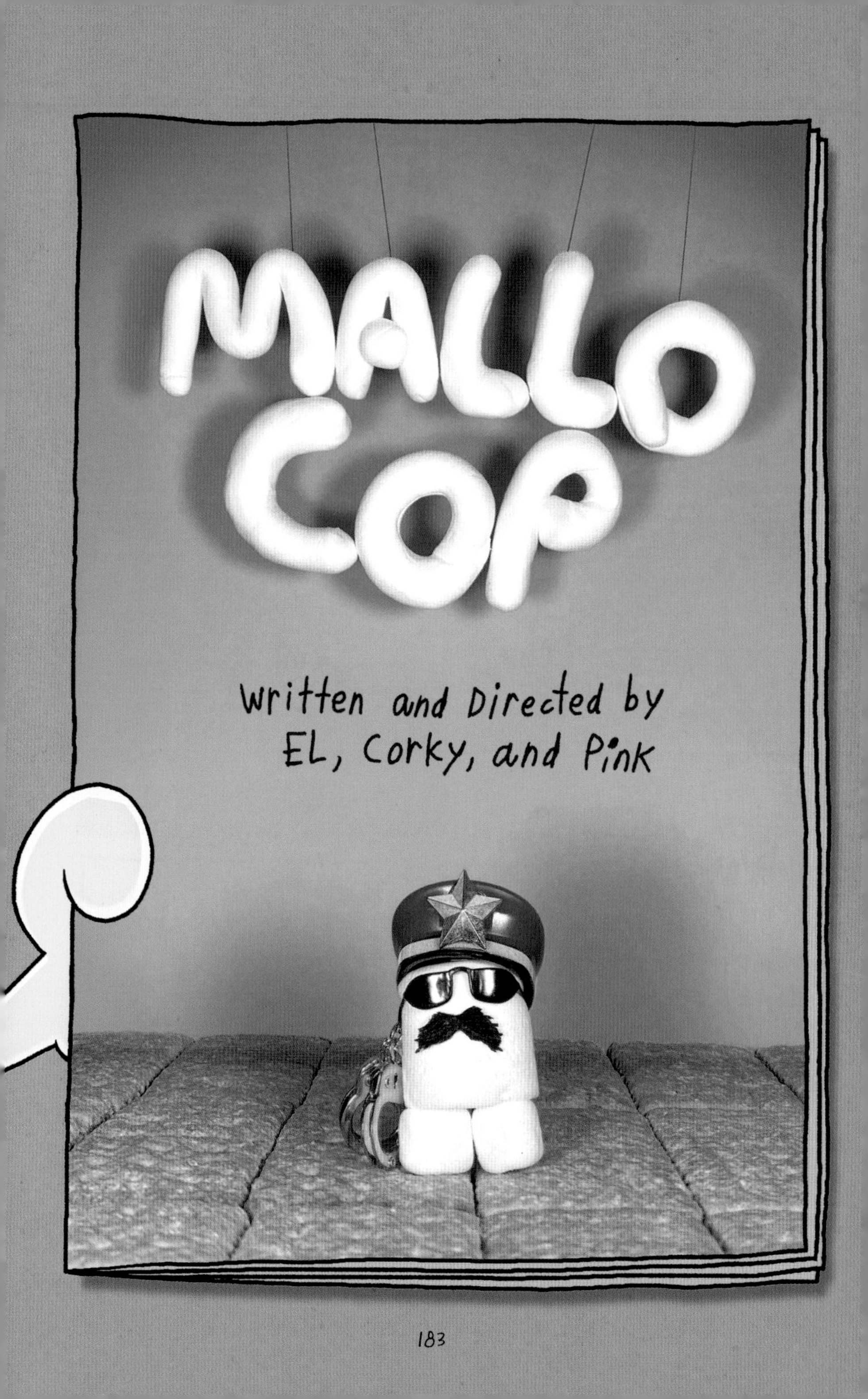
MALLO COP
Written and Directed by
EL, Corky, and Pink

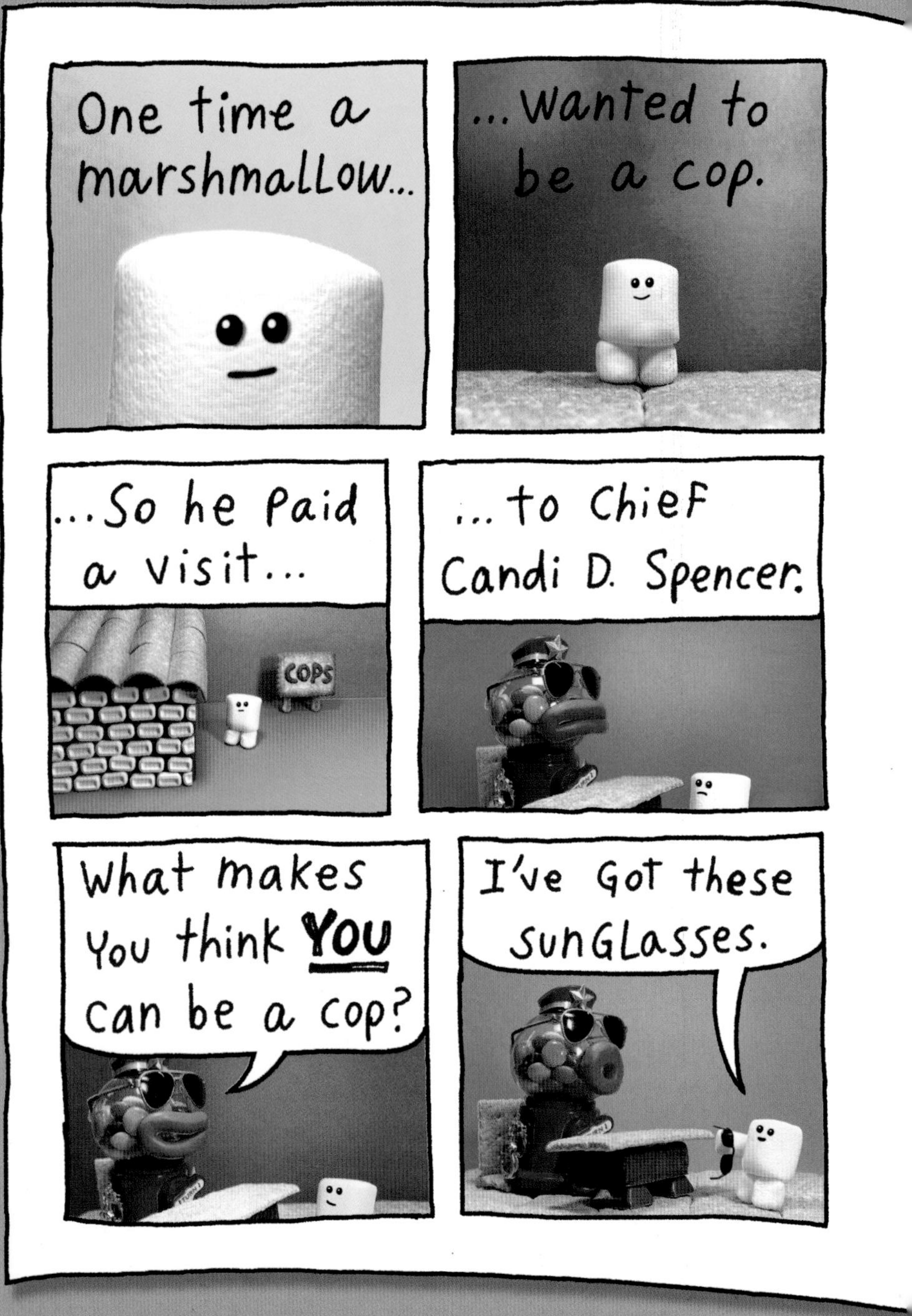
One time a marshmallow...
...wanted to be a cop.
COPS
...So he paid a visit...
...to Chief Candi D. Spencer.
What makes you think YOU can be a cop?
I've got these sunglasses.

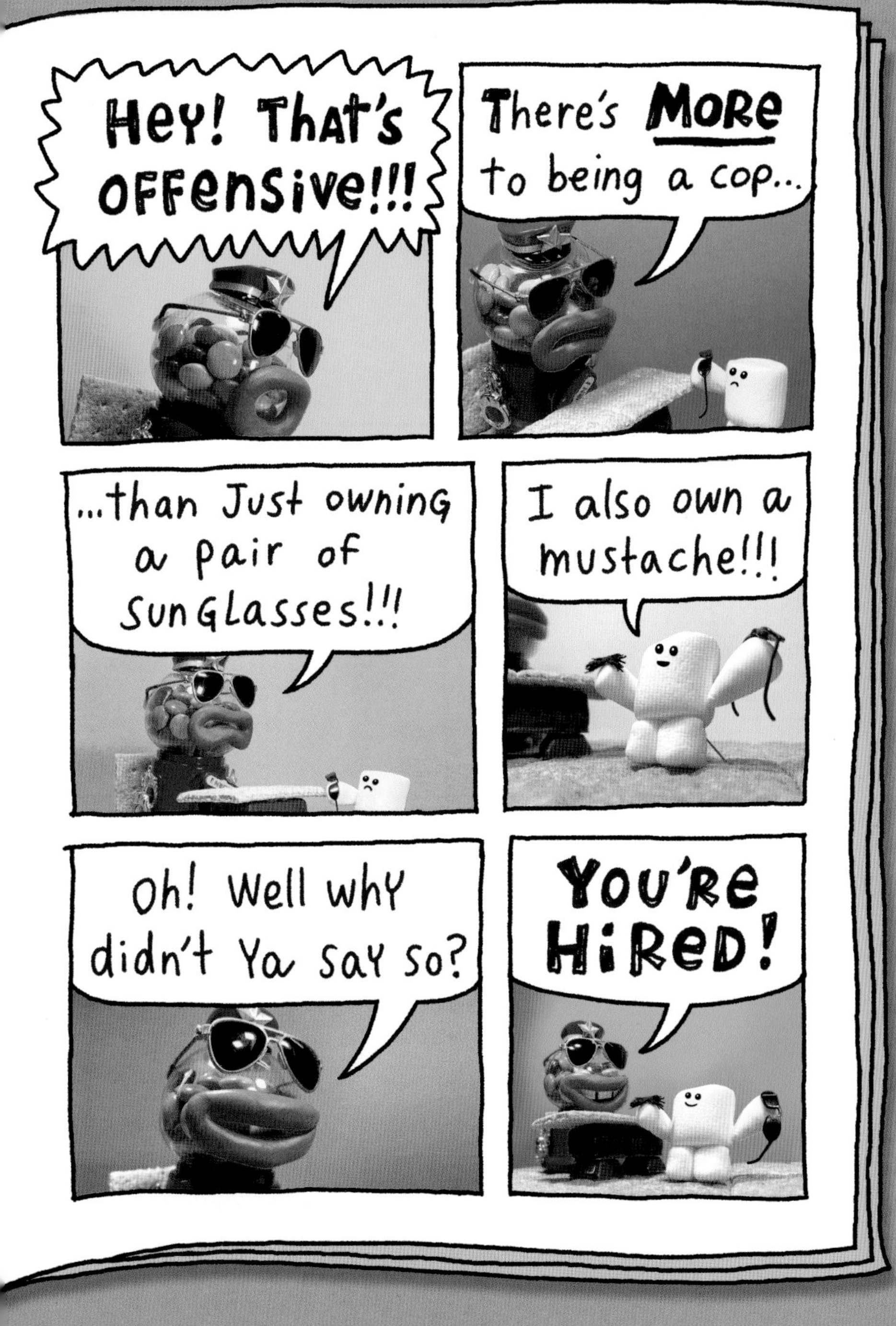
Hey! That's OFFensive!!!
There's MORE to being a cop...
...than Just owning a pair of sunGlasses!!!
I also own a mustache!!!
Oh! Well why didn't Ya say so?
You're Hired!

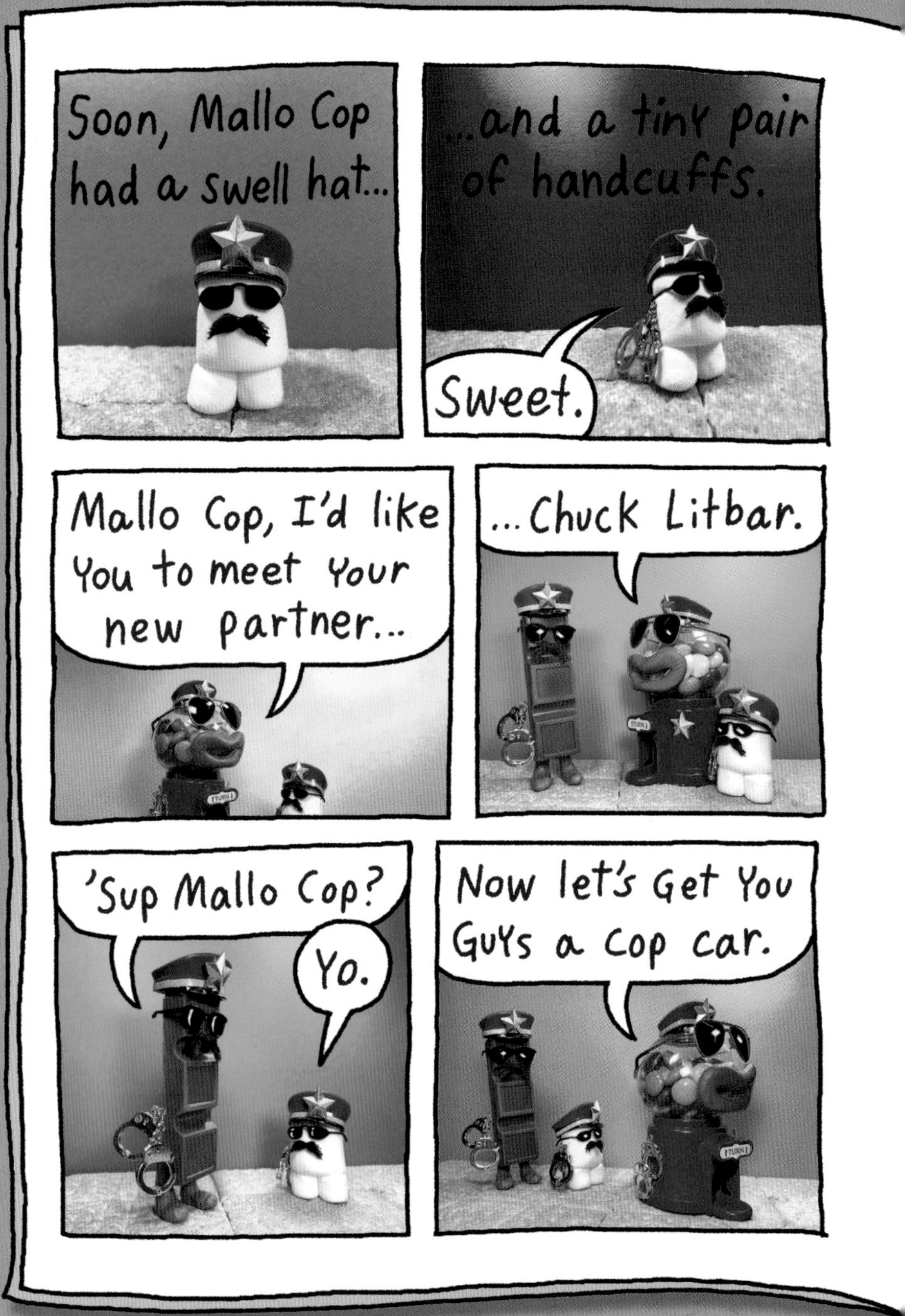
Soon, Mallo Cop had a swell hat...
...and a tiny pair of handcuffs.
Sweet.
Mallo Cop, I'd like You to meet Your new partner...
...Chuck Litbar.
'Sup Mallo Cop?
Yo.
Now let's Get You Guys a Cop car.

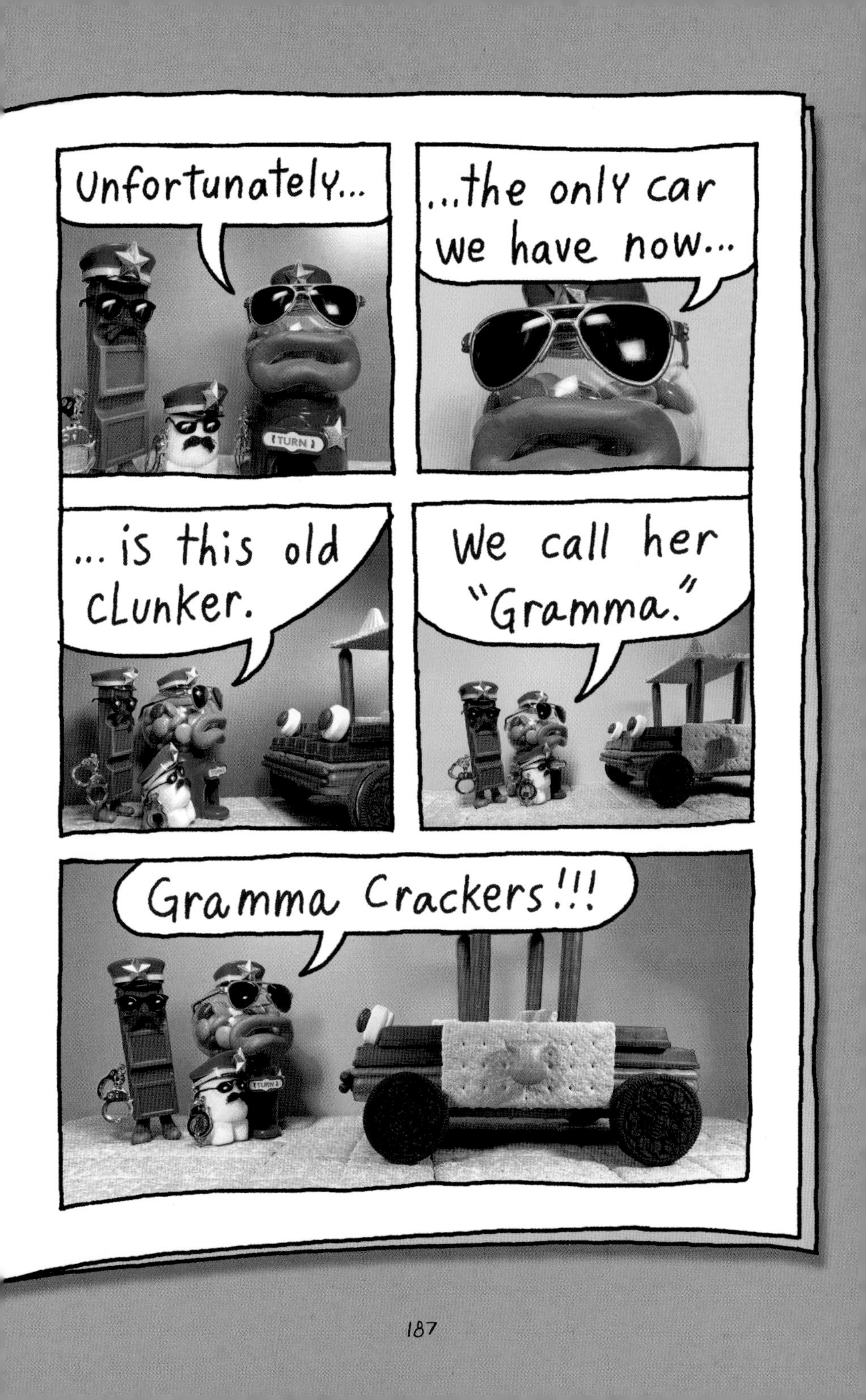
Unfortunately...
...the only car we have now...
TURN
... is this old clunker.
We call her "Gramma."
Gramma Crackers!!!

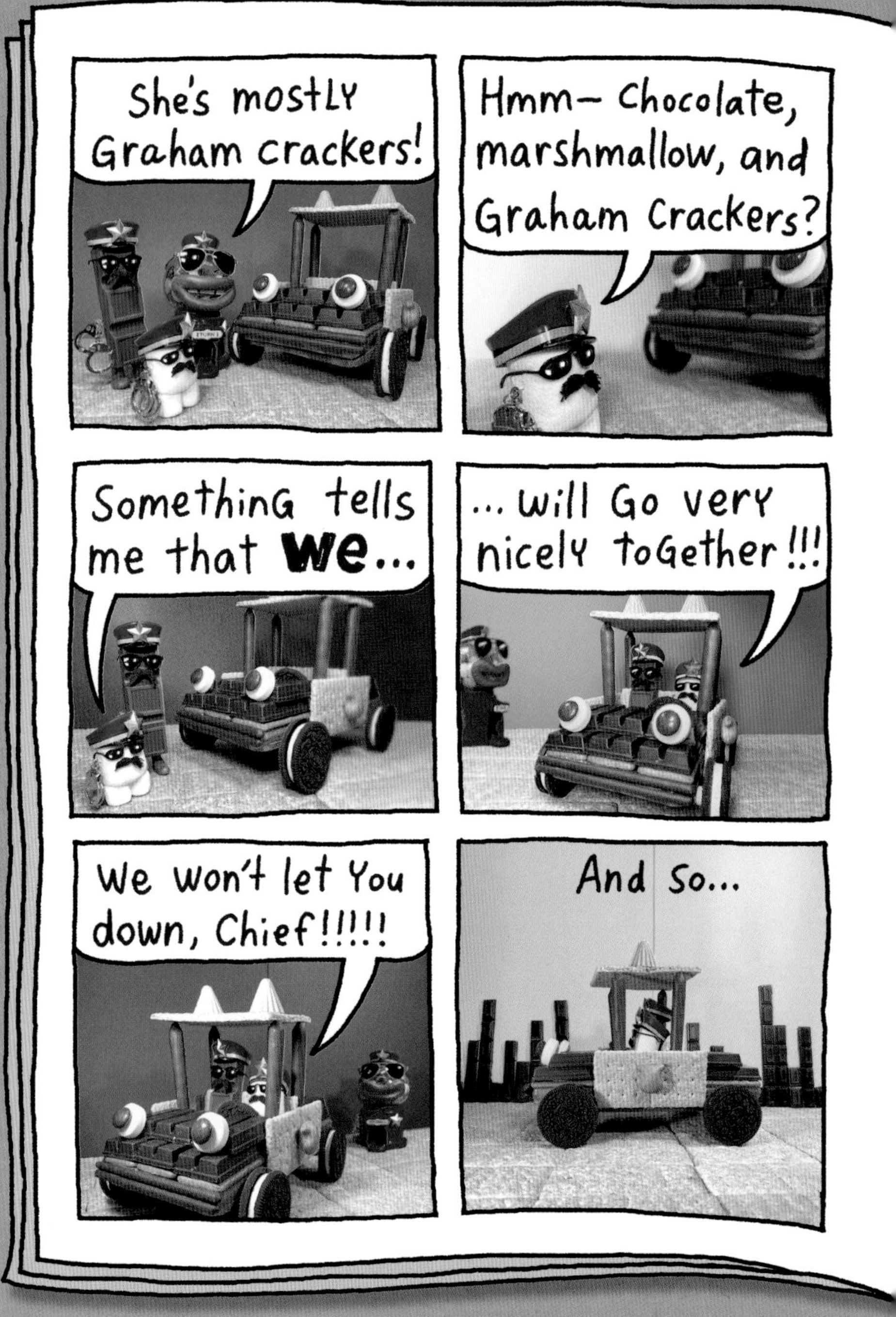
She's mostly Graham crackers!
Hmm– Chocolate, marshmallow, and Graham Crackers?
Something tells me that **we**...
...will Go very nicely toGether!!!
We won't let You down, Chief!!!!!
And so...

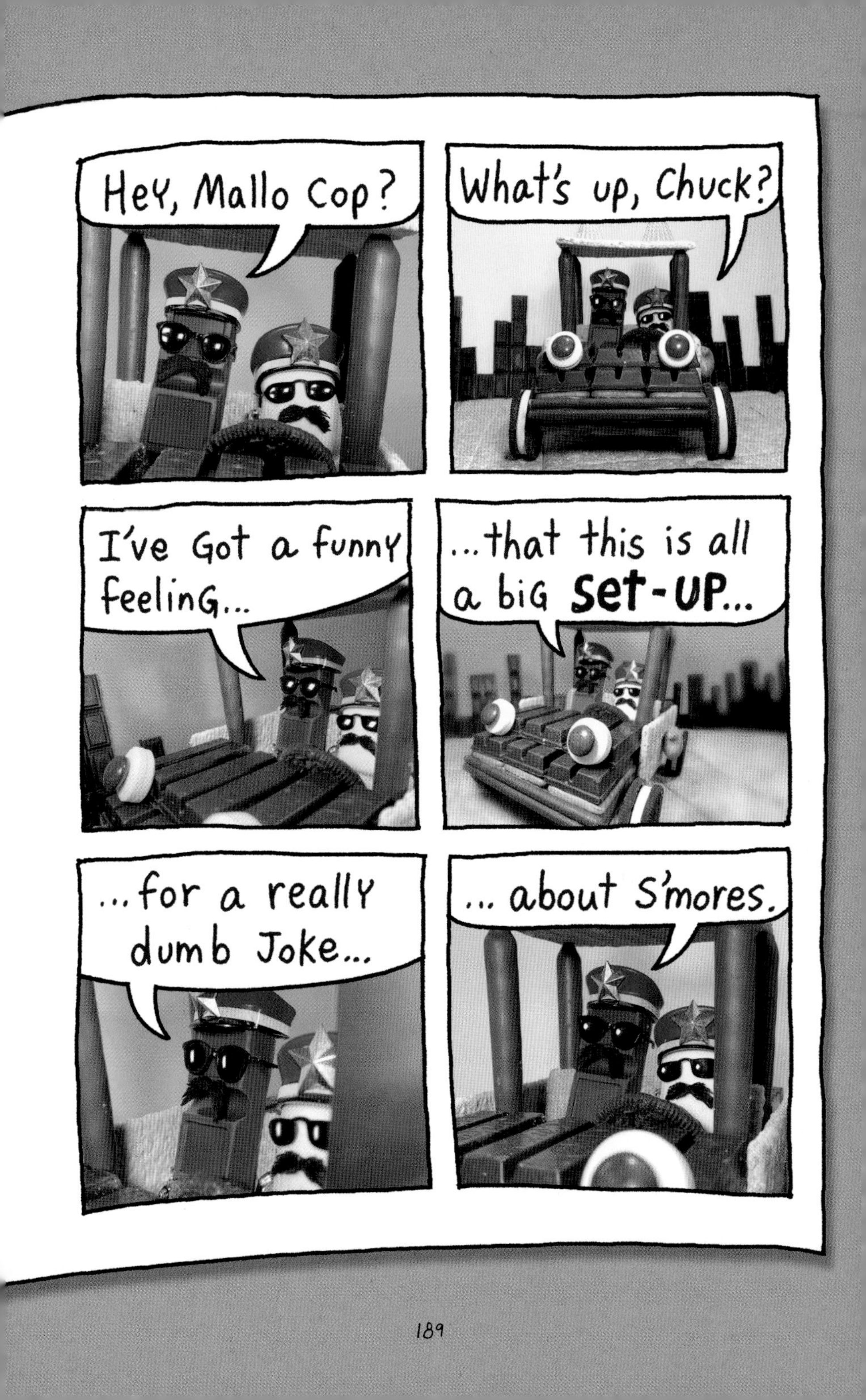

Hey, Mallo Cop?
What's up, Chuck?
I've Got a funny feeling...
...that this is all a big SET-UP...
...for a really dumb Joke...
... about S'mores.

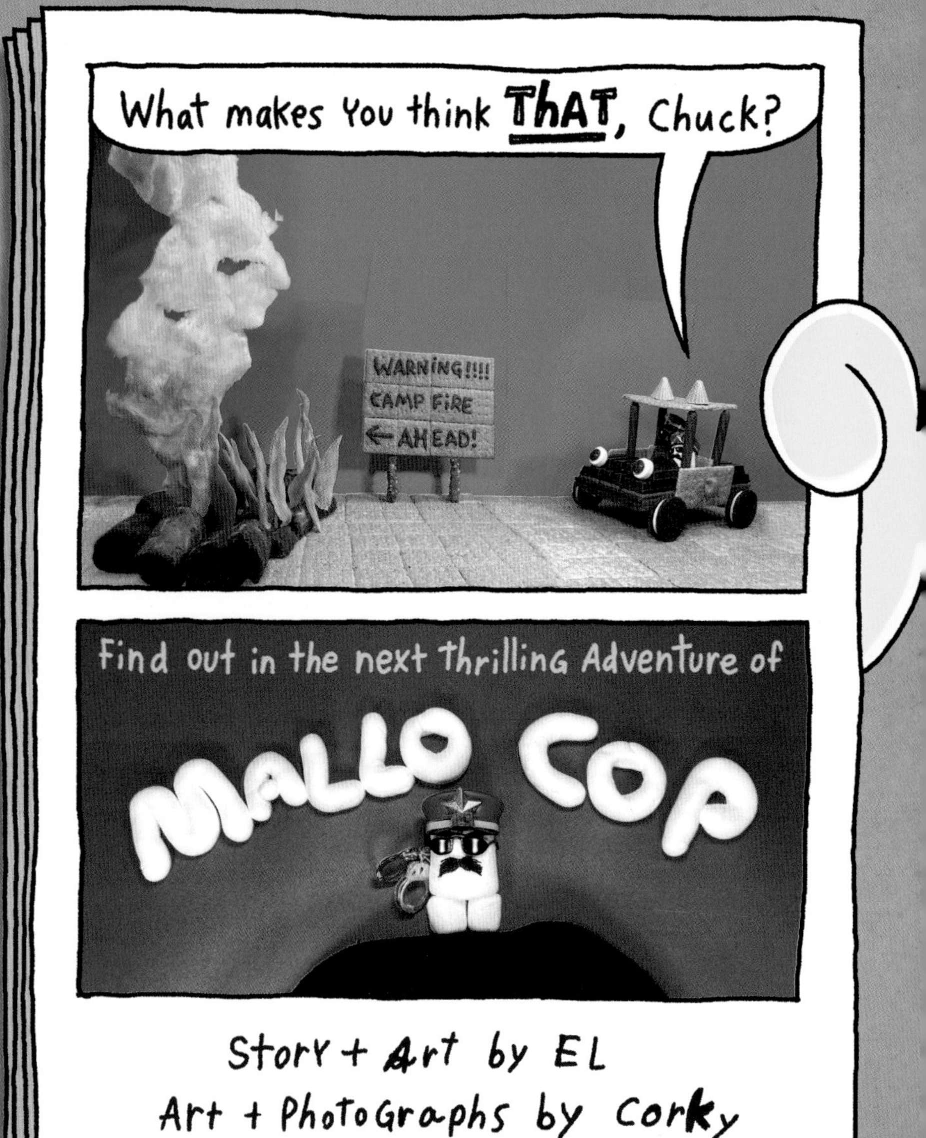
What makes You think ThAT, Chuck?
WARNiNG!!!!
CAMP FiRE
← AHEAD!
Find out in the next thrilling Adventure of
MALLO COP
Story + Art by EL
Art + PhotoGraphs by Corky
ArT + DiGital Wizardry by Pink
copyriGht © by ELPiCO ProDuctions, Inc.
ALL RiGhts Reserved

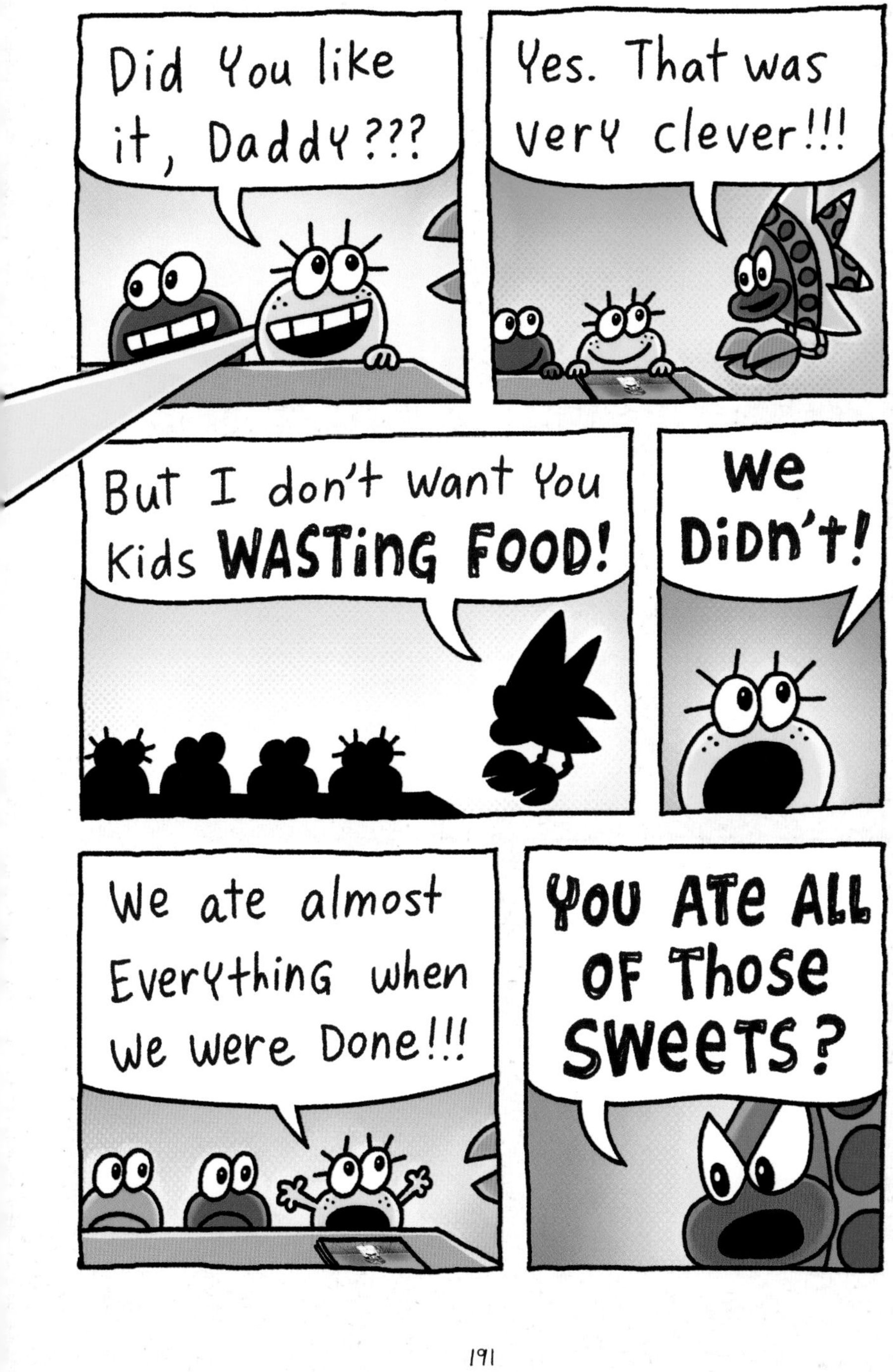
Did You like it, Daddy???
Yes. That was very clever!!!
But I don't want You Kids WASTinG FOOD!
We DiDn't!
We ate almost Everything when we were Done!!!
YOU ATE ALL OF Those SWEETS?

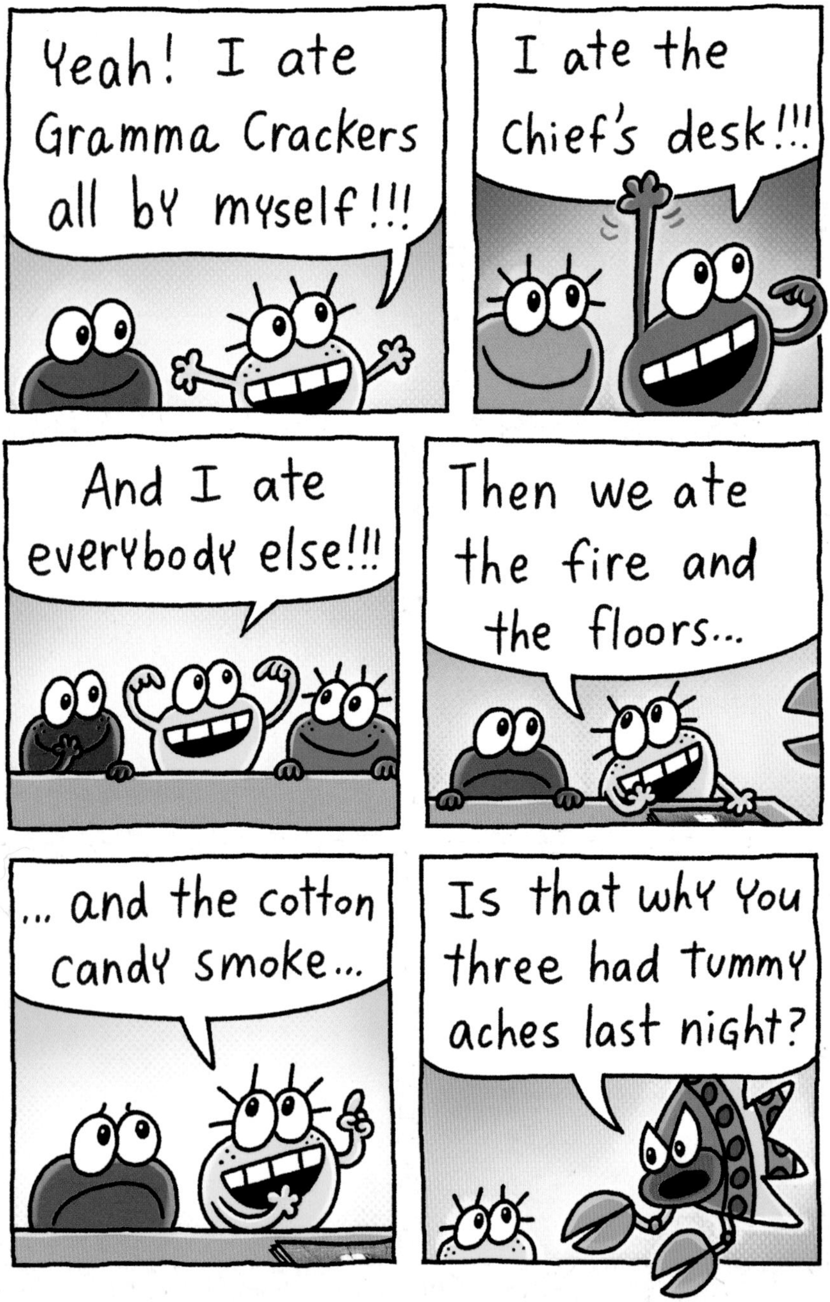
Yeah! I ate Gramma Crackers all by myself!!!
I ate the Chief's desk!!!
And I ate everybody else!!!
Then we ate the fire and the floors...
... and the cotton candy smoke...
Is that why you three had tummy aches last night?

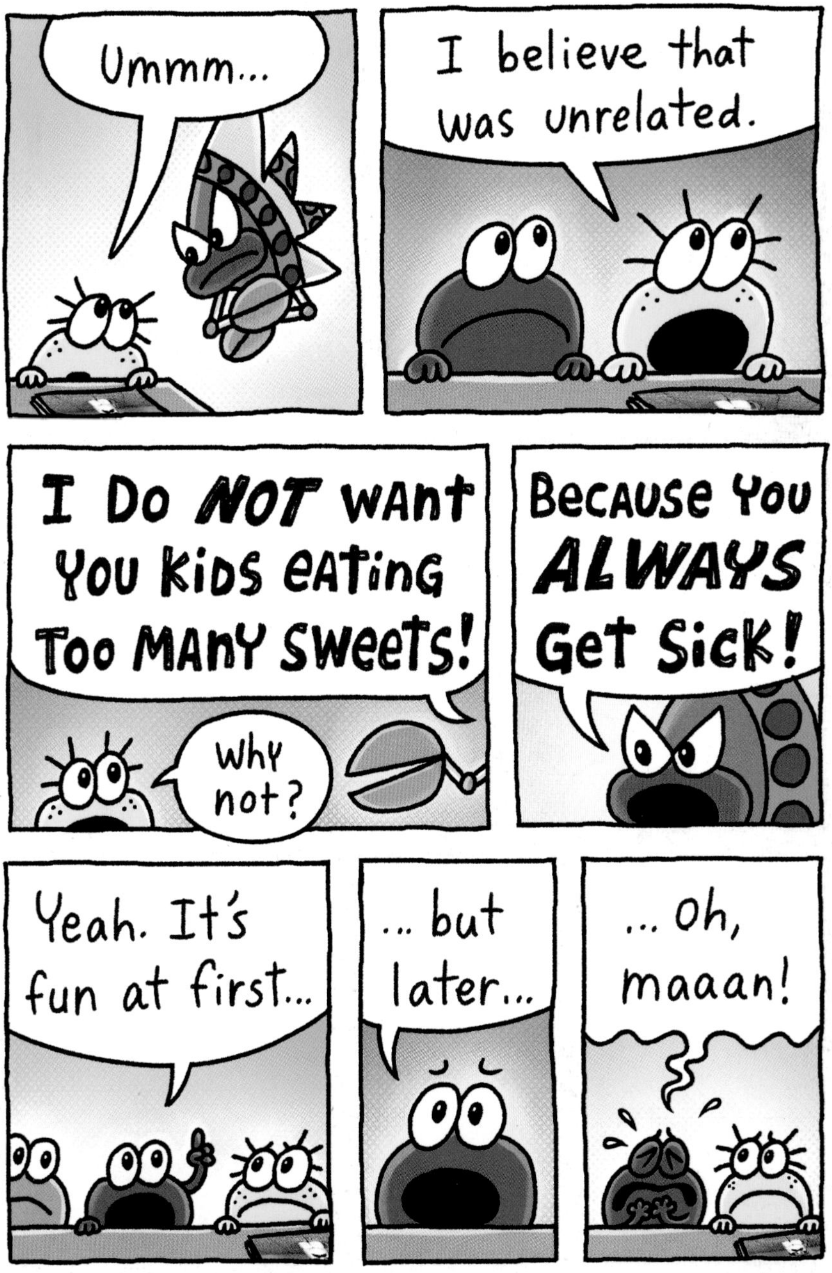
Ummm...
I believe that was unrelated.
I DO NOT WANT YOU KIDS EATING TOO MANY SWEETS!
Why not?
BECAUSE YOU ALWAYS GET SICK!
Yeah. It's fun at first...
... but later...
... Oh, maaan!

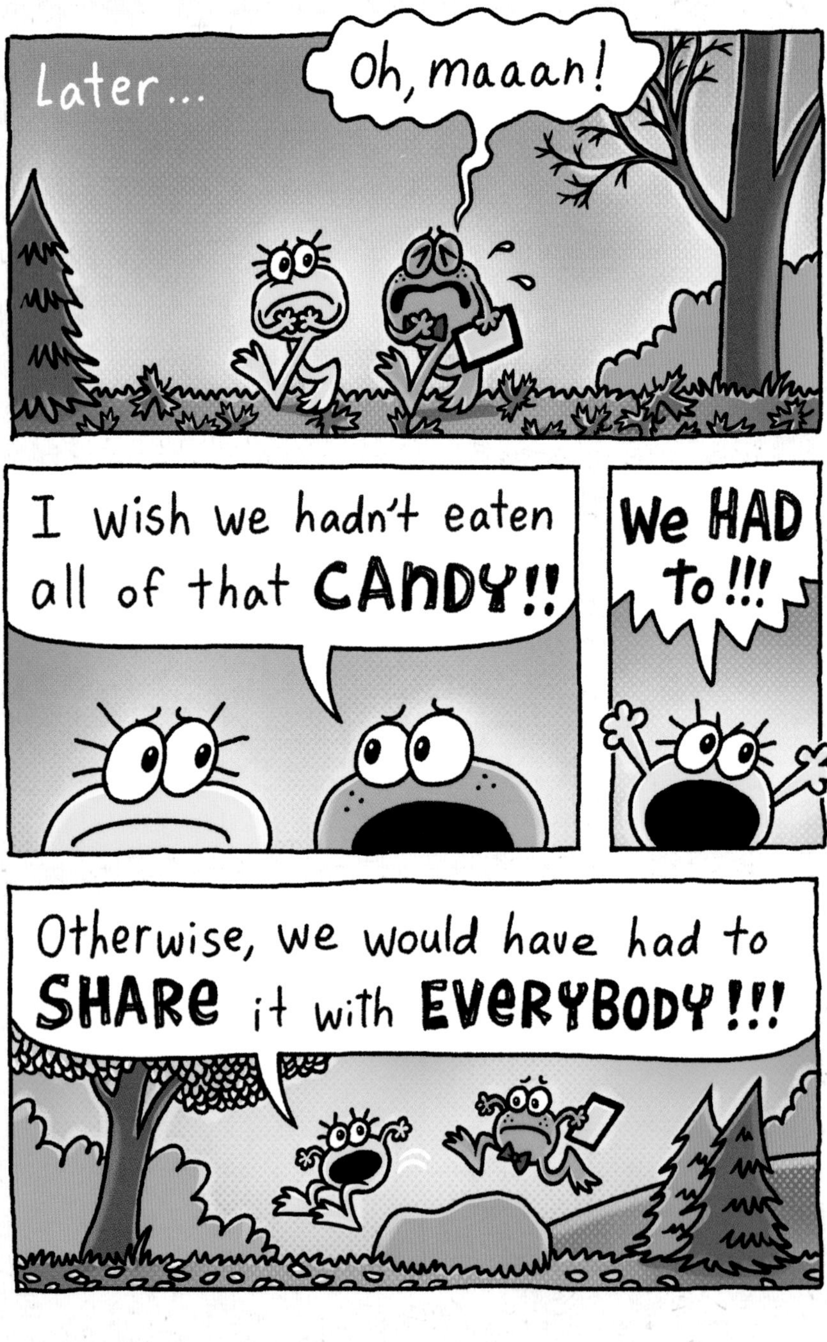
Later...
Oh, maaan!
I wish we hadn't eaten all of that CANDY!!
We HAD to!!!
Otherwise, we would have had to SHARE it with EVERYBODY!!!

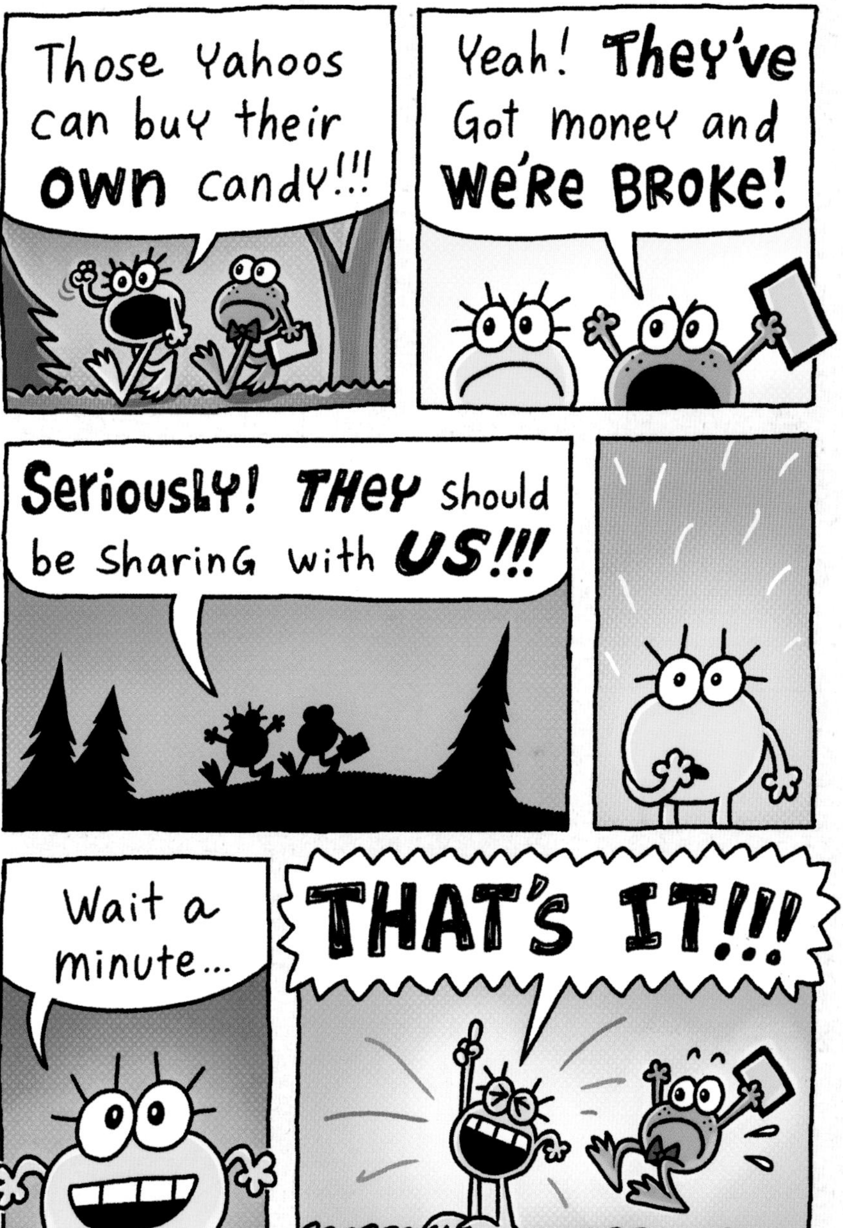
Those Yahoos can buy their OWN candy!!!
Yeah! They've Got money and WE'RE BROKE!
Seriously! THEY should be sharinG with US!!!
Wait a minute...
THAT'S IT!!!

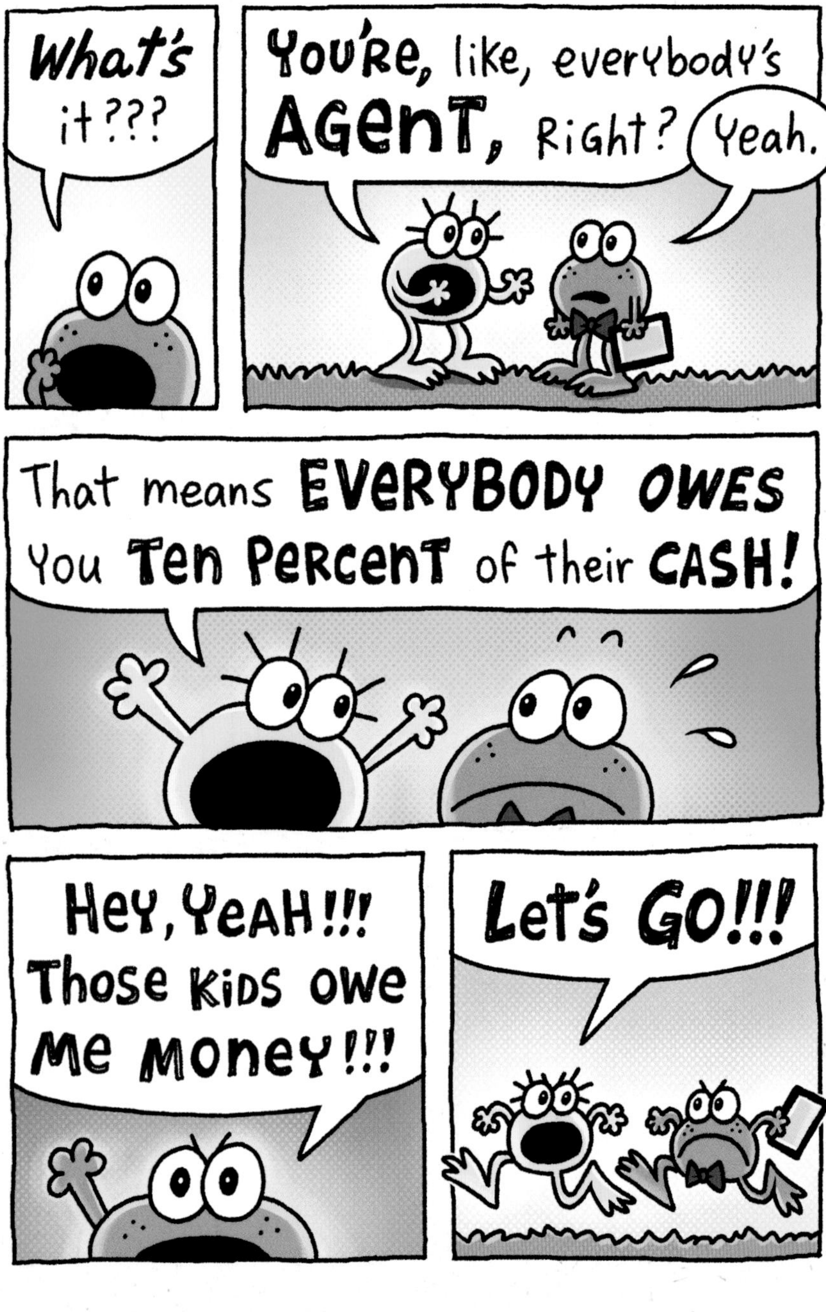
What's it???
You're, like, everybody's AGENT, Right?
Yeah.
That means EVERYBODY OWES You TEN PERCENT of their CASH!
Hey, YEAH!!! Those KIDS OWE ME MONEY!!!
Let's GO!!!

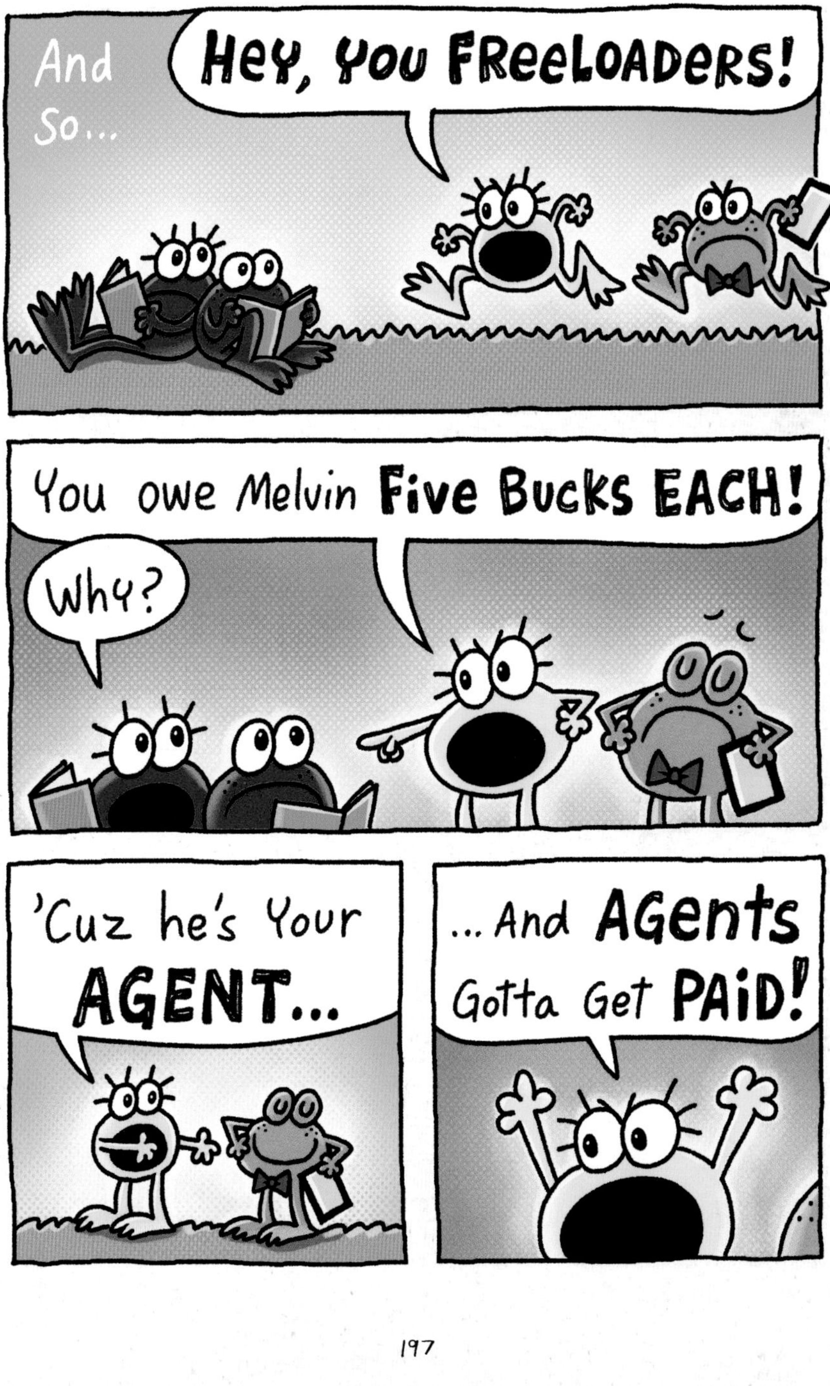
And So...
HEY, YOU FREELOADERS!
You owe Melvin Five Bucks EACH!
Why?
'Cuz he's Your AGENT...
...And AGents Gotta Get PAID!

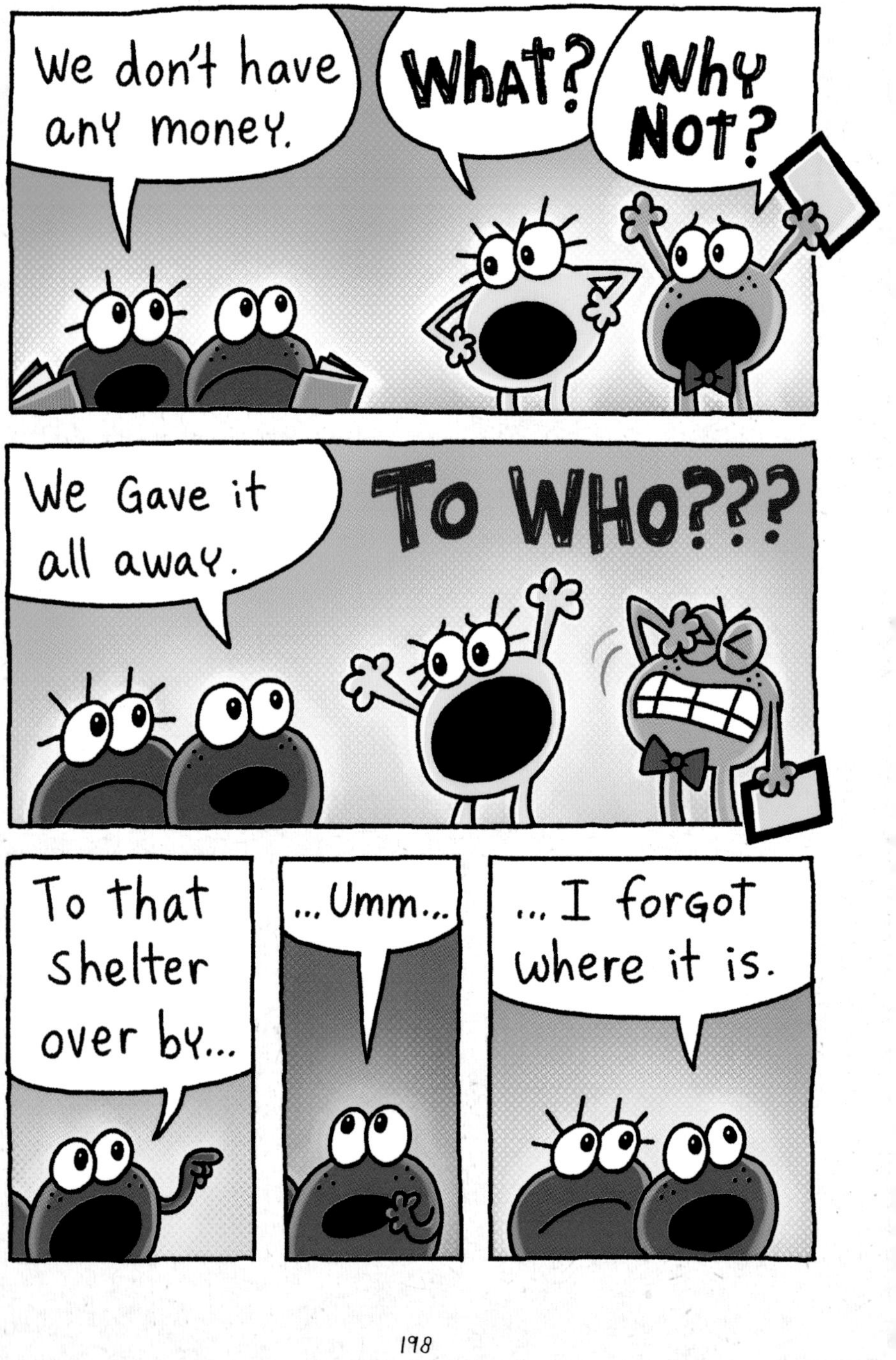
We don't have any money.
WHAT?
Why Not?
We Gave it all away.
TO WHO???
To that Shelter over by...
...Umm...
...I forgot where it is.

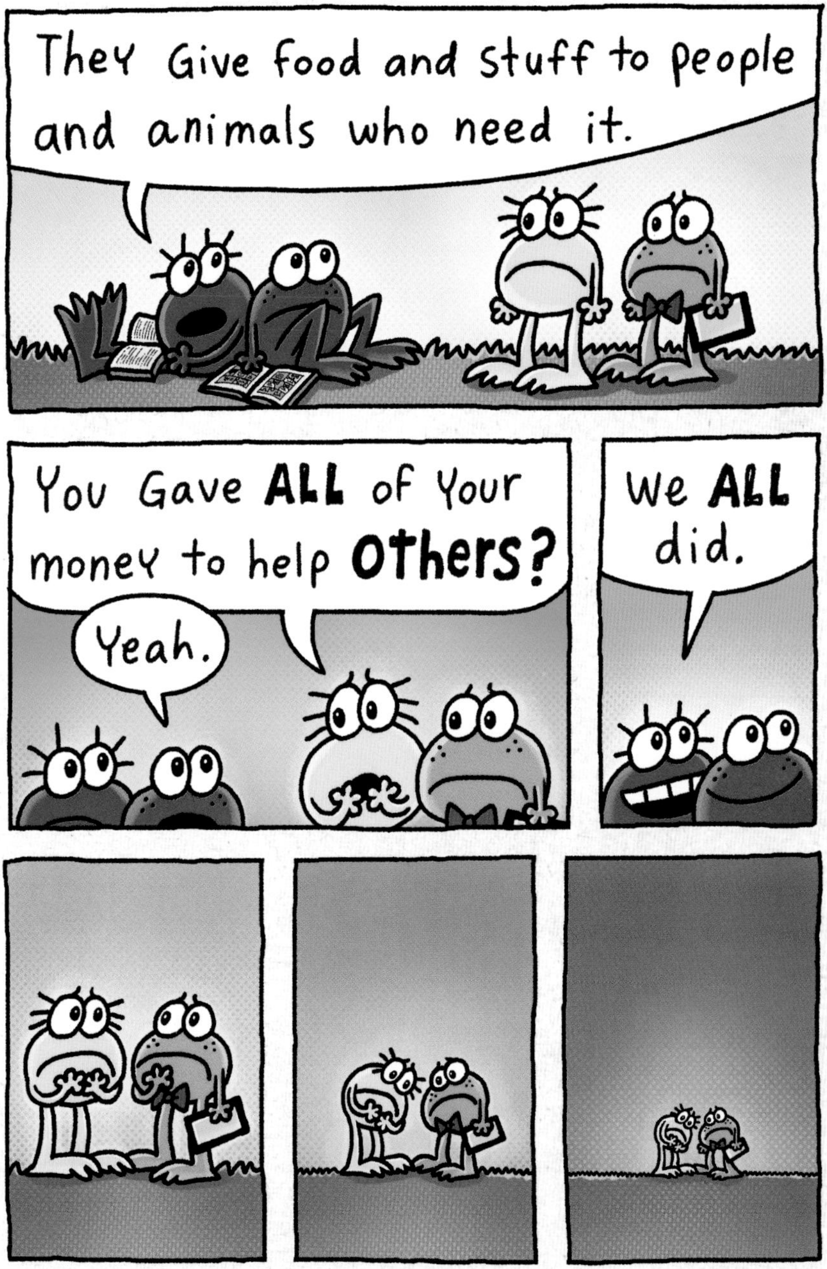
They Give food and stuff to people and animals who need it.
You Gave **ALL** of Your money to help **Others?**
Yeah.
We **ALL** did.

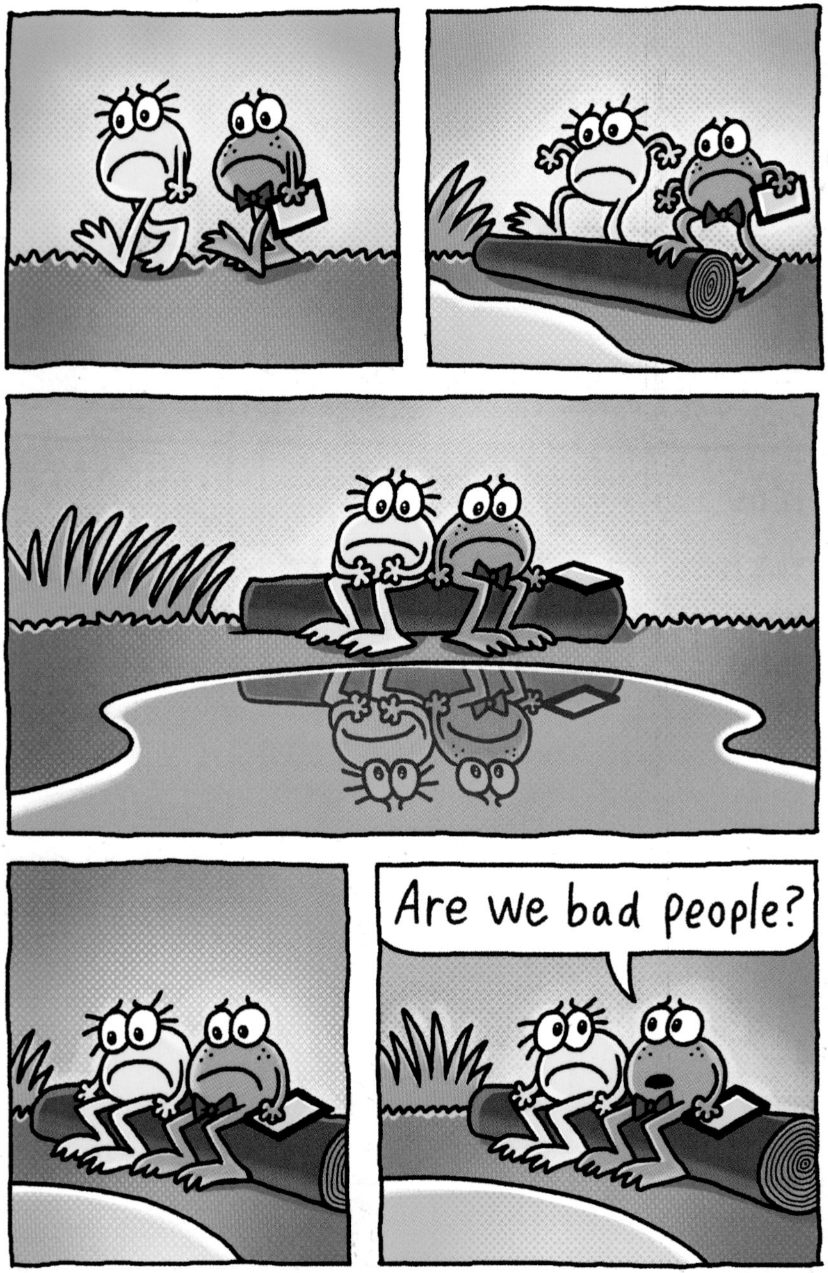
Are we bad people?

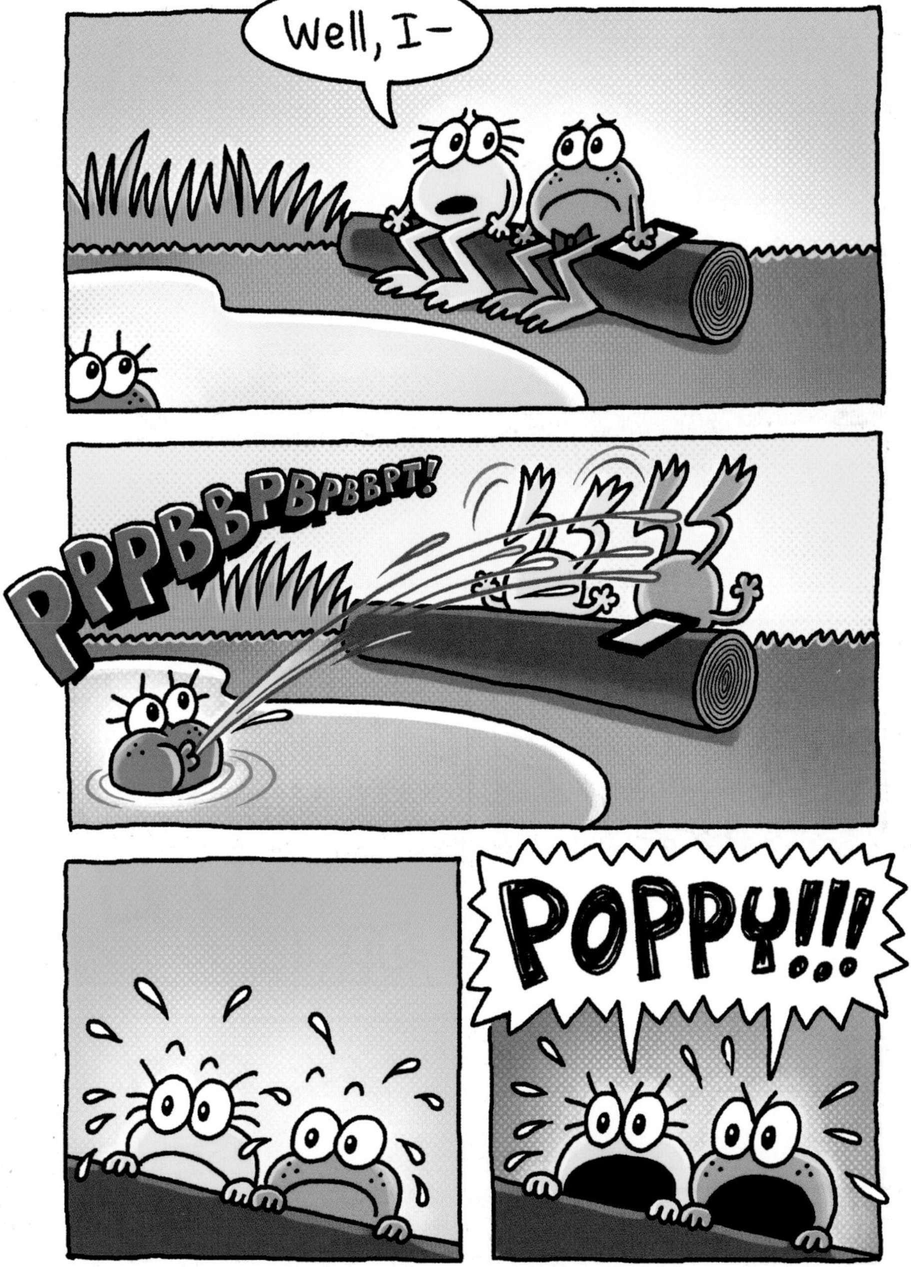
Well, I-
PPPBBBPBPBBBPT!
POPPY!!!

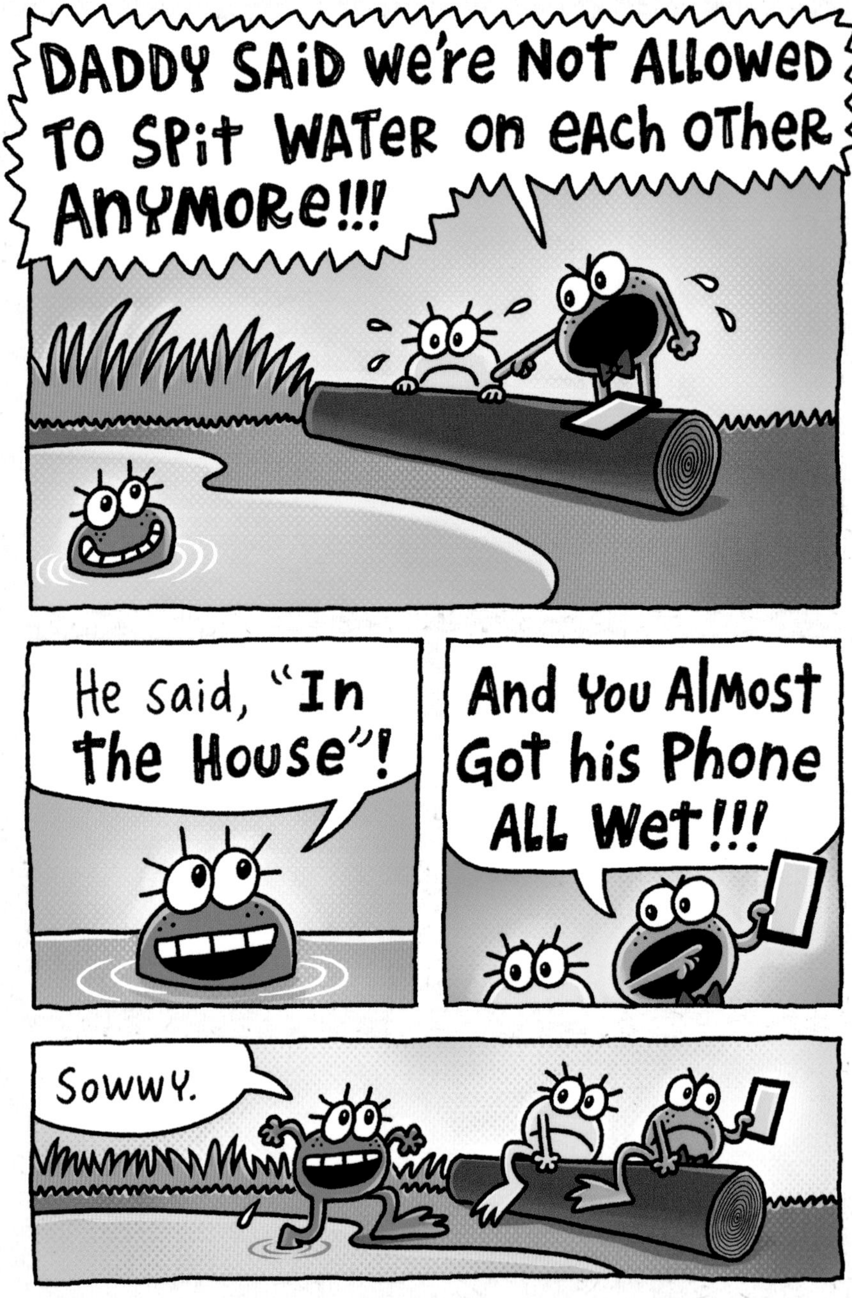
DADDY SAID we're NOT ALLOWED TO SPiT WATER on eACh OTHER ANYMORE!!!
He said, "In the House"!
And You Almost Got his Phone ALL Wet!!!
SOWWY.

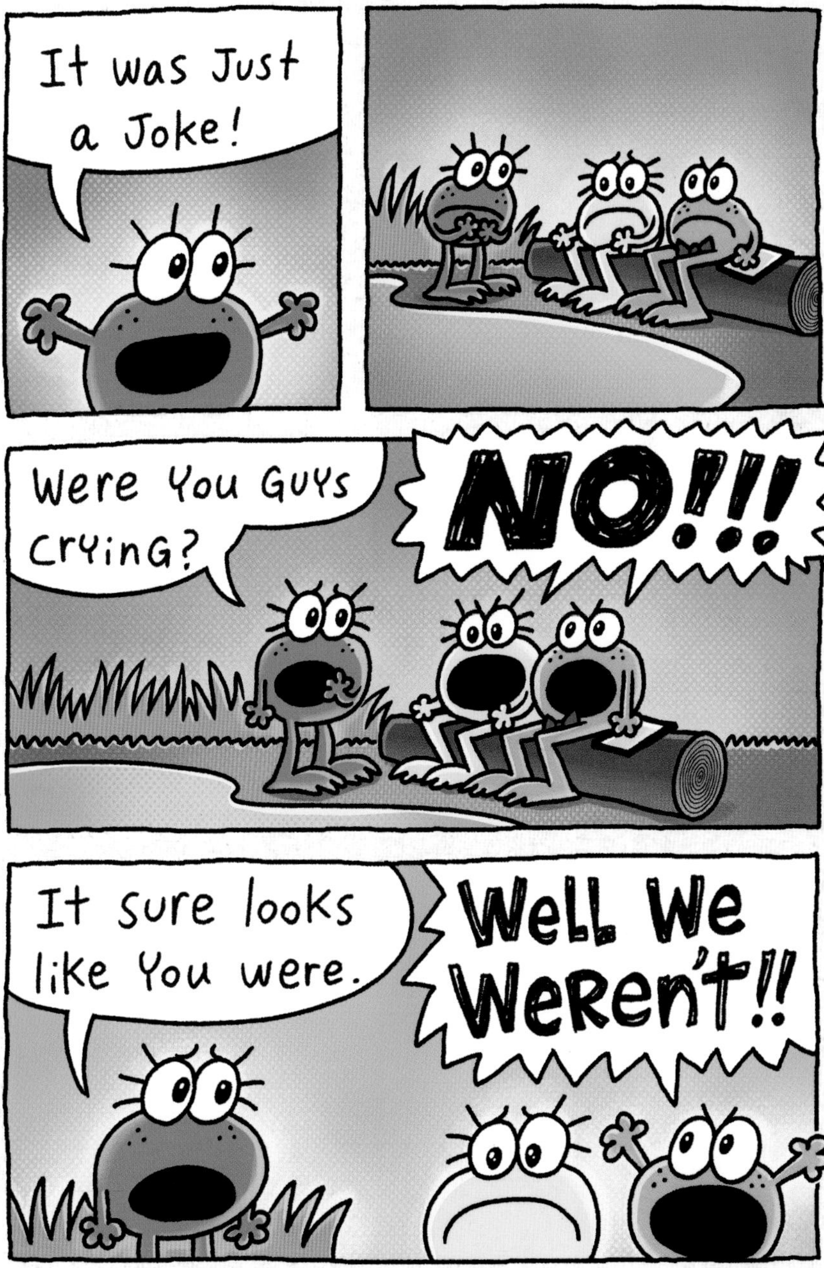
It was Just a Joke!
Were You GUYS crYing?
NO!!!
It sure looks like You were.
Well We Weren't!!

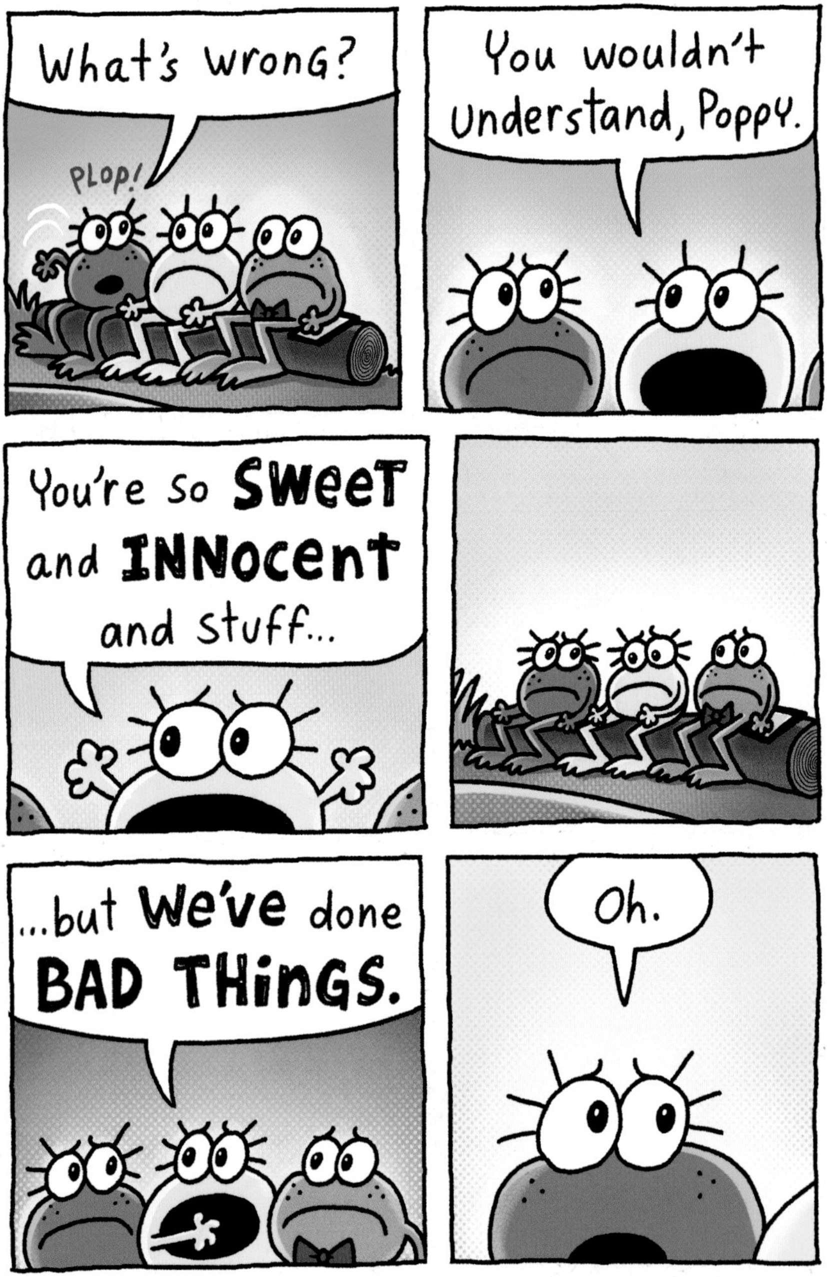
What's WRONG?
PLOP!
You wouldn't understand, Poppy.
You're so SWEET and INNOCENT and stuff...
...but We've done BAD THiNGS.
Oh.

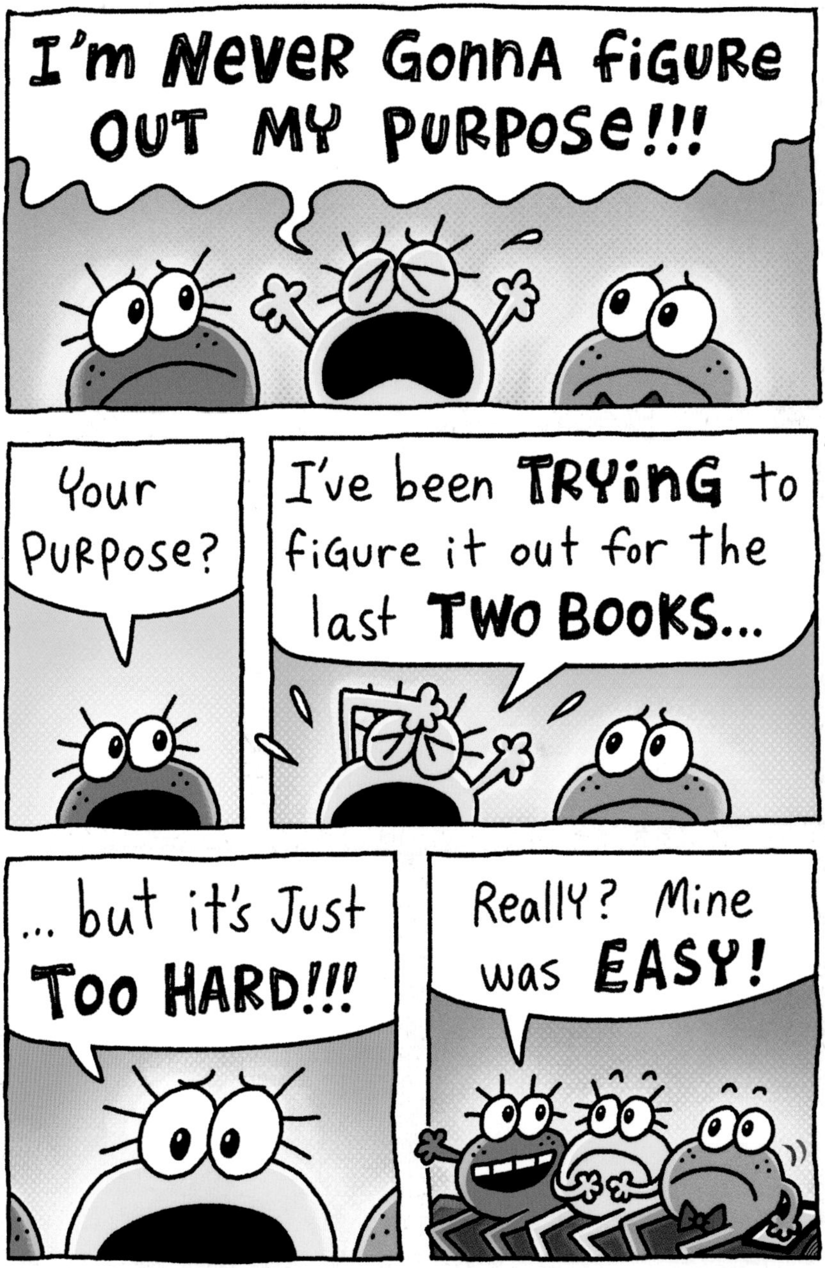
I'm NEVER GONNA FIGURE OUT MY PURPOSE!!!
Your PURPOSE?
I've been TRYING to figure it out for the last TWO BOOKS...
... but it's Just TOO HARD!!!
Really? Mine was EASY!

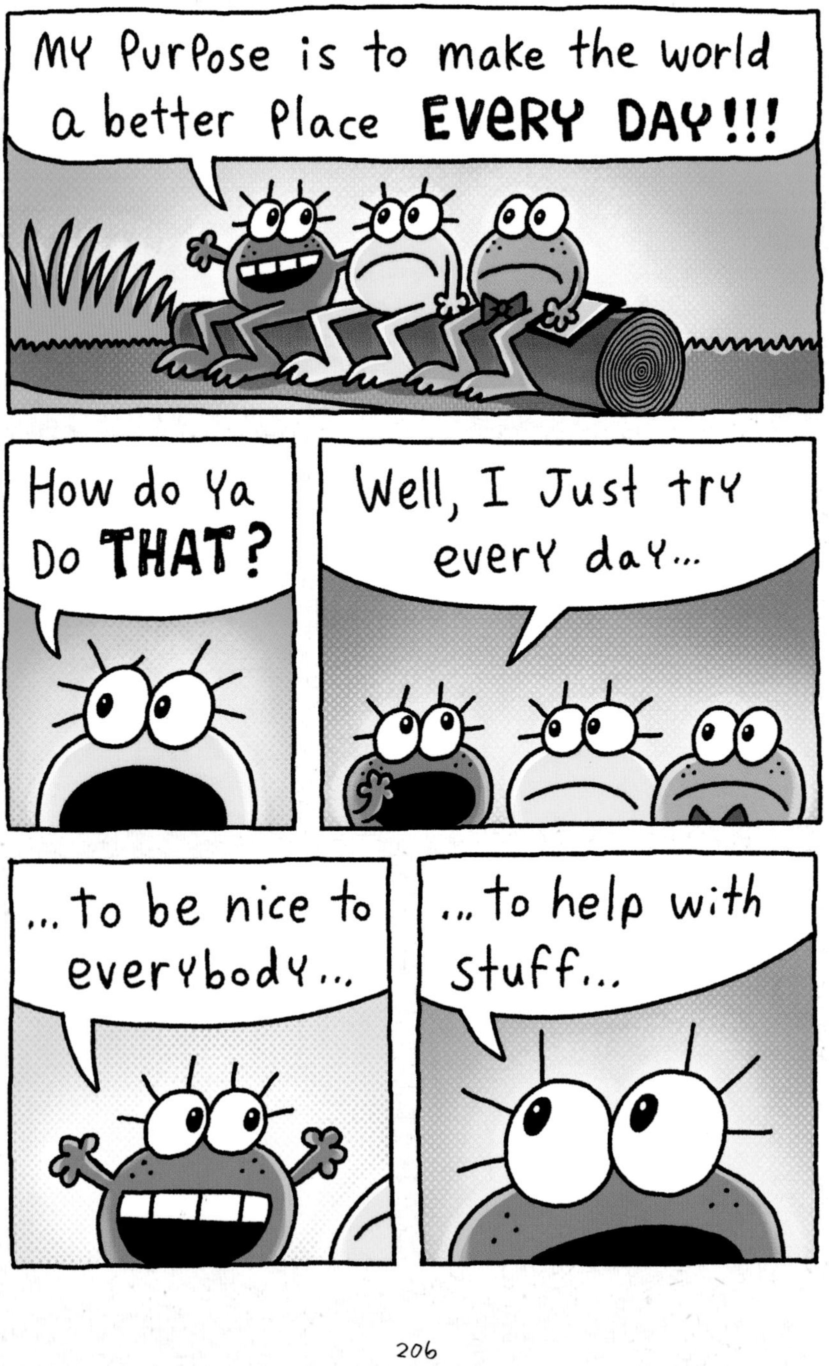
My purpose is to make the world a better place EVERY DAY!!!
How do ya do THAT?
Well, I just try every day...
...to be nice to everybody...
...to help with stuff...

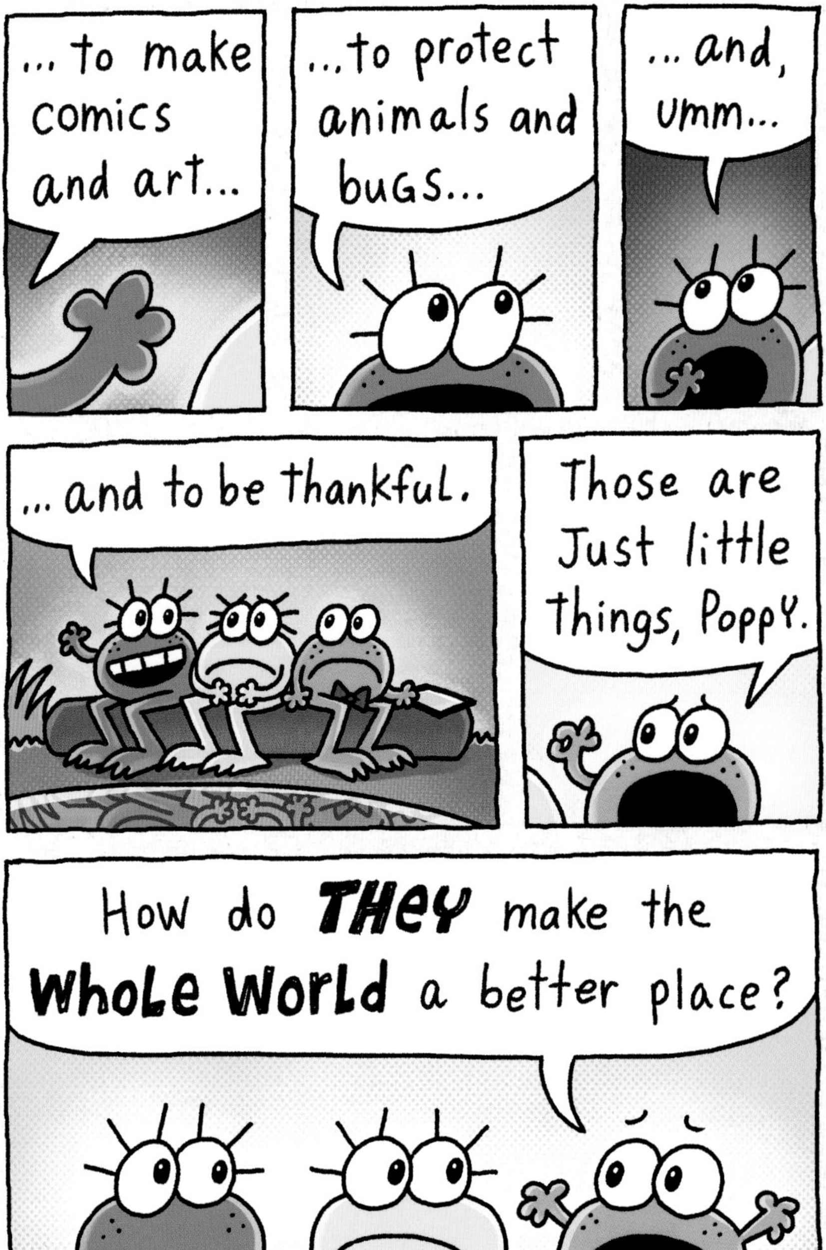
... to make comics and art...
...to protect animals and bugs...
... and, umm...
... and to be thankful.
Those are Just little things, Poppy.
How do THEY make the WHOLE WORLD a better place?

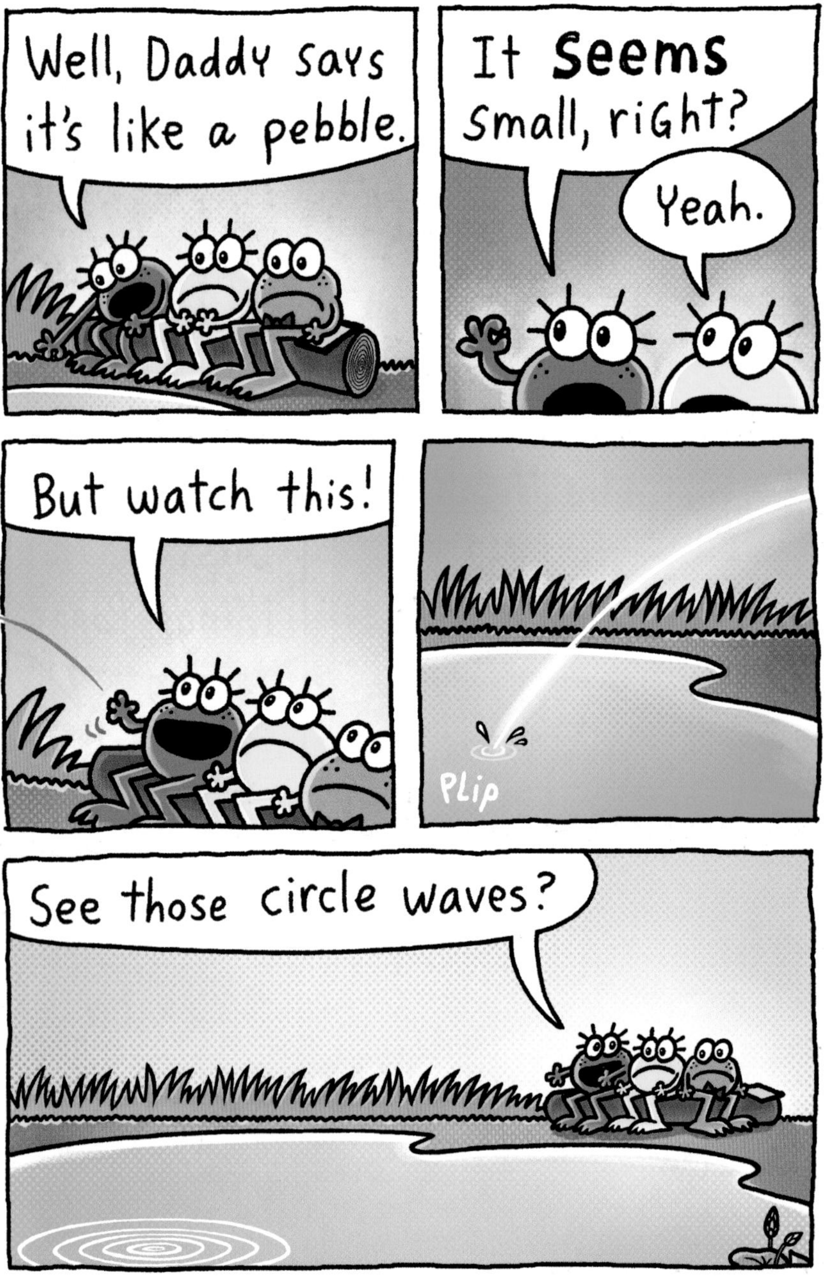
Well, Daddy says it's like a pebble.
It **seems** small, right?
Yeah.
But watch this!
PLip
See those circle waves?

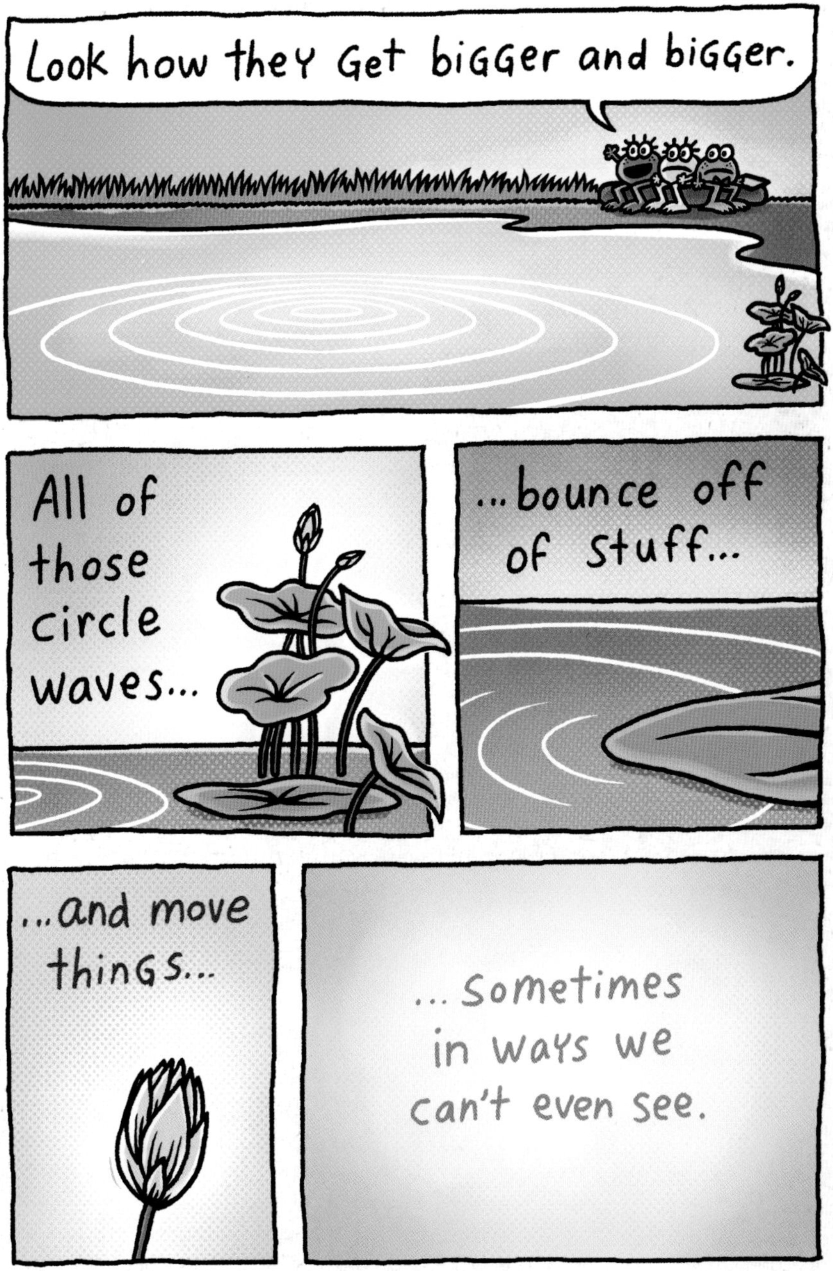
Look how they get bigger and bigger.
All of those circle waves...
...bounce off of stuff...
...and move things...
...sometimes in ways we can't even see.

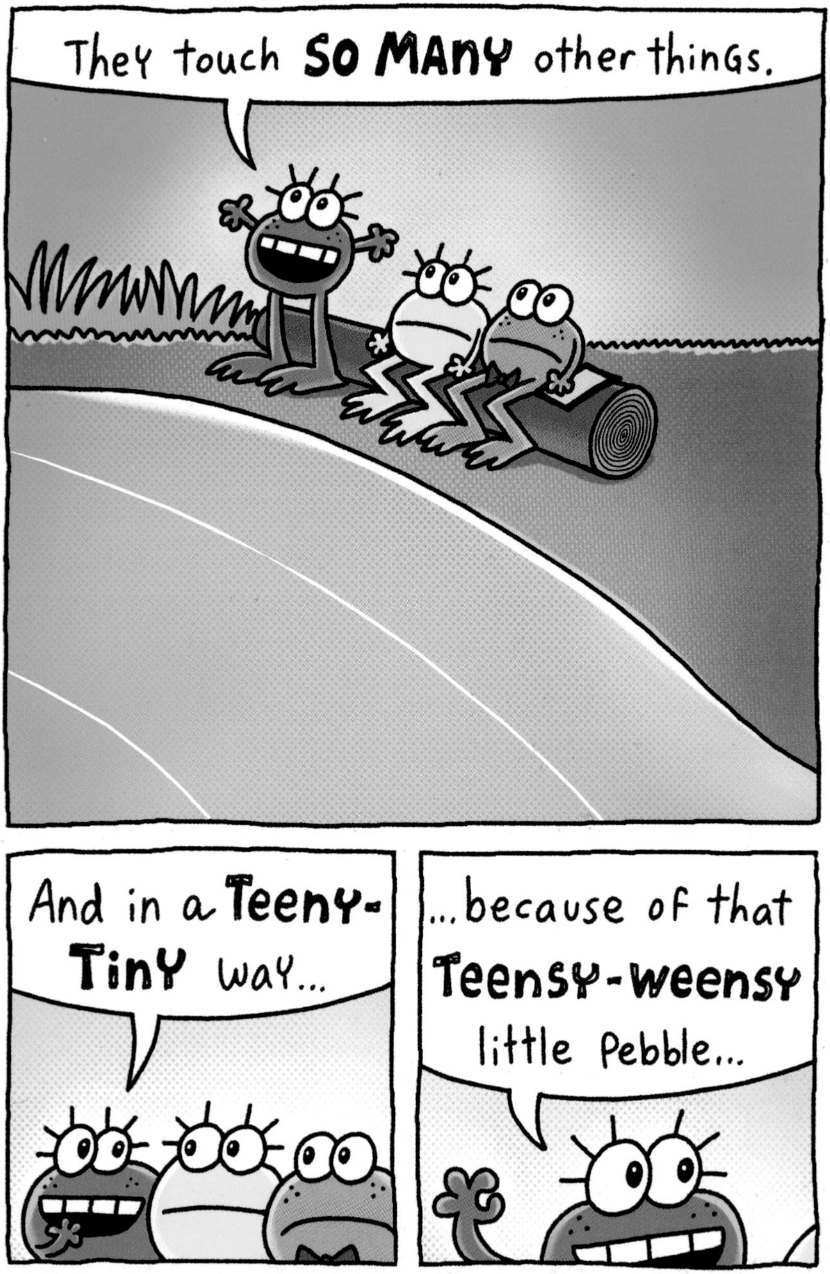
They touch SO MANY other things.
And in a Teeny-Tiny way...
...because of that Teensy-weensy little pebble...

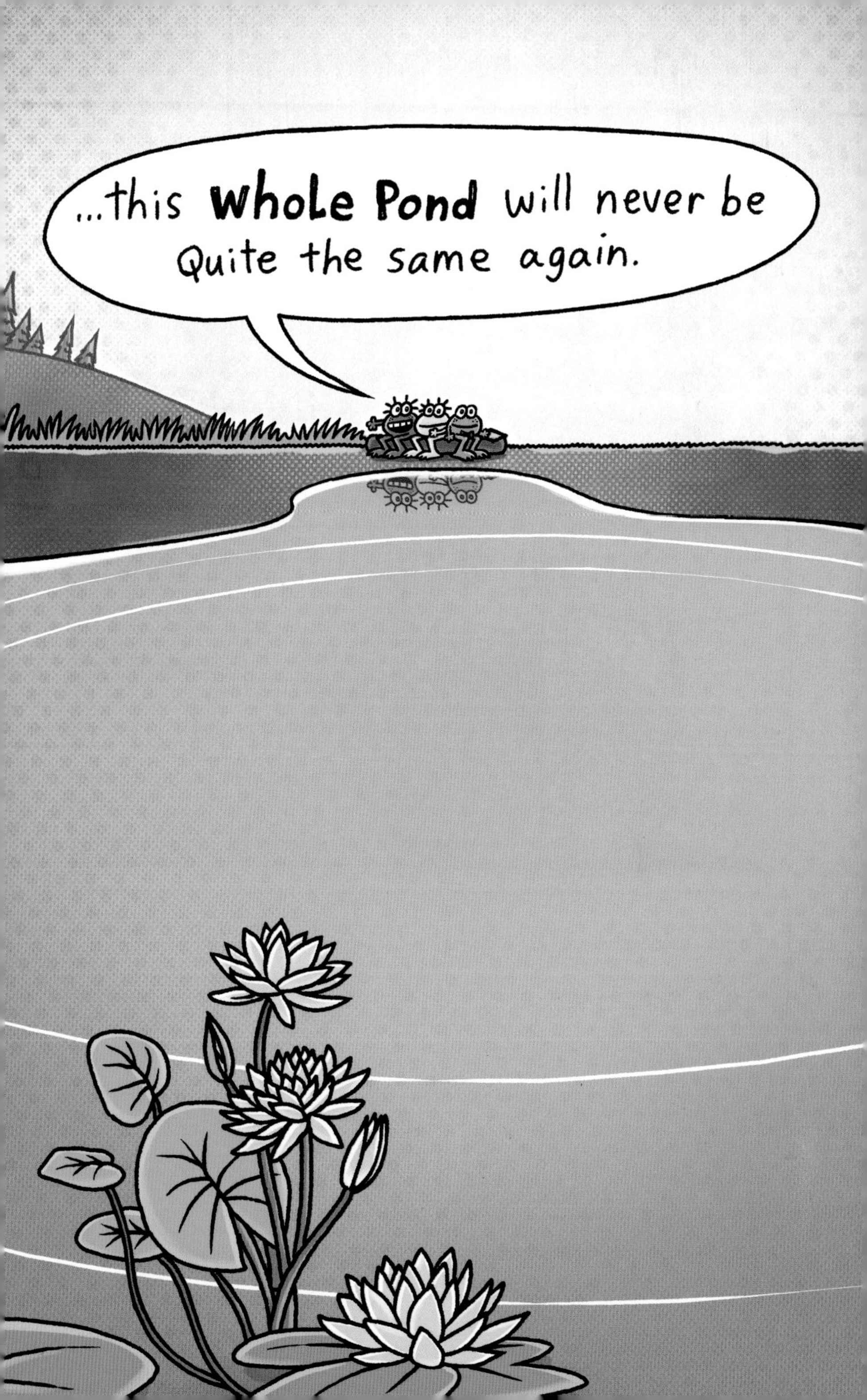
...this **Whole Pond** will never be Quite the same again.

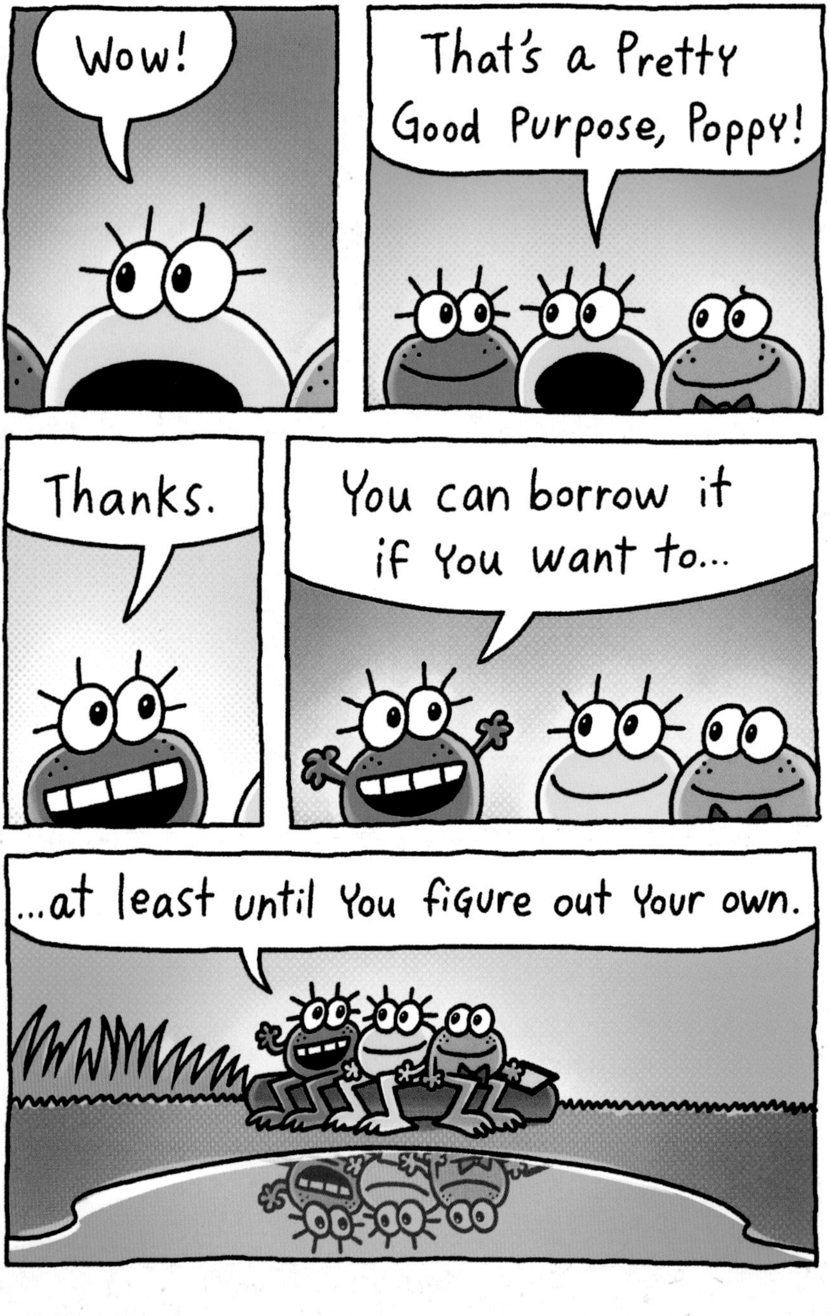
Wow!
That's a Pretty Good Purpose, Poppy!
Thanks.
You can borrow it if You want to...
...at least until You figure out Your own.

CHAPTER 10

NAOMI AND MELVIN LEARN THEIR LESSON (SORT OF)

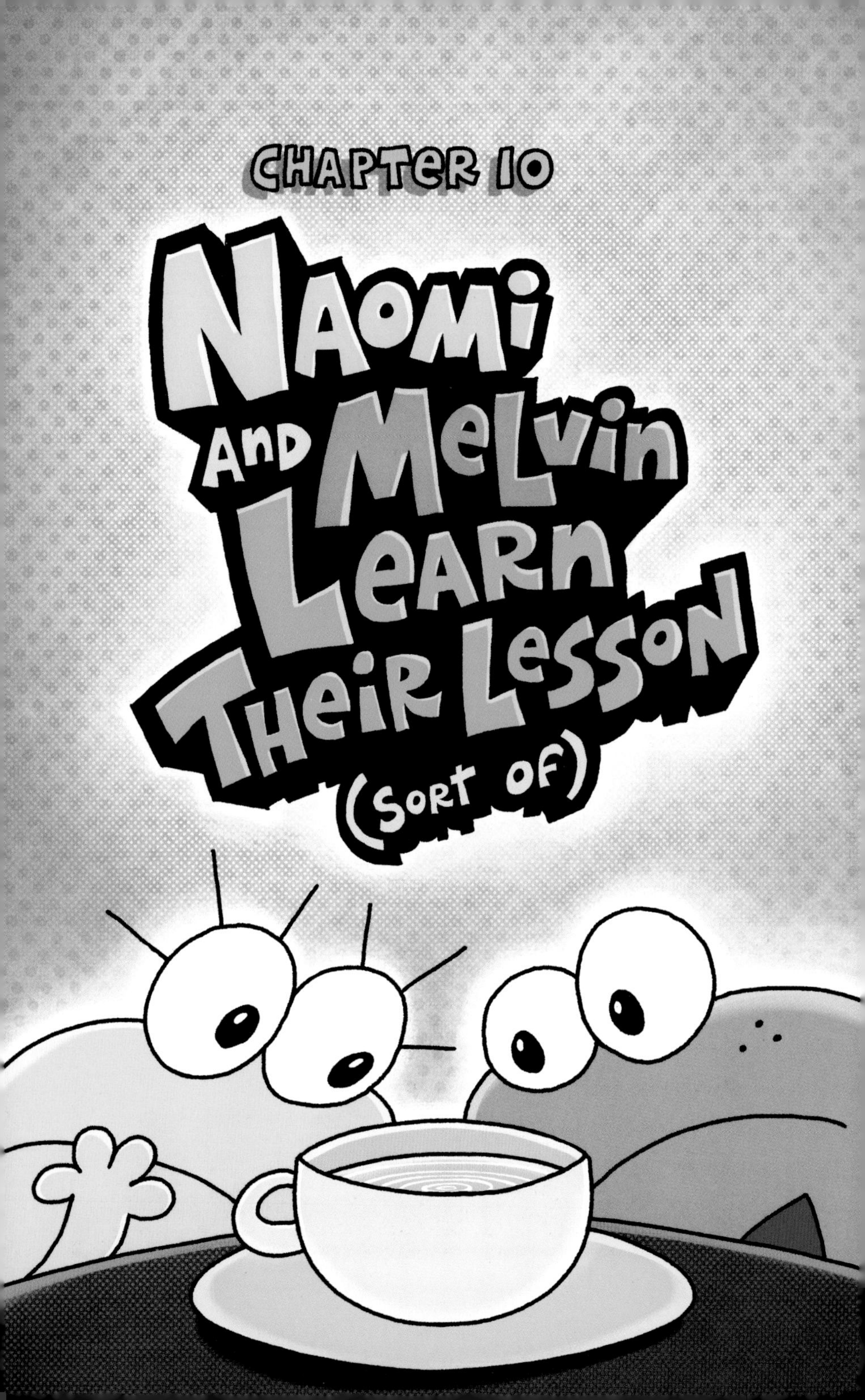

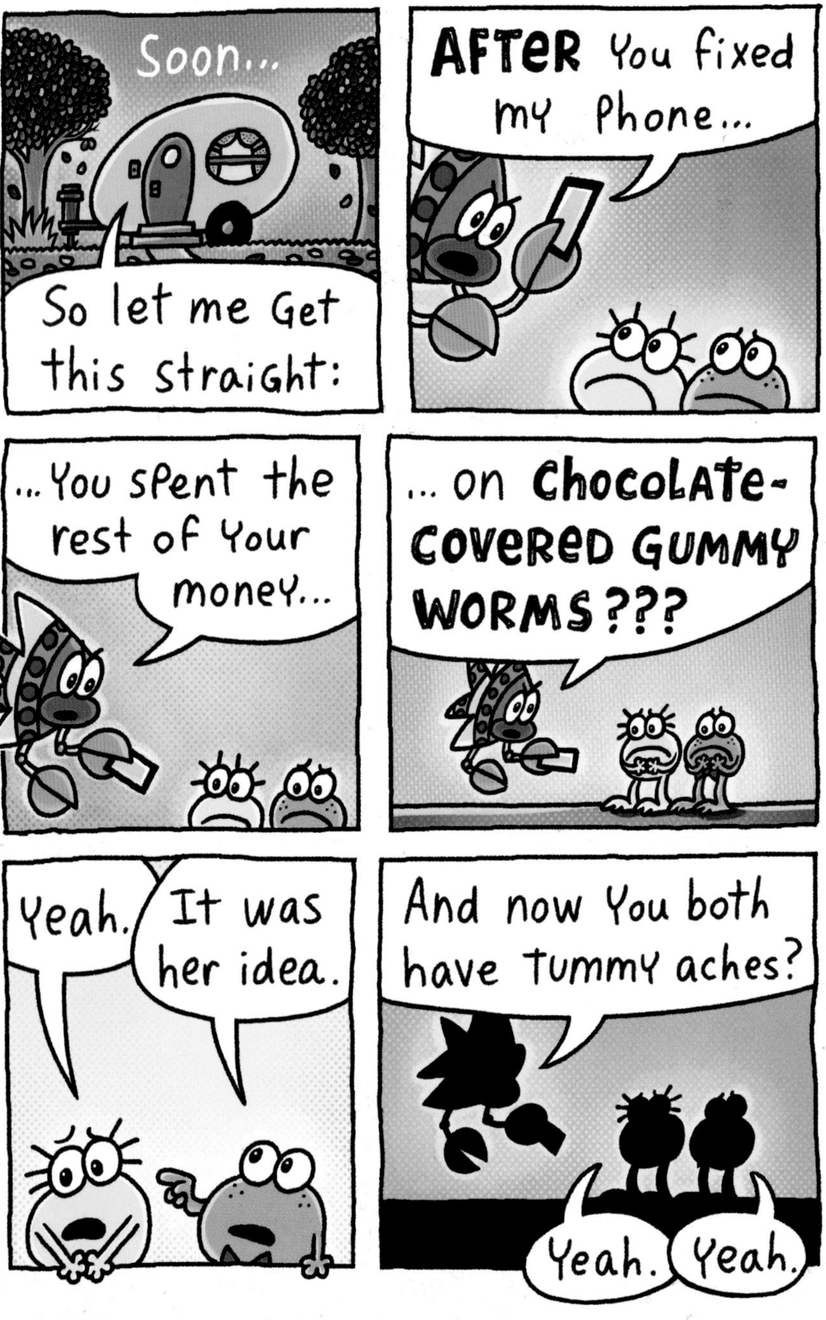
Soon...
So let me Get this straight:
AFTER you fixed my phone...
...you spent the rest of your money...
...on CHOCOLATE-COVERED GUMMY WORMS???
Yeah.
It was her idea.
And now you both have tummy aches?
Yeah.
Yeah.

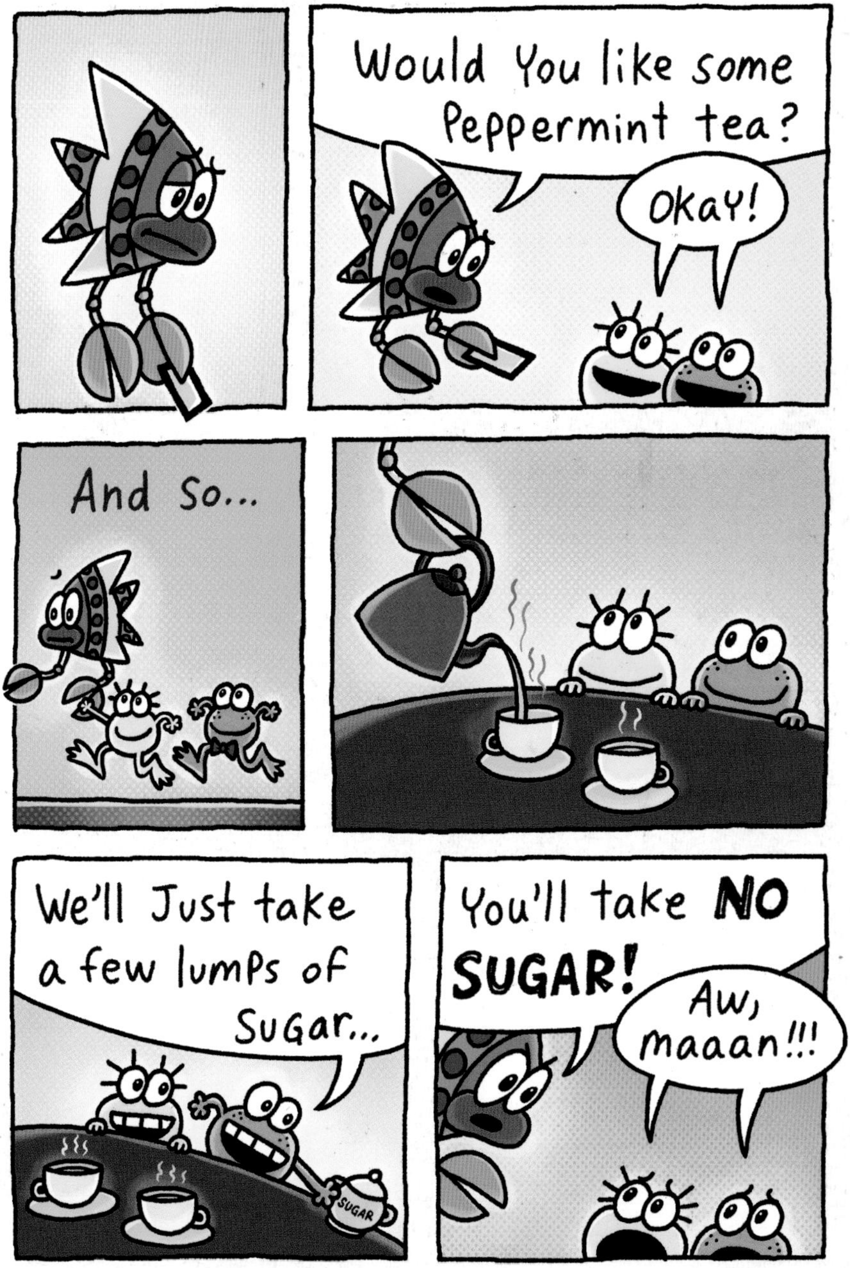
Would You like some Peppermint tea?
OKAY!
And so...
We'll Just take a few lumps of Sugar...
SUGAR
You'll take **NO SUGAR!**
Aw, maaan!!!

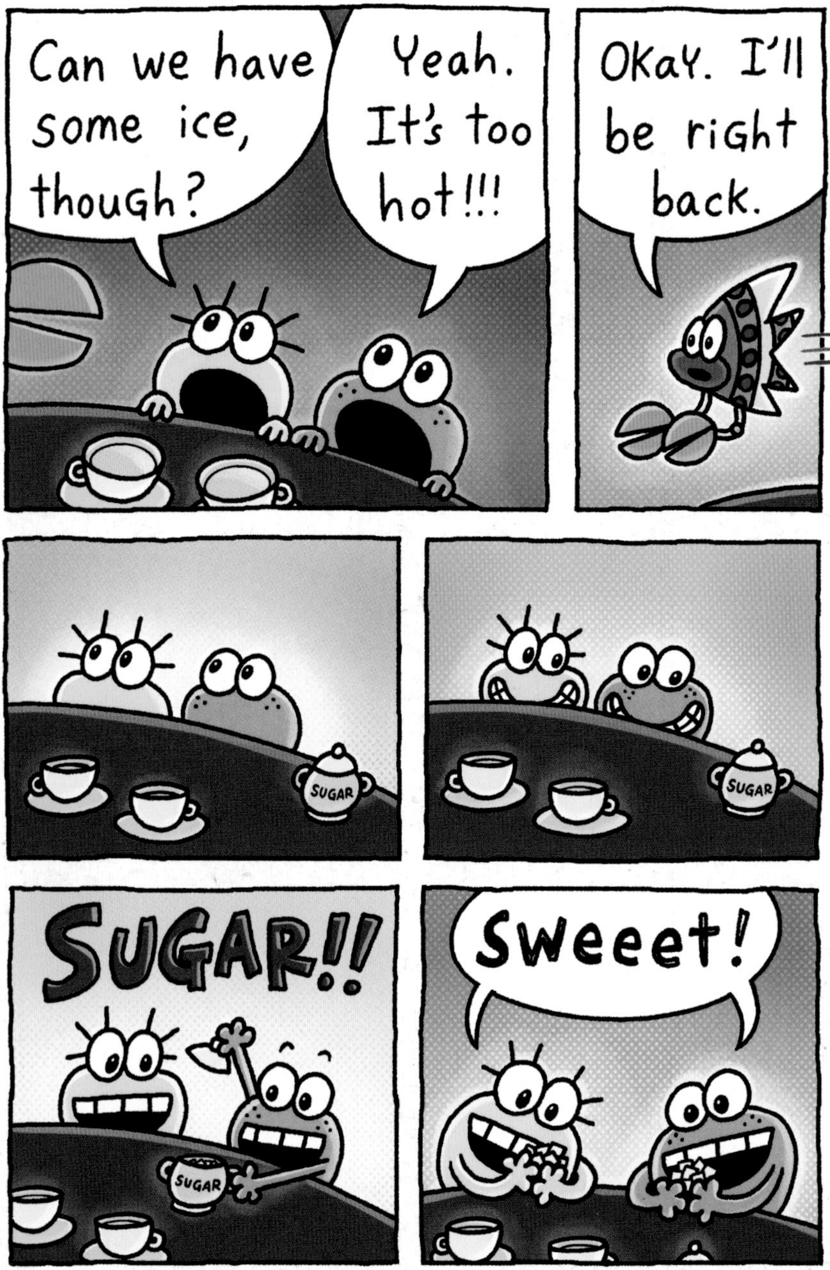
Can we have some ice, though?
Yeah. It's too hot!!!
OKAY. I'll be right back.
SUGAR
SUGAR
SUGAR!!
SUGAR
Sweeet!

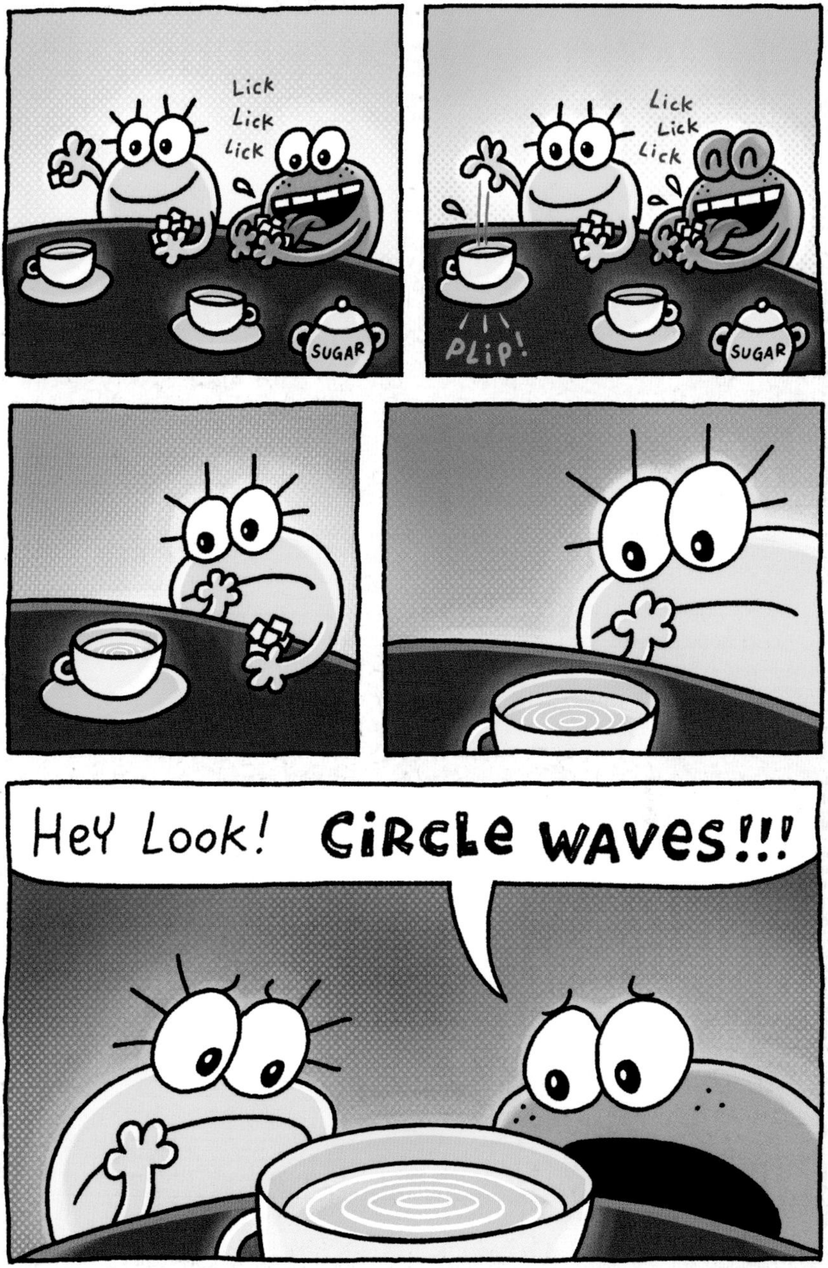
Lick
Lick
Lick
SUGAR
Lick
Lick
Lick
PLIP!
SUGAR
Hey Look! CIRCLE WAVES!!!

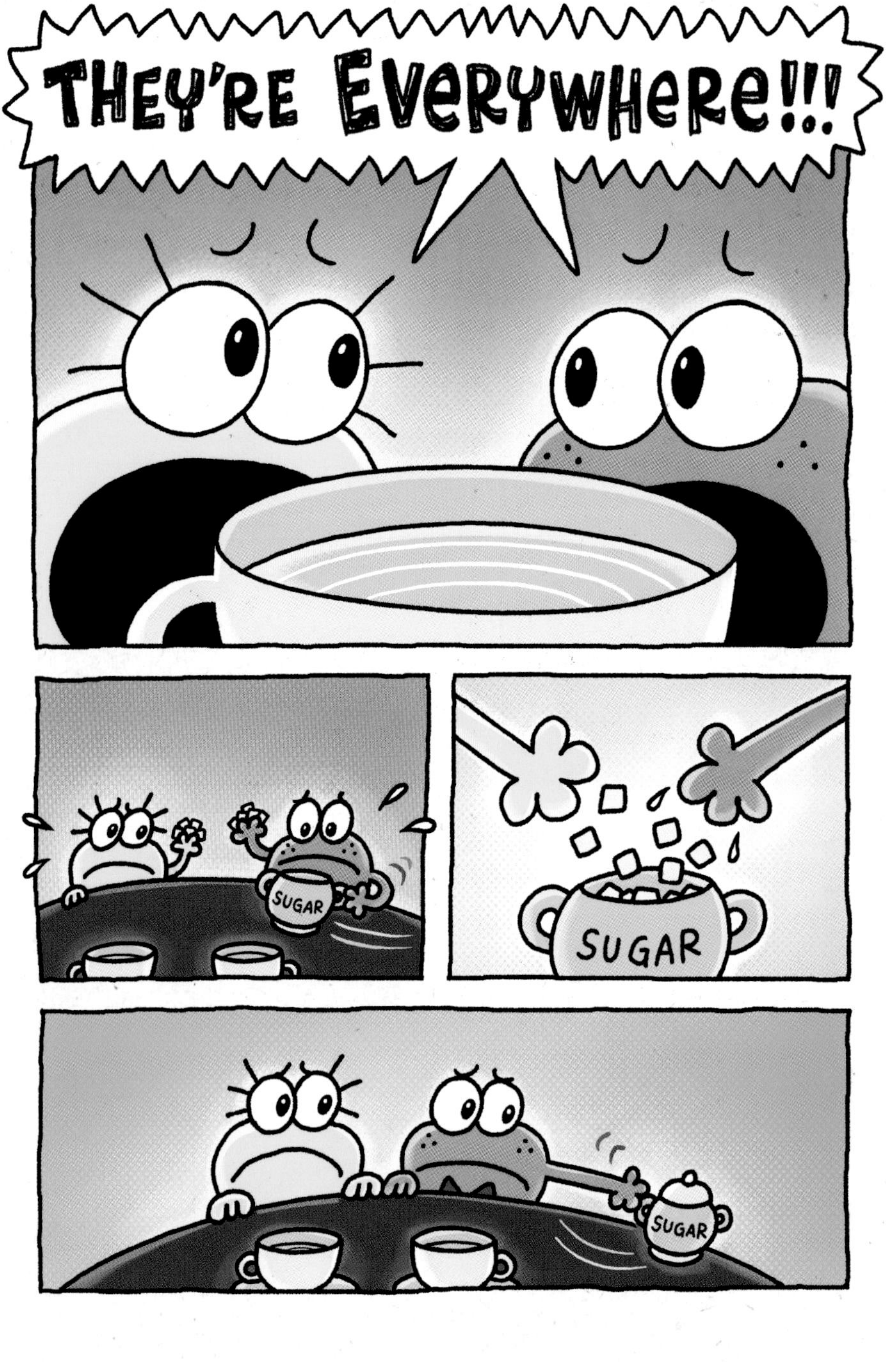
THEY'RE EVERYWHERE!!!
SUGAR
SUGAR
SUGAR

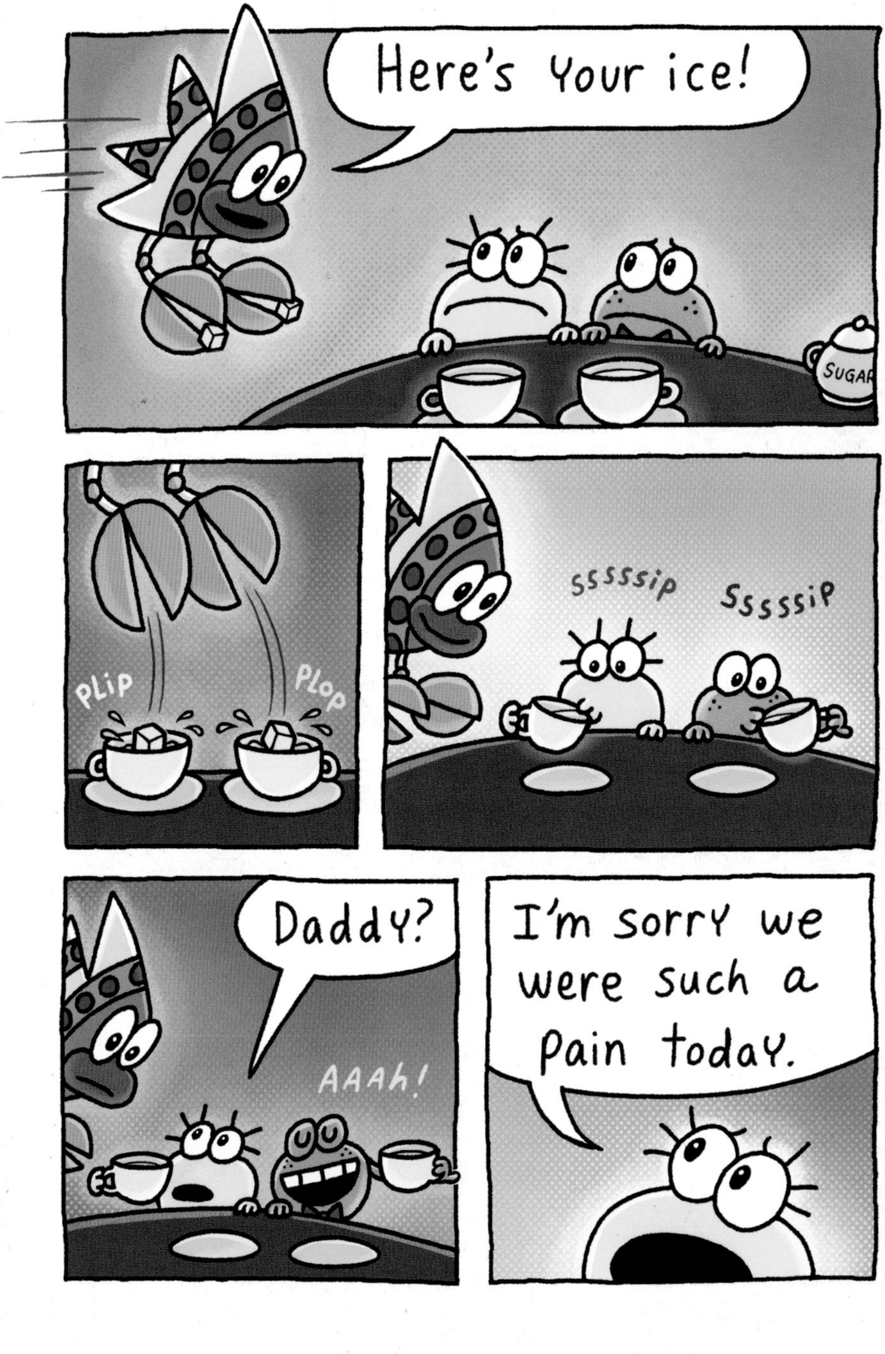
Here's your ice!
SUGAR
PLIP
PLOP
SSSSSip
SSSSSiP
Daddy?
AAAh!
I'm sorry we were such a pain today.

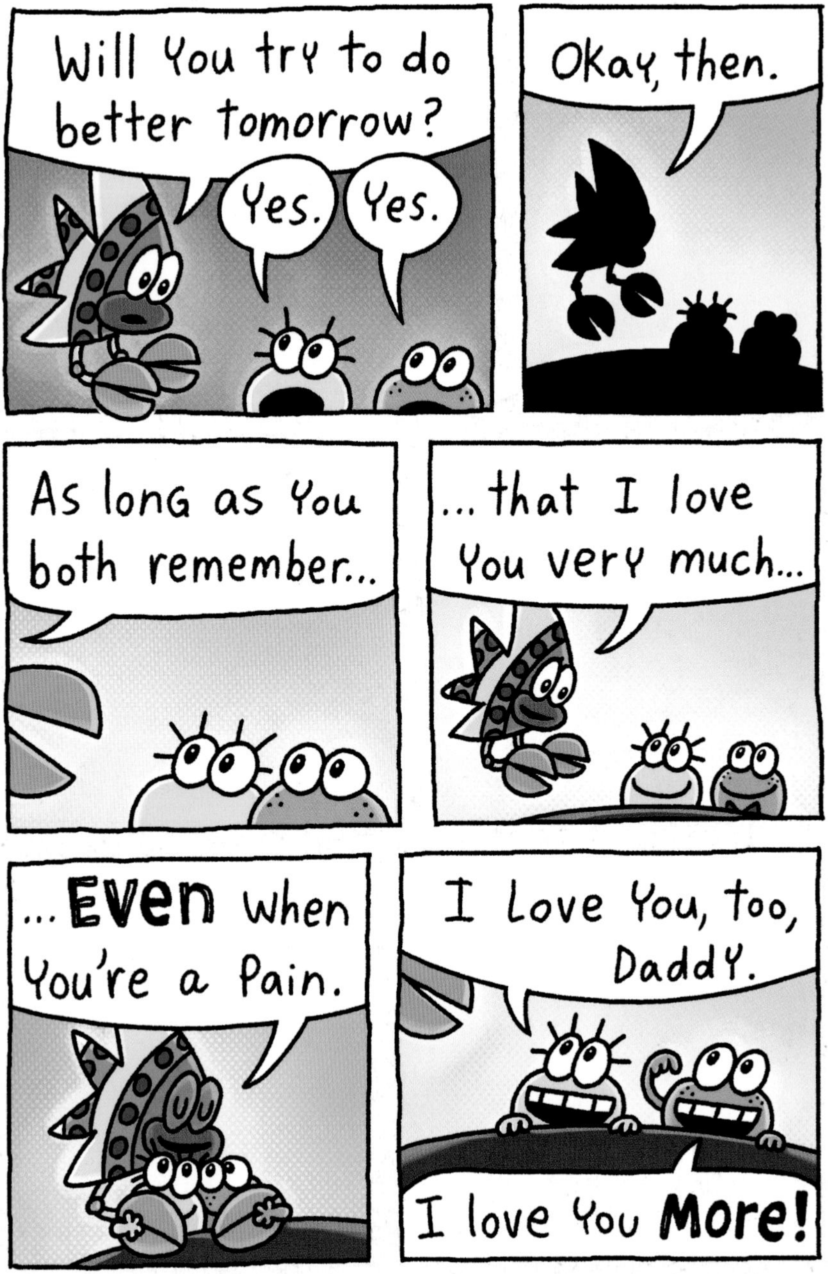
Will You try to do better tomorrow?
Yes.
Yes.
Okay, then.
As long as You both remember...
... that I love You very much...
... Even when You're a Pain.
I Love You, too, Daddy.
I love You More!

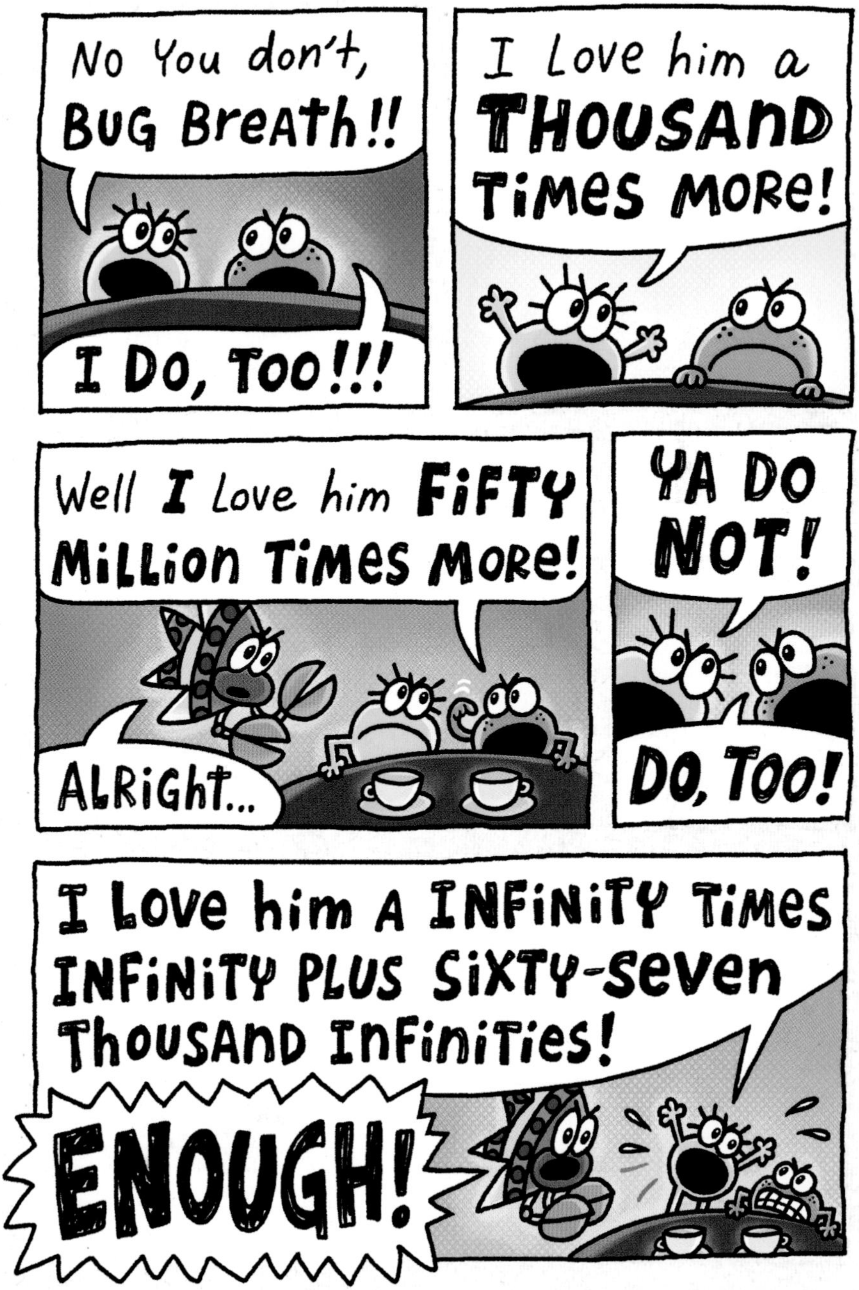
No You don't, BUG BreATh!!
I DO, TOO!!!
I Love him a THOUSAND TiMeS MORe!
Well I Love him FiFTY MiLLion TiMeS MORe!
ALRiGhT...
YA DO NOT!
DO, TOO!
I LOVe him A INFiNiTY TiMeS INFiNiTY PLUS SiXTY-Seven ThOUSAND InFiniTies!
ENOUGH!

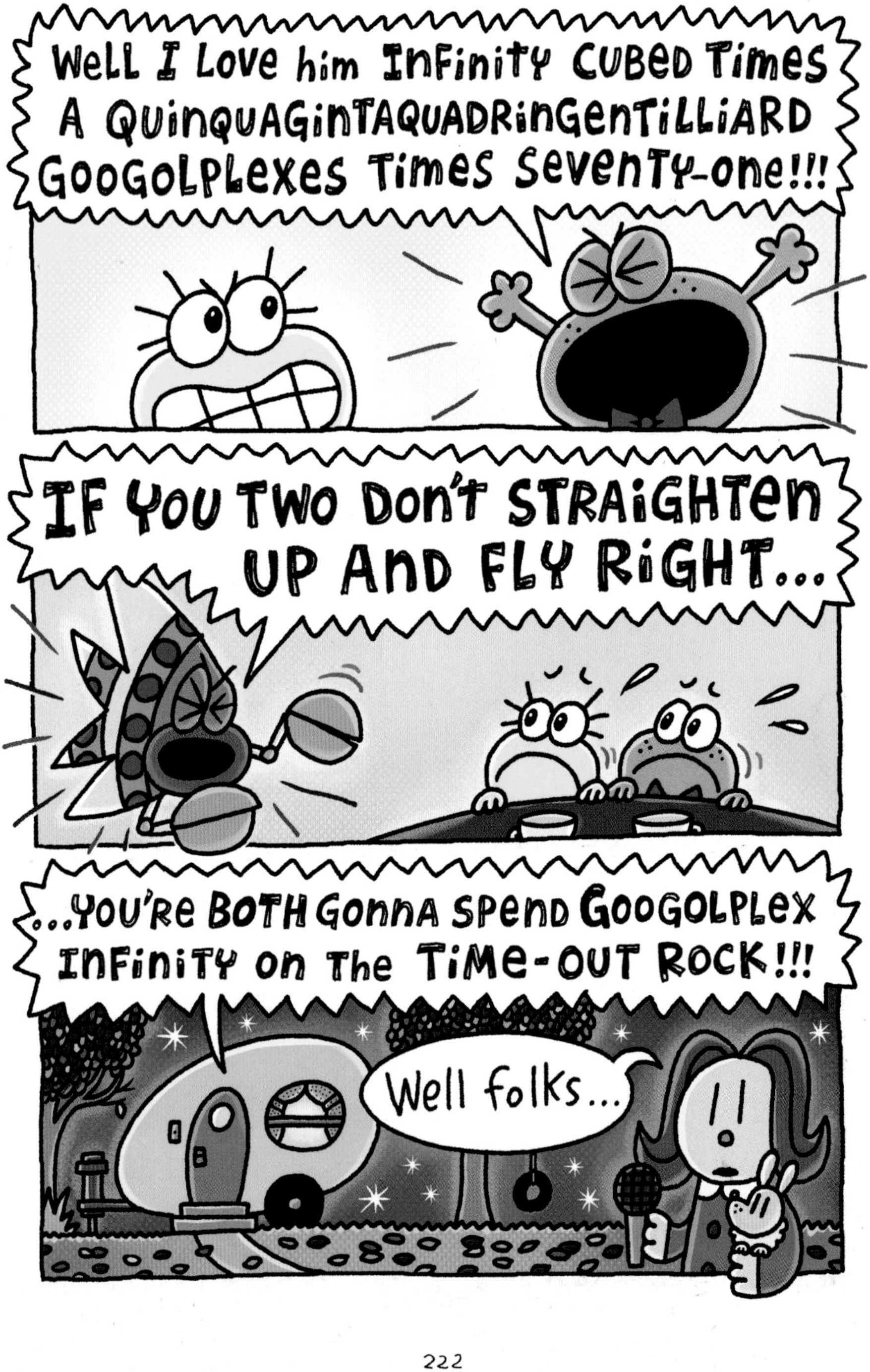
WELL I LOVE HIM INFINITY CUBED TIMES A QUINQUAGINTAQUADRINGENTILLIARD GOOGOLPLEXES TIMES SEVENTY-ONE!!!
IF YOU TWO DON'T STRAIGHTEN UP AND FLY RIGHT...
...YOU'RE BOTH GONNA SPEND GOOGOLPLEX INFINITY ON THE TIME-OUT ROCK!!!
Well folks...

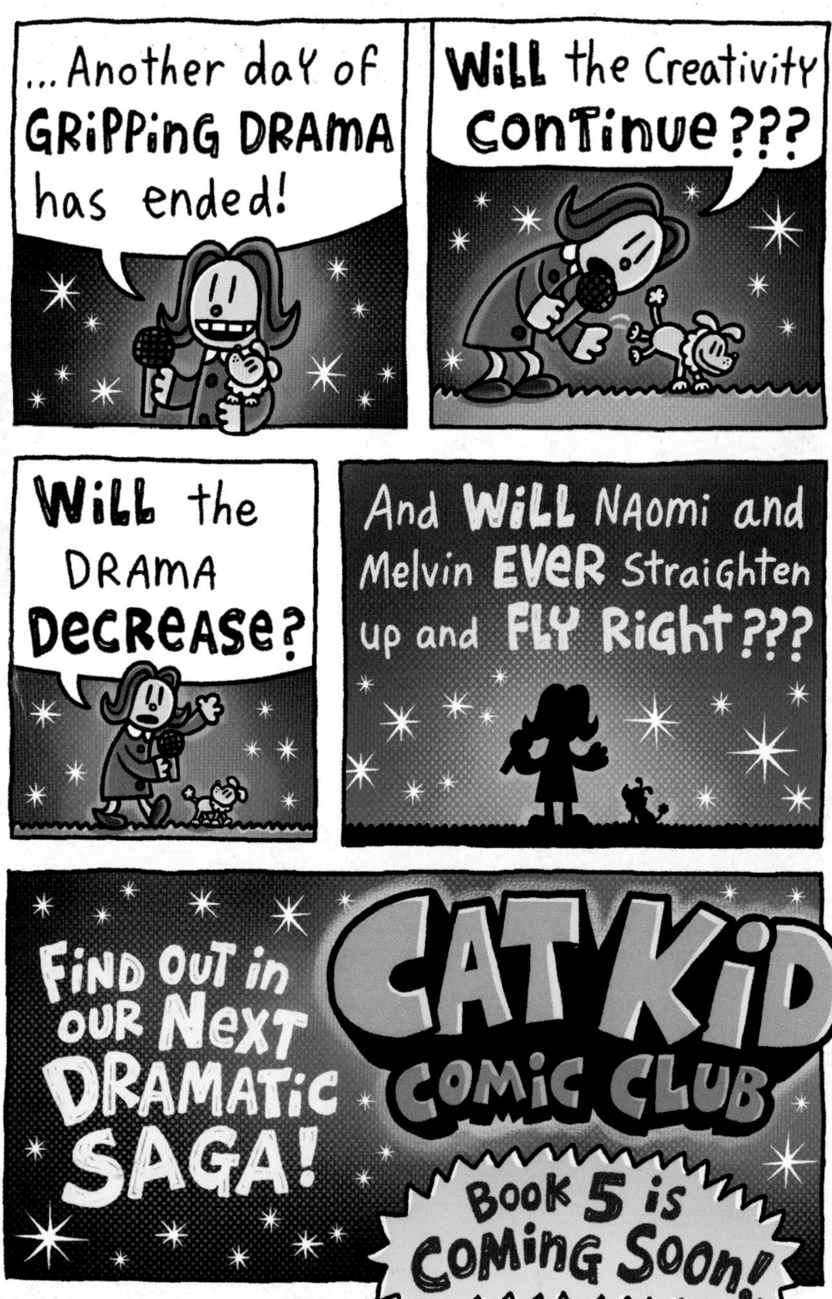

...Another day of GRIPPING DRAMA has ended!
Will the Creativity CONTINUE???
Will the DRAMA DECREASE?
And WILL NAOMI and Melvin EVER Straighten up and FLY RIGHT???
FIND OUT in OUR NEXT DRAMATIC SAGA!
CAT KID COMIC CLUB
Book 5 is COMING Soon!

NOTES & FUN FACTS

⭐ The theme of this book (small things can have great effects) was inspired by the following quote: "Behold also the ships, which though they be so great, and are driven of fierce winds, yet are they turned about with a very small helm..." – James 3:4 (KJV)

⭐ Poppy's purpose (pages 206-211) is based on a scientific ideology and branch of mathematics known as "chaos theory." This concept proposes that things that appear random and insignificant actually display underlying patterns and interconnectedness, which can have a profound effect on other seemingly independent things.

⭐ Quinquagintaquadringentilliard (page 222) is a real number equal to 10^{2703}, or 1 with 2,703 zeros after it. It would take about two pages to write the entire number.

⭐ Googolplex is also a real number, equal to $10^{10^{100}}$, or a 1 with so many zeros after it, it would be impossible to write. If you could, the number of pages you'd need would fill up enough books to overflow the observable universe.

⭐ The number "googolplex" was coined in 1920 by a nine-year-old named Milton Sirotta, who described the number as "one, followed by writing zeros until you get tired." Milton's uncle, mathematician Edward Kasner, adapted this number to the standardized $10^{10^{100}}$.

⭐ The video game cabinets in EASY SPIDER were made (hacked) from toys that actually work. Each game still works and can be played— although the games are different than what is shown.

⭐ All the smoke in EASY SPIDER was made out of polyester stuffing (from an old pillow) glued to recycled paper.

⭐ The campfire in MALLO COP was made from strips of dried mango "toothpicked" to wheat gluten "logs." The smoke was cotton candy.

⭐ "Wee-wee" really does mean "yes, yes" (or "yeah, yeah") in French. It's spelled "oui, oui," but it's pronounced "wee-wee."

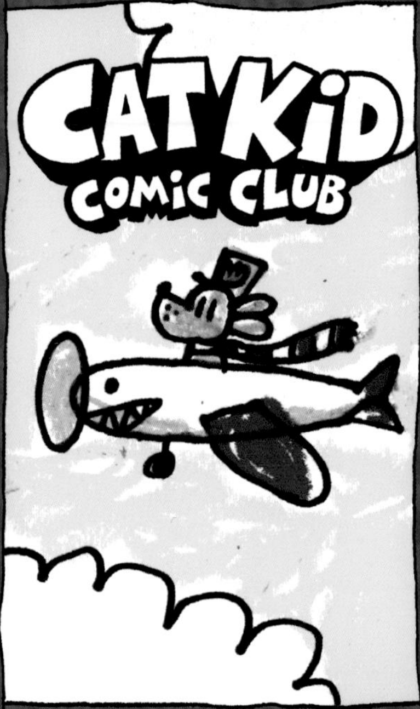
CAT KID
COMIC CLUB

DOG MAN

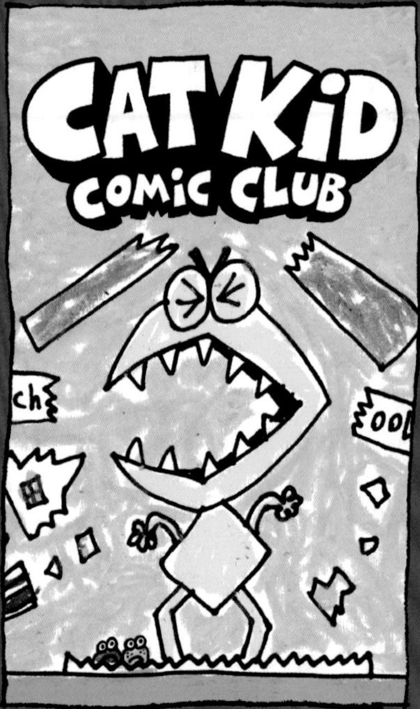
CAT KID
COMIC CLUB

FROGZILLA

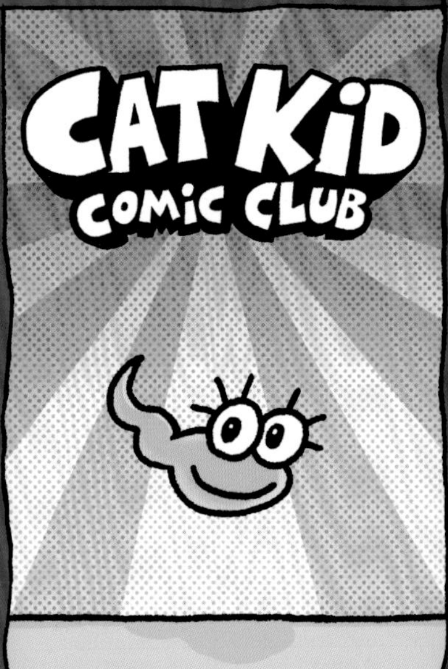
CAT KID
COMIC CLUB

MOLLY

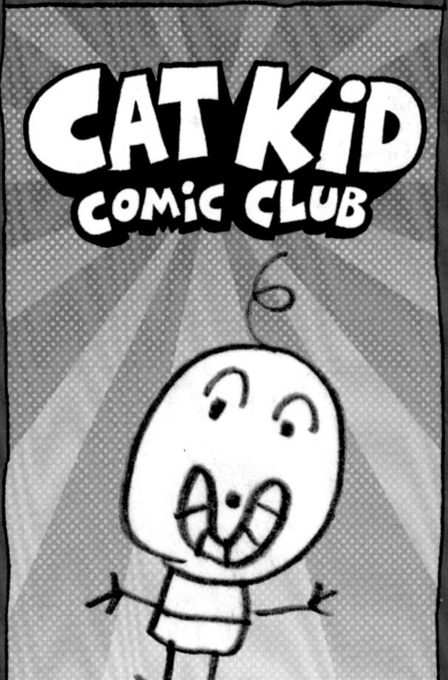
CAT KID
COMIC CLUB

LITTLE BABY

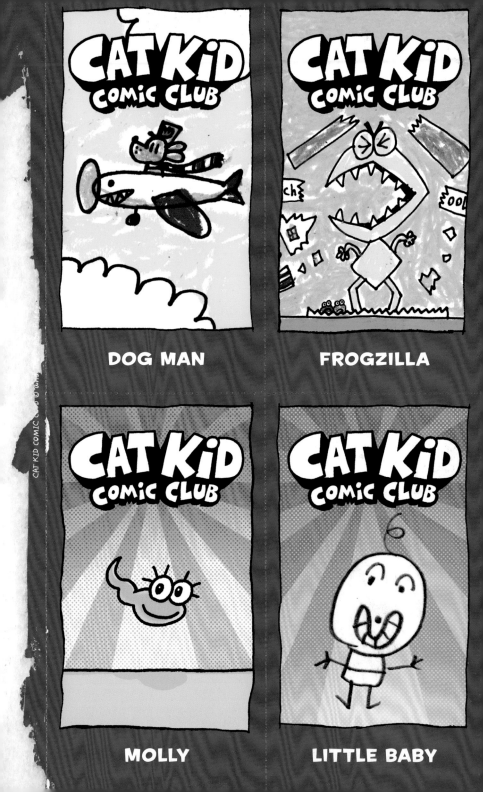

FROGZILLA

INGREDIENTS:
Dead frog, growth formula, dangerous atomic waste

GOAL:
To destroy the city

PARODY OF:
Godzilla

CREATED BY:
Gilbert and Curly

CREATE AND SHARE YOUR OWN COMICS AT PLANETPILKEY.COM

DOG MAN

MISSION:
To stop Frogzilla before he ruins someone else's video game

SECONDARY MISSION:
To not make any mistakes

EQUIPMENT:
Borrowed jet and cute little scarf

CREATED BY:
Gilbert and Curly

CREATE AND SHARE YOUR OWN COMICS AT PLANETPILKEY.COM

LITTLE BABY

COMIC TITLE:
Run, Little Baby, Run!

CREATED BY:
Billie, Corky, and Pink

SUMMARY:
A food order goes wrong and Little Baby has to run from two French flies and a supa-sized snake.

MEDIUM:
Pencil and marker

CREATE AND SHARE YOUR OWN COMICS AT PLANETPILKEY.COM

MOLLY

COMIC TITLE:
Squid Kid and Katydid

CREATED BY:
Molly and Li'l Petey

SUMMARY:
Two misfits become best friends and change the world.

MEDIUM:
Pen and cut-out construction paper

CHECK OUT "SQUID KID AND KATYDID" IN CAT KID COMIC CLUB: PERSPECTIVES!

CREATE AND SHARE YOUR OWN COMICS AT PLANETPILKEY.COM